# TWO LEFTS DON'T MAKE A RIGHT

*A Dylan Tomassi Novel*

## Dan Romanello

*Two Lefts Don't Make a Right*
(A Dylan Tomassi Novel, Book Three)
Copyright © 2025 by Dan Romanello, Sanitas Publishing, Inc.

For more about this author, please visit authordanromanello.com

This is a work of fiction. Names, characters, businesses, places, events, locales, and incidents are either the products of the author's imagination or used in a fictitious manner. Any resemblance to actual persons, living or dead, or actual events is purely coincidental.

All rights reserved. No part of this publication may be reproduced, distributed, or transmitted in any form or by any means, including photocopying, recording, or other electronic or mechanical methods, without the prior written permission of the publisher, except in the case of brief quotations embodied in critical reviews and certain other noncommercial uses permitted by copyright law. Please do not participate in or encourage piracy of copyrighted materials in violation of the author's rights.

For permission requests, write to: authordanromanello@gmail.com

Editing by The Pro Book Editor
Interior and Cover Design by IAPS.rocks
Cover Art by Camilo A. Cuervo

eBook ISBN: 979-8-9863151-5-7
Paperback ISBN: 979-8-9863151-4-0

    1. Main category—FICTION / Action & Adventure
    2. Other category—FICTION / Thrillers / Suspense
    3. Other category—FICTION / Literary

# CHAPTER ONE

Barry Filmore rolled over in his bed and stared at the taut body of the young woman lying next to him. She was naked, positioned on her side, with her back to him. What little he could see of her face was obscured by a nest of tousled brown hair. He thought of the Charlie Sheen line, "I don't pay them for sex—I pay them to leave," and immediately regretted not hiring an escort for last evening's New Year's Eve party, held at the nearby Pound Ridge, New York, estate of a furniture heiress. He slithered out of bed and made his way into the well-appointed master bathroom.

He regarded his naked self in the mirror. Barry Filmore was not an attractive man. He was in his late forties with a long face highlighted by a prominent nose and chin, courtesy of his Puritan ancestry. His thinning hair was gradually being consumed by an ever-expanding forehead. He had a sallow complexion; long, spindly extremities; and a sunken chest, the result of a sedentary lifestyle. He had met the striking young woman, half his age, at the party. She had initially dismissed him until she found herself in a small gathering where Filmore had the opportunity to introduce himself as an associate climate envoy for the US Department of the Interior.

He had watched amusedly as the woman underwent a transformation, with her attention redirected toward him. She had hung back as the group conversation waned and the others moved on. Soon after, she began ranting about climate change and her concern for the planet, and he knew he had her hooked, as it almost never failed.

He donned a thick terry cloth robe and a pair of lined leather slippers, exited the sprawling master suite, and took the elevator downstairs in search of his houseman. After wandering the expansive main floor layout without success, he exited the back entrance, traversed past the winterized pool area, and made his way down the dirt path toward the horse stables. He found his man tending to the animals. "Max," he shouted.

The tall, sturdy man, a decade his senior, turned slowly and observed his boss. "Good morning, sir. Is there something you need?"

"That's why I'm out here looking for you," he snapped. "There's a young woman in my bed who requires extraction and transport to wherever she wants to go, so long as it's not here."

"What shall I say if she inquires about your whereabouts, sir?" he asked with a hint of his old English accent.

"Tell her I had an emergency meeting with the secretary of the Department of Interior."

"Yes, sir." Max had become proficient in covering for his inconsiderately hedonistic employer and required only basic instruction.

As Max headed back toward the house, Filmore hung around the barn a moment before trudging farther down the path in the direction of a small manmade lake. It was an unseasonably mild morning on the first day of the new year, and he was comfortable in the robe. He had no interest in horses, the obligatory cow that lived on the property, or even the picturesque scenery of his twenty-acre estate. It was all about the agricultural tax break, set up to avoid the brunt of the exorbitant Westchester County property taxes. He figured he would embark on a rare fifteen-minute walk, and when he returned to the house, Max would have removed his no-longer-welcome guest from the premises.

Filmore's estimation proved correct when he reentered the house and all was quiet. He went upstairs to his suite and found no trace of the woman who had just shared his bed and willingly attended to his selfish carnal needs. He opened the nightstand, fished out a remote control, and positioned himself comfortably on the bed. He pressed a button on the remote, and a razor-thin screen ascended from the large footboard. Soon a split screen with four images was replaying the earlier activities, captured by the cameras mounted clandestinely around the bedroom. He was tactless and not much of a lover, but he enjoyed watching the replays more than he enjoyed the live performances. He selected one of the camera angles and was about to settle in when his phone buzzed. Annoyed, he grabbed it and then looked at the screen. "Ly, happy New Year! How's everything in Washington?"

Lymon Scott was deputy chief assistant to the secretary of the Department of the Interior. Barry and Lymon had become friends during their time at Georgetown University. Midway through their senior year, the two had been arrested following an undercover investigation into drug dealing on campus. Lymon was the mastermind behind the operation, but Filmore had been the one caught selling a dime bag to an undercover officer posing as a student. After some quick maneuvering, Filmore agreed to take the fall and preserve Lymon's promising career in Washington. He was convicted of drug trafficking, but through Lymon's already established contacts, adjudication was withheld, and he had avoided jail time. Lymon had promised Filmore he would be well taken care of, and he had kept his word.

"Happy New Year, Barry. By any chance, did you see what happened at the Winter Classic last night?"

"Uh, what's the Winter Classic?"

"Right, you don't follow sports. Anyway, every year, the National Hockey League hosts a game in a large outdoor stadium. They lay some type of expansive plumbing under the rink to keep the ice at the optimum temperature required for play. This year's game was scheduled for last night, a New Year's Eve rivalry between the New York Rangers and the Bruins at Fenway Park in Boston. But it was so warm and humid they couldn't get the ice playable and had to cancel the game. Forty-five thousand fans showed up and left disappointed. This is a great opportunity for you to work your magic. Could be very good for us."

"Sounds like I need to get up to Boston."

"And right away. I've scheduled a press conference for you at one o'clock, so you've got a few hours. We want maximum exposure on this, and the timing is perfect. People will be up celebrating New Year's Day and tuned into their televisions, watching football."

He looked at the time. "All right, I'll order up the jet and be wheels up out of Westchester Airport in an hour. I'll get there in plenty of time."

"Perfect. Call me from the plane, and we can strategize. I have some ideas."

# CHAPTER TWO

A week later, Dylan Tomassi awoke just before sunrise, dressed in gym shorts, a tattered T-shirt, and old running shoes, and headed down the three flights of stairs to the garage level of his palatial waterfront home overlooking Boca Ciega Bay in St. Petersburg, Florida. He entered the fitness center, glided past the free weights, machines, and cardio equipment, and stretched out the lean musculature of his six-foot two-inch frame on the mats.

After fifteen minutes, he made his way into the front area where his vehicles were parked and lifted his Trek Domane SL 5 down from the hook on which it hung by its rear wheel. He checked the air pressure in both tires before exiting the garage and riding down the winding driveway of his four-acre property. He stopped at the street to open the gate and observed the Monday morning traffic on the first full week after the New Year's holiday. As the gates closed behind him, he remounted his bike and pedaled south on the narrow shoulder of the brick-paved street, passing the other exclusive waterfront estates, collectively known as Millionaires' Row.

He turned left on Country Club Road at Admiral Farragut Academy and observed the buzz of activity at the iconic military school as the faculty, staff, and students settled back into their postholiday routines. After a short ride, he arrived at the Pinellas Trail and headed north for his fifteen-mile jaunt along the recreational trail, shared by cyclists, walkers, Rollerbladers, and an occasional sprinkling of eccentric characters. Dylan never wore headphones when he rode, rather opting for the peacefulness of being alone with his thoughts.

As he pedaled up the straightaway past the Tyrone Square Mall in the direction of Seminole his thoughts turned toward his schedule. The Tomassi

Youth Center grand opening, the crown jewel of his Tomassi Family Charitable Foundation, had been held in November and had been a huge success. The center provided after-school tutoring, medical services, recreational activities, and competitive club sports opportunities for underprivileged youth in the St. Petersburg area.

Dylan had grown up poor in Connecticut, raised by a single mother. Through the love and support of his mom and her family and a mysteriously reclusive widow he had met on his paper route as a child, he'd prospered and was now a private investor with a net worth approaching a half-billion dollars.

The youth center was now officially open, and students had begun arriving last week when Pinellas County schools resumed. On the advice of his best friend, Alex Malloy, he had hired Claire Semanski as the youth center director, and the running of the day-to-day operations was in her capable hands.

His next project was about to be unveiled at a ceremony the following week at St. Mary School in Stamford, Connecticut. Dylan's mother, Cheryl, had been a fourth-grade teacher at the Catholic elementary school, and Dylan had been able to attend as a benefit of his mother's position. He had previously funded scholarships at the school and had donated the money necessary to complete the school renovation project.

The initial phase, expanding and updating the classrooms and offices, had been finished several years ago, but plans to build a new field house and gymnasium had been put on hold because of a lack of funding until Dylan had stepped forward a year and a half ago. In addition to the gym, construction of the field house included a state-of-the-art performance theater, which doubled as an assembly hall with stadium-style seating for 300. The project was now complete, and the grand opening was scheduled for a week from Tuesday.

St. Mary was known throughout Fairfield County for the quality of its annual student-produced play, which rivaled that of a Broadway production. As the sole donor, he had been given the opportunity to select the naming rights. The facility would be named after his mother and be known as the Cheryl Tomassi Field House. He wanted to include his mentor, who was in large part responsible for his success because of her wisdom and generosity. Accordingly, the theater would be named the Esther Lott Theater.

As he made his turnaround on the trail just past the Seminole Boulevard overpass, Dylan began running the guest list through his head. Esther lived in Connecticut, but all his other invitees were in Florida. In addition to his mother and her boyfriend, retired US Coast Guard Rear Admiral Rick Landry, his grandparents, Anthony and Isabella Tomassi, lived in Indian Rocks Beach. Alex, his best friend since childhood, was an attorney who split his time between his New York and Tampa offices and was in town. Shirley Taylor, his personal assistant, who ran his business and personal lives and served as the Tomassi Foundation administrator, would also be attending. She would be bringing her boyfriend, Tampa Bay Buccaneers running back Quentin Ali, whose season had just ended with a loss on Sunday. He and Dylan both had foundations dedicated to helping underprivileged youth and had become friends. Along the way, Quentin had met Shirley, and the two had now been dating for a few months.

Upon returning to the house, Dylan showered in his upper-level master suite, returned to the second floor, grabbed a protein bar and bottled water from the state-of-the-art gourmet kitchen, and walked down the hallway, provisions in hand, until he reached the adjacent offices. He passed his own office and found Shirley speaking to a vendor on her headset. He leaned in her doorway and observed patiently while she completed her call.

Shirley was an attractive woman with streaked blonde hair and a compact body with curves in all the right places. They had met more than twenty years ago when they'd worked together in the Tampa office of a national brokerage house. His initial impression was that she was an aging party girl, but he soon came to admire her two best qualities: a tremendous work ethic and undying loyalty. She'd been a single mother living in St. Petersburg and raising her son, Ronnie, when Dylan left to start his own firm. Dylan offered her a job, and they had worked together ever since. He considered her family and had come to her aid last year when Ronnie was the victim of an overzealous prosecutor who charged him with murder after he shot and killed an intruder in his North Tampa apartment during a failed home invasion.

She looked up at him and met his gaze as she disconnected her call. "Good morning, Dylan. What's on the agenda for today? I don't see anything on your calendar other than your dinner tonight with Alex and Parker

Gough. How are those two getting along? I'm worried about that fine young man being exposed to Alex's corruptive influences."

He laughed. "I've been mentoring him on making good choices, and interaction with Alex is a good test for him. Have you finalized travel and lodging arrangements for next week?"

"Yes. I booked the four suites at the Delamar in Greenwich, and the hotel hooked us up with a van and driver. It's one of those Mercedes Sprinter executive editions with seating for eight. It will pick us up at the airport and be at our disposal for the balance of the trip. The charter flight leaves out of Clearwater Airport, and we have a two-hour takeoff window. I understand Alex will be catching a ride up with us, correct?"

"Yeah. I've never flown private, and neither have my mom or grandparents. It'll be a nice treat for them."

"I spoke with Quentin, and we decided to stay an extra day. We're going to *MJ the Musical* on Broadway while we're up there, so we'll find our own way back."

Dylan looked at her thoughtfully for a moment. "Is that the Michael Jackson musical?"

"Yes."

"I heard about it. It would be great if we all went to see it together. We can extend our stay another night and have the driver take us to the city in the van."

"That's a great idea."

It was now past nine thirty, so he returned to his office and fired up his computer, and the two large screens on his desk came to life. He checked the markets. Dylan had become slightly more risk-averse over the past several years, and his holdings were now weighted in a diversified basket of blue-chip dividend stocks, ETFs, and treasury bonds. Interest rates had skyrocketed to levels not seen in almost a quarter century, and fixed-income investments had once again become attractive alternatives.

Satisfied with his review, he switched to the newspapers and read the online versions of the *Wall Street Journal* and *Investor's Business Daily*. Dylan had been closely following the increase in demand for mining materials necessary to build government-induced green energy products, such as windmills, solar panels, and electric vehicles. He clicked away at his keyboard, making several purchases in the mining sector.

His extensive research on the subject revealed that the global pledge to transition away from fossil fuels on the aggressive deadlines spearheaded by US and European policymakers was unobtainable, and worldwide demand for conventional energy sources would remain robust into the foreseeable future. Accordingly, he continued to maintain significant holdings in the oil, natural gas, and pipeline sectors. After about an hour, he stood and stretched his legs before grabbing another bottle of water from his small office fridge. He thought about Penel and decided to give her a call.

Penelope Stanhill was a prominent family law attorney in New York. Dylan had met her as a teen, and the two had shared a brief summer romance. He had not seen her again until they ran into each other a few years ago on a flight to New York during the time he was assisting Alex as he was going through his divorce. They had reconnected, saw each other several times in New York, and Penel had traveled down to Florida for a visit. The pair made an attractive couple and always enjoyed each other's company but had gone their separate ways for almost a year, until Penel called to congratulate him on the youth center opening. They had spoken on the phone a few times since.

Dylan dialed her cell number, and she picked up immediately. "Dylan, how are you?" she answered with an air of enthusiasm.

"I'm doing well. How are things in New York?"

"Everything's fine here. The weather has been unseasonably warm, but it's a nice break from the bitter cold we had last month. I'm looking forward to seeing you next week when you're in town. It's been too long."

"About that. I wanted to invite you to the ribbon-cutting ceremony at St. Mary. I'll be staying at the Greenwich Delamar, and you're welcome to stay with me."

"Oh, Dylan, that's great! I have such good memories of our time there together."

"Same here. I'm planning on arriving next Monday. The ceremony is Tuesday evening, and I'll be spending a few extra days if you can get away from work."

"My clients may have to stay married a bit longer, but I'll work it out," she chortled.

"Great."

"I can't wait to see you."

"I'm looking forward to it. I'll be in touch with the details and talk to you soon," he replied as he disconnected the call.

# CHAPTER THREE

That same afternoon, Barry Filmore paced back and forth in his home office as he wrapped up his radio interview with NPR. "Look at the overwhelming evidence. In addition to the record hot winter temperatures in New England that caused the NHL to cancel their annual outdoor game, we've had wildfires in California and Hawaii, record flooding throughout the Midwest, and unprecedented hurricane activity in the Gulf and Atlantic regions. If anyone fails to see these are all direct consequences of climate change, they're either not paying attention, or they're in denial."

The radio host took on a solemn tone. "So, what can we as Americans do to help combat climate change?"

"First, accept that the threat is existential and has reached crisis proportions. Everyone listening to my voice needs to act now. Not tomorrow or next week. Not next month or next year, but today. Go to my website, domypartfortheplanet.org, and become a member. For just ninety-nine dollars a year, you'll receive a membership card made from repurposed materials, our monthly online newsletter, and an immediate action plan you can take right now. Additionally, we ask all individuals to pledge one percent of their income and businesses one percent of their annual revenue to help us fund our mission. In addition to our programs to help accelerate the transition to renewable energy, we're developing cutting-edge technology that will block the sun's rays, essentially acting like a pair of giant sunglasses for the earth. It will cool down the planet, bring down ocean temperatures, and mitigate global warming. This work needs to be fast-tracked to avoid a climate apocalypse."

"Please give our listeners an idea of some things they can do right now to help make a difference."

"There's no simple, short answer, but here are some steps people can take immediately. Get rid of your cars. Walk, ride a bike, or take public transportation. Stop eating meat and dairy. Cattle ranches and dairy farms are some of the worst producers of greenhouse gas emissions. At home, jettison your gas appliances, air conditioners, ceiling fans, and toasters. If everyone did these things today, we could reduce emissions by twenty-five percent overnight."

"All right, sir, well, thank you for that invaluable information and everything you and your organization are doing to combat climate change. Once again, you can reach Mr. Filmore's organization through his website at domypartfortheplanet.org. Thanks again for speaking with me today."

"You're welcome," he concluded as he disconnected the call. He exhaled, sat down at his desk, and immediately clicked away at his computer keyboard. He observed delightedly as the two numbers in the upper right corner of the screen accelerated rapidly at an indecipherable pace. The first number represented new membership signups, and the second one fresh donation pledges. Satisfied, he left the office and went into the bar, where he poured himself a double Scotch. He had just slid onto one of the padded leather barstools when his phone rang. It was Lymon.

"Hey, Ly, what's up?"

"Barry, I caught your interview on NPR. Very powerful stuff."

"Did you hear the others today?"

"No, I've been busy working on the DEI project for the national parks program. A bunch of crap about increasing minority visitor numbers and assigning pronouns to the various species of trees in the parks."

"Well, I did television all morning: the networks, World News Now, CNBC, and MSNBC. It was a brilliant strategy to leverage the canceled hockey game to increase visibility. We've reached a lot of new people with this campaign. I just checked, and we're doing great on the numbers."

"That's good news. Your performance at Fenway was legendary. I especially enjoyed the footage of you riding up to the stadium on the bicycle. Where'd you come up with that?"

"I've used that move a few times. I stow the bike in the back of one of the SUVs in my security detail, and have my driver drop me off a few blocks from the TV cameras."

"Very nice touch. Listen. I have to be in New York next week for meetings, and I'd like to see you. There's someone I want to introduce you to."

"Who's that?"

"Her name is Kari Baldwin. She's the leader of NYMATU."

"What's that?"

"The New York Metro Area Teachers' Union. It would be good for you to get to know her."

"Whatever you say. Is she a looker?"

"Far from it. But she's a powerful woman and could be a strong ally."

"Fine. When will you be here?"

"I'm flying in early Tuesday and will be tied up all day and probably the next. She's based in Bridgeport, so we'll probably meet her in Connecticut. Plan on dinner either Wednesday evening or Thursday. I'll be in touch," he said just before the phone went dead.

# CHAPTER FOUR

Dylan awoke before sunrise the following morning and headed downstairs to his home gym. After completing a vigorous ninety-minute weightlifting workout, he showered, dressed, and made his way to the kitchen. He mixed peanut butter, oatmeal, banana, blueberries, and protein powder into his Vitamix blender. He poured the concoction into a large Tervis tumbler and took the smoothie down to his office. Shirley buzzed his phone. "Quentin's on the line for you."

He picked up the receiver. "Good morning."

"Hey, Dylan."

"Quentin, how are you?"

"Pretty sore. I managed to stay on the field all season, but I'm pretty beat up. Now that it's over, I'm looking forward to taking a few weeks off and letting my body heal before beginning off-season workouts. Anyway, I wanted to thank you for inviting me to the school field house opening next week. Shirley's told me all about it. I also wanted to let you know I'm taking care of the theater tickets for the group. My agent hooked us up, and we'll be sitting in a box."

"Thanks, Quentin, that's very generous. I heard that show is completely sold out."

"My pleasure. I understand you want to go on Wednesday. There are matinee and evening performances. Which do you prefer?"

"Why don't we go to the matinee, and then we can have dinner? There's an Italian restaurant, Carmine's on Broadway. Some of the best food I've had, outside of my grandmother's cooking."

"Sounds great. You know I love to eat."

"We've rented a van that will take us to the city and back to the hotel in Greenwich."

"I'm looking forward to the trip. Talk soon."

As soon as he hung up, Dylan called Esther. As usual, Franklin answered. He was her estate manager and had been with Esther since Dylan had known her. She lived in a large Victorian-style home on considerable acreage at the end of a street in a working-class neighborhood in Stamford, not far from where Dylan had grown up.

"Good morning, sir," he replied in his usual formal tone. "Please hold for Mrs. Lott." Dylan had referred to her by her surname from the time he'd first met her as a child until his college graduation when she requested he call her Esther. He had done so for the past twenty years, but either that privilege didn't apply to Franklin, or he refused to indulge in such informalities.

"Good morning, Dylan. How are you?"

"Doing well, Esther, and you?"

"I'm doing wonderful. I just finished my morning walk. The weather has been nice up here lately, so I've been walking outside. Usually, I take laps in the greenhouse this time of year."

"I heard the weather's been mild, but I also heard the forecast is calling for snow next week."

"Yes. It's going to be cold, but I don't expect we'll get more than a dusting. I'm glad you called. I want to host a dinner party for you and your family when you're in town."

Dylan sat in silence for a moment. He and Esther were extremely close, and he thought of her as family. He'd shared his most intimate thoughts with her throughout the years and valued her advice and friendship. However, as smart and engaging as she was with him, one on one, he privately found her to be eccentric and quite the recluse. He recalled that she had met his family on one occasion many years ago after he'd graduated from college and before his move to Florida. "That's very generous of you, Esther. In addition to my mother and grandparents, my mom's boyfriend and my assistant, Shirley, and her boyfriend are traveling with us. I don't want to put you out."

"Don't be silly. We have plenty of room for you and your family and friends, and I'm going to invite a few other people. I look forward to seeing your mother and grandparents again and meeting the people in your life. Please send me each person's email address, and I'll send out invitations to everyone with the details."

"Of course. I have everyone's email; I'll have them sent right over." He pondered for a moment. "Alex will be in town and my friend Penel is going to be staying with me while I'm in Connecticut. Okay if they're included as well?"

"Of course, I recall many of our conversations involving those two. I look forward to meeting them. The opening is on Tuesday evening. Will you all be here on Monday?"

"Yes. We're all flying up together on Monday afternoon. The group has plans on Wednesday to go see a show in the city, so Monday should be fine."

"Well, I'll let you get back to your day. I have a lot of planning to do."

"Take care, Esther."

"You do the same, Dylan. I'll talk with you soon."

He hung up the phone and stared off in bemusement, a smile on his face. He had never seen this side of Esther, the social party host. This trip was indeed getting more interesting.

# CHAPTER FIVE

On Friday afternoon, Francis Nagle sat alone at a small table in the first-floor dining hall of the Park City Plaza building on Middle Street in downtown Bridgeport, Connecticut. As she finished her brown bag lunch, she gazed out the window at her view of a slice of the Long Island Sound waterfront and reflected on her good fortune.

Fanci, as she was known to her friends, was a senior at Turing University, an Ivy League school on Philadelphia's Main Line. She was an education major scheduled to graduate in May. Saddled with student loan debt, she had read about a loan forgiveness program tied to working in the Connecticut public-school system. She had wanted to be a teacher since she was a little girl growing up in Danbury and, to improve her prospects, had applied for and received an internship with the New York Metro Area Teachers' Union headquartered in Bridgeport. It was a paid position, and she would receive the last of the nine credits required for graduation.

Fanci was tall and thin, with long black hair, dark eyes, and mocha skin, courtesy of her Ecuadorian-American mother. She was attractive, with looks similar to the models currently in high demand. Her mother, Graciela Cruz, had raised Fanci alone in Danbury after she split with her boyfriend, a local named Nagle, not long after Fanci was born. Fanci was a product of the Danbury public-school system, had graduated near the top of her class at Danbury High School, and was named salutatorian. She'd applied to every Ivy League college and was rejected by all of them except Turing.

According to her high school guidance counselor, the decisive factor in Turing's admission decision was the moving essay about her humble background as the only child of a single Ecuadorian immigrant mother who toiled at dual jobs at Broadview Junior High School, working in the school cafeteria by day and as a custodian at night. Fanci often stayed after school, studying in the library well into the evening hours while her mother worked cleaning the classrooms. She had decided to become a teacher since those long days spent at Broadview.

She was finishing up the first week of the fourteen-week internship and thinking about the weekend as she scrolled through her emails. One jumped out at her with the subject line "Meeting Invite Confirm ASAP." It was from Kari Baldwin, president of the teachers' union. Fighting off the nervous pit forming in her stomach, she read the text of the email: "Your presence is required in my office for a meeting at 2:00 p.m. this afternoon. Reply with your confirmation."

Fanci looked at her phone; the time was one thirty-five. She hit the reply symbol, typed Confirmed, and pressed Send. She quickly gathered up her things and ran frantically to the elevator. She could feel the heat emanating from her frontal lobe as the elevator ascended to the twentieth floor.

*I don't even know where her office is located. Is it even in this building?* she thought as the elevator doors opened. She rushed out and ran right into the arms of a man standing four feet from the elevator doors.

"Whoa there, young lady. What's the hurry?" the man asked as he stopped her, placing his hands on her shoulders to soften the impact. She didn't look up, lost in the thoughts ricocheting through her brain.

"Excuse me," she replied as she extricated herself from his grasp and ran in the direction of her desk. She sat down, put her head in her hands, and allowed herself to rerun the first four and a half days on the job through her memory banks. Day one was spent in an unremarkable orientation session with three other people, all of whom were starting in various positions. She'd spent Tuesday and Wednesday shadowing her supervisor, Marion Bishop, a curriculum analyst, and since that time had been working on a project, researching the merits of eliminating standardized testing. She was making good progress on her assignment and hadn't yet turned in any work.

*What could this possibly be about? Have I done something wrong?* She thought about every interaction she could recall during the work week and came up empty,

Her hands trembling slightly, she took a deep breath, nervously arranged her hair down the back of her shoulders, and walked timidly to the inner cubicle where Marion worked.

She knocked on the soft-sided wall. "Hello," she uttered softly.

Marion looked up from her computer screen, reading glasses resting on her disproportionately large nose. "Yes, Francis. Is there something you need?" she said in a monotone inflection.

Fanci hesitated for a beat, taken aback by the coldness of the reply. "Uh, if you have a moment, I wanted to ask you about an email I just received."

"What is it?"

"It's from Kari Baldwin, requesting me in a meeting in her office at two o'clock. I wanted to ask if you knew anything about it."

She observed as Marion glanced quickly at the digital clock on her desk and then looked back at her while removing her glasses from their perch on her nose. She folded them in her hands as she spoke. "I'm not aware of any meeting. Are you sure it's from Ms. Baldwin?"

It hadn't occurred to her to investigate the validity of the email. She pressed a few times on her phone screen and handed the device to Marion.

Replacing the reading glasses, she stared at the screen. "Hmm. I don't know anything about this. It's almost two, so I suggest you present yourself to Ms. Baldwin's office."

"Can you tell me where it's located?"

"Upper management offices are on the twenty-first floor," she replied, handing back her phone. "Let me know what this is about after the meeting."

"Yes, ma'am," she said as she turned and headed back to the elevators.

The car opened to an expansive reception area on the executive floor. There was a large built-in counter in the middle and thick double-glass doors on either side. Two security officers in blazers manned the counter. "May I help you, young lady?" the older of the two men inquired after she had barely stepped out of the elevator.

A wave of clear-headed calmness swept over her. She said nothing but walked confidently toward the security man, shoulders back, head up, maintaining eye contact the entire time. "Francis Nagle to see Kari Baldwin," she stated confidently in a clear voice.

She watched as his eyes shifted to the ID badge resting on her chest, held in place by a lanyard around her neck. "Young lady, this is the executive floor. Interns are not permitted up here without an appointment."

"My appointment with Ms. Baldwin is for two o'clock. Kindly ring her office and let her know I'm here."

The man regarded her a moment longer before pressing some keys on the computer keyboard in front of him. He sat focused on the screen, avoiding further eye contact. She stared back at him, not looking away. After about a minute, he looked back up at her. "Please have a seat, Ms. Nagle. Someone will be out for you shortly."

She nodded but said nothing before turning on her heels and walking to a small couch off to one side of the lobby. She sat down and looked around. The walls were decorated with what appeared to be original oil paintings of school buildings from around the tristate area. She recognized the post-renovation picture of Danbury High, its three-story main building and single-level entrance with the decorative steel-framed glass panels above the school's name.

After taking in the lobby, she glanced down at her clothing. Her mother had splurged for Christmas and bought her several business outfits for the new job. Today, she was wearing one of them: a tailored houndstooth skirt and tan turtleneck under a black wool blazer. Knee-high black boots completed the ensemble.

She began thinking about Kari Baldwin and wished she'd had time to do some research. She had seen her on television a few times and recalled an older woman with short, graying hair and a plain face with soft features. She vaguely recalled that she was a lawyer by training but couldn't be sure about that.

After a few minutes, she heard a loud buzzing sound just as an attractive young woman came through the set of glass doors across from where she was seated. The woman was wearing tailored dark-wool pants over boots with a high heel. Her tight sweater highlighted large breasts. She stared at Fanci for a moment with a slight grimace that Fanci interpreted as a sympathetic expression. "Ms. Nagle?"

Fanci stood and walked in her direction. "I'm Francis Nagle."

"Please follow me," she instructed as she turned and scanned her badge against a black box mounted on the wall. The buzzing sound returned as she opened the door and walked down a long plush-carpeted hallway. Fanci followed along in silence. When they reached a set of heavy dark wooden doors, the woman pushed her way through. It opened into a sitting area with a modest desk off to one side. "I'm Cindy Seravisi, Ms. Baldwin's personal assistant. Please have a seat," she instructed with a nod, indicating a set of couches across from the desk.

"Thank you," she replied as she took a seat on the couch with a view of the desk and another set of double doors that presumably led to an inner office. The assistant took her seat behind the desk.

Shortly, Kari Baldwin emerged from behind the doors, looking at her assistant as she spoke. "Cindy, I'll be tied up in a meeting. Please hold all calls and do not allow any disturbances."

"Of course, Ms. Baldwin," she replied.

The short exchange gave Fanci an opportunity to observe Kari Baldwin. Her face was as she recalled from television, but she was somewhat surprised by her size. The woman had broad shoulders, thick arms and legs, and appeared to stand close to six feet. She was dressed in a tailored pink pantsuit and matching pink running shoes. She turned toward Fanci, who instinctively stood but remained in place. The woman took a few steps in her direction and stopped. "Francis, I'm Kari Baldwin."

Fanci walked toward her and extended her right hand. "Ms. Baldwin, I'm Francis Nagle."

"It's very nice to meet you," she replied with a thin smile as she accepted her hand, holding it and retaining the smile for an extended period. Fanci stood motionless, maintaining eye contact with an expressionless mien.

"All right, then," she said, finally releasing her grip on Fanci's hand. "Please come. We have some business to discuss," as she turned and led her through the doors to her office suite.

Fanci followed behind and was awestruck by the opulence of the office. It appeared to take up at least a quarter of the square footage of the entire floor. Two full walls were floor-to-ceiling glass and offered expansive views of the waterfront, extending out to the horizon of Long Island Sound.

The room appeared to be divided into three parts. In the center of the room was an oversized executive office desk with matching credenza, seating for four, and an antique oak cabinet that served as a bar. Off to one side was a conference room equipped with a large screen and seating for twenty. The opposite side of the space reminded Fanci of a well-furnished sitting room she had seen in magazines featuring fancy estate homes.

Kari Baldwin sat behind her massive desk, and Fanci took a chair directly in front of her. She settled in, her five-foot-nine-inch frame positioned erect on the hardback chair, yet uncomfortably low, with the union leader towering over her from an ergonomic executive chair. "Ms. Nagle, I asked you here to discuss an important matter, but before we get into that, please tell me a little about yourself."

Fanci launched into a thirty-second bio, highlighting her personal background, educational history, and her passion for a career in education, leaving out the part about her student loan debt. Baldwin sat rapt, taking her in, chin resting on a closed fist.

After Fanci had finished, Baldwin folded her hands in front of her, resting her arms on the desk. She leaned forward, displaying a broader smile of slightly discolored teeth. "I'm pleased to learn about your desire for a career in public education because we, as an institution, are under attack by extremist groups. We're in a constant battle in the court of public opinion, getting our messaging out in front of the negative propaganda put forth by our enemies. And, of course, we are engaged in the relentless fight for the funding necessary to maintain our high standards of educating students while simultaneously protecting our membership and continuing to fulfill our objectives advancing equity and inclusion policies while closing the racial performance disparity gap."

Fanci sat silently and nodded, so Baldwin continued. "The rhetoric behind school choice and parental rights is similar to what was heard during the pre-*Brown v. Board of Education* era. It is separatist and segregationist and pits parents against our teachers."

Fanci remained quiet. Baldwin stood and stretched her considerable frame. "It's getting on in the afternoon, I could use a drink. Please join me," she commanded, walking toward the bar. She raised a sliding door and plucked cubes from a portable ice machine with a pair of tongs, placing them into a couple of Waterford glasses. She poured two healthy fingers of Scotch into each glass, picked up the drinks, and walked over to the sitting area. Fanci reluctantly followed behind her, confounded by an invitation to imbibe during working hours but cognizant that declining was not an option. "Please, take a seat and make yourself comfortable," Baldwin instructed.

"Thank you, ma'am," she quietly murmured as Baldwin handed her one of the glasses. She accepted it, grasping it awkwardly while positioning herself at one end of the couch.

Baldwin sat down uncomfortably close to her. She clinked her glass against Fanci's. "It's five o'clock somewhere. Here's to meeting new friends," she remarked before taking a healthy gulp.

Fanci politely took the smallest of sips before removing a coaster from a stack on the glass table in front of her and placing the drink upon it. She subtly slid away from Baldwin, practically wedging her back against the arm of the couch, as she turned to face her. She could smell the overbearing scent of Scotch masking that of the stale coffee on her breath. Baldwin took another generous sip of her drink before placing it on a coaster alongside Fanci's.

She turned to Fanci, gently brushing her arm. "Now I have an important assignment for you. It requires after-hours work." She then stared at her in silence, waiting for a reply.

Fanci said nothing but nodded again, so Baldwin continued. "It is important for us to monitor the progress of what is happening with our colleagues in the private sector. There is a Catholic elementary school in Stamford that's thriving; it's expanded and grown significantly over the past several years. This is concerning to our membership as it defies the trend of the contraction of Catholic schools over the past decade. A grand opening is scheduled there for next Tuesday night. I would like you to attend and report back to me with your findings."

"What specifically am I looking for?"

"The scope of the expansion, the identity of any major players, including the big money donors, anything you hear during the remarks you consider important to our mission. It would be ideal if you could record any public statements. Identify and mingle with some of the key players and see what information you can extract from them about future fundraising and expansion plans."

"What shall I say if I'm asked about why I'm present?"

Baldwin picked up her drink and took another sip before replacing her glass. She smiled and leaned in uncomfortably close, violating Fanci's personal space. "You're an attractive, intelligent young woman. Use those qualities to your advantage. Say as little as possible, but if pressed, explain that you're an education major doing a research paper on the success of school choice and private school expansion. That should get people to open up and share information."

Fanci was still unsure about the specifics of what she was supposed to do but declined to request any further instruction. "All right, I understand the assignment. And thank you for the opportunity, Ms. Baldwin."

She leaned in again, placing her hand on Fanci's thigh. "Please. Since we'll be working together, call me Kari. Do you go by Francis?"

"My friends call me Fanci," she said instinctively, immediately regretting her reply.

Baldwin leaned back and let out a hearty laugh. "I love it!" she belched out. "Fanci it is. This is an important assignment, and I need the information quickly. The event is on Tuesday evening next week. I live in Greenwich, about ten minutes from the school. Stop by my house right after for a debriefing."

Fanci said nothing, so Baldwin stood. "See Cindy on the way out. She has all the information you'll need, including my home address and personal cell phone number. I look forward to seeing you at the house on Tuesday evening. And don't worry about the time. I'll be waiting for you," she concluded, displaying a cringy tight-lipped smile.

"Yes, ma'am. Nice meeting you," Fanci murmured as she stood and made her way out of the office.

## CHAPTER SIX

Dylan awoke early on Monday morning. After a workout in his home gym, he showered and packed before heading down to his office. He answered some emails and was reading the newspapers when his phone rang. He answered and pressed the speaker button on his cell phone lying on the desk.

"Good morning, Dylan. All set for the trip?"

"Hey, Alex. I think so. I'm all packed and taking care of some last-minute stuff in the office before Aengus takes me to the airport."

Aengus Lobo was Dylan's property manager. He lived on the premises in an apartment above the auxiliary garage and occasionally served as Dylan's driver.

"How are you getting to the airport?" Dylan inquired.

"I'll take an Uber. I really appreciate the lift up to Connecticut. I bet your family is excited. When was the last time they all were back up there?"

"My mom and I were there together about a year ago when we stopped by the old house. I can't remember the last time my grandparents were there. I'm not sure they have been since they moved to Florida. They love it here and have become quite the beach bums."

"It's quite an entourage we're traveling with. How's everyone else getting to the airport?"

"Rick's driving my mom and grandparents, and Shirley and Quentin are meeting us there."

"Well, I'm looking forward to seeing everyone and meeting your mysterious friend, Esther. You've managed to keep me away from her all these years."

"She's like family. The least I could do was shield her from you as long as possible."

"Very funny," he snickered.

"Seriously, though, you'll really like her. She's one of the smartest and most interesting people I've ever known."

"Boy, that really hurts." His voice cracked in what sounded like mock disappointment. "I thought I was the smartest and most interesting person you knew."

"You are very interesting, but in a completely different sort of way."

"I'll take that as a compliment."

"You really shouldn't," Dylan replied, leaning back in his chair and interlacing his fingers behind his head.

"Who else is going to be at the party tonight?" Alex asked, changing the subject.

"No idea. Esther mentioned she invited other guests. We'll just have to wait and see."

"Maybe there'll be some eligible young ladies present."

"For their sake, I hope not," he replied, glancing at the digital clock on his computer screen. "It's about time for me to head to the airport. I'll see you shortly."

He hung up, grabbed his suitcase, and headed downstairs, where he found Aengus in the kitchen. "If you're ready to leave, sir, I have the Escalade pulled up out front."

Dylan followed him outside, and Aengus rushed over and held the rear door open.

"Really, Aengus? I prefer to sit up front with you."

"As you wish, sir," he replied with a subtle sigh, closing the door.

"We're going to Clearwater, not Tampa," Dylan instructed as they headed down the driveway. Aengus nodded, turned left, and drove north.

Clearwater International Airport was a small, intimate operation, handling a fraction of the passenger count of its big brother across the bay, Tampa International. In addition to the single main terminal, it housed a small executive jet center for private planes.

"Please pull up to the executive jet building. You can drop me off in front," Dylan instructed. He thanked Aengus, grabbed his bag, and wheeled it into the center. He immediately spotted an attractive female with a head of thick, full-blown blonde hair and a face obscured by oversized sunglasses. She was dressed in a blue button-down sweater that was cut above mid-thigh and served as a dress. White ankle boots completed the outfit. She was surrounded by a set of matching Louis Vuitton luggage of various sizes and shapes. The woman appeared to be staring at Dylan from behind her shades. As he walked in her direction she smiled, waved, and yelled out, "Dylan."

Slack-jawed, he said nothing but continued to walk toward her. The woman removed her sunglasses, and he smiled bashfully. "Shirley, I'm sorry I didn't recognize you at first," he replied. "Whose luggage is all this?" he asked, indicating with a wave of his hand.

"It's mine. Well, it's Quentin's, actually."

"Even the handbag?" he said with a smirk, nodding at the matching oversized purse on her shoulder.

"Ha, ha," she retorted with a tight smile and tilt of her head. "Quentin bought it for me to match the luggage."

"Very thoughtful and generous of him."

"You're not the only gentleman around here," she teased.

"Apparently not," he retorted. "So where is this gentleman of yours?"

"He's parking the car."

Quentin entered the building, and Dylan observed his mother, Rick, and his grandparents a short distance behind. The men were simultaneously pulling and carrying bags. Cheryl was also pulling a large rolling suitcase. As they gathered together, Dylan hugged his mother and grandmother and introduced everyone to Quentin. Hands were shaken all around. Anthony Tomassi clenched his jaw as he firmly shook Quentin's hand. "It's a pleasure to meet you. You're a hell of a football player."

"Thank you for the kind words. It's a pleasure to meet *you*."

"You know, Dylan was quite a ballplayer when he was young. Growing up, I thought he would end up in your profession."

"I heard something about that," Quentin replied with a look of amusement.

"Okay, Grandpa. Enough about the glory days," Dylan interjected.

"Christ's sakes there, I'm just saying. Can't an old man brag about his only grandson once in a while?"

As they were commiserating, two men dressed in pressed blue overalls emerged from the back doors leading to the tarmac. Each was pushing a luggage cart. "Mr. Tomassi?" the older of the two inquired as he approached the group.

"I'm Dylan Tomassi."

"Welcome, sir. My name is Matt, and this is Jorge," he said, indicating the other man. "We'll be handling your luggage and loading it into the aircraft."

The two men made quick work of the bags, and after they were expertly stacked on the carts, Matt continued, "We'll have your luggage stowed in no time. Whenever your group is ready, go out those doors," he instructed, pointing in the direction where he'd entered. "Your plane is right outside, and the pilots and crew are ready for you."

"Thank you, Matt," Dylan remarked as he watched the porters scurry out the doors. Alex appeared, pulling his suitcase and carrying an attaché in his other hand. He greeted everyone.

After a few minutes, Dylan observed the group engaged in relaxed chitchat. "Hey, everyone," he said in a raised voice above the chatter, "the plane's ready. Let's do this."

He began walking toward the rear doors, with the rest of his party following casually behind, still engaged in conversation. He stepped outside into the late morning sun and observed a single sleek, white aircraft, its stairway extended in place. A bright blue logo outlined in gold contained the letters PGF painted on the front of the fuselage. Two pilots and a pair of flight attendants stood at the foot of the stairs.

As Dylan approached, the sole man in the group stepped forward. "Mr. Tomassi?" he inquired.

"I'm Dylan."

"Good morning, I'm Captain Chuck Fiedler. I'll be your pilot today. This is First Officer Penny Carlson. We'll be flying you to New Jersey."

"Nice to meet you," Dylan replied, shaking both their hands.

Captain Fiedler turned to the two younger women standing behind him. "This is Kay and Rose. They'll be taking care of your group during the flight."

Dylan nodded and smiled. Both women were slim and attractive, their skirts short and their heels high.

The captain glanced at the cargo hold. "We've completed our preflight check, and we're wheels up whenever you're ready."

Dylan turned and looked behind him to find everyone silent and staring in his direction. "Looks like we're ready."

Positioning herself at the base of the stairs, Kay observed as Rose ascended the short stairwell before turning and addressing the group. "Welcome aboard, everyone," she announced.

As everyone began to climb aboard, Dylan's phone rang. He looked at the screen. It was Penel. He turned and took a few steps away from the aircraft, cradling the phone to the side of his face. "Good morning."

"Hey, Dylan. How are you?"

"We're at the airport, ready to board the plane. We should be taking off shortly."

"What time do you think you'll arrive in Greenwich?"

Holding the phone away from his ear, he glanced at the time. "It's eleven thirty now. We'll probably land at Teterboro no later than two thirty. A van will be waiting to take us to the hotel. Traffic shouldn't be too bad at that hour, so we should check in no later than four."

"I'm at the office, and I have my bags with me. Text me when you land, and I'll head to the train station."

"Okay, I'll meet you at the train," he replied, looking back at the plane and seeing no one. "Looks like everyone's aboard. I need to get going."

"Okay, safe travels, and see you soon," she gushed.

"Looking forward." He hung up and hurried toward the aircraft.

Rose was standing just inside the cabin as he entered. "Welcome, I'm glad you could make it," she said with an extra big smile, holding his gaze.

"Thanks for waiting," he said, returning the smile before breaking eye contact and turning to take in the cabin. It was furnished in white leather upholstery with a contrasting dark hardwood floor. His mother, Rick, and grandparents were sitting in chairs opposite each other on one side, separated by a table. Shirley and Quentin were seated closer to the rear on a couch. Alex was sitting toward the rear of the plane, engaged in conversation with Kay. There were several open swivel chairs toward the front. Dylan noticed the PGF logo prominently displayed on the walls and embroidered in the chair headrests. "What's PGF?" he asked Rose.

"It stands for Premier Global Finance. This is their plane. It's a Falcon 8X that seats fourteen." Dylan looked at her inquisitively, so she continued. "PGF is a hedge fund. Company management flew in last night for a conference. They'll be here until Wednesday morning. Rather than have the plane sit idle, it's leased out during the downtime."

"I see," Dylan replied, nodding. He moved toward the front of the plane and took a seat on the same side as his family, swiveling his chair in their direction. He observed Kay reemerge from what appeared to be a rear galley, carrying a tray of champagne flutes. As she served the passengers, his grandmother giggled. "Oh, thank you so much."

"No, thanks," his grandfather said with a wave of the hand. "If you have any beer, I'll take one of those."

"We have Blue Moon, Heineken, and Michelob Ultra."

"Not a fan of diet beer, but I'll have a bottle of the plain old American brew."

"Yes, sir. Let me serve the rest of the champagne, and I'll be right back."

"Thank you, darling."

Isabella nudged him under the table. "What?" he inquired with a puzzled look.

"She's a woman, not your darling."

"So? Who did I offend, you or her?"

"Both of us," she replied, taking a healthy sip of her champagne as the jet began to move.

Once the plane took off and they were at cruising altitude, a lunch of chicken piccata was served with wild rice and asparagus. Dylan passed on lunch, choosing instead to nibble on a few beef short rib appetizers wrapped in bacon. After a second glass of champagne, he put in his headphones, reclined his chair, and listened to a music station that played classic rock. He dozed off almost immediately and woke up to the sound of the plane's wheels touching down.

The plane taxied to a staging area and came to a stop. Dylan watched out the window as the lineman who had directed the aircraft chocked the tires. A black Mercedes Sprinter van appeared from behind the building and pulled up adjacent to the jet. Two other men were unloading the luggage from the cargo hold and placing it in the rear of the van. Dylan was impressed with the efficiency of the entire operation.

As everyone began to deplane, the cockpit door opened, and the entire crew stood by, exchanging pleasantries as they departed. As Dylan exited the plane, he felt the blast of cold air hit him. He stopped, pulled his down puffer jacket out of his carry-on bag, and zipped it to his neck.

*I don't miss winters up north,* he thought as he descended the stairwell. Once on the ground, he pulled out his phone and texted Penel. "Just landed at Teterboro. See you soon."

Everyone was standing around when the driver of the van approached. "Welcome, everyone. My name is Hugo. I'll be taking you to Greenwich, and I'll be your driver for the rest of the day."

Cheryl approached Dylan and pulled him aside. "Thank you so much for organizing this trip. Your grandparents, Rick, and I really appreciate it," she whispered before planting a kiss on his cheek.

"You're welcome, Mom," he replied. "Actually, we need to thank Shirley." He raised his voice to get everyone's attention. "I hope everyone enjoyed the flight."

Various expressions in the affirmative followed. "We all owe a measure of gratitude to Shirley for organizing the travel. You hit it out of the park as usual," he said, looking in her direction. She brushed her hair back and blushed slightly.

"Thanks, Shirley," everyone said in unison.

She leaned into Quentin. "You can thank me tonight."

"I fully plan on it," he whispered in a hushed tone.

They piled into the van, which reminded Dylan of a scaled-down version of the aircraft cabin. There was a row of captain's chairs across the rear with a bar set up between two of the seats. Leather couches were situated on either side. Toward the front were two additional swivel chairs. The seating was finished in napa leather and floors in stained black wood. The walls and fixtures were a shade of French vanilla.

Hugo took the New Jersey Turnpike to I-287. Traffic was moderate, and they arrived at the Delamar in forty-five minutes. The van pulled up to the front entrance, and they were met by bellmen who promptly began unloading their luggage. While they waited, Dylan pulled Shirley aside. "Can you please check everyone in and have my luggage delivered to my suite? I'm going to have Hugo drop off Alex and take me to the train station and pick up Penel."

"Sure thing."

"Hugo, when we're done here, we need to make one stop and then a pick up at the train station."

"Yes, Mr. Tomassi. We'll be ready as soon as the luggage is unloaded."

After Alex was delivered to his house, Dylan thought about Penel on the drive over to the train. They hadn't seen each other for several months after she had announced she'd met someone in New York. Dylan was saddened but not devastated by the news. He had been consumed with work and getting the youth center opened when he received a phone call from Penel congratulating him on the grand opening. During the course of the conversation, she admitted that she missed him and that her other relationship had been short-lived. They'd talked on the phone regularly since then and made plans to get together while Dylan was in Connecticut.

Hugo found a parking spot across from the train station. "Wait here, Hugo. I shouldn't be long."

"As you wish, sir."

Dylan hurried inside the warm station building and scanned the crowd. He immediately recognized Penel standing against a wall next to a row of vending machines. Her tall stature and expensively cut, shoulder-length dark hair created an air of combined beauty and sophistication. She was dressed in a camel-colored overcoat and brown knee-high boots. A brown cashmere scarf was wrapped around her neck.

Dylan approached her, careful to downplay the surge of anticipation and excitement that began to rush over him. Suddenly, she turned and looked in his direction.

"Oh, my God!" she exclaimed, taking several hurried steps toward him. She leaped off the ground and into his arms, wrapping both sets of her extremities around him. Their eyes met, and she kissed him on the lips. She broke the embrace enough to set her feet back on the floor, keeping her arms around him. Without saying another word, she kissed him again, this time locking mouths and holding him tightly for an extended time. Dylan took in the familiarity of her touch and scent. "It's so good to see you," she breathed.

"It's great to see you," he replied, gently breaking the embrace and steadying her on her feet while he held her at arm's length.

"My bags are right there," she said, indicating with a twist of her neck.

"I'll get those. Our ride is waiting outside."

Dylan handled her bags and led them out the automatic front doors and across the street. Hugo jumped out, took over the handling of the bags, and placed them in the rear cargo compartment. Dylan held the side door for Penel as she stepped inside and selected a seat on the couch. Dylan cozied up next to her. She smiled and leaned her head on his shoulder. "How was your trip from New York?" he asked.

"Uneventful. It wasn't crowded, so I got some work done. I can relax now and enjoy these next few days," she answered, kissing him lightly on the cheek.

"That's good to hear," he replied with a smile.

"Tell me more about this party tonight?"

"I don't know much more than Esther invited my family and friends over and said there would be some others in attendance. That's about it, other than the information contained in the invitation."

"A black-tie optional dinner. That's pretty old-school, especially these days."

"I've known Esther practically all my life. She is definitely old-school, somewhat mysterious at times, and often full of surprises. I've never known her to be much of the entertaining type, so we'll have to wait and see."

"Anyway, I'm looking forward to seeing your family and meeting your friends," she replied, caressing his leg.

Dylan felt a stirring of desire. Attempting to maintain his composure, he refocused his thoughts. "Here we are," he announced as the van pulled up to the Delamar's front entrance. He glanced at his phone. "We have a few hours before the party. Why don't we go up to the room, unpack, and relax."

"I'd like that," she purred, nibbling on his ear.

He extracted himself from the couch just as Hugo opened the side door. A uniformed bellman approached him as soon as he stepped outside. "Mr. Tomassi?"

"Yes," he replied with an inquisitive look.

"We've been expecting you. Your assistant left your keys at the front desk when she checked in," he said, handing him a sleeve of magnetic cards. "You're in suite 410. Your bags have already been delivered. Will there be additional luggage?"

"It's in the van," Dylan replied, gesturing to the rear.

"I'll bring them up right away."

Dylan and Penel entered the lobby, hand in hand, and headed directly over to the elevator. They arrived in the room, and the bellman showed up a moment later. Dylan thanked him and tipped the man. "Thank you, sir. Please let me know if there's anything else you require."

As soon as he left, Dylan began to unpack. Penel approached him from behind, placed her arms around his waist and snuggled up to him. "I'm a little tired from the trip. What do you say we take a nap before we get ready for the party?"

"I say that sounds like a fine idea."

He watched as Penel took off her overcoat to reveal a pair of tan riding pants tucked into her boots and a form-fitting mocha knit top. "Wow, you look wonderful."

"Come and take a closer look," she said in a throaty voice, taking him by the hand and leading him to the bedroom. Soon they were in each other's arms, conjoined on the bed, kissing and undressing each other. They'd always been physically compatible, and the heightened sexual familiarity returned as they began to indulge in carnal pleasure. Fifteen minutes later, they were sound asleep in each other's arms.

# CHAPTER SEVEN

Dylan awoke to the sound of the shower running. He stretched and sat up in bed, feeling relaxed and refreshed, unable to recall the last time he had taken two naps in a single day. He checked his phone while he waited for Penel to emerge from the bathroom, and there was a voicemail message from Esther asking him to call. He dialed her number and waited patiently for someone, presumably Franklin, to answer. He uncharacteristically picked up on the fifth ring. "Good afternoon," he said breathlessly, "Lott residence."

"Hello, Franklin. It's Dylan, returning Esther's call."

"Yes, sir. Please hold while I locate her."

A moment later, Esther came onto the phone and, after they'd exchanged pleasantries, got to the point. "I wanted to give you a heads-up. One of the guests tonight is a reporter for *Connecticut Today*. She called earlier to let me know that she's writing an article on school choice and the role of private schools. She's aware of your work with the Catholic school systems here and in Florida and would like to interview you for her piece."

"What do you think?"

"Her name is Scotland Kerns, but she goes by Scottie. I've known her a long time, and she's one of several people I invited this evening in addition to you and your family and friends. From a reporter's perspective, I've always found her to be a straight shooter, but it's entirely up to you. I had no idea she was working on such a project when I extended the invite."

"I see," he replied, rubbing his temples while evaluating his decision. There was silence on the other end, and a moment later, he responded. "Sure, I'll speak with her."

"Good. Now that we have that out of the way, I'm looking forward to seeing everyone tonight."

"Same here. I know my mom and grandparents are excited as well. You haven't seen them since I moved to Florida."

"You are correct. I was thinking about that when I put this party together. Well, the catering staff is here, and we still have a good deal of work to do. I'll see you in a couple hours."

As he hung up the phone, Penel emerged from the bathroom wearing a hotel robe, her hair wrapped in a towel. "Hey, there, sailor. The bathroom's yours if you want to take a shower."

"You do know I didn't arrive here by boat."

She laughed hysterically before coming over and wrapping her arms around his neck. She kissed him gently on the lips. "I've missed you *and* your sense of humor."

He kissed her back, this time longer and more passionately. As they broke the embrace, he suggested, "Why don't you take your time and get ready? I think I'll head downstairs and grab a drink. I only need fifteen minutes to shower and get dressed."

"Another thing I like about you." She consulted her Piaget wristwatch. "Give me a half hour, and the bathroom's yours."

"Perfect," he replied, pulling on a pair of joggers and a sweatshirt. He made his way to the lounge and found Rick and his grandfather sitting at the bar, his grandfather wearing a pinstripe gray suit and Rick in his dress blue Coast Guard uniform.

"Good evening, gentlemen," he said as he approached. Both men turned in unison.

"Dylan," his grandfather replied, taking him in. "Please tell me you're not wearing *that* to the party."

Dylan glanced down before assuming a distressful look. "What's wrong with what I'm wearing?" he replied in mock indignation.

"Nothing if you're going out to do a little road work."

"Relax, Grandpa. Penel is getting ready. I'll shower and change when she's done. I thought I would come down here and grab a drink."

"Great minds think alike," he said, sliding out the barstool on his opposite side from Rick. "Saddle up. We just got our drinks, so we're not far ahead of you."

"What are you drinking?"

"Oban single malt."

The bartender approached, wiping down the space in front of Dylan and placing a paper napkin in front of him. "Good evening, sir. What can I get you?"

"I'll have the same as these fine gentlemen."

"Very good, sir," the man said approvingly as he hurried off.

"How is Penel?" Rick inquired, leaning back in his seat.

"She's doing well and looking forward to seeing everyone."

"We're looking forward to seeing her as well," Anthony added. "She's a mighty fine woman."

His drink was served, sparing him from replying to his grandfather's comment.

The three men chatted for a while before Dylan consulted his phone. "Looks like it's time for me to get ready. I'll meet you all in the lobby in twenty minutes."

"Sounds good," Anthony exclaimed, holding up his glass in the direction of the bartender. "Just enough time for us to have a second drink."

Dylan opened the door to the suite and found Penel standing in front of a full-length mirror, wearing nothing but sheer black stockings and matching lace garter belt, bra, and thong. She turned as he entered. "I hope that's your outfit for the evening," he commented. "You'll make quite a splash at the party, particularly with the male guests."

She smiled somewhat seductively. "I am wearing this. . .underneath that gown hanging in the closet. If you're a good boy, I could be convinced to lose the dress when we get back tonight."

He raised his right hand. "I swear I will be on my best behavior."

She smiled and shook her head as he made his way into the bathroom. Fifteen minutes later, he was dressed in a black suit and tie, and they were in the lobby as the rest of the group arrived. Dylan made the introductions. Penel had met his family once before, but he was introducing her to Shirley and Quentin for the first time. "Pleasure to meet you," Shirley said, somewhat aloof.

Quentin held her hand a moment longer. "It is certainly a pleasure to meet a friend of Dylan's. He's a good man and a close friend of mine as well."

"Thank you, Quentin."

Shirley, dressed in a gold chiffon wrap gown, broke away from the foursome and pulled her phone out of a small clutch purse. Quentin stood by looking dapper in black tuxedo pants and a white dinner jacket over a white shirt and black bow tie. "That was Hugo, our driver," she announced. "He's just pulled up and is waiting for us outside."

As the group piled into the van, Dylan helped Penel into a seat on one of the couches before leaning over the two front captain's chairs to speak with Hugo. "Good evening, Hugo. We're going to 216 Travis Avenue in Stamford."

"Yes, sir. Shirley informed me earlier when she called for the pickup. I've already keyed the address into the navigation system. We should be there in about fifteen minutes."

He turned back and looked at Shirley, who was snuggled next to Quentin on the opposite couch, his massive arm resting gently across her petite shoulders. She made eye contact and twitched a smile simultaneously with a slight tilt of the head. Dylan sat down next to Penel and took in the couple. "You're looking quite spectacular tonight," he commented in their general direction. "And you look lovely also, Shirley."

She displayed a tight smile which scrunched up her nose and eyes.

"Thank you, Dylan. Penel, would you like to switch seats?" Quentin asked, feigning seriousness. Dylan glanced toward the rear of the van, where his mother, grandparents, and Rick looked on in amusement.

"Was he always this way?" Quentin asked, looking back at his family.

"Christ sakes," Anthony said. "It's starting to sound like Alex is here."

"Alex will be at the party," Cheryl reminded him.

"I'm gonna need another drink. Why didn't we stock this van with booze?"

"Take it easy," Isabella said, gently clutching his arm. "You can wait until we get to the party. And besides, you miss the days when Dylan and Alex used to come by the house and visit."

"I suppose you're right."

Penel grazed Dylan's arm before her hand came to rest on his thigh. "Isn't this great? Having your family and friends all together?"

He hesitated for a moment while everyone looked on. "I'll have to get back to you on that," he decided as they all burst into laughter.

As Esther's large gray Victorian house came into view, Dylan's mind flashed back to his daily trips as a boy, delivering her newspaper in the old cedar box on the porch. Large outdoor floodlights illuminated the stately manor, and a half-dozen cars were parked in the driveway.

Dylan led the group to the front door, and Franklin answered dressed in a classic black tuxedo with tails, ramrod straight in posture, and in full formal manner, per usual. "Good evening," he announced as they entered. "Mrs. Lott is accepting guests in the parlor just off to your right."

Dylan escorted Penel by the arm, and the others fell in behind them. Esther was wearing a long black dress and black walking shoes. She was standing with a champagne flute in her hand, talking to an older woman, when she turned toward Dylan. "Excuse me," she said to the woman as she placed her glass on a nearby end table and moved toward him. She gave Dylan a gentle hug, squeezing tightly once they had established the embrace. "It's so good to see you. I'm so glad you could attend." He thought he noticed a small tear forming in her left eye.

"Thank you for inviting us. The house looks beautiful, as usual. Let me introduce you to everyone," he said, taking charge. "This is my friend Penel. You know my mom, Cheryl, and this is her companion, retired US Coast Guard Rear Admiral Rick Landry."

Dylan stepped aside and observed silently as they all exchanged pleasantries. When the balance of the introductions were complete, Esther concluded, "Welcome again, everyone. There is a bar set up on the other side of the room, and hors d'oeuvres will be served shortly. Dinner is at eight."

Everyone scattered while Dylan hung back with Esther. "I'm very impressed," he said leaning into her. "I've never seen this side of you, Esther, the social hostess."

She regarded him for a moment. "Even though we've known each other a long time, there are many things you may be unaware of when it comes to me."

"I can see that," he replied, looking around the room. "There must be a dozen other people here."

"Twenty-two guests at the moment, including your family. I believe we're only waiting for your friend Alex. He and I will make it an even two dozen. I wanted everyone to fit comfortably in the dining room, and that's the capacity."

"That figures. Alex is all about making the splashy entrance."

"Did someone mention my name?" Dylan turned and saw Alex enter the room, escorted by the ubiquitous Franklin. He came over, ignoring Dylan, and extended his hand in Esther's direction. "And who might this fair young woman be?"

"This fair, not-so-young woman would be Esther Lott. I assume you are Alex," she replied, accepting his hand.

"Alex Malloy, at your service," he said with a slight bow.

"I've heard quite a bit about you over the years."

"Please understand, where I am the subject and Dylan the source, things tend to get quite distorted and greatly exaggerated."

"I'll reserve ruling on that, but the fact that you and Dylan are best friends starts you off on favorable footing."

"I apologize in advance for Alex," Dylan added. "Unfortunately, the statute of limitations has run, and he has been grandfathered in for quite some time. I couldn't get rid of him if I tried."

He could see she was delighted with the exchange, but then her expression turned semiserious. "Lifelong friends are a rarity in this world. You two should consider yourselves lucky and treasure that relationship."

Alex appeared speechless, a rarity for him. Dylan looked around the room. "Is there anything I can help you with?"

"No, dear. Franklin and the caterers have everything in hand. Please grab a drink."

"We will, thank you." He led Alex in the direction of the bar, where Penel was standing alongside Cheryl and Rick. "Hello, Ms. T. It's great to see you," Alex blurted, giving Cheryl a bear hug. As a child, Alex had referred to her as Ms. McD, a reference to her former married name, and thought of her as a second mom. Dylan and Cheryl had their last name legally changed just before he moved to Florida.

"Alex, you never change, and that's not necessarily a bad thing," she said with a smile.

Rick extended his hand. "Nice to see you again, Alex."

"Rick," he said with a nod. "You certainly are a lucky man." He glanced in Cheryl's direction.

"I am well aware of my good fortune."

Finally, Alex turned his attention to Penel, taking her hand and kissing it gently. "And how are you, my dear?"

Dylan looked on with amusement as Alex was clearly in his usual zone. "You know, when we all first met, why didn't we end up together?" he continued, referring to the time he and Dylan had first met Penel and her friend at a hockey game at Madison Square Garden when they were teenagers. "Things might have turned out differently, and you would have been spared spending time in the company of this guy."

"If you recall, Alex, you had your choice, and you picked my former roommate. As far as I'm concerned, everything worked out just fine," she replied with a smile.

Clutching his chest with his right hand, "Ouch, that hurts,"

"Somehow, I think you'll recover just fine."

Esther approached with a young woman in tow. She had straight, long brown hair and a mousey face and was dressed in a British tan pantsuit. "May I grab Dylan for a moment?" she asked, gently taking hold of his elbow. "There's someone I want you to meet."

"Excuse me," Dylan replied, breaking off from the group. The threesome gathered in a section of the parlor by the fireplace, which was burning a brilliant orange red.

"Dylan, this is Scotland Kerns," Esther continued. "She's the reporter from the newspaper I was telling you about."

"Hello, Dylan. Please, call me Scottie. Everyone does. I'm with *Connecticut Today*, and I've been working on a feature article on school choice. It's scheduled to go to press on Wednesday, and I understand you're in town for the grand opening of an addition to St. Mary school and that you're a supporter of Catholic education. I'd like to speak with you about that. Should only take ten, fifteen minutes at the most."

"Sure."

"You can use my office," Esther interjected. "It'll be quieter there and give me a chance to chat with your family and friends."

Once they were seated in the two upholstered chairs in front of Esther's somewhat cluttered desk, Scottie pulled out her phone. "Okay if I record this?"

"Yes."

"Could you start by stating your name and spelling it, please."

"Dylan Tomassi. D-Y-L-A-N T-O-M-A-S-S-I."

Leaning forward in her chair, she said, "As I mentioned, I'm writing a feature on school choice. I'd like to get your perspective on the state of our education system and how you got involved in supporting private schools, particularly Catholic primary education. But first, could you give me a summary of your background and educational history?"

"I was born and raised right here in Stamford. Attended St. Mary and then graduated from Stamford High School. I have a finance degree from the University of Connecticut."

"I understand you now live in Florida. You appear very youthful," she commented with a smile. "Tell me about your professional career and how you were able to attain a degree of success at such a relatively young age that enabled you to get involved in philanthropy?"

Dylan leaned back in his chair, placing his hands behind his head as he gathered his thoughts. "I made the decision to move to Florida after college and selected the Tampa Bay area because it was an up-and-coming center for business and finance. I worked in a Tampa brokerage for several years before I struck out on my own. Since that time, I manage my personal investment portfolio and run a real estate company that develops and manages residential and commercial properties."

"How did you come to get involved in philanthropy?"

"Honestly, I'd never thought about it until a couple years ago when I was approached by a friend about getting involved in charitable giving. I passed on the idea he proposed, but it opened my mind to the concept, and I began thinking about the best way I could help other people. Ultimately, I looked back at my own life growing up and how education and the people in my life were pivotal in my success. I always felt my education at St. Mary provided me a solid foundation in the fundamentals of math, reading, writing, and history, which have served me well to this day. So I started a charitable foundation. We began with funding scholarships at Catholic elementary schools here and in Florida, and then it just grew organically from there."

"How would you respond to the argument that moving students out of the public-school system and into private schools takes away critical funding and resources that hurt the district schools?"

Dylan made eye contact with Scottie and held her gaze for an uncomfortable period. "I don't think I understand your question."

"Allow me to explain. A school district receives local, state, and federal funding based on the number of students enrolled. If, for example, through vouchers, charter schools and programs, or in the case where a private foundation like yours is funding scholarships, headcount is reduced, and thus, the public schools receive less funding, which means less money for teachers, books, computers, and other education materials, support staff, buildings, et cetera. The current trend holds for virtually every state in the nation, and as it continues, the district education system is drained of resources, and the quality of public education will continue in a hopelessly downward spiral."

Dylan winced. "I approach this from a realistic perspective. As one person, I can only do so much. My objective is to carefully select promising young people who come from underprivileged or disadvantaged backgrounds and provide them with the tools and resources to be successful in life. I was raised by a single mom, and as I mentioned earlier, I credit my family, a Catholic education, and the mentors and coaches who took an interest in me growing up for the level of success I enjoy today. I want to try to duplicate that experience for others. Children grow up faster today, and these are their formative years, where a quality education and positive role models are critical to building a solid foundation for adulthood. That's why we built the youth center in St. Petersburg. To help them and keep them engaged outside of the classroom."

"I appreciate that, but I want to stay focused on your involvement in education. What do you think of the public education system today?"

"It's not my place to make a judgment on that. Remember, I attended public high school and graduated from a fine state university. I can only go by my own experience, and I feel that, during those formative years, a Catholic education at the elementary and junior high levels served me well."

"What other Catholic schools do you support other than St. Mary?"

"In Florida, I fund scholarships at St. Gregory School in St. Petersburg."

"How did you go about selecting that particular school?"

"My mother taught at St. Gregory before she retired, and I was a member of the parish finance committee, so I was very familiar with the school."

"Do you have plans to fund other Catholic or private schools?"

"We just had the grand opening of the youth center, and, of course, I'm in town for the opening of an addition to St. Mary that I was involved with, so no immediate plans beyond those projects."

"Do you believe a Catholic education is inherently superior to one in the public-school system?"

Narrowing his eyes, he carefully selected his words. "I don't think you can make a sweeping generalization like that. Although I was familiar with both St. Mary and St. Gregory, before I made the financial commitment, due diligence was performed to make certain it was a good match."

"What did that involve?"

"Visiting the schools in session and observing, reviewing curriculums and textbooks, speaking with teachers and administrators, that type of thing."

"What were you looking for?"

Dylan exhaled deeply. "Like I said, I wanted to have a certain comfort level with how the school was being run."

"Was school culture something you looked at during this process?"

"What do you mean by school culture?"

"Are you concerned about the claims by certain groups that schools have become indoctrination factories?"

"Yes, it is a cause of concern."

"Let me get more specific. What is your position on teaching critical race theory as part of the curriculum?"

He leaned forward in his seat. "Before I got involved in supporting education, I'd never heard of critical race theory. It certainly wasn't around when I was in school. After doing a lot of study on trends in academia, I have concluded that categorizing students based on skin color as a primary identifying characteristic and treating them accordingly is a horrible idea on many levels."

"How would you describe yourself politically?"

"I'm not into politics. I'm into trying to help people. And I've made the decision that I can do the most good working with young people."

She glanced at her phone. "I don't want to keep you much longer. Just a few more questions. What do you think of the Department of Education?"

"Not much."

"What does that mean?"

"When Jimmy Carter formed the department, the United States was number one in the world in education. Today, we're number twenty-four. It certainly hasn't helped."

"Finally, do you support universal school choice?"

Dylan rubbed his neck in an effort to relieve the building tension. "I will say this. In Chicago, the public-school budget is $27,000 per student. It costs $11,000 for a private school education in that same city, where student math and reading scores outperform the public schools by a wide margin. Something's wrong with the system, and it needs fixing. I support a system where the students are the focal point, and the money follows them rather than the other way around. It's currently trending in that direction, and I predict it will continue."

She turned off the recording function on her phone, stood up, and smiled, extending her right hand. "Thank you so much, Dylan, for speaking with me."

"Sure, no problem," he mumbled, grateful it was over. "If you'll excuse me, I'm going to get back to the party."

"Yeah, okay. I'll be right behind you."

Dylan scurried out of the office and made his way toward the living room. People were milling about, others conversing in small groups. He observed Esther and Penel engaged in discussion, both holding champagne flutes. "Hello, ladies. I could certainly use one of those," he said, nodding at their drink glasses.

"Penel and I were just having a marvelous conversation," Esther commented. "What a lovely friend you have, Dylan."

"Thank you, Esther," he replied, observing Penel smiling silently, "but you are respectfully inaccurate in your assessment of the situation."

"Oh. And why is that?"

"Yeah, Dylan, what *does* that mean?" Penel chimed in, poking him on the side with her free hand.

"A more precise statement would be that I have two lovely friends."

They both laughed in unison. "Okay, you got me there," Penel retorted.

Suddenly, Franklin entered the dining room. "May I have your attention, please!" he belted out. "Dinner will be served in ten minutes."

Dylan shook his head in amusement. "Esther, Franklin is as eccentric as he is efficient."

"I can't argue with you there. If you'll excuse me, I want to check on things in the kitchen," she said before heading in that direction.

"What were the two of you talking about?" he asked when they were alone.

"Girl talk, that type of stuff."

"Can you be more specific?"

"Do you mean were we talking about you?"

"That's not necessarily what I meant," he replied, looking up as Alex approached. It appeared he had just finished a conversation with a distinguished-looking woman with gray hair and black highlights wearing horn-rimmed glasses.

"Where'd you disappear off to, Dylan?" he asked as he approached.

"I was in Esther's office talking to a reporter."

"There's a reporter here?" he asked, looking around.

"Relax. No one's here to disclose the sordid details of your escapades."

"You can never be too sure."

"Who was that you were just speaking with?" Penel chimed in.

"Oh, that's Dr. Freeman."

"Who's she?" Dylan asked.

"*She* is Leslie Freeman, the dean of Yale Law School. She's been there since my time at Yale. I haven't seen her in years, so we were catching up."

"I bet she could tell some classic tales of your exploits. How do she and Esther know each other?"

"She said they've known each other for years. Told me they're both alumni of Endicott. Said Esther's pretty involved in higher education and sits on a few boards."

"Wow," Dylan replied.

"Looks like there's much you don't know about your friend Esther," Penel observed.

"It does appear that way."

Franklin reappeared, holding a sterling silver triangular dinner bell. He clanged it three times with a matching call striker. "Ladies and gentlemen, dinner is now being served in the dining room," he announced.

"That's certainly old school," Alex whispered, nudging Dylan in the arm.

"Classic Franklin," Dylan replied with a grin as he took Penel's arm and escorted her to dinner. When they entered the room, Esther was already seated at the head of the large table on the far side of the room. Dylan observed nameplates at each setting and found Penel's about halfway down. An older, distinguished-looking man was already seated to her right, and the other side was marked with a woman's name he didn't recognize. He assisted her into her chair and moved down the table until he found his seat at the end directly to Esther's left.

Once everyone was seated, a white wine was served by two caterers dressed in black slacks and white tuxedo shirts. "What type of wine is being served?" he asked as a young woman was filling his glass.

"It's a 2018 Far Niente chardonnay," the woman replied, presenting the label. He nodded approvingly.

After the wine was poured, Esther clanked her glass with a spoon. "May I have your attention, please? First, thank you all for coming this evening and joining me for dinner and fellowship. You may have observed that you are all seated next to people you may not know. That was by design so you will all have an opportunity to get acquainted. Please introduce yourselves and enjoy some good conversation while we dine. I have known many of you for years, while some I've just met tonight. So welcome again, and here's to friendships, old and new. Please enjoy," she concluded, raising her glass.

A chorus of "Hear, hear" followed as the guests lifted their own glasses in reply.

A garden salad with Gorgonzola dressing was served, followed by a main entrée of sauteed chicken with a marsala wine sauce and fresh mushrooms.

Dylan glanced to his left and observed an older man with a full head of expensively cut white hair dressed in a classic black tuxedo. "Good evening, sir. I haven't had the pleasure of meeting you. I'm Dylan Tomassi."

"Ah, Mr. Tomassi. It's a pleasure to meet you. I'm Chance Allen. I understand your presence in town was the catalyst for our gathering tonight."

He glanced over at Esther, who was engaged in conversation with a younger woman to her right. "What brings you to our fair state?" he continued.

"My family, friends, and I are in town for the grand opening of a new wing at a school here in Stamford."

"I see. Where are you from?"

"I grew up in Connecticut, but I've lived in Florida for the past twenty-five years."

"Moving to the Sunshine State from this neck of the woods is certainly the trend these days."

"Where are you from, Chance?"

"Born and raised in Manhattan. Attended Columbia and spent my entire career at Goldman Sachs. I always lived in the city but kept a weekend house in Westport. After I retired, my wife and I—she's here somewhere," he said, glancing down the long table. "Anyway, we downsized our apartment in New York and bought a larger place in Greenwich. We live here full time now and spend our time traveling and visiting with the grandkids. More room for them here too. We use the apartment when we visit the city."

"How do you know Esther?" he asked.

"I met her years ago at an investment seminar. As a partner at Goldman, I had access to some great minds in the fields of finance and investment, and I would put Esther up against any of them. How about you? How do you know Esther?" he asked with an expression that led Dylan to the impression she'd never mentioned him other than as the impetus for the evening's event.

"I've known Esther since I was a child. Met her when I was a paperboy delivering the *Stamford Advocate*."

"Interesting," he replied with a raised brow, confirming Dylan's suspicion that Esther had never spoken about their relationship.

"How are the two of you getting along?" Esther chimed in.

"We're just getting acquainted," Chance replied.

Dylan smiled and continued the light conversation through dinner. After coffee and dessert, which featured a cheesecake topped with a strawberry coulis on a graham cracker-crumb crust, the group began retiring back into the grand parlor room. Dylan stopped where Penel was still seated and touched her lightly on the shoulder before leaning in. "Come here often? Can I buy you a drink?" he whispered in her ear.

"Dylan, this is Dr. Spencer Leahy," she said, referring to the man seated to her right. "He's a retired ob-gyn. Dr. Leahy lost his wife in the past year."

"Nice to meet you, sir, and I am sorry for your loss."

"Thank you, Dylan. That's very kind of you. I certainly enjoyed the company of your friend Penel this evening."

"I enjoyed meeting you as well, Dr. Leahy. Good evening," she replied as she stood and led Dylan toward the parlor.

"Where's the fire?" he whispered as they left the room.

"The good doctor was coming on pretty strong during dinner."

"Are you sure?"

"He invited me on a Polynesian Island cruise. Said he bought the tickets over a year ago, just before his wife died."

"Maybe he's lonely and still grieving?"

"Dylan, he had his hand on my leg and was massaging my thigh when he asked."

"What did you say?"

"Told him I would've considered it, but I'd be concerned for his personal safety. I pointed you out, told him your last name and that you were the jealous type, and explained in somewhat vague terms your connection to a certain element of organized crime."

"Did that slow him down?"

"Not really."

"Well, at least he picked the right profession."

She nudged him affectionately. "I guess so. He probably misses his work."

They approached Cheryl and Rick, who were speaking with his grandparents. "Hell of a party your friend Esther throws, Dylan," his grandfather commented. "Met some really interesting people here tonight."

"Glad you enjoyed yourself, Grandpa."

"Esther is very pleasant and a generous host," his mother added. "I'm so glad we got to see her again."

"It's getting late, Dylan," his grandmother added, "and your grandfather here has been drinking since before we left the hotel. We're ready to leave whenever you are?"

"Christ sakes, Isabella, it's barely past ten o'clock. I think I'll have a nightcap," he retorted. "Come on, Rick, let's grab a drink."

"Go ahead, dear," Cheryl said, kissing him on the cheek. "Please keep an eye on him."

"Sure thing," Rick replied, following Anthony back to the bar.

"I'll go find Shirley and have her contact Hugo for a ten forty-five pickup. That should give us all time to say our goodbyes to our gracious host," Dylan said.

He found Shirley and Quentin off in a corner, engaged in quiet conversation. "How was your evening?" he asked.

"We had a wonderful time, Dylan," Shirley replied. "Apparently, none of these people recognized Quentin. It was quite refreshing."

"One person did ask me if I was a superhero," he chimed in.

"What did you say?" Dylan asked.

"I told her I fight for truth, justice, and the American way, but only Sundays during football season."

"Did she figure out you played in the NFL?"

"I don't think so."

"Well, I'm glad you enjoyed yourselves. Shirley, please text Hugo and arrange for him to pick us up in a half hour."

"Will do."

Dylan searched out Esther, who was saying goodbye to a woman he had not met. He waited for her to turn and head toward the door. "Esther, I want to thank you again for putting this evening together. We all had a wonderful time."

"I'm so glad to hear that, Dylan. I enjoyed seeing your family again and meeting all your friends. I'm very impressed with Shirley and Quentin, and I think Rick is a wonderful companion for your mother. She certainly deserves to be happy."

"I agree with everything you just said."

"Now as to your friend Alex, he's quite the rascal. Please keep an eye on that young man."

"That appears to be my lot in life," he replied with a smile. "We're going to be leaving soon. I just wanted to say thank you again, and I'll see you tomorrow night."

"You're so welcome," she said, her voice cracking slightly as she embraced him.

They arrived back at the hotel just past eleven o'clock. Dylan and Penel said goodnight as everyone departed the fourth-floor elevator and made their way to their rooms. "Well?" he said after they were inside their suite.

"Well, what?" Penel replied.

"Time for my report card. Do I get an A for good behavior?"

"From what I was able to observe that is an affirmative."

"Then I expect the reward I was promised." He stood and watched as she reached behind and expertly dropped her full-length gown to the floor. She stepped out and, clad only in black patent leather pumps and lingerie, took him by the hand and led him to the bedroom where he received his just due.

# CHAPTER EIGHT

Fanci worked late on Tuesday evening, toiling away in her cubicle until just before six. There was a daily stampede for the elevators at five as it was rare for anyone at the teachers' union to put in extra time. It didn't hurt that the managers had to pass by Fanci's desk and see her working as they left for the day. It was about twenty miles from her Bridgeport office to St. Mary School, normally about a half-hour drive. She planned to take the bus and Uber back to Ms. Baldwin's home, given the anticipated late hour.

The bus dropped her off just before seven. A modern-style church sat on the front of the expansive property, and she had to walk up the sidewalk that ran along a winding driveway to the school, which was set back on considerable acreage. She observed a nearly full parking lot with cars still dropping off passengers in front as she approached the entrance.

One of the vehicles caught her attention. An older sturdy-looking man in a chauffeur's cap exited from behind the wheel of a vintage Rolls Royce. The man opened the rear door, and an even older woman with well-coiffed gray hair exited, ensconced in a long off-white overcoat. Fanci followed a comfortable distance behind as the older woman entered the main lobby and approached a middle-aged female in a navy business dress. Skirting off to the side, Fanci glanced at the name plate pinned above her right breast, which confirmed she was the school principal.

"Good evening and welcome. I'm Rebecca O'Brien," she said, greeting the older woman.

"Good evening, I'm Esther Lott."

"Oh, Ms. Lott," Principal O'Brien enthusiastically exclaimed, extending her right hand. "I've been waiting for you. It's so nice to meet you. We are so honored you could be here this evening."

"It is certainly my pleasure."

"Dylan and his family have already arrived. We have seating reserved for you. Please, may I escort you to the field house?"

"Of course." The volume of their conversation waned as the two women walked together down a shimmering glass-enclosed walkway. A group of about half-dozen people arrived and headed in the same direction, so Fanci fell in behind them.

The walkway led to what appeared to be a recent addition. The sign above the grand entrance read Cheryl Tomassi Field House. Fanci followed the group into a lobby, larger than the main one at the entrance. It smelled of new construction, clean with hints of paint and burled wood.

As the crowd milled about, Fanci stood off to the side and took in the layout. On one side was a series of glass double doors. The opposite side contained sets of solid wood doors with a large sign above that read Esther Lott Theater. She made mental notes of the names and decided to proceed through the glass doors. Once inside, she was amazed at the opulence of the gymnasium. Several courts ran across a gleaming hardwood floor, the baskets tucked away high into the ceiling. High-gloss polished bleachers were set up on both sides of what appeared to be the main court that ran in the opposite direction. A state-of-the-art electronic scoreboard was suspended down from the middle and featured large display screens on all four sides. The electronic message read Welcome to St. Mary School's Grand Opening of the Cheryl Tomassi Field House and Esther Lott Theater.

Folding tables and chairs were set up across the floor and temporary refreshment stands on either end. People were clustered around both, so Fanci made her way to the one that appeared slightly less crowded and found soft drinks and alcoholic beverages were available. She stepped up and a male server dressed in all black asked what she would like to drink.

"A glass of champagne will be fine, thank you."

The man handed her a plastic flute and smiled. "Welcome to St. Mary. You look too young to be a parent. What brings you here this evening?" he inquired.

She quickly squelched a small flash of trepidation. "I'm a college student studying education administration. I'm here as part of my research for a paper I'm writing."

"Well, we're glad to have you. My name is Derek. Please Ms., uh . . ."

"It's Francis," she replied.

"Well, Francis. Welcome again and let me know if there's anything I can get you."

It was now clear this was not an interrogation but rather more of a come-on. "I will certainly do that. Thank you, Derek," she said with a smile and tip of her glass as she moved away.

She found a spot along the bleachers on the opposite end of the doors she had come through. The only exits on her side consisted of solid-gray metal doors with emergency exit signs displayed above.

She sipped her drink as she took in the scene. There were men's and women's locker rooms and restrooms and a permanent concession stand, all situated on the opposite side. The crowd appeared to be mostly adults, probably a mix of parents, teachers, staff, and guests. There were a handful of well-dressed students present who appeared to be older, probably eighth graders, she figured.

After a few moments, people began moving toward the exits. She blended into the crowd as it made its way through the lobby and into the theater. Once inside, a long hallway covered in commercial-grade carpeting led her to a perpendicular walkway. The upper level to her right consisted of tiered seating, and the main section to the left was one level featuring pitched flooring that allowed for a view of an elevated stage, complete with banks of spotlights and speakers suspended from above, all finished in matte black. A live orchestra played light jazz from a sunken pit off to the right. The stage itself was empty except for a podium set up in the center.

Fanci decided to trek up into the second level and found a pair of empty seats in an otherwise full row about halfway from the top. She selected one of the two, reasoning it provided an excellent bird's-eye view, comfortably away from the action with a slim chance of another single occupying the seat next to her.

She sank into the plush chair, upholstered in a velvety navy-colored material. Blue and white appeared to be the school colors, she surmised from decor and the large St. Mary Saints logo prominently displayed in the gymnasium.

*There was certainly no expense spared in the construction of this addition,* she concluded.

The presentations lasted about fifty minutes. Fanci made note of a tall, handsome man named Dylan Tomassi, the single donor responsible for funding construction of the addition, who spoke briefly. She thought his speech was as elegantly pleasing as his appearance. Other people were taking pictures with their phones, and she took the opportunity to snap several as well.

Cheryl Tomassi was his mother, but it was unclear what his relationship was with the older woman, Esther Lott. During Principal O'Brien's introductions, she also took note of Tomassi's grandparents. A petite blonde and a thickly muscled Black man also appeared to be part of their group, but no introductions were made, and she was unable to ascertain who they were.

Afterward, she hung back as people headed for the exits. She stood along the walkway that divided the lower from the upper seating levels as the Tomassi entourage passed by. Dylan Tomassi was accompanied by a striking brunette, tall and quite sophisticated in dress and manner.

A single male with dark hair was also with the group. He was shorter and smaller in stature than Dylan and dressed in a finely tailored suit. He made eye contact with her as he passed and held her gaze as he veered off and headed directly toward her.

"Excuse me, but I noticed you looking in my direction. Do we know each other?" he inquired.

Managing a small smile, "No, I don't think so," she replied.

"Well, I can fix that," he said, displaying what she perceived as his best smile as he thrust his right hand in her direction. "I'm Alex Malloy."

"Hello, Alex."

"I'm here with the Tomassi family. What brings you here this evening? With all due respect, it's clear you're too old to be a student and *much* too young to be a parent."

"Correct on both counts."

"Do you work at the school?"

"No," she mumbled, thinking he might get the hint with her short and direct answers.

"Well, I'm out of guesses. What brings such a beautiful woman out this evening?"

Concluding the man was not discouraged by her apparent lack of interest, she changed course. "I'm a college student majoring in education. I'm doing my senior research paper on school choice and heard about tonight's event. Thought I might come and observe as part of my project."

"I see. Where do you go to school?"

"The University of Bridgeport," she lied.

"Oh," he replied with a raise of his brow, which he quickly extinguished. "Learn anything interesting tonight?"

"I think so, but, please, tell me about yourself. How do you know Mr. Tomassi?"

"Dylan? We've known each other since we were kids. I consider him to be my best friend and the brother I never had."

"He certainly appears to have achieved a great deal of success at a relatively young age. What does he do?"

"Dylan? He does all right. Runs his own businesses down in Florida where he lives."

"And what about you?"

"I'm an attorney. I split my time between here and Tampa, where my firm has a satellite office."

She thought quickly. "That's all very interesting. Are you here alone this evening?"

"As a matter of fact, I am. And you?"

"Of course."

"I can fix that problem for both of us. Would you like to grab a drink somewhere where we can continue this conversation?"

"I would love to," she said with a smile glancing down at her watch, "but my academic adviser asked me to stop by tonight to give her an update on my senior paper."

"At this hour?"

"My adviser's very hands-on and prefers to meet after hours. I was scheduled to see her earlier, but when I told her I would be attending the opening here tonight, she insisted on my coming by afterward rather than postponing. Sorry, there's no way around it."

"I see," he said, clearly disappointed yet undeterred. "How about we do it another time? I'm sorry, forgive me, but I haven't even asked your name."

"My friends call me Liz," she fabricated.

"Well, Liz, I now consider you a friend. Let's exchange numbers, and I'll call to have that drink another time."

"I'd like that. Where do you live?"

"I have a house in Old Greenwich?"

"Really?" she said with a look of delight.

"Really. You like Greenwich?"

"Of course. It's beautiful. I was just wondering; I took the bus here and my adviser lives in Greenwich. Do you think you could give me a ride?"

"I not only think I can, but it would be my pleasure to be of service. Give me a few minutes to say goodbye to my friends, and I'll be right with you."

They made small talk on the ride to Kari Baldwin's home. Fanci was careful to keep the conversation interesting without revealing too much personal information and kept the disinformation to a minimum.

"I guess this is it," she said as they arrived, pointing to a large mansion set back behind a stone wall with a beautifully manicured lawn, all illuminated by an impressive night-scaping system.

"Wow," Alex exclaimed taking in the property as he drove up the driveway. "This an awfully nice home for someone who works in academia."

"Yeah. She's mentioned something about her deceased husband having left her very well off, from what I understand."

"Still, that's quite a crib. Well, listen, I have your number, so I'll be in touch."

"Look forward to it, Alex," she replied with a smile as she exited the car. She straightened her clothes and ran her fingers through her long black hair as she watched him leave before heading for the front door.

She rang the doorbell and heard a multitone ring permeating from inside. A moment later, Kari Baldwin answered the door, clad in a white lace robe with some type of black undergarment bleeding through. She wore dress slippers on her feet. Extending a meaty hand, she said, "Good evening, Fanci. Please come in."

Fanci reluctantly entered and followed behind as Baldwin led her through a large foyer and into what appeared to be a well-furnished formal living room. She sat down on one of the couches and patted the seat next to her. "Please sit, dear," she instructed, displaying her smile of slightly discolored teeth.

Fanci sat down, a short distance from her, and observed as Baldwin scooted over and placed a hand on her thigh. "That's better. I want to hear all about your evening, but first, I think you should be honored that I've taken an interest in you."

"I am," she interrupted in a meek voice." Please don't get the wrong impression."

"That's very reassuring to hear, Fanci. You know, as the leader of the teachers' union, one of the tenets I live by is that in any successful relationship it's important to create win-win situations. Do you understand?"

"I think so."

"What I mean is, for example, we are forced to deal with politicians for a seat at the table in order to advocate for our membership. These politicians expect something from me and in return I obligate them to look out for our teachers' best interests."

She nodded demurely but said nothing.

"The same thing applies to personal relationships. I understand you will be graduating at the end of the semester, and I have the ability to positively affect the trajectory of your career path. But, of course, I require loyalty in return."

Again, she nodded in reply but said nothing.

"You may be wondering, *What can I do for Ms. Baldwin?* Is that what you're thinking, Fanci?"

"Yes, ma'am," she murmured, barely above a whisper.

"Good. Then it's time to have that discussion. Have you ever been with a woman?" she asked, reaching around Fanci's shoulder and gently massaging her neck.

"No, ma'am," Fanci mumbled, eyes wide open and masking a frown.

"Well, of course, I studied education. I will teach you. Would you like that, Fanci?"

She sat quietly for a moment, frozen in place. Baldwin glared at her awaiting a response. Finally, she spoke. "I'm very eager and a fast learner, Ms. Baldwin. What would you like to do?"

She leaned in and flicked her tongue in Fanci's ear. "Do you like oral pleasure?" she whispered.

"Oh, yes. I want to do that with you, and I want you to teach me first so I can do it properly. But tonight's not a good time."

"Why's that?" she blurted in obvious frustration.

"I really want our first time to be special, but I'm not, you know, in the right condition to initiate things tonight," she explained, glancing down at her crotch. "That time of the month."

Baldwin's frustration waned, and she exhaled deeply before her voice took on a conciliatory tone. "All right, dear. We'll do this another time. It's getting late anyway, and I still want a briefing about your assignment tonight. I'll be in touch to reschedule."

"Thank you, ma'am. I appreciate your understanding, and I look forward to next time. I promise you it'll be worth the wait."

"That's very good to hear, Francis. If you stay true to your word, things may work out very well for you."

"Yes, ma'am."

"I think I like your attitude." She stood, stretching her considerable frame and raising her meaty arms above her head. "Well, I'm ready for bed. How did you get here?"

"I took an Uber."

"I'll arrange for a ride. Feel free to wait in the foyer and close the door on your way out," she instructed as she turned and headed down a hallway.

# CHAPTER NINE

DYLAN, HIS FAMILY, AND FRIENDS were finishing an early dinner at Carmine's. As they shared the family-style meal of antipasto, salad, pasta, and veal in a private corner of the second-floor dining room, the group discussed their plans to return to Florida the following day. The charter flight would leave Teterboro for Clearwater by noon. Dylan was going to spend the night at Penel's apartment in the city and take an early train back to Greenwich in the morning in time to pack and make the drive over to New Jersey with them. They made their way out of the restaurant and said their goodbyes against a biting cold wind as the rest of the group piled into the warm confines of the Sprinter van.

As the van pulled away, Penel huddled against Dylan while he hailed a cab. Mercifully, one pulled over on his second attempt and the pair jumped into the back. "Park Avenue and East Sixty-Second Street. My building's on the corner," Penel instructed the driver.

He nodded but said nothing as he inched the cab back into the perpetual traffic gridlock on Broadway. "Quite a meal," Dylan commented grazing his hand across his belly before it came to rest in her lap.

"It was great, but I feel like I won't be able to eat again for the rest of the week," she agreed before turning toward him and lowering her voice. "I'm glad you're staying the night, but I was hoping for a longer visit."

"That was the original plan, but when Quentin came up with the theater tickets, that extended everyone's stay, and it made sense for us to all travel back home together."

"I suppose. When will I see you again?"

"Soon, I promise." She rested her head on his shoulder, and they rode along quietly for a spell as the cab crawled through traffic.

"What did you think of the play?" he finally asked, breaking the silence.

"It was wonderful, and what a thrill to meet the young man who played Michael Jackson. He can certainly sing and dance."

"He is definitely talented, and who would have thought someone who grew up in DC would be a Tampa Bay Bucs fan? He seemed just as excited to meet Quentin."

When they arrived at Penel's apartment, they were greeted by the doorman. "Good evening, Ms. Stanhill. Sir," he said and nodded in Dylan's direction.

The elevator took them to the top floor, which opened directly into her apartment. He had not been there in more than a year, but the sights and smells were familiar. He immediately walked into the living room and stood at the floor-to-ceiling window with a view of an illuminated Central Park.

"Can I get you something?" she offered.

"What do you feel like?"

"I was thinking coffee with a shot of brandy, a shower, and then bed."

"Sounds perfect."

They soon found themselves together in bed. Their lean bodies fit together felicitously, and they exhausted themselves, cognizant of the fact it was their final time together for a while.

Barry Filmore drove his jet-black Mercedes S63 AMG at a high rate of speed down the Merritt Parkway. Traffic was light on a Wednesday evening, and he arrived at Blackstone's Steakhouse in Greenwich just before seven. He had no idea as to the purpose of the dinner meeting except Lymon had told him it was important.

He walked into the restaurant and observed Lymon seated at a corner table occupying the gunner's seat. A large-framed person sat beside him with close-cropped graying hair. He presumed this was the Kari Baldwin he had to meet. Approaching the table, he greeted Lymon.

"Hello, Ly. Nice to see you."

The woman remained seated and turned toward him. "Kari Baldwin," she said, extending a beefy right hand.

"Hello, Barry Filmore. My pleasure." He sat down and observed that wine had already been served and poured. "What are we drinking tonight?"

"*We* are drinking a Chateau Lafleur. It's French," she answered snidely.

Lymon poured Barry a glass, ignoring the comment, just as a waiter approached. Lymon gestured with the bottle. "We'll have another of these, and please give us some time to order."

"Yes, sir," the waiter replied and hurried away.

"We were just talking about the state of the public school system," Lymon explained. "Kari was telling me that traditional district schools are under attack from extremists who want to destroy the education system in this country."

"Just today, there was a feature article in *Connecticut Today* discussing how school choice has continued to gain momentum across the country," she lamented. "Pointed out that from 2019 through last year charter schools alone have increased enrollment while traditional schools lost students. And, of course, we are under siege here in the tristate area. Just this week, some boy scout funded a major expansion at a Catholic school in Stamford, and he's also funding scholarships. Every time we lose a student, it costs us money and, ultimately, membership. This shit's gotta stop."

Filmore, bored with the conversation, nodded in agreement.

"Perhaps we can help, at least on a microlevel," Lymon interjected.

"Oh, how's that?" she asked, taking a healthy gulp of her wine, draining her glass.

Lymon refilled her drink, finishing off the first bottle. "Barry, here, is a man of many talents. Perhaps he can have a conversation with this guy."

She looked over at him skeptically. "Really? What can you do?"

Lymon nodded, so Barry dove in. "Probably better you don't know. Let's say I have ways of asserting influence that will cause this, uh, boy scout to focus his energies in other directions."

"Think of it as a favor to the union," Lymon added. "Barry here is eager to be of service."

"And what do you want?" She sneered in his direction.

The waiter appeared, presenting the new bottle and refilling the glasses. "Are you all ready to order?" he asked once the task was complete.

"I'll have the lobster bisque. Porterhouse, medium rare, loaded baked potato, and creamed spinach," she said.

"The porterhouse cut tonight is fifty-four ounces, I'd recommend it for two," he gently suggested.

"So?" she replied glaring at him. "I'll take home whatever I don't finish."

"Yes, ma'am," he acquiesced.

After the men ordered and the waiter departed, she continued. "So, Mr. Filmore. What is it you want in return?"

"Nothing," Lymon interrupted. "We work as a team. Maybe there will come a time when you can do something for us. Then again, maybe not."

She stared at him for a moment. "All right. Go ahead," she finally said.

"What information do you have on this guy?" Lymon asked.

"Enough to get started. Name's Tomassi. He resides in Florida and supports a private school down there as well. I'll send over what we have on him."

"Good. Get it to me, and I'll forward it to Barry," he replied, glancing in his direction.

Barry nodded, gleaning that the woman was as much a major player as she was imperious.

After dinner and dessert, they were on coffee when Barry explored an exit strategy. "Ms. Baldwin, may I call you Kari?"

"My friends call me Kari. You can call me Ms. Baldwin for now. Let's see how you do with Mr. Tomassi, and we'll go from there."

"Fair enough," he continued. "Well, I've got some research to do, but my initial thought is to pay this man a personal visit. I've got a decent ride back to Westchester County, so I think I'll be going."

"Hold on there, cowboy," she said. "The night is young. I say we head over to Beamer's Café. You boys can treat me to some lap dances."

He thought about asking whether the dancers were of the male or female persuasion but thought better of it.

"I think you'll enjoy the place," Lymon remarked. "The ladies are, uh, very accommodating."

"I'll say," Baldwin added. "Things didn't fall my way with my date last night, and I could really use some female companionship."

The waiter reappeared. "Will there be anything else this evening?"

"No, sir. Just the check, please," Lymon said.

He pulled a leather portfolio from his apron and placed it in the middle of the table. "Barry will get that," Lymon offered, nudging the check in his direction and rising from the table. "We'll meet you at Beamer's." He winked at his colleague as he and Baldwin left together.

# CHAPTER TEN

A week later, Barry Filmore received a call from Lymon Scott. The two had not spoken since their meeting in Connecticut. "Hello, Barry. I'm following up on our dinner with Kari Baldwin."

"Hey, Ly. I have been meaning to get back with you on that. She's quite a character. Not to mention butt ugly."

"She reminds me of George Hackett."

"Who's that?"

"George 'Fatty' Hackett, an old-time baseball player. Look him up, and tell me you don't see the resemblance. Anyway, as you know, she's a very powerful woman and one we want on our side. What have you come up with that will assist with what she's asked you to do?"

"I gotta say," he replied, ignoring the question, "I've never seen a woman eat like that. She devoured an entire porterhouse and drank the better part of two bottles of wine by herself. And the way she devoured those two young ladies at the strip club. I can only imagine what went on when the three of them retired to the champagne room. My Amex card is still smarting from that evening, between dinner and the club. Thank God she prefers women."

"Forget all that, and think of your assignment as an investment. Now, what have you come up with?"

"Did some deep-dive research on Tomassi. All his business interests are closely held private companies. There was a little more information available on his nonprofit, but not as much as you would expect, as the 501(c)3 was established just recently. But to answer your question, yes, I've come up with a plan that will be mutually beneficial to her and us. It's taken some doing, but I've got an appointment with him on Friday."

"Very good. Keep me posted."

That same afternoon, Fanci was tidying up her desk at the close of the business day. It had been more than a week since her meeting at Kari Baldwin's home, and she had not heard from her. Several reasons crossed her mind for the lack of follow-up, not the least of which was the possibility the task had been a pretext to get her alone at Baldwin's home.

Her phone buzzed. She picked it up and looked at the screen. The text message read, "My office at five thirty to discuss your assignment last week." It was from the personal phone number that Kari Baldwin had given her. Fanci continued to work at her desk while everyone else on the floor headed for the elevators. By five twenty-five, she didn't see or hear a soul.

She took the elevator up to the executive floor and found the lobby empty except for a single security guard who appeared to be the one of the men from her visit last week. She approached the desk with an air of authority, making eye contact with the guard at the first opportunity. "Good evening, Ms. Nagle. Ms. Baldwin is expecting you. Please go right in," he said, pressing a button that buzzed the large doors.

She made her way back and noted that neither Baldwin's assistant, Cindy Seravisi, nor anyone else was around. She continued into the inner office and found Baldwin seated on a couch sipping a Scotch. A crystal decanter and another glass sat on the table in front of her.

"Hello, Fanci. What a pleasure it is to see you again," she said in her husky voice, patting the seat next to her. "Please sit." Fanci obliged and sat down while she leaned forward, poured another drink, and handed it to her. "Please join me."

Fanci accepted the drink, took a sip, and exhaled. "Nice to see you again, Ms. Baldwin."

"Come now, dear," she said, placing her free hand on Fanci's thigh. "We're good friends now. I insist you call me Kari when we're alone."

"Yes, ma'am, I mean Kari," she replied sheepishly.

"Now, I'd like to hear all about your evening at St. Mary."

Fanci gave her a summary from memory while Kari appeared to listen intently, nodding when she was discussing Dylan Tomassi's role in the project, and her chance meeting with his friend, Alex Malloy. As she concluded her report, she picked up her glass, drained the contents, and sat silently waiting for Kari's reply.

"That's all very interesting, Fanci. You know what else is interesting to me? The way you drank that Scotch. You have a very seductive mouth."

Fanci instinctively licked her lips in silence.

Kari stood and positioned herself in front of Fanci. She began unbuttoning her pants, but then her cell phone buzzed on the table.

"Damn." She turned and looked at the screen. She picked it up and read the message before pressing a button and holding the phone to her ear. "Yeah, what is it?" she barked. "I'm in a meeting."

Fanci observed as she walked away, listening and pacing the room. "Uh-huh," she muttered into the phone several times before looking at her watch. "All right. I'll be there by seven."

She made another call to her driver. "I need to go to the New Haven School Board meeting right away." A moment later, she spoke again. "Okay, I'll meet you downstairs in ten minutes."

She hung up, exasperated. "I was really looking forward to spending some quality time together, but I've got to get to New Haven. There's a referendum on the ballot to increase property taxes to raise funds to combat homelessness, which will also provide revenue for subsidizing teacher and staff housing. We're organizing a presentation for eligible students in the area high schools to make their voices heard by registering to vote and supporting the measure. I have to go, but *we will* do this again." She glanced at her watch. "There is one other thing I want you to do." She provided Fanci with general instructions and made it clear it was off the books and up to Fanci's discretion as to how to proceed.

Fanci went back down to her office, grabbed her coat, and headed out for the bus stop just outside the building. As soon as she pushed through the revolving door, the biting January wind struck, blowing right through her and down to the bone. She huddled against the fiberglass wall of the bus stop, which provided little relief from the winter chill. She heard her phone buzz in her bag and fished it out. "Hey, Liz, how are you?"

"Pretty uncomfortably cold at the moment."

"I'm well aware of your beauty and have no desire to mess with that, but perhaps I can assist with a climate adjustment."

"Who is this?"

"It's Alex. We met at St. Mary last week. The kind gentleman who gave you a ride."

"Oh, Alex, hi! Sorry, I didn't recognize the number. I must've keyed it into my phone wrong or something. Anyway, I'm just leaving work and it's freezing outside. I'm very interested to hear how you can remedy that. You're not a weatherman, are you?"

"In a manner of speaking. How about dinner on Saturday night?"

"How is that going to help with the weather?"

"I'm calling from my office in Tampa, where it's eighty-two degrees outside. I'll be down here this weekend."

"But I'm in Connecticut."

"We can fix that. It's what airports are for."

"Alex, I'm a college student working an internship for minimum wage. I can't afford a plane ticket to Florida."

"Do you have a credit card?"

"Yes."

"Charge the ticket, and I'll reimburse you when you get here."

"And where will I stay while I'm in Florida?"

"I live at the Edition in Tampa. It's a hotel. You'll have your own room, of course."

"I have to admit that sounds like a very nice offer, given that I may not have all my toes when I see you on account of frostbite," she commented, shivering against a bluster of cold air.

"I'll take that as a yes. Book yourself a first-class ticket and text me the flight info. I'll pick you up at the airport."

"Okay," she replied. "I'll find a flight on Saturday morning, but I'm coming back on Sunday. I have to be at work the next day."

"Fair enough. Looking forward to seeing you."

She hung up the phone just in time to see her bus pull up. She hurried inside as soon as the doors swung open, thankful for the warmth of the heat inside.

*Timing is everything,* she thought to herself as she selected a window seat in an empty row near the front.

# CHAPTER ELEVEN

Dylan was in his office early on Friday when Shirley poked her head in the door. "Good morning. It's not on your calendar, but you have a meeting at one today at the youth center."

"Good morning," he replied, looking up from his computer screen. "Sorry, I was in the middle of an article. Did you say something about a meeting?"

"Yes. You have an appointment with a Barry Filmore."

"Who's that?"

"He's from the US Department of the Interior. He called five or six times, very persistent. I originally blew him off, but he sent a follow-up letter on Department of the Interior letterhead," she explained, dropping her reading glasses down from the top of her head and referring to a piece of paper in her hand. "Apparently, at some point, the foundation land received federal funding when it was a public park, and because of that, the property is subject to a federal audit. It was assigned to him by the department, and he has scheduled this meeting to discuss the results as you are the nonprofit's president."

"Really," he replied with a raised eyebrow. "May I see the letter?" After scanning the document, he sighed. "All right, I guess I'll be seeing Mr. Filmore this afternoon."

He worked in his office until just before noon, then hopped in his pickup and drove in the direction of the youth center. As he headed down Park Street, he felt a pang in his stomach and realized he hadn't eaten all day. He continued toward South Pasadena to a little sandwich shop he'd recently discovered. He pulled into the strip center adjacent to Palms of Pasadena Hospital and ordered a Big Beach, no onion, no mayo, to go.

Arriving at the youth center, he parked in front of the administration building, walked inside, and found Claire in her office. "Hello, Claire, how are you?"

"I'm doing well, Dylan. You're early," she noted. "I thought your appointment was at one."

"Apparently, until a few hours ago, I was the only person who didn't know about my one o'clock."

"Shirley called me this morning to let me know," she said, smiling. "I reserved the conference room for you."

"Perfect. I'll have enough time to eat my sandwich," he said, holding up the bag. He stopped off in the small kitchen and selected a bottled water from the fridge before setting up in the conference room. He was finishing his lunch when his phone rang. "Hey, Dylan, what's going on?"

"Hi, Alex. I'm over at the youth center. I've got a one o'clock appointment, so I only have a few minutes."

"What appointment can possibly be more important than speaking with me?"

"Actually, most. But in this case you do win, so talk away. The meeting can wait."

"I knew you'd see things my way. Anyway, I'm not going to be around this weekend."

"I thought you were in town until next week."

"I am, but I will be entertaining an out-of-town guest this weekend."

Dylan smiled to himself and remained silent, sensing Alex couldn't help himself.

"Don't you want details?"

"Somehow I knew you'd volunteer. Do tell."

Alex recounted the story of how he'd met the young woman at St. Mary.

"You met this young lady once, and she agreed to spend the night with you?"

"Well, she's staying at the Edition. I booked her a hotel room, but it's a start. At least we're under the same roof."

"You never cease to amaze me. I didn't see you speaking with any college students at the grand opening."

"I met her as we were leaving. We just hit it off. I really felt a connection."

"I've heard you say that before. Particularly about another college student who formerly lived down the road from me and now resides in a cemetery."

"Why do you always have to drag up the past when I'm looking forward toward the future."

"Just be careful. That's all."

"She's a college student. How dangerous could she be?"

"I just reminded you how dangerous getting involved with a college student can be."

"That's the difference between you and me. You worry too much."

"That's because I have to worry for both of us."

"Please continue to do that while I'm out enjoying myself. I'm picking her up at the airport on Saturday, and she's flying back on Sunday, so hopefully, I'll be contentedly worn out and recovering on Sunday night."

"All right, that's enough. I've got to get to my meeting," he said, terminating the call. Suddenly, speaking with some government bureaucrat didn't seem so bad.

He was still sitting alone in the conference room reading an article on his phone when the intercom buzzed. It was Claire. "Mr. Barry Filmore is in the lobby to see you."

He cleared the article on his phone, and the home screen read 1:17. *Typical government flunky; right on time,* he thought as he made his way down the hallway. He entered the lobby and observed the back of a thin man in a well-tailored suit, hands jammed in his pockets, looking out the window toward the athletic fields. Dylan stood there for a moment in silence, but the man didn't turn around. Finally, he said, "Mr. Filmore?"

The man turned and revealed a long, thin face topped with an expensive haircut designed to conceal a receding hairline. His silk striped tie, expertly fashioned around the wing collar of a light patterned shirt, and expensive designer shoes did not fit Dylan's profile of a typical G-man lackey.

"I'm Barry Filmore," the man replied, handing him a business card. "Is there somewhere where we can speak in private?"

He said nothing and looked at the business card. It was plain white with black embossed lettering and read "Barry Filmore, Climate Envoy, United States Department of the Interior, Washington, DC." A phone number with a 202-area code appeared at the bottom.

"What can I do for you?" he asked, ignoring the request for a more intimate setting.

"I'm here on official business as a representative of the Department of the Interior. This is a sensitive matter of a confidential nature. I would request again that we speak in private."

"You just said a lot without saying anything. I'll need more information before I decide how long to keep this conversation going," Dylan replied, a muted forcefulness of authority in his voice.

He stared at the man in silence, awaiting a reply. Filmore appeared neither nervous nor confrontational. Rather, he stood and looked back in a relaxed, almost detached manner until he finally spoke in a measured tone. "Mr. Tomassi, consider this a courtesy call, an initial meeting, if you will. I am here at the request of the department, following the results of a periodic audit on the property on which we stand." His accent held a hint of old New England upper crust. "This property was once owned by the city of St. Petersburg and before that by Pinellas County. Both entities received federal funding for park maintenance and improvements. Accordingly, it falls under the department's jurisdiction, and I am here to discuss official business in a, uh, less formal manner, than, say, the setting under a federal subpoena or, God forbid, a lawsuit."

Dylan stood silently as he processed the response. "All right, you have fifteen minutes," he finally replied as he turned and walked back down the hallway to the conference room. Upon arrival he opened the door and took a seat at the head of the table. Only then did he confirm that Filmore had followed and taken a chair to his left. Dylan noted he had no briefcase, laptop, or even a folder with him.

The man placed his arms on the table, folding soft, manicured hands that stuck out from the surgeon's cuffs of his suit jacket. "As time is at a premium, I'll dispense with the informalities and get right down to it. As I mentioned, I'm here at the behest of the department. Your audit revealed that your nonprofit purchased this property a little over a year ago. The transfer of title and a recent grant proposal submitted by your 501(c)3 is what prompted the investigation into your nonprofit as well as your personal business holdings. Are you familiar with ESG scoring, Mr. Tomassi?"

"At this point, I'm here to listen. If I have any questions, I'll ask. Otherwise, please continue."

"Very well, sir. ESG, or Environmental, Social, and Governance scoring, has become a very relevant metric for evaluating an organization's commitment to corporate sustainability and social responsibility, not the least of which is their commitment to environmental issues such as energy efficiency and carbon footprint reduction. There are various rating agencies and data providers, and scores will vary given the range of evaluation criteria, but in your case they are all strikingly similar."

It was clear to Dylan he was eliciting a response, but he chose to remain silent, displaying a blank stare.

"I'll tell you what your scores are, son. To quote the learned Dean Wormer, 'Zero. Point. Zero.' I've looked into your business dealings as your personal holdings are a primary source of the nonprofit's funding, and we have a problem, sir."

"Which is it?"

"Which is what?"

"Son or sir? You've referred to me as both."

"You think this is a joke? Or some laughing matter? The department did not send me down here at taxpayer expense for your amusement."

Discerning a crack in his bureaucratic locution, he asked, "Why exactly are you here?"

He observed as the man pulled up something on his phone. "Your business assets include commercial properties, farming and ranch lands, and a considerable stock portfolio."

Dylan maintained an indifferent expression, fighting the instinct to express surprise as to the extent of the detail of the man's information.

"Let's look at a sampling of each," he continued, scrolling down his phone. "In the past five years, you've been involved in nine construction projects along the Florida Gulf Coast, including residential condominiums and townhomes, hotels, and retail buildings, all of which exclusively used concrete construction materials. Concrete, and cement specifically, is one of the world's worst pollutants, accounting for seven percent of global carbon emissions. That's double the amount produced by the entire worldwide aviation industry. The land you own in South Dakota is occupied by more than 10,000 head of cattle. Cows, pigs, and other animals account for more than half of all food production emissions. And your stock holdings are weighted heavily in the energy sector, particularly oil and gas, pipeline, and other fossil fuel companies. It's probably a good thing no one has rated your holdings, Mr. Tomassi, or you would in fact find yourself in good company with the miscreants of Delta House. You should begin to get the picture."

Filmore concluded, looking up from his phone and glaring directly into his eyes. "And as it comes into focus you now find yourself firmly entrenched in the crosshairs of the federal government."

Dylan lifted his own phone from the table and consulted the screen. "Looks like you have four minutes, should you care to wrap things up."

"Mr. Tomassi, you and I have clearly gotten off on a contentious footing, but I am, in fact, here to offer a solution to your problem. Not only do I have the solution, but I have the authority to extricate you from the unfortunate position you find yourself in."

Dylan sat in silence staring past Filmore as if he were not in the room.

"In sum, the solution involves carbon offsets. My time is about up, so I will be sending you a proposal via your foundation email account, and I expect to hear from you by the deadline set forth therein. If I don't, I promise you, things will deteriorate quickly for you on this matter. Good day," he concluded, as he stood and exited the room.

Dylan sat there for a few minutes, processing what he had heard. He did, in fact, find it somewhat disconcerting that a purported government official knew so much about his private business affairs, but, then again, everything he'd just heard was a matter of public record. Finally, he decided to table the issue for now and ignore the last half hour he would never get back.

# CHAPTER TWELVE

The American Airlines flight from LaGuardia to Tampa International circled the airport just before noon. Fanci, ensconced in the soft leather of seat 2A in the first-class cabin, had enjoyed a breakfast fruit plate and a mimosa. She was comfortably dressed in black leggings and a light pullover. Alex had arranged for a limousine that had picked her up at her apartment and delivered her directly to the American terminal so she was able to dispense with bringing a heavy coat, which would have otherwise been required to navigate the biting cold currently paralyzing the tristate area.

She listened as the pilot broadcasted the weather over the intercom. "Welcome to Tampa. It's currently sunny, eighty-four degrees with a light breeze."

After the plane landed and taxied to the terminal, Fanci grabbed her rolling bag from the overhead compartment and proceeded down the walkway, the mild weather from outside permeating the jet bridge. She followed the signs to the tram, which took her to the main terminal. She had never been to Florida before, and she took in the bright sunshine and swaying palm trees through the tram's glass enclosure on the short ride.

"I've arrived," she texted Alex's number once she departed the tram.

A moment later, she received a reply. "I'm parked in the cell phone lot. Meet me outside at arrivals. I'm driving a black Porsche Taycan. Be there in a few."

Once again, following the signs, she took the escalator downstairs and walked outside. The air felt warm and soothing. She watched as an endless stream of vehicles drove through, uniformed traffic officers moving along those that were not actively loading passengers. A shiny, sleek sports car pulled up beside her. Alex got out and gave her a gentle hug. "Liz, it's so good to see you. How was the trip?"

"Wonderful. I've never flown first class before," she said, neglecting to add she'd never even been on an airplane in her twenty-two years.

"Did my secretary reimburse you for the flight and the limo ride?" he asked as he loaded her bag into the trunk.

"Yes, she Venmo'd me the funds. Thank you."

"You're certainly welcome and thank you for coming. Next time I'll just have her book your transportation."

She smiled but said nothing. They left the airport and merged onto Interstate 275 toward downtown. "This car rides so quietly," she observed.

"That's because it's electric. Doing my part for the environment. We've got to take care of the planet for you youngsters."

"Youngster? You're not much older than me."

"I don't know about that, but you'll find I'm young at heart. It more than makes up for any age difference."

"I won't ask, but you look wonderful," she replied, briefly brushing her hand against his arm.

He smiled but did not respond, so she looked out the window for a spell, taking in the scenery. "I've never been to Tampa before. Where exactly to you live.?"

"Downtown," he replied, his head on a swivel as he changed lanes, navigating his way in the direction of the Ashley Street exit. "I have a condo in the Edition. I reserved you a room for the night in the hotel downstairs."

"Where are we going for dinner?"

"I made reservations at Ponte. The owner-chef is amazing."

"Sounds yummy. It's only twelve thirty. What would you like to do before then?"

"I would love to hang out, but work requires me to spend another few hours in the office. I broke away to come pick you up. I figured you can get settled in your room, maybe take a nap if you're tired from the flight. The hotel has a wonderful pool if you want to check that out."

"You have to work on a Saturday?"

"Unfortunately, I do today. The associates are typically in the office all day, but we're working on a merger for a client, and there's a big presentation scheduled for Monday. As the managing partner, my presence is required today."

She turned and gazed out the window again, taking in the skyline as they drove toward downtown. She looked back at Alex. "How far is Ybor City from where you live?"

He glanced back at her. "Not far. Why?"

"I was reading about it in the in-flight magazine. Sounds like an interesting place. I thought I'd check it out."

"I'd love to show you around, but duty calls. There is a shuttle not far from the hotel that will take you there if you'd like. It's definitely better for a female traveling alone to visit in the daytime."

"Why? Is it dangerous or something?"

"Not really, but the nightlife can get crazy. I wouldn't want some young buck to snatch you up," he said with a smile.

Ignoring the comment, she said, "What time will you be done with work?"

"No later than four. I can meet you for a drink at the bar at, say, five. Our reservation is for seven."

"That sounds good. I think I'll get settled and then maybe explore the city a bit until then."

They pulled up to the front entrance and a uniformed man standing behind a valet stand jumped to attention and greeted them, opening Fanci's door. "Good afternoon, ma'am, Mr. Malloy. Shall I leave the car up here, sir?"

"No, thanks, Henry. Please put it in the garage. I won't need it until this evening."

"Very good, sir," the man said, pulling the car away in the direction of the parking garage.

"I'm going to walk over to my office. Go ahead and check in. The room's under my account. Just mention my name."

"Will do," she whispered, kissing him on the cheek.

After checking in and putting away her things, she walked outside and approached the valet stand. "Hello again, Henry. How would I find the shuttle to Ybor City?"

"There's a free tram you can take. Pick it up at the Whiting Station, and it will drop you at Centro Ybor," he said, handing her a map. She thanked the man and began walking. She took the River Walk over to Channelside, exploring Sparkman Wharf before walking past the Florida Aquarium and looking at the massive cruise ships moored in the nearby port.

She finally made her way back toward Whiting Street, and less than a half hour later, she was standing on Seventh Avenue. The street and bars were crowded with people. She continued farther east past the Columbia Restaurant until she came across a small dive bar. The doors were opened to the outside. She peered into the dimly lit room and observed a bar occupied by several men. The single bartender was a sturdy-looking, middle-aged female dressed in tight blue jeans and low-cut T-shirt.

Everyone in the place stared as she selected an empty stool at the short end of the bar. The bartender came over quickly. "What can I get you, honey?" she asked.

"How about a glass of wine?"

"Sweetheart, this is a beer and shot joint."

"Okay, then, make it a gin and tonic."

The woman turned and went to work on the drink. Fanci looked around and saw everyone had gone back to their conversations, men occasionally stealing a glance in her direction. The bartender came back and served the drink. "Here you are. If you need anything else, my name's Sue."

"Thanks, Sue. You're very kind. I'm Beth."

"Nice to meet you. And don't let these animals bother you," she said, raising her voice to a decibel she was certain the men all heard. "Anyone gives you a problem in here, they have to deal with me."

"We may be animals, but we don't bite," retorted a large man with long, unkept hair and a beard that appeared to have never been trimmed. "That is, unless you want us to."

A man of similar proportion and grooming habits slapped him on the back and let out a roar. The pair resembled a couple of actors straight out of central casting for a biker bar movie scene.

"That comment just cost you," Sue replied to the man with a glare. "Her next drink is on you."

"Be my pleasure," he said, raising his beer mug in her direction.

Fanci spent the next hour commiserating with the local patrons before making her way back to the hotel.

She showered and applied light makeup before slipping into a teal-patterned minidress she'd bought online for twenty-four dollars. The long sleeves covered her slender arms, and the hem line cut just above mid-thigh, highlighting her thin, shapely legs. She slipped her feet into a pair of bone-colored pumps and headed downstairs to the bar. It was a few minutes after five.

Alex was already seated at the bar, a drink in front of him and engaged in an animated conversation with the bartender. She approached him from behind and gently placed her hands on his shoulders, leaning her head close to his.

"Come here often?" she whispered in his ear.

"Probably more than I should, but I'll let Dennis here be the judge of that. Dennis, this is Liz. Dennis is the head bartender here."

"Nice to meet you, ma'am. Any friend of Alex is always welcome at the Edition."

"Thank you, Dennis," she replied with a smile as she slid onto the stool next to Alex.

"What can I get you this evening?"

"I think I'll stick with wine. Do you have a rosé?"

"We do serve a rosé by the glass. I'll bring it right over."

"What are you drinking tonight?" she asked Alex.

"Soldier Horse. It's fast becoming my favorite bourbon. What did you do this afternoon?"

"Walked around the city for a while. Checked out Riverwalk and looked at the cruise ships in the port. This is quite a bustling downtown."

"It is indeed, but it wasn't always that way, from what I understand. Not long ago, it was busy all day with business and commerce and pretty much a ghost town at night after people headed for the suburbs. That all changed when the owner of the hockey team renovated the arena and then developed Water Street around it. Residential buildings, restaurants, shopping, and entertainment followed. Now it's a destination for living, working, and playing."

Dennis came back over and served the wine. "Please let me know if there's anything else I can get you."

"Thank you, Dennis," she replied, turning back to Alex as the bartender disappeared. "Do you spend all your time downtown when you're here?"

"Pretty much, since my home and office are within walking distance.

My friend Dylan lives across the bay in St. Petersburg, so I'm over there quite a bit when I'm not working."

"Is that the guy who was honored at the St. Mary event where we met?"

"The very same. He donated the money to build the gym and theater, which was the final phase of renovations for the school. He was granted the naming rights and named the field house after his mother and the theater after a longtime friend."

"What exactly does he do again to have that kind of money?"

"Mostly, he's involved with finance and investments, and he owns a commercial real estate development company. A couple years ago, he got involved in philanthropy, and now that takes up a lot of his time. But enough about him. He's quite boring, actually. Let's talk more about you. All I know, besides being a beautiful woman who looks fantastic in that dress, is that you go to school at the University of Bridgeport."

She twisted her hair back over her ear and smiled bashfully. "You are too kind. I'll graduate this spring, and my plan is to go into teaching. Maybe go back to Danbury, where I grew up."

"Well, I do spend half my time in Connecticut, so that would be convenient. But we're here in Florida tonight, so let's enjoy the evening," he said, glancing at his watch. "We have to drive to the restaurant, and it sounds like you walked around downtown a bit. How about if we head out and I show you around the rest of the town?"

They left the bar and exited out through the lobby to the front of the hotel, where Alex's Porsche was backed into a parking spot, sandwiched between two exotic sports cars.

Fanci stared in their direction while Henry pulled the car up. "What are those other two cars?" she asked.

"The orange one is a McLaren and the blue one's a Ferrari," Alex explained, pointing out the pair.

"Hmm. I thought all Ferraris were red."

"Seriously? I think you've watched too many episodes of *Magnum, P.I.*"

"Oh, my gosh, I love that show," she exclaimed. She turned toward him. "You kind of remind me of the Magnum character."

"Tom Selleck? Now that guy *is* old. Plus, he has a mustache."

"No, silly, the new Magnum, in the reboot show."

"I've never seen that. I'll have to check it out and get back to you."

"Trust me: it's a compliment," she said, brushing his arm with her fingers.

They drove west through downtown as Alex pointed out the convention center, Harbor Island, and the University of Tampa. They then headed south toward Bayshore Boulevard, where mansions set back on well-manicured lawns looked out over Old Tampa Bay toward Davis Island and downtown. "This is where the annual Gasparilla parade is held."

"What's that?"

"You don't know the tale of José Gaspar?"

"Please enlighten me."

"Every year, usually the end of January or beginning of February, the city holds the Gasparilla Pirate Festival. José Gaspar and his band of merry men invade Tampa by ship, right here in the basin," he explained, indicating toward the waterfront. "The mayor then surrenders the key to the city."

"That's it?" she said with a look of confusion.

"Oh, no. That's just the ceremonial aspect, which serves as an excuse for the entire city to dress up like pirates and get stinking drunk. There's a big parade down Bayshore, and residents and visitors line the streets for miles. Huge parties are thrown at all these big homes."

"So it's just an excuse to party and get drunk?"

"Pretty much. It's kind of like Tampa's version of Mardi Gras."

He turned off Bayshore Boulevard and weaved through Hyde Park before heading up Dale Mabry Highway. "That's Raymond James Stadium," he said out as soon as they passed the Kennedy Boulevard intersection. "It's where the football team plays. The restaurant's not far from here."

He pulled into Midtown, a newer shopping-and-entertainment district, and handed his car off to a valet at the parking garage adjacent to the restaurant. They walked next door, where the maître d' directed them to an intimate corner table, and they were seated in curved back, cushioned chairs. A male waiter, clad in a black apron over black pants, white dress shirt, and striped necktie, greeted them promptly.

"Good evening. My name is Jackson. I'll be your server this evening. Have you dined with us before?"

"I have," Alex replied. "This is the young lady's first visit."

"Welcome, miss, and welcome back, sir. I thought you looked familiar," he responded, handing out menus and placing an iPad that contained an electronic wine list in the center of the table as a second, younger man filled water glasses. A third man displayed and served a tray of various gourmet breads.

"Tonight we are featuring a rosemary sourdough, a roasted tomato and herb focaccia, and a cheddar breadstick," he explained, pointing each one out. "What can I get you?"

"Please leave us one of each in the middle of the table, and we'll share," Alex replied.

As the breadman obliged, the waiter stepped forward. "What can I get you to drink?"

Alex looked at her. "I think I'll have wine," she said.

"Please give us a few moments, and we'll select something from your wine list."

"Very good, sir. Please take your time, and I'll check back with you shortly."

Fanci looked around after the servers had departed and leaned forward, lowering her voice. "This is a very intimate place, and everything looks amazing."

"I have to credit Dylan with that. The chef's original restaurant was in St. Petersburg, and we used to go there. When it closed down many people, including yours truly, were highly disappointed. He opened this one in Tampa, and now I come here regularly."

"How often to you go over to St. Petersburg?"

"Before I bought my condo, quite often. I stayed with Dylan when I was visiting and sometimes when I was here for work. If I got tired of the commute, I would stay at a hotel in Tampa, usually the Marriott, before the Edition was built."

"How often do you see your friend now when you're in town?"

"Pretty regularly. We take turns going back and forth. But enough about me and him, especially him. He's boring, as I mentioned earlier. If you like what've you've seen so far, wait until you see the food. Everything the chef prepares here is a work of art. What do you feel like eating tonight?"

"I'm not sure yet. I'll have to look at the menu."

"We can get started on the wine. What would you like?" he added as he began perusing the list.

"Whatever you decide will be fine."

"Well, you had a rosé back at the hotel. How about a pinot noir?"

"What exactly is that? I'm no expert."

"We can fix that," he replied with a smile. "You'll just have to spend more time with me. It's a light red, close in proximity to a rosé. We can start with that, and if you don't like it, we can select something else. We can always take the leftovers home."

"Even wine?"

"Yeah. The local ordinance has been around for a while now. It encourages people not to over imbibe, as one may be inclined to do after spending a hefty sum on a bottle if it would have to be consumed on the premises or otherwise left behind."

"Makes sense," she commented as she began to examine the menu.

They enjoyed an intimate two-hour dinner, and the conversation flowed naturally. Fanci found Alex as charming as he was disarming and felt somewhat regretful about using a pseudonym and fibbing about other details when they'd met, but she had reflexively done so, concerned about the clandestine nature of her assignment.

She had never expected to see or hear from him again, but she was enjoying his company, and the opportunity to travel to Florida for a couple days and escape the frigid cold of the northeast was a concomitant bonus.

The conversation was more muted on the ride back to the hotel. After they entered the lobby Alex asked, "It's still early. Is there anything else you would like to do?"

"I would like to see your apartment, if that's okay," she replied unpretentiously.

"It's more than okay. It's an excellent idea. We can have a nightcap, and I'll give you the nickel tour."

They took the private elevator to his residence, and upon entering, Fanci was impressed with the openness, high-end finishes, and furnishings of the great room that comprised the kitchen, dining, and living areas. She looked around the space before walking over and gazing out the floor-to-ceiling glass windows that offered eastern views of the illuminated city and waterfront.

Alex approached her from behind, gently placing his hands on her petite shoulders, and nuzzled up to her ear. "Let me show you the rest of the place," he said, taking her by the hand.

He pointed out Ben's nursery and Helen's room, decorated in a manner that indicated it clearly belonged to a woman. "You mentioned you had a young son, but what about this room?" she asked with a sideways glance. "It clearly belongs to a woman. You aren't married, are you?"

He laughed. "That's Helen's room. She's Ben's nanny. She travels with my son when he visits me here." He turned her around and looked her in the eye, their faces close together. "And what kind of husband would I be if my wife slept in a separate room?"

"You do have a point there."

"Come on. I'll show you the master."

Once they entered and Fanci had an opportunity to briefly look around, Alex maneuvered behind her and massaged her shoulders. She did not resist but rather lightly moaned with pleasure, signifying approval. Taking the cue, he turned her around and kissed her gently on the lips. She put her arms around his neck, and they kissed, this time longer and more passionately as his hands explored her upper body before moving to her chest.

"I'm going to use your bathroom," she said softly, gently breaking the embrace.

"Certainly," he replied in a hushed tone, indicating the direction.

Fanci closed the door before shutting her eyes and allowing her mind to clear. She checked herself in the mirror and washed her hands before fixing her hair. Taking a deep breath, she opened the door to find Alex sitting up on the bed, shoes off but otherwise dressed. "Come sit," he commanded, patting the space next to him on the quilted mattress.

She instinctively obeyed, and he leaned across, continuing the petting, increasing the passion and frequency. "I don't have a lot of experience," she uttered when they came up for air.

He smiled disarmingly. "Don't worry. I'll be gentle."

"Oh, no," she replied. "That's not what I meant. I need an experienced man to teach me properly."

"You came to the right place." He started slowly and worked his way down her body. Fanci allowed herself to relax, and it soon became evident he possessed the skill set as advertised. The tingling of warm anticipation built until a torrent of sensuality coursed through her body. Afterward, she felt a contented buoyancy she had never experienced before. After a brief respite, they continued kissing and caressing before she fell into a deep slumber.

# CHAPTER THIRTEEN

ON WEDNESDAY OF THE FOLLOWING week, Dylan was in his office when Alex called. "Hey, Dylan. It's been a minute. I thought I'd check in and see if you want to have dinner tomorrow night."

"Sounds good. How was your weekend with the college student from Connecticut?"

"Outstanding. Thank you very much. Which side of the bay do you want to dine on?"

"You came over here last time, so I'll come to you. How about Ponte? I haven't been there in a while, and I really miss the place since they closed the restaurant over here."

"Liz and I just had dinner there on Saturday night, but I'm ready to go back."

He leaned back in his chair, smiled, and shook his head. "Ponte, huh? Was the young lady impressed?"

"I believe so. And she enjoyed the restaurant as well."

He laughed. "Okay, I teed that one up for you. Make the reservation for seven, and I'll meet you there."

"Will do. See you then."

As soon as he hung up with Alex, his cell phone rang again. He looked at the screen and saw it was Penel.

"Hi, how are you?"

"I'm well, Penel. And how about yourself?"

"Other than the fact that the temperatures up here have been frigid, I'm doing fine. I miss you, though. It may be time for a visit soon. Maybe I'll come to you and thaw out my frozen bones."

"I've heard about the record cold you've had up there since we were all together a few weeks ago. You're always welcome here, and the weather's been spectacular."

"Thank you, Dylan. I'll take a look at my work calendar and carve out some time. I'll let you know."

"I look forward to it."

"Well, I've got to run. I have to get to court, but I had a few minutes and wanted to check in and say hello."

"All right, take care, and we'll talk again soon."

As soon as he disconnected the call, Shirley came in and dropped a pile of mail on his desk. "There's some interesting reading in the packet from Barry Filmore. It just arrived by overnight delivery. I put it on the bottom of the pile. The important stuff's on top."

"Thanks, Shirley. I'll check out Mr. Filmore's correspondence when I'm bored and looking for some light entertainment."

"He's already called twice to confirm that his package was received and to see whether you're prepared to go forward with his proposal," she said with a smile.

"What's that look for? You're not secretly working for"—he sifted through the mail and pulling the cover letter from the packet on the bottom of the pile—"Barry Filmore and Associates Consulting Group, are you?"

"Busted. And I'm working on commission. So when you do start doing business with him, I'll be out shopping."

"I wouldn't make those shopping plans anytime soon."

"That's what I figured," she said with a smirk as she sashayed out of the office.

That afternoon, Barry Filmore presented himself to the downtown New York corporate offices of BubbleRap, Incorporated, a Fortune 500 conglomerate that got its start when a small Ohio chewing gum factory purchased another local family-owned business that produced the wax paper formerly used in butcher shops to wrap customers' meat orders. Since that time, it had functioned as a holding company for various acquisitions in the consumer products space and owned a myriad of best-selling, brand-name products in categories ranging from soap and laundry detergent to snacks and beverages.

"Barry Filmore to see Hans Petersen," he barked at a pair of receptionists at the lobby front desk before sitting down in a chair with views of Central Park. He heard a woman's throat clear and then, "Mr. Petersen will be with you shortly, sir. Is there anything I can get you?"

"You can get me Mr. Petersen," he snapped, looking at the steel Rolex Daytona strapped to his wrist. "It's eleven fifteen, and we had an eleven o'clock. My time is extremely valuable."

"Sir," the woman replied in a raised voice, "Mr. Petersen is the CEO of the company and an extremely busy man. He will be with you shortly, as I indicated."

Filmore stood and stared at the woman in icy silence until he sensed she had become uncomfortable. "Perhaps you didn't understand me the first time. Did you speak with Mr. Petersen directly when I was announced?"

"I spoke with his private secretary."

"I suggest you call again and confirm that he is aware I'm waiting in the lobby."

The woman hesitated before picking up a phone and dialing a few numbers. She spoke softly into the mouthpiece before placing it back in its cradle. "My apologies, sir. Mr. Petersen's secretary did not immediately notify him as he was on a conference call. She just went into his office and slipped him a note."

They both looked up as a distinguished-looking man dressed in a tailored suit entered the lobby. The receptionist who had been subject of Filmore's derision nudged her coworker.

"Mr. Filmore, I most certainly apologize for the delay. It's nice to see you again. Please come on back," he said in a conciliatory tone, extending his right hand.

"Mr. Petersen," he said with a nod, accepting the handshake.

"Please, follow me. We can speak in my office."

Filmore followed the CEO back to his office, glaring at the receptionist as he strode past.

The two men were seated in an outer office that doubled as an intimate conference room and took chairs opposite each other. Filmore selected the seat with the view of the park, folded his hands in his lap, and stared silently at the CEO.

"That's a beautiful timepiece. Is that a Rolex?"

"Yes, sir. It's a vintage Daytona. Picked it up at a horological auction."

"Excuse me."

"An auction specializing in timepieces."

"I see. Well, thank you, Mr. Filmore, for coming to see me personally again. I know your time is valuable."

"You are correct, sir, but since you've agreed to hire my firm, I am available to guide your journey on the pathway to sustainable business practices."

"And I appreciate your expertise in this area. As you are aware, we have a vast product line, and this is quite a complex and expensive commitment."

"I acknowledge that, sir, and your devotion to the cause is admirable. But may I remind you, this is not without benefit to your stakeholders. In addition to reducing your carbon footprint, you will be ahead of the curve, meeting the new SEC requirements for disclosure of greenhouse gas emissions. This, in turn, will attract ESG investment and positively affect your market capitalization."

"I've run this by our board, and they are committed as well."

"That's good to hear. I trust you've given further consideration to my recommendation to add a board member with climate skills to assist in managing this new venture?"

"We have. The board was a bit more equivocal on that point, but I'm working on it. I've also been tasked with requesting whether there is any wiggle room on your fees."

Filmore glared at him until the executive looked away. "Mr. Petersen. As you have acknowledged multiple times, including this very day, this is a huge undertaking, given the vast and diversified product line of your holdings. Never mind the complexities of quantifying and standardizing the direct emissions, the intricacies of reporting the indirect Scope Two and Three emissions from your supply chains and customers' use of your products is a huge undertaking. Only my company, the preeminent firm in the industry, has the resources, expertise, and government contacts to make this venture a success. Once we complete our audit and submit our recommendations, your firm will be a leader in corporate climate responsibility.

In addition to increasing your market cap, you will be eligible for generous grants and subsidies. This will be a win-win all the way around. Working with the preeminent climate consulting firm will benefit your company environmentally as well as financially, and you personally will be seen as a trailblazer in the field of corporate responsibility."

Filmore stood, and Petersen followed suit. "Again, Mr. Filmore, I appreciate your agreeing to partner with us on this."

"Thank you, sir. I'll send over the documentation necessary to complete our work. I trust the nondisclosure agreement we sent over was acceptable."

"Our corporate and outside counsel have reviewed it and given it the green light. It's been signed and sent back to your office."

"Excellent. I'll leave you to it then," he replied, shaking the man's hand. "I'll see myself out. Good day, sir."

Filmore turned and walked calmly back in the direction of the lobby. Once outside the building his phone rang. "Hey, Ly, what's up?"

"I'm checking on the progress of your dealings with our philanthropic friend in Florida. Our union friend has developed a real interest in this guy. I want to give her an update."

"I'm in the city right now. Just closed a seven-figure annual consulting fee commitment from another of these C-suite schmucks chomping at the bit to tout his company's sustainability program."

"Excellent, got to keep that pump primed, but again, we need to redirect our Florida guy's focus. We do this for our union friend, and we can count on her as another trusted partner in our campaign."

"The plan is in place and being executed with the usual precision as we speak. I'll have an update for you shortly."

"Good. Let me know right away when you have something I can report back."

"Will do."

# CHAPTER FOURTEEN

The following evening, Dylan left the house about six fifteen, figuring the traffic into Tampa would begin to recede by the time he reached the Howard Frankland Bridge. He was dressed in gray slacks, tan polo, and dress sneakers, but grabbed a blue blazer at the last moment, recalling the semi-formality of the dinner crowd at Ponte. His calculations as to the commuter traffic proved prescient, and he arrived at the restaurant precisely at seven. Alex pulled up to the valet station right behind him, wearing what appeared to be that day's business suit. "You're looking dapper. Good to see you're on time. I like that in a man," he observed.

Dylan stared at him for a moment. "Good to know, but I have to say that sounds quite effeminate."

"That from a guy who uses 'quite' as an adverb?" he retorted.

Dylan shook his head and let the matter drop. As soon as they were seated, a waiter approached. "Good evening, Mr. Malloy. Nice to see you again so soon."

"Jackson, nice to see you as well. I apologize in advance, sir."

"Oh?" the waiter replied with a dubious stare.

"I apologize for the lack of resplendence in my dining companion this evening. I am painfully aware of the devolution since my visit on Saturday."

"Your companion is quite appropriate, sir. It will be my pleasure to serve you both this evening. What can I get you to drink?"

"Water will be fine for now," Dylan replied. "May we have a wine menu, please?"

"Certainly, sir," Jackson replied, handing him the wine list.

"I'll have a splash of that water on top of a Macallen," Alex added.

"Very good, sir, I'll be back with your drink. Please take your time and let me know when you're ready to order."

"What's been happening in your world?" Alex inquired.

"You won't believe this one," he said, explaining the visit from Barry Filmore and the proposal he'd received in the mail earlier in the day. "The guy claims he can guarantee me an ESG score in the eightieth percentile if I do business with him."

Alex had been listening with apparent interest, leaning forward in his chair, a hand under his chin. "And explain to me again why you, operating essentially a financial business out of a home office, are such a burden on the environment that you're a major contributor to 'the existential climate crisis'?" he asked, emphasizing the last phrase with air quotes.

"The guy sent this detailed proposal quantifying my carbon footprint on every construction project for the past five years, including building materials, equipment, and the current usage of the buildings down to the utilities and human toll. Apparently, my name is also listed in the public data available from many of the energy companies I've invested in, including a number of master limited partnerships. I have no idea how he compiled all this information on me. He even provided a breakdown of climate-related issues on the land I own out west that's leased to farmers and ranchers. The proposal included specifics on greenhouse gas emissions as well as effects on weather patterns and the water supply. Even claims the agriculture industry threatens the well-being of farm workers and contributes to food insecurity for people below the poverty threshold. How is that all possible? The farms employ hundreds of people who provide for their families. And how does raising crops result in more people going hungry? This stuff seems crazy."

Alex glanced in the direction of Jackson, who was approaching their table. "Well, I, for one, am part of the solution."

"Really? Please enlighten me."

"It's quite simple, really. I'm a secondhand vegetarian. Cows eat grass. I eat cows."

Jackson served Alex his drink. "Are you gentlemen ready to order?"

"After consultation with my dinner companion here," Alex said, "I'm most certainly going to have the Kansas City strip steak with asparagus and your lobster mac and cheese."

"How would you like your steak prepared?"

"Medium rare, please."

"And you, sir?"

"I'll have the filet medium rare. And we'll share the sides."

"Very good. Have you made your wine selection?"

"I haven't had a chance to peruse the wine list. Do you have a recommendation?"

"With the beef, I would suggest a Bordeaux. Perhaps the Chateau Lassegue Saint-Emilion," he articulated with a perfect French accent.

"That will be fine, thank you."

Jackson departed, and Dylan decided to change the subject, struggling to figure out why he was allowing this Filmore character's recent intrusion into his life to consume his thoughts. "So, are you going to see the young lady from Connecticut again anytime soon?"

"Oh, no. You're not getting off that easy. It sounds to me like this climate scold is living rent-free inside your head."

Dylan winced. "Is it that obvious? It's just that the guy completely blindsided me, and I suppose I never thought much about the issue. The guy talks a good game, but it appears to be nothing more than a money grab."

"I take it this charlatan has made you an offer you can't refuse, and it involves a substantial amount of cash."

"Right again. Basically, he concluded that since I'm not involved in any of the day-to-day activities firsthand, the only viable solution is to purchase carbon credits through his company. Claims he holds all these government and private entity designations as a gold-standard certified carbon credit dealer."

"What exactly does he do in return for your writing him hefty checks?"

"Apparently, he purchases carbon offsets and credits from entities that are engaged in projects that produce renewable energy or capture and destroy pollutants."

"So, what are you going to do?"

"The guy gives me the creeps. I was pretty aggressive with him from the start. I'm going to blow him off, but I may look into this whole climate change thing a little deeper."

"Uh oh," Alex uttered.

"Uh oh what?"

"The last time someone approached you about charitable giving, you went all in and started your own foundation. Please don't tell me you're about to become one of those guys."

"One of what guys?" he said, narrowing his eyes.

"A card-carrying member of the climate clerisy. I don't think I could handle that."

"Well, in that case, I'll just drop the whole subject."

"That's the smartest thing you've said since we got here." And it was the last word on the matter for the balance of the evening.

# CHAPTER FIFTEEN

On Friday morning, Dylan spent a full two and a half hours in his home gym, putting himself through a vigorous full-body workout as he tried to clear his mind. He spent the last thirty minutes on the treadmill pushing through an incline climb. Afterward, he showered and mixed a protein shake, taking the concoction to the main level outdoor balcony. He was sitting in a lounge chair and sipping his drink while gazing out over the bright blue-green waters of Boca Ciega Bay, glistening in the early morning sun, when his phone rang.

"Hi, Dylan. It's Parker."

"Hey. What's going on?"

"We haven't spoken in a few weeks since dinner with Alex, so I thought I'd touch base. How've you been?"

Parker was in his midtwenties with movie star good looks, highlighted by piercing blue eyes, classic chiseled features, and a killer jawline. Originally from Wisconsin, he'd relocated to Florida after graduating from college and, less than a year ago, was working for an upstart community bank involved in money laundering and other nefarious activities. He cooperated with the FBI, was granted whistleblower status, and the matter was resolved quickly.

The bank and the cartel agreed to pay a hundred-million-dollar fine, with the cartel funding ninety percent. Parker received an eight-figure fee after taxes. Just as significantly, the case file was sealed, and his identity was never released. Dylan had met him through a mutual business contact and had taken a liking to the young man. After the case was resolved, Parker sought advice, and Dylan agreed.

"I'm doing well," Dylan replied. "We had a good time in Connecticut.

The opening of the new school addition up there was a success, and I got to see some old friends. How about yourself?"

"I just got back from the driving range. Been working on my golf game."

"How'd you hit 'em?"

"Not bad. I bought new clubs, and I'm getting more consistent. I feel like hitting the links if you're up to it."

"Where've you been playing?"

"Just the public courses around here, but I'm really enjoying it. I'm thinking about joining a club, maybe Pasadena."

"Pasadena's nice. I've played there a few times. The entire course underwent a complete renovation a few years back. How much golf have you played before?"

"A little back in high school and college during the summers in Wisconsin. Since I moved down here, it's mostly customer golf as a working stiff in the financial world. With my newfound freedom, I'm thinking about getting serious, maybe taking some lessons."

"That's probably a good idea. I can hook you up with the pro at the Vinoy. How about we play a round there and I introduce you?" he suggested, pulling up his calendar on his phone. "How about next Friday morning?"

"Sounds good."

Dylan leaned back and ran his hand through his hair. "Speaking of working stiffs, how is early retirement treating you?"

"I've been busy furnishing and decorating the condo. That's done now, but I'll start volunteering at your youth center soon and schedule the rest of my day around that."

"Have you thought about what you want to do there?"

"I have. I'd like to work with the club sports teams."

"What experience do you have?"

"I played baseball in high school. Was pretty good, got a few feelers to play in college but no serious scholarship money, and I wasn't the greatest student. That's how I ended up at Wisconsin-La Crosse. In-state tuition was really all I could afford, and that was only with student loan assistance."

"Do you have any coaching experience?"

"I helped coach a Little League team for a year, and then the town where I lived hired me to umpire. I've done games up through the Babe Ruth level and some men's softball."

"I've got an experienced guy to handle managerial duties, but he needs an assistant coach. How do you feel about that?"

"That's perfect. I know the game on the field, but I have a lot to learn about instruction and coaching strategy."

"Great. I'll get you in touch with him. His name is Evan Fedorko. We call him Junior. I played for his dad's travel team when I was in high school. He was legendary, and I learned a lot from him. Junior's probably a dozen years older than me, and he used to help his dad coach back in the day. They both live in St. Pete Beach, and I convinced Junior to coach. His dad will also be around, helping out. He's in his seventies and still in great shape. I'll get a tee time and plan on picking you up on Friday. I'll text you the time."

"Looking forward to it. I'll continue to practice and see you then."

He hung up and, after a moment, decided to call Esther. "Good morning," he said after she got on the line. "I wanted to check in and see how you're doing."

"I'm doing very well. I'm hoping this cold snap we've been having up here breaks soon. We got eight inches of snow last night."

"Wow. That's quite a bit for your area."

"Indeed. What's been happening in your world?"

Dylan spent the next twenty minutes unburdening himself about his encounter with Barry Filmore and his recent thoughts about climate change. "It's kind of strange. This guy is clearly a scoundrel, but—I have to admit—he's given me pause to consider a subject I never paid much attention to. Now that I think about it, it does appear that there have been more extreme weather patterns in recent times. Floods, fires, droughts, blizzards, hurricanes. My first decade living in Florida, I hardly recall any hurricane warnings. Now it seems like we're required to evacuate every year. I've left a few times thinking my house might not be standing when I returned."

Esther listened patiently until there was a lull in his narrative. "Dylan, your concerns are not uncommon. Over my lifetime, I've heard all the alarmist pundits' predictions. Threats of an ice age, acid rain and the deterioration of the ozone layer, global warming, and the disappearance of ice caps. However, those threats mostly fell on the ears of a small radical minority, and, of course, none of those things came to pass. The difference I see today is that climate is now a matter of a core cultural identity, achieving an almost religious-like status on a not-insignificant portion of the population, resulting in widespread hysteria. There's no shortage of those with a platform who blame every major weather event on climate change and take the opportunity to capitalize on it by imposing their values on others and exerting more control over their lives. And, of course, profiting off fearmongering is a tried-and-true venture, and that appears to be flourishing. All major institutions, from government, academia, media, and even Wall Street, are pushing the agenda. Most corporate entities now have an entire department dedicated to sustainable business practices. I'm surprised it hasn't landed on your radar until now."

"Of course, I'm aware of ESG investing. I've steered clear of it the same way I have with any new investment fad, like cryptocurrency or NFTs, so I never gave it much thought. What do you think about it?"

"I think studying climate science is a good thing. And when a consensus is reached through robust scientific research, testing, and debate, and a measured long-term plan is formulated to include things like reducing greenhouse gases and replacing conventional energy sources with something cleaner and more efficient, that's real progress. But that isn't what's happening, not even close. Sky-is-falling alarmism has been the catalyst for drastic, unproven, cost-prohibitive measures to replace conventional methods of transportation, food production, energy, and construction. And that's highly irresponsible, inefficient, and intrusive. Have you done any research on this Barry Filmore and his companies?"

"No, because I haven't taken him seriously enough to go through the exercise. He does have me thinking about the subject, though. It's like a few years ago when I was approached with the opportunity to invest in the newspaper industry as an altruistic endeavor. I quickly dismissed the idea, but it got me thinking about philanthropy, and I started the foundation to help with a cause I truly believe in."

"You're a good and decent person, Dylan, and I understand your thought process. I won't burden you with details, but I just googled Mr. Filmore. In addition to his consulting company, he runs a nonprofit called Do My Part for the Planet, which is also his website domain name. He has a degree in history from Georgetown University, so he's clearly no scientist. I also came across a recent interview. He advocates for drastic lifestyle changes like getting rid of cars and household appliances and eating bugs for sustenance. My initial impression is that he falls somewhere between a crackpot and a swindler."

"I appreciate your advice on this, Esther, as usual. I won't give Mr. Filmore another thought once I make it clear to him that we won't be doing business. I am going to continue looking into the climate issue, though."

"There's nothing wrong with that. There's a lot more to discuss on the subject when you're ready."

He went back inside and pulled Filmore's proposal from the stack of papers on his desk. He read the cover letter, which stated that the proposal was valid for seven days, at which time it would be revoked.

His office phone buzzed. "Barry Filmore is on line one for you," Shirley announced.

He put down the letter and picked up the phone. "Dylan Tomassi."

"Dylan, Barry Filmore. I'm following up on the proposal I sent you. Can I count on your commitment?"

"You can count on this. I have no interest in doing business with you or your firm, now or ever. Kindly refrain from contacting me again."

"That's very disappointing, Dylan. I have to say you will come to regret this shortsighted decision."

"Is that a threat, sir?"

"No. It is simply a prediction of future events. As a climate envoy, I am obligated to report your noncompliance to my superiors with the department and the other appropriate federal agencies. I am certain you have not heard the last word on this matter. You should tread lightly, sir," he admonished as he disconnected the call.

# CHAPTER SIXTEEN

EARLY WEDNESDAY MORNING, DYLAN WAS in his office reviewing the progress reports on a new residential development in Largo. He had purchased a six-and-half-acre property that had once been a drive-in movie theater but had fallen into disrepair and, in the past decade, had become a magnet for homelessness, drug use, and other nefarious activities. The city of Largo had commended him on purchasing and cleaning up the property and building much-needed housing. When completed, the development, known as Largo Palms, would be comprised of an apartment building, twenty townhomes, and ten single-family residences. Amenities included a community pool, clubhouse, and fitness center.

Site development and infrastructure work had been concluded months ago. Foundations were poured, and buildings had begun rising from the earth. Dylan was meeting the building contractor, Rock Wright of Ronco Design Group, at seven thirty, just after the construction crews started work for the day.

He was driving his old pickup north on Starkey Road as the sun began to rise above the horizon when his phone rang. It was Rock. "Uh, Dylan, you on your way?" His words oozed with trepidation.

"Yes. I'm on Starkey. Should be there within ten minutes. What's up?"

"Um, I'll tell you when you get here. Please hurry."

Dylan pulled up to the job site, greeted by the bright custom-painted sign posted at the grand entrance, the temporary sales and leasing office set just behind it. As he drove onto the property, he observed a black Chevy SUV with US government plates and a late-model white sedan, both out of place with the pickups and construction trucks scattered around, workers uncharacteristically hanging around their vehicles past starting time. Rock began walking stiffly in his direction as soon as he dismounted his truck. Two other men stood some distance behind him. One was tan and well-built, dressed in a black suit and wearing sunglasses. The other man was short and pudgy with a pasty complexion and wore khaki pants, a short-sleeve gingham shirt, and soft-sole work shoes.

"Dylan, we've got a major problem here," Rock whispered, handing Dylan a piece of paper and gesturing with his chin in the direction of the two dubious visitors. "Those guys arrived shortly after I did this morning. They're G-men. Told me they're shutting down the job site indefinitely."

"Who are they?" Dylan asked, holding the paper at his side while taking in the two men.

"One's FBI, and the other is from the Department of the Interior. Both showed me badges and IDs before they handed me the letter," he replied, gazing down at Dylan's hand.

"I'll speak with them in a moment, but tell me what this is all about."

"The short guy did most of the talking. Says a federal investigation revealed possible unmarked Indigenous burial sites on the property. Said the federal government issued an immediate cease-work order. He ordered my crews to stop working immediately. Apparently, the FBI guy is here to oversee enforcement."

Dylan looked at the paper printed on US Department of the Interior letterhead. It was dated for that same day and addressed to his company, DAT Real Estate Holding, LLC. The caption read:

> By Order of the United States Secretary of the Interior
> IMMEDIATE CEASE WORK ORDER
> Largo Palms Development
> 3105 Plumtree Heights
> Largo Florida

He approached the two men, engaging the one in the suit. "I'm Dylan Tomassi. I own the company that's developing this property. What is this all about?"

The shorter man stepped in front of the FBI agent. "Stanley Hodges, Department of the Interior. This is *about* what's contained within the four corners of the letter you're holding in your hand. I'm just the messenger. Received notice of this yesterday in my Atlanta office and was told to fly down here and shut down the job site. My colleague here is local, and his agency will be enforcing the order."

The agent stood expressionless behind his shades, suit jacket open enough to expose a badge and holstered sidearm attached to his belt.

Dylan stood and read the balance of the letter. "We'll comply for now while I have my legal team review this. I don't see a name on here other than the secretary's signature. Who is the contact person on this?"

"Not my concern," Hodges replied. "I'm going to enjoy a few hours in the Florida sunshine, grab some lunch, and be home in time for dinner. You boys have any good barbeque places around here?"

Dylan glared at the man. "Not my concern," he said, detecting a small smile from the otherwise stoic FBI agent as he turned and walked back toward Rock.

"I'll get this to my lawyers right away, but for now, we need to clear this place of all personnel, marketing staff included, and lock the front gate."

"Okay, Dylan."

"Let me look into this, and I'll get back with you as soon as I have something."

"I'm on it."

Dylan got back in his truck and dialed his attorney's office. "Good morning, Driscoll Williams. How may I direct your call?"

"Dylan Tomassi calling for Walt Jackman."

"Good morning, Mr. Tomassi. I'll connect you with Mr. Jackman's office."

Driscoll Williams was a full-service law firm that occupied several upper floors of the Bank of America tower in downtown Tampa. The white-shoe firm handled all Dylan's legal work, including his business, personal, and foundation matters. He was an important client who received white-glove treatment. Walt was the head of the firm's tax department and the point person responsible for his account.

"Good morning, Dylan. What can I do for you?"

"I wish I could say it was a good morning, but, unfortunately, it's not off to a particularly auspicious start," he said before filling Walt in on the morning's events.

"That is certainly odd."

"Especially considering we now include geological and archeological studies as part of our overall environmental due diligence on all new properties we acquire."

"And one was done on the Largo property, correct?"

"Of course. We worked very closely with the city on it."

"Where are you now?"

"Driving back home as we speak."

"Send me a copy of the letter when you get there. I'll get with Tina Fischer in our land use and environmental law department. She's the go-to person for these types of matters."

"I'll do it. Thanks, Walt."

Dylan got home and headed straight to his office. As soon as he was seated Shirley came in with a stack of mail. "How did your meeting go at Largo?"

"Not good. We've been shut down by the federal government."

She winced as she handed him a page from the stack of mail. "You should take a look at this. It came in a plain envelope with no return address."

Dylan stared in confused silence at the three cutout images pasted across the page.

Fanci was in her cubicle toiling away at five o'clock when the daily stampede to the elevators commenced. Ten minutes later, per usual, she could not see or hear a soul on the floor. She kept herself busy until six, when she headed upstairs to meet Kari Baldwin as requested. All she was told was that she would be accompanying her to a dinner meeting and to wear something she thought Kari would like. She had selected a pair of well-fitting wool pants, a black sweater, and ankle boots.

She texted the number for Kari's personal cell phone to let her know she was on her way up. Five minutes later, she was standing in the union chief's office undergoing a physical inspection. "You are a very sexy young woman. I want you to wear something tonight that accents that luscious figure of yours." Glancing at her oversized men's sterling silver watch, she said, "We have time to do a little shopping before dinner."

They headed over to the Arcade, a downtown shopping mall, and Kari led the way to an expensive-looking women's boutique. A saleswoman approached. "Good evening. How may I be of service to you ladies this evening?"

"We're looking for some lingerie and a dress for my friend here," Baldwin replied. "We'll look around and let you know when we require assistance."

"Please do so and let me know if you need anything at all. Can I get you both something to drink, champagne perhaps?"

"Yes. That will do nicely."

Kari selected a few dresses for Fanci and lingerie for both of them and then sat in a chair in the dressing room while Fanci modeled for her. Kari approved of a snow-white knit dress with a front cutout across the chest and a pair of black leather thigh-high boots with a generous heel that zipped snugly against her legs. She insisted Fanci wear the new outfit with the black matching lace bra and panties she had picked out.

Fanci nodded affirmatively but said nothing.

Ralph-n-Rich's Restaurant was near their office building, and they arrived a few minutes early. Kari continued through the narrow reception area and led Fanci to the bar, where she ordered two dirty martinis. She handed one to Fanci and took a seat at a high-top table, patting the chair next to her. "We're having dinner with Fred Mason. He's a partner with Jensen Wheeler, one of the firms that manages the union pension fund. He usually has a few associates with him." She leaned in closer. "Order whatever you want and maintain a low profile. Your work begins when we get back to my house," she breathed in a hushed voice.

They sat silently for a few minutes sipping their drinks until a distinguished-looking man with gray hair and a blue pinstripe suit appeared, waving in their direction. He was accompanied by two attractive younger women. Both were well endowed and meticulously dressed and coiffed, probably for Kari's benefit, Fanci thought. They were introduced as Adriel and Barbara, associates who worked on the union account.

"It's nice to see you both again," Kari said with a smile.

"The maître d' told me you were in the bar. Our table is ready."

The group was seated in a private corner with views of Main Street. A waiter quickly approached and introduced himself. "What are we drinking this evening?" he inquired.

"Is everyone good with champagne?" Fred asked, looking in Kari and Fanci's direction.

"That will be fine," Kari replied.

"A bottle of Louis Roederer, Cristal, five glasses."

"Very good, sir," the waiter commented, and he meant it.

The champagne was promptly presented and served. "We're going to need a second bottle," Fred informed the waiter.

"Yes, sir," he said, hurrying off.

He lifted his glass. "Here's to Kari and her union and to a fine year for the fund. As you know, it returned twenty-eight point five percent last year."

"Hear, hear," Kari quipped, taking a healthy sip.

Fanci felt an immediate buzz from the champagne and was tempted to look at the wine list set in the center of the table to ascertain the price but thought better of it. The waiter promptly returned, setting up a stand-alone sterling silver ice bucket, opening the second bottle, and wrapping the top portion with a white linen napkin before setting it in the bucket. "Will there be anything else at the moment, some appetizers, perhaps?"

"We'll have two dozen raw oysters," Kari said.

"Very good, ma'am," he said, and he was off again.

"Oysters are quite the aphrodisiac," she commented to the two associates with a smile, placing her hand under the tablecloth, where it came to rest on Fanci's thigh.

The dinner conversation was dominated by Fred and Kari, confirming Fanci's initial impression that the women were eye candy for Kari's pleasure.

More wine was served with dinner, and Kari regularly refilled her glass. After the two-hour fete, Fanci was contented, still feeling buzzed from the excessive drinking. They were sitting comfortably close together in the back of the Uber on the ride to Kari's home when her phone rang. Fanci was pressed up against her and could hear both ends of the conversation.

"Kari, Barry Filmore."

"Yeah, Barry, what can I do for you.? I only have a moment."

"Just wanted to let you know Mr. Tomassi was unreceptive to my initial offer, but I've made a counterproposal, and I believe he will come around."

"And what the hell does all that mean?"

"We just shut down one of his construction sites in Florida. I expect an adjustment in his attitude toward his future business plans will be forthcoming, which will ultimately be of benefit to the union."

"I'm a very busy person. In the future, there's no need to provide me with progress reports. Let me know when you have something concrete," she snapped as she hung up the phone. Turning her attention back to Fanci, she began running her hand up her dress as she leaned over and whispered, "Now, where were we?"

"Who was that?"

"Just another person trying to gain favor who's out to please me. You want to please me, don't you, Fanci?" she asked, narrowing her eyes while she held her gaze.

"Yes, ma'am," she replied sheepishly, glancing away.

Kari leaned in further, kissing her passionately on the mouth. Fanci went numb, her mind a blank slate, feeling as if she were observing the experience from outside her own body.

The heavy petting continued until they reached Kari's residence. They entered the house, and Kari handed her the shopping bag from their earlier excursion. "Go take a shower in the guest room, put on the lingerie I bought you, and meet me in my bedroom," she instructed. Fanci said nothing and marched into the bathroom. She took a long hot shower, dried herself, and put on a white teddy, the only garment in the bag.

She made her way to the master, where the lights were dimmed, and found Kari sprawled out on her back, completely naked. She was amazed at the enormous size of the woman, filling out the better part of the king-size bed.

"Come to momma," Kari ordered, arms spread wide. Fanci complied and took orders from her for the next hour, fulfilling each of her heteroclite sexual demands.

# CHAPTER SEVENTEEN

DYLAN SPENT THE ENTIRE NEXT morning on the phone, juggling calls between his attorneys, contractors, and the bankers financing the Largo Palms project. He had just hung up with Tina Fischer, who had briefed him with a sobering assessment of the situation. He stood and stretched, his back and neck aching from the built-up tension, then Shirley buzzed him. "Mayor James is on line two."

Wincing, he picked up the desk phone. "Good morning, Madison."

"Good morning, Dylan. I'm returning your call from yesterday. Sorry I couldn't get back to you sooner. My staff has briefed me on Largo Palms. How could this happen? It's very disappointing, to say the least."

"I received a call yesterday morning and met with the FBI and the government official who delivered the stop-work order. My attorneys have been in contact with the federal government, and we've retained an archeology team from the University of South Florida to conduct a thorough investigation."

"Dylan, this project is very important to the city as well as my administration. Cleaning up a long-festering nuisance property and providing much-needed housing will be a tremendous improvement, but it has to get done. I have to say I'm more than a little concerned. And I don't have to remind you that I personally went out on a limb to get the tax credits and subsidies you needed."

"As I told you before, I appreciate your confidence in me and my company, and we will work through this. You have my word on that."

"I would think buying me dinner and spending a little more time convincing me is in order."

"Of course. How about Saturday night?"

"Sure, I'm available. You select the restaurant and let me know what time you'll pick me up. Oh, and one more thing. Can we take that wonderful sports car of yours?"

"Sure. How about Villa Gallace? I'll get a reservation for seven and pick you up at six thirty."

"Perfect. See you then. And hopefully, you'll have some good news for me on this."

Hanging up the phone, he breathed a heavy sigh. Dylan was cognizant of the Honorable Madison James's fondness for him, and she had certainly been an asset in paving the way for generous incentives and smoothing the path to obtaining the necessary permits. Still, as was his practice, Dylan had been thorough in his due diligence in investigating and planning the project, and he remained flummoxed as to how his team could have failed to discover an old burial ground beneath the property.

He was thinking about the Largo project and contemplating the delicate manner in which he would navigate his dinner date with the mayor when his cell phone rang and Penel's name appeared. "Hi, Dylan, what's going on in sunny Florida?"

"Hello, Penel. Actually, things appear quite stormy at the moment."

"Oh? Do tell."

He filled her in on the details involving the Largo project, leaving out any mention of the mayor. "So, what do you think?"

"I'm not sure. Do you think maybe it has something to do with this guy who presented you with the climate proposal who you, in turn, told to go pack sand?"

"I don't know. There is a connection. He's affiliated with the Department of the Interior, and they are the ones that shut down the project. And the next day, I get some cryptic cartoon message in the mail that makes absolutely no sense."

"I wish I could see the paper. It's strange the way you describe it."

He took a photo and texted it to her. "See? There's no other way to describe it: no writing, just a cutout picture of a wristwatch, a plus sign, a picture of a sheep, another plus sign, and a picture of a donkey. That's it."

"Weird, to say the least. And no clue of who sent it or where it came from?"

"I haven't the slightest idea. It came in a plain white envelope addressed to me at my home. No return address."

"I'm sorry to hear all this is happening to you. Perhaps I can cheer you up. I want to come down and see you in a couple weeks if you're available to host me."

"That can certainly be arranged. When were you thinking?"

"I can work on clearing my work calendar and shoot for, say, the first week of March."

"That sounds good. It'll be nice to have you down here, and maybe some of this stuff will be resolved by then."

"Okay, good. Well, I have to run. I have a client meeting, but I'll start working on travel plans and be back in touch with the specifics."

"All right. Penel. Always good to hear from you. Take care."

"Dylan, please take care of yourself as well."

Five minutes later, Alex called. With everything going on since yesterday, they hadn't spoken, and Dylan unburdened himself, bringing him up to date on his current tribulations.

"What you need is a good night out, and Dr. Malloy has office hours available this evening. I'll pick you up, take you to dinner, and we'll go from there."

Dylan found the thought appealing. "Where do you recommend we conduct this therapy session?"

"It's the height of tourist season. Somewhere on the beach where the fairer sex gathers."

"How about Castile? The food's great, and we can have a drink afterward on the rooftop lounge."

"A perfect setting to administer the modalities to fix what ails you. I can get to your house by six thirty. Make the dinner reservation for seven."

"Done. I'll see you then."

Dylan completed his last phone conference shortly after five thirty. Shirley had already left for the day, so he headed upstairs, showered, and changed into tan slacks, navy pullover, and tan dress sneakers. He headed downstairs to the barroom and poured himself a Scotch. He sipped his drink while staring at the bizarre anonymous letter he'd received. He folded it up and placed it in his back pocket just as his phone buzzed. "It's me. I'm at the gate."

He punched a code into his phone. "Come on up. I'll meet you out in front," he said, throwing back the last of his drink.

Thirty minutes later, they were seated at a table in the crowded restaurant overlooking the Intracoastal waterway.

"So, what's been going on?" Alex asked while they looked over menus. "Talk to me?"

"A lot of strange stuff's been happening since we got back from Connecticut. What do you *really* think about climate change?"

"I think climate change is good," he replied, taking in the crowded dining room. "It gets cold up north, and all these fine women seek a change in the climate, so they head south, in search of warmth and companionship."

"You're a wealth of knowledge and a fine help, as usual. Allow me to confuse you with some facts. Did you know that cement is one of the planet's biggest polluters?"

"I didn't know that. I thought it was farting cows. That's why I eat as much steak as possible. Less cows, less farting, less greenhouse gas. I try to do my part for the planet."

The waitress appeared. She was trim and blonde. "Good evening, gentlemen. My name is Jennifer. I'll be your server this evening. Can I get you something to drink?"

"Good evening to you, Jennifer. How are you this fine evening?" Alex inquired, flashing his best smile.

"Very well, sir. Thank you for asking."

"I think I'll start with an old-fashioned."

She turned to Dylan. "And how about you, sir?"

"I'll stick with water for now. Can you bring us a wine list?"

"Certainly," she replied. "I'll get that drink and be back to take your order."

"I like our waitress," Alex commented. "Now, where were we?"

"Two things, Alex. First, it's apparent you have no chance with the waitress, so forget it. Leave her alone and let her do her job. Second, never mind about where we were. I see I can't have a serious conversation with you tonight."

"All right. I admit I've been lacking in female companionship for a while. I'm sorry. I promise I'll be more attentive."

Dylan stared at him askance. "You just had that young girl fly in from Connecticut not long ago."

"Exactly. That tells you how desperate I've become. I could have waited to see her until I was back up there. I've got nothing going on down here."

"What about Ann?"

"I really like her. She's a fine woman, and we have a good time when we get together. But that's the problem. She hasn't been available much these days. Busy with work seems to be the issue. She's very career-oriented."

"She is at that, and she's very good at what she does. That's a good quality for an attorney to have, especially when she happens to be one of my attorneys. But could it also be she doesn't find you as charming as you think you are?"

"Ouch, that really hurts," he bemoaned, clutching his chest.

Dylan looked up and saw Jennifer staring concernedly in Alex's direction, a drink and wine list in her hands. "Are you all right, sir?" she asked earnestly.

"Yes, dear. I was just making a point with my friend here."

"He's fine, Jennifer. Alex tends to be overly dramatic at times. We sometimes refer to him as the 'Drama Llama.'"

She placed the drink in front of Alex and handed Dylan the wine list, a warm smile on her face. "May I be honest?"

"Please do. Honesty is a valued trait in these difficult and trying times in which we find ourselves," Alex replied.

"I initially thought the two of you were gonna be a couple of serious businessmen. You guys are fun."

"Thanks for that," Dylan replied, "but I must stop you. You'll only encourage him."

"Too late. I'm already encouraged. What time do you get off work?"

The waitress looked at him, and Dylan observed the color draining from her face. "Sorry. I'm closing tonight and also working the rooftop lounge, so I won't get out of here until well after midnight. It's pretty crowded out there. Lots of beautiful women. You guys should head out there after dinner, have a drink, and check it out."

"Thanks for the suggestion, Jennifer. I think we'll do just that," Alex replied.

Fully recovered from Alex's awkward pass, she smiled, turning her attention to Dylan. "Please look over the wine list, and I'll check back with you shortly," she said before quickly departing.

Dylan stared at Alex and smiled. "What?" he finally asked after taking a pull on his drink and looking up.

"I give her a nine-point-five on the recovery," Dylan commented.

"What recovery?"

"Come on, Alex. You made a pass at our server, and a cringy and awkward one at that. I thought she recovered from the shock quite nicely and handled it well."

He stared back at his friend in silence before taking another thoughtful sip of his drink. Putting the glass down, he folded his hands and stared across the table. "My dear friend. You are an unseasoned hunter when it comes to the pursuit of the opposite sex. I don't think of it like you do. I flirted with her and never gave her response a second thought. I'm like one of those old-time Fuller Brush salesman. I knock on several doors before I can close a deal. It's part of the game. Door slams in your face. Walk next door and knock on the next one."

Dylan looked up and saw Jennifer standing there, trying but failing to suppress a smile. "What's this about slamming doors and going next door? The food and drinks are much better here. Not to mention the service."

"Touché," Alex replied, lifting his glass.

"Have you decided on a wine selection?" she asked Dylan.

"I think so. We'll have a bottle of the Banfi Pinot Grigio."

"Very good choice," she commented with an approving smile.

Turning to Alex, "Would you like another drink, sir?"

"No, thank you. I'll share the wine with my friend here. Please bring two glasses."

"Very well. Are you gentlemen ready to order?"

"I'll have the short ribs," Alex replied.

"And you, sir?"

"I'll have the scallops."

"An excellent choice. And it pairs well with the wine. I'll get that right out and put your dinner orders in," she said, collecting the wine list and menus.

After dinner was served, Dylan found himself relaxing and enjoying the company of his ebullient friend, whose head remained on a swivel, checking out the throngs of women who appeared to be dining and drinking in groups sans male companions.

"I'm glad you picked this place," he commented, fixing his gaze back on his dining companion. "The place is crawling with talent tonight."

"Don't you mean unsuspecting victims?" Dylan replied.

"I don't see them as victims. I see them as new friends I haven't had the pleasure of meeting yet."

"I was looking at it from the female perspective."

"How progressive of you." Dylan looked over to find Jennifer standing there. Her timing was impeccable. "Sorry. I couldn't help myself. I didn't mean to interrupt your conversation. Will there be anything else this evening?"

"Just the check, please," Alex replied, flashing his omnipresent undeterred smile. "We're going to retire over to the rooftop bar for an after-dinner drink."

"Great idea. It's pretty crowded out there. Let me see if I can find you a table."

She hurried off and returned a short time later. "Please follow me, gentlemen. I've secured you a table. We can take care of the check out there."

They followed Jennifer outside to the crowded bar. Dylan observed that the seats at the bar were all occupied, and people were standing two and three deep around the bar. Their table was along the balcony overlooking Gulf Boulevard and the hotels across the street. The sun had set, and rays of orange and red clung to the horizon above the dark waters of the Gulf of Mexico.

As they were seated, Alex ordered two beers and took care of the bill. Dylan could not help overhearing the resounding banter and laughter coming from the adjacent table. He glanced over past Alex and saw two women, appearing to be in their late thirties or early forties, with florid complexions that manifested overexposure to sunshine and alcohol.

Dylan pulled the note from his back pocket and spread it out in front of Alex. "What do you think of this?"

Alex stared at the three images on the paper for a moment until his attention was diverted to the noise coming from behind him. *It was only a matter of time before he noticed those two,* Dylan thought. *Here we go.*

He spun around on his stool. "Ladies," greeting them with a nod. "How are you two enjoying yourselves this fine evening?"

The one with light brown hair, dressed in a white midriff shirt, white shorts, and white tennis shoes, lifted her cocktail glass. "Carping the snot out of the diem."

"Hell, yeah! You go, girl," replied the blonde in a sundress and sandals. They clinked glasses and drained the contents before simultaneously slamming their glasses onto the table, drawing a few stares from surrounding patrons.

"It looks like the two of you are in need of refills. I wish to oblige, but we haven't been properly introduced. I'm Alex."

"Hi, Alex, I'm Carmen," the blonde replied. "And this here's Christie. I have to ask you a question first." She slurred as she spoke. "How come you're wearing a suit out here on the beach?"

"Fair question, Carmen. I'm an attorney in Tampa. I rushed over after work to assist my friend in need over here," indicating with the beer bottle in his hand. "This is Dylan."

Dylan nodded, unable to suppress the grimace on his face.

"Nice to meet you both," Christie added in a tone louder than was necessary. "And what is it that ails you, Dylan?"

"Why don't we pull our tables together? Order more drinks, and I promise to fully brief you on the situation."

Dylan observed as the two women clumsily slid off their stools while Alex pulled the table toward theirs and helped relocate the women, who were obviously unsteady on their feet. "Excuse me for a moment, ladies. I need to use the restroom," Dylan said, and he disappeared back into the restaurant.

He returned a few minutes later to find Alex conversing with the two women as if they were long-lost friends. "Carmen and Christie are from Michigan. They're staying at the Sea Towers across the street. They invited us over for a nightcap as soon as we finish these drinks."

"Sorry, ladies, but I have an early day tomorrow. I just texted for a ride. He should be here shortly, so I'm going to meet him downstairs."

The two women seemed unfazed by his departure.

"Whatever you say, Dylan. Who's coming to pick you up?" Alex inquired.

"Aengus is on his way, so I should get downstairs."

"Nice meeting you," Christie yelled out, waving furiously with her right hand in the air.

As he turned to leave, Alex grabbed him by the arm. "You almost forget this," he said, handing him the folded-up letter. "Watch your ass."

"Excuse me?" Dylan replied.

"Watch. Ewe. Ass. The note. It's a warning."

Dylan stared at him for a moment before putting the letter back in his pocket and leaving the bar.

# CHAPTER EIGHTEEN

The next afternoon, Dylan and Parker sat in the Vinoy Club Grill enjoying an early afternoon lunch after eighteen holes of golf. "I must say, Dylan, I really enjoyed myself today. The course is beautiful, and I'm impressed with your game. What was your final score?"

"Eighty-one. That's the best I've hit the ball in a while. It's a funny game you're getting yourself involved in, Parker."

"Now that I have the time and the funds, I'm going to get serious. How difficult is it to become a member here?"

"It wasn't bad when I joined, but I understand there's now an extensive wait list. I recently heard a former Tampa Bay Buccaneer who's a member of the Pro Football Hall of Fame applied for membership and was told he would have to put his name on the wait list like everyone else."

"That's pretty discouraging," Parker replied with a frown. "I don't suppose you could pull some strings."

Dylan laughed. "Unfortunately, I have no sway around here. I could introduce you to the golf pro. You should take some lessons if you want to improve your game. You're a natural athlete, and because you're a newbie, you haven't had much opportunity to develop bad habits. Taking lessons now would be a good way to see rapid improvement. That and a lot of practice."

"That's a great idea. Can we go see him now?"

Dylan smiled. "That's one of the things I like about you, Parker. You're charmingly aggressive." He pondered the statement for a moment. "And you never know. Working with Zach and getting to know him may get you an in with a fast-track membership."

"Zach?"

"He's the golf professional here."

"Great. Let's knock this out right now. Lunch is on me."

"Sorry. Your money's no good here. Literally. Lunch goes on my tab."

Dylan signed the check, and they walked through the clubhouse. He approached the young woman at the cash register. She had sundrenched blonde hair and wore a white tennis skirt and matching tank top that revealed a perfect tan on her well-toned arms and long legs. She smiled at Dylan, and her smile broadened as her gaze fixated on Parker.

"What can I do for you, gentlemen?"

"Good afternoon. Is Zach available?"

"Let me check. Who should I say is asking?"

"Dylan Tomassi. Please let him know I have a friend with me who's interested in taking lessons."

"And what would your friend's name be?" she inquired, giving Parker the full once-over.

"I'm Parker Gough," he replied, extending a hand. "It's very nice to meet you, Brooke Mitchell from Ithaca, New York. That's quite a commute to work you have every day."

She giggled as she glanced down at the name tag pinned just above her perky breasts. "I'm a student at Cornell studying hospitality management. I'm here for the spring doing an internship. It's *very* nice to meet you, Parker Gough."

"Smart move. Ditching upstate New York during the winter months for the warmth and sunshine in Florida."

"You're not kidding. It's beautiful here. It's just, with working so much, I haven't had much of a chance to go out and meet people."

"Well, we can fix that. After we speak with the golf pro, I'll get your number and show you around town. Do you like the beach?"

"Of course."

"I live on Treasure Island, so I would be happy to show you that part of town. All the good spots the tourists don't know about."

"Thank you. That's so kind," she said, the smile never leaving her face. "Let me go see if Zach is available," she added as she scurried down the hallway.

Dylan looked at him and remained silent but managed to suppress a smile.

"What?"

"Nothing."

"I can tell you're trying not to laugh."

"Laugh about what?" a tall, athletic-looking man dressed in a Vinoy Club golf shirt and tan slacks asked as he approached.

"Zach. Nice to see you. This is my friend Parker. I'm pretty sure he was referring to his golf game. That's why we sought you out. Parker's just getting started, and I thought you would be an excellent teacher."

"You've come to the right place. Zach Loyer," he said, extending a hand to Parker.

"Parker Gough."

"Nice to meet you. Are you a member here?"

"No, sir. I do plan on applying for membership."

"I see. Well, we can get you started as long as Dylan here will vouch for you," he replied with a smile.

"Parker's a good man."

Zach studied him a moment longer. "You look familiar. Have I seen you around here before?"

"Yes, sir, it's quite possible. The company I worked for had a corporate membership, and I utilized that quite a bit, meeting with clients."

"Ah," he replied with a look of approval. "What company?"

"Uh, I no longer work for them. I'm recently retired."

The golf pro looked at him dubiously. "I see."

"Anyway, I'd like to get started as soon as your schedule allows. I'm fairly flexible on the times."

The man consulted his phone. "Can you be out here next Wednesday at eight?"

"Sure thing."

"Great. Here's my business card. Please send me an email, and I'll forward you a form to fill out. And then I'll meet you on the driving range Wednesday morning, and we'll see what we're working with."

"Very good, sir. I appreciate it. See you then."

They shook hands, and the man turned and headed back down the hallway toward his office.

Brooke was back at her station, and Parker looked at her. "And here's my card," she said, handing it to Parker.

"Great. What days are you off?"

"Right now just Mondays."

"Then let's plan on getting together on Monday. I'll be in touch before then to confirm the details," he said with a smile as he turned and headed out of the pro shop. Dylan watched with amusement before falling in behind and following him out the door.

Twenty minutes later, Dylan pulled his Escalade up to the security gate at Treasure Sands as the guard slid his window open. "Good afternoon, I have Parker Gough with me," Dylan said, indicating the passenger seat. "I'm dropping him off at home."

The guard peered in and gave a short salute. "Good afternoon, Mr. Gough. Go right in," he said as the gate arm lifted. Dylan pulled up to the front of Parker's building and pressed a button, lifting the rear tailgate. Parker retrieved his clubs and walked over to the driver's side.

"Thanks for a great day of golf and for introducing me to Zach. I'll see you later."

"Sure thing, Parker." He refrained from making a comment about the young intern he'd just met and drove off for the short ride home.

Dylan crossed the Treasure Island Bridge and merged into the left lane as he approached the intersection of Park Street, a few minutes from his house. He was stopped at the red light in the left turn lane when he glanced into the rearview mirror and observed two pickup trucks, one white, one black, traveling side by side in the two through-travel lanes. They both appeared to be moving at high rates of speed. He looked to his right and noticed a car stopped in the curb lane, but no vehicle was occupying the lane directly adjacent to him.

Dylan continued to observe the two trucks in his rearview mirror as they bore down on the light. Neither was slowing, and he could not see the occupants as both had heavily tinted windows. The truck in the right lane pulled in front of the black one, cutting it off, and then locked up its brakes. The black truck had no place to go and moved over into Dylan's lane.

It was clear it wasn't going to stop, so he braced himself. The black truck slammed into the rear of the Escalade, throwing him violently back and then forward within the confines of his seat belt. His head smacked against the steering wheel, and he saw a flash of light. He blinked rapidly, then peered into his sideview mirror and watched the black truck pull around to his left, cross the low brick-paved median, and drive into an oncoming lane of traffic. He heard what sounded like muted explosions coming from his right. Turning, he saw the barrel of a gun pointed in his direction from the driver's side of the white truck just as the Escalade's front passenger-side window shattered and everything went dark.

# CHAPTER NINETEEN

Dylan opened his eyes and found himself lying on a gurney in the back of an ambulance with two young paramedics. He felt a stinging sensation on his right side, particularly in his face and arm. One of the medics stood watch as the other sat next to Dylan and plucked pieces of shattered glass from his arm using surgical gloves and tweezers.

"How are you feeling?" the man standing asked.

"My head hurts, and my right side is painful, particularly my face and arm. Was I shot?"

"No, but you're covered in glass fragments. We extracted most of it out of your face and applied an antiseptic and pain analgesic. He's almost done with your arm. We're taking you to the hospital for further evaluation."

"What happened exactly?"

"That's probably a better question for the police. They're waiting to speak with you, but I recommend you let me tell them to wait until we get to the hospital. From a clinical standpoint, it appears your vehicle was rear-ended at a moderate rate of speed, causing you to strike the back of your head on the headrest, and then you were thrown forward and struck your forehead on the steering wheel. At some point thereafter, you were shot at from the right side of your vehicle. Miraculously, no bullet struck you, but you were covered in shattered glass. Your symptoms and the physical injuries on your head, face, and right arm bear that out."

"Can you transport me to St. Anthony's?"

"If that's where you wish to go."

"Yes, please. Could you also retrieve my cell phone and wallet from my car?"

"That's already been done," he explained, holding up a clear plastic bag containing the items. "Because you were unconscious, the police went through your wallet to ascertain your identity, as the vehicle is registered to an LLC. They also provided us with your health insurance information. What's your current pain level on a scale of one to ten?"

"I'd say about a six," he replied as he watched the man apply a topical and bandage to his right arm.

"Current medical history?"

"None to speak of."

"Do you take any prescription medication?"

"No."

"Have you consumed any alcohol or recreational drugs today?"

"No, sir."

"Okay. We're about done here. I'll let law enforcement know you're being transported to St. Anthony's."

"Thank you."

He watched as the man with whom he was speaking exited the back of the truck and shut the double doors. The one who had been working on him strapped himself into a jump seat facing the gurney. He heard sirens and saw flashing red lights as the ambulance began moving.

The medic in the back was quiet for a time. "How are you doing?"

"I'm okay."

"That Escalade *was* a sweet ride," he commented. "I see a lot of different stuff out here, but this was one I'll remember for a while. The entire right side of your SUV is riddled with bullet holes. The ones that went through the passenger side window miraculously missed you."

Dylan turned his head toward the man slightly. "Do you know what's happening with my vehicle?"

"The police took possession of it. You'll have to speak with them."

Suddenly, the ambulance came to an abrupt stop. He was rolled out down a ramp and rushed into the emergency entrance. Medical personnel immediately surrounded him, and a nurse began checking his vital signs. He heard her say, "Pulse is 110 and blood pressure 122 over 77," followed by the sound of tearing Velcro.

A man in a lab coat spoke in soft, measured tones. "Please state your name and date of birth."

Dylan recited the information.

"I'm Dr. Damalos. We're going to do some blood work and send you for X-rays, and then you'll be admitted and assigned to a room. I will see you there, and we'll speak again after we get the test results. Is there anything else you need at the moment?"

"What time is it, Doctor?"

Consulting his watch, he said, "It's five twenty-five."

"Thank you. May I make a phone call?"

"Certainly. The EMS personnel provided us with your personal effects. I'll have your phone brought to radiology."

He was on the move again as an orderly expertly navigated his way through the hallway and to a bank of elevators. A few moments later, Dylan was handed his phone. "Do you think you can get up and sit for a series of X-rays?" the man inquired.

"Of course. Please give me a few moments, and I'll be right with you."

He thought about who to call before dialing Shirley's cell phone number. She picked up right away. "Dylan, where are you? I expected you back at the house after lunch. I've been calling and texting you all afternoon."

"Sorry about that. There's been an incident, and I just got my cell phone handed back to me this instant. You were the first person I called." He provided a summary of the events since he'd dropped off Parker.

"Oh, my God! How are you feeling?"

"Under the circumstances, better than terrible. I need to have some tests done, and I'll probably be here overnight. Could you bring me a few things?"

"Of course."

He provided her with a list. "By the time you get here, I should be assigned to a room."

"Do you want me to call anyone else?"

"No. I don't want to worry my family, and I can't think of anyone else who needs to know about this at the moment."

"Okay, I'll be there soon."

Dylan had his eyes closed when Shirley knocked on the doorjamb.

He opened them to find her standing over him with a duffel bag in hand. "How are you feeling?"

"Better since we last spoke. They gave me something for pain that seems to be working."

The doctor walked in. "Good evening, ma'am. Are you the significant other?"

"No," she replied.

"Yes, she is," Dylan interrupted. "Not in the conventional sense. She's my personal assistant. You can discuss my condition in front of her."

"Very well. I'm Theo Damalos," he replied, directing his introduction to Shirley before turning back to Dylan and consulting a chart in his right hand. "You are very fortunate, Mr. Tomassi, and I attribute your good fortune, in large part, to your excellent physical condition. You obviously take good care of yourself. You have no fractures or internal injuries. Based upon my examination and the results of your diagnostic studies, my impression is that you've suffered a concussion. Additionally, X-rays reveal residual foreign bodies remain present in your face and neck on the right side as well as your right arm, consistent with glass fragments. I recommend you undergo surgery through a process called dermatoscopy. It's a minimally invasive procedure that allows the surgeon to visualize the foreign microbodies with a tool similar to a high-powered magnifying glass and then extract the superficial material. This will minimize injury to the tissues and promote healing with little to no visible scarring. However, because the affected areas involve the face and neck, I recommend the operation be performed by a plastic surgeon. He'll be able to revise any potential scarring in the event incision is necessary to enlarge the affected areas."

"When can this be performed?"

"Dr. Manny Sapienza is on call tonight. He's a colleague and an excellent plastic surgeon. I do these procedures myself, but I highly recommend Dr. Sapienza given the trauma site." He then went over the risks and benefits of the surgery and explained the procedure in more detail, including the use of a local anesthetic. "Do you have any questions?" he concluded.

"I take it this is considered elective?"

"Elective in the sense that it is not a medical emergency as your condition is currently stable. However, there is a high risk of infection, chronic pain, and neurovascular impairment if the glass fragments are left in your body."

"How long will I need to be in the hospital?"

"You'll be kept overnight for observation and most likely be discharged tomorrow."

"Can you give me a moment, Doctor?"

"Certainly. I've got a few other patients to see, and then I'll check back with you."

After he left, Dylan asked Shirley to close the door. "How bad do I look?"

"I'll let you see for yourself," she replied, handing him a compact mirror from her purse.

He peered into the mirror and observed swelling and redness in his cheek, forehead, and neck. He was tempted to touch his face but thought better of it. Handing her back the mirror, he said, "Please go to the nurses' station and let them know I want to have the procedure done tonight."

A short time later, a nurse came in and introduced herself. "I'm Wanda," she said, writing her name on a blackboard that contained Dylan's name and medical information. "I'll be your nurse on the night shift, which runs until six in the morning. Dr. Sapienza has been called and is on his way. We should have you in surgery within forty-five minutes. I'll need you to sign some forms, and I have some medicine for you to take."

Dylan accepted a clipboard and signed the forms, beginning with the one on top entitled Informed Consent. He handed the nurse back the clipboard, and she handed him a small paper cup filled with a liquid substance. "What is this?" he asked.

"It's Percocet, a muscle relaxant and pain reliever. You'll also be given local pain blocks, but you'll be awake during the procedure. Trust me, honey, you won't feel a thing."

He accepted the medication and drank it down. Before long, he began to feel relaxed as he vaguely noticed being wheeled out of his room to the elevators and down to a sectioned-off area with high-tech machines and a rolling cart. Dr. Sapienza introduced himself and administered several injections of lidocaine into his face, neck, and arm, and before long, the surgeon was hovering over him wearing large eyeglasses, holding a giant illuminated magnifying glass in one hand and a tweezer-like instrument in the other. Occasionally, he could hear the clinking sound of a tiny hard object being dropped into a metal dish. He felt completely relaxed, devoid of any feeling in his body, almost like he was observing from above. After a while, he had a hard time keeping his eyes open until everything went dark.

# CHAPTER TWENTY

Dylan was discharged from the hospital shortly before noon the next day, and Shirley was there to pick him up and deliver him home. She went upstairs with him and got him settled in the kitchen.

"I made you some chicken and rice soup. It's in the fridge. You can heat it up in the microwave. Aengus is aware of the situation, and he's in his apartment. He'll be available all weekend to get you whatever you need until I'm back on Monday. And if you need anything else from me before then, promise me you'll call."

"Thanks for everything, Shirley, but amazingly, I don't feel that bad. I'm just a little tired. I don't think I slept in that hospital bed for more than an hour at a time."

"After I leave, you should take a shower and go sleep in your own bed. You'll probably feel better after that." She hesitated for a moment. "What did the doctor say about showering? Your face and arm are all bandaged up."

"He said it's okay to remove the bandages and shower and wash the affected areas with a hypoallergenic product. They gave me a sample bottle of an antiseptic skin cleanser."

"Okay. If you're all set, I'll leave you to rest, but please promise you'll call if you need something."

"Scout's honor," he replied, holding up his right hand.

She looked at him with a frown. "Does it hurt to raise your arm like that?"

"Not really."

"All right. I'll see you later."

Dylan went upstairs and carefully removed his bandages before taking a long, hot shower. He lay down on his bed and closed his eyes but felt fidgety, concluding he was too wired to sleep. He called Alex, who answered on the first ring. "Dylan, what's going on?"

"Are you sitting down?"

"Should I be?"

"It's probably a good idea." He explained the events of Friday afternoon and his hospital experience.

After he finished, Alex was uncharacteristically quiet for a moment before he spoke. "That's crazy. How are you feeling now?"

"Not too bad, all things considered."

"Unfortunately, I may have been right."

"Right about what?"

"That weird anonymous note you received in the mail. 'Watch Your Ass.'"

Dylan started to touch his face and continued the movement of his hand upward, making a last second adjustment, and ran it through his hair. "I didn't even think about that."

"Well, maybe it's time to start. You have any idea who those guys were?"

"None. All I saw before the collision were two pickup trucks bearing down on me, and I couldn't see in the windows because the glass was tinted. Then I lost consciousness, and when I came to, I was in the back of the ambulance."

"Can you think of anyone who you've pissed off lately?"

"Not really," he replied, glancing upward. "About the only unusual thing that's happened, besides receiving that letter, which may or may not mean what you say it does, is that guy from the Department of the Interior who presented me with the climate mitigation proposal and who I told to get lost. He said I would be hearing from the government again, but it's ludicrous to think our government agencies are resorting to violence over rejections of their proposals, with which compliance is completely optional."

"And yet that same department is the one that's shut down your construction project."

"That I'll accept could possibly be related, even though I have zero proof."

Suddenly, Dylan's phone buzzed, and he saw a call coming in from

Leroy Thompson. "Alex I've got to run. There's a call coming in from Chief Thompson of the St. Pete PD." He pressed a button on his cell phone that disconnected Alex and connected the chief. "Hello."

"Dylan. Leroy Thompson. Word reached me this morning about your incident yesterday. I wanted to call personally and see how you're doing."

The chief and Dylan had originally met following Alex's dealings with the department and had since seen each other occasionally at social functions. Most recently, the chief and his wife were guests at the grand opening of the foundation's youth center. "All things considered, I'm doing okay."

"That's certainly good news. I wanted to give you a heads-up. My investigator will be contacting you to take a statement. We can do that at a time and place that's convenient for you."

"I can come down to the station. Will Monday morning work?"

"That's fine. The investigator's name is Dunn. Andrew Dunn. I'll let him know. Say ten o'clock Monday morning?"

"Sure."

"Another thing. We're done processing your vehicle, and it's in pretty bad shape. Severe rearend damage and the entire right side is riddled with bullet holes. We pulled two different caliber slugs from the body, which indicates there were at least two shooters. Fortunately, they weren't very good shots if they were aiming at you."

"Who else could they have been shooting at?"

"At this point, we can't rule out any possibilities, and there was the other vehicle that rear-ended you and took off. We found shells and bullets that were fired directionally in front of your vehicle as well."

"I see."

"Anyway, I'm pleased to hear you're going to be okay. If you need anything, you have my cell number."

"Thanks, Chief. I appreciate that."

"Sure thing. Take care of yourself."

He hung up and sat there silently in thought, fingers interlaced behind his head. After a while, he got up and stared at his face in the mirror. He decided he looked like he'd undergone one of those facial treatments in which they peel back layers of skin, except just the right side of his face was red and swollen. He finally decided he was presentable enough to go forward with his dinner meeting with Madison James.

That evening, he changed clothes and grabbed the keys to the Porsche for the drive to Largo to pick her up. He had been to her home on one other occasion and understood it was the family home before her divorce, which she now shared with her two teenage sons. He knocked on the door, and she answered with a smile, before giving him a double take.

She was wearing form-fitting black pants, black heels, and a beige knit top, and her shoulder-length black hair was perfectly cut. "Hello, Dylan," she said with a look of concern. "Is everything okay?"

"I suppose I should get that out of the way first," he replied with a smile. "I was involved in a car accident yesterday."

"Oh, my gosh. What happened?"

"I got hit and ended up covered in glass. I should be fine once my skin clears up."

She redirected her gaze to the driveway. "You obviously weren't driving the Porsche."

"No. I was in the Escalade. It was towed away, and it's probably a total loss."

They stood at the front door for an awkward moment of silence. He was hoping there'd be no more questions about the incident, as he was intent on keeping the dinner a friendly business affair while ameliorating her concerns about the construction project. A discussion of whether he might be the subject of threats or physical harm was not going to help.

"Well, I'm ready. I just need to grab my purse," she finally said.

"How are your boys doing?" he inquired once they were cruising along in the 911 on the way to Indian Rocks Beach.

"They are well, back to school after the holiday break. They're with their father this weekend." She was staring at his face. "Are you in any pain?"

"Not really."

"Are you sure you're up to going out tonight? Should you be at home resting?"

"The doctor didn't place me on any restrictions, and I wanted to see you and bring you up to date on the Largo Palms project."

"That's very considerate of you, Dylan, but I already knew you were a man of character and integrity," she said with a smile, brushing his arm lightly.

He smiled back. "You are too kind."

"I mean that sincerely. The people I deal with in politics and business, particularly the construction industry, often lack those qualities."

When they arrived at Villa Gallace, Dylan handed off the car to the valet, and they walked inside, where they were greeted by the owner, Luigi. "Dylan, Your Honor, good evening. It's a pleasure to see you both. I have a table for you in the corner where you'll have some privacy. Please follow me."

They were seated at the back of the restaurant along the double-paned glass windows that separated the outdoor dining section. Dylan sat in the gunner's seat with a complete view of the dining room.

The waiter approached and greeted them while a younger man served waters and a basket of bread. "What would you like to drink this evening?" the waiter inquired after he had handed out menus.

Dylan looked over at Madison. "Are you okay with wine?" she asked.

"Whatever you like."

"How about white wine? Will you pick something nice, Dylan."

"Please bring us a wine list."

"Do you know what you're having for dinner?" he asked once the waiter departed. "It'll help me select the wine."

"I think I'll have the chicken marsala."

The waiter appeared with the wine list, and he perused it quickly. "We'll have a bottle of the Cakebread sauvignon blanc."

"Very good, sir," the waiter replied before departing again.

Once dinner was ordered and the wine and salads served, Dylan brought up the construction project. "My lawyers have advised me that the drive-in movie theater was built on the property in 1958. A title search revealed prior to that it was a family-owned citrus grove that had been in the family for three generations. That takes us back to the early to mid-nineteenth century. Before that, property records are somewhat incomplete, but it appears the land was owned by the county."

"I know how you do business, Dylan, and I have confidence that you've done all your due diligence. If the property turns out to contain old gravesites, the problem is not about assigning blame. It becomes a very thorny sociopolitical controversy. Most of the gravesites discovered beneath developed property in the Tampa Bay area belonged to poor and marginalized groups, and the matters have garnered a great deal of publicity. The FrankCrum company is dealing with the issue presently with their Clearwater corporate headquarters property, and it's become a national news story. There was even a *60 Minutes* feature. We certainly don't want that kind of publicity in Largo, especially with what will likely be characterized as a joint public-private project."

"I understand your concerns, and we're dealing with this on a very proactive basis. The archeology team will begin their study next week, and my lawyers are working closely with the appropriate federal government officials. I would be happy to have my legal team draft a statement if you think we should get out in front of this."

She took a sip of wine and daintily dabbed her lips with the black linen napkin in her lap. "I think it's a good idea. Please send it to me, and I'll run it by our people and get a consensus on the matter."

They enjoyed their dinner, and the conversation eventually turned away from the business at hand to a light and friendly discourse. It appeared to Dylan that his accident had somewhat dampened her enthusiasm for a discussion of a more personally intimate nature, and for that he was thankful. The evening ended when he walked Madison to her door and received a gentle hug.

"Thank you for a nice dinner and a pleasant evening. Please take care of yourself, and I want you to know I trust you will successfully navigate us through this business with our project. Good night, Dylan," she said as she unlocked her front door and went inside, closing it gently behind her.

# CHAPTER TWENTY-ONE

TEN DAYS LATER, DYLAN RECEIVED a phone call from an adjuster for his insurance company informing him that the collision damage claim was resolved and that a settlement check was being issued. He was further advised that he had three days to return the Chevy Tahoe rental car he had been driving. After lunch, he drove the Tahoe to the Cadillac dealership and walked into the showroom. He was looking at a new Escalade when a salesman approached him.

"Good afternoon, sir. How may I be of service today?"

"I'm interested in an Escalade, but I see they have gone up in price significantly since I bought my last one," he replied, referring to the six-figure price tag on the window sticker. "This one here seems to be what I'm looking for."

"It's certainly a beauty. It's a 2025 Sport model, fully loaded with every available option, including twenty-two-inch wheels and the blackout package. The badging, door handles, and moldings are all blacked out. The windows are tinted to the darkest level permissible under Florida law." He opened the driver's side door. "The interior is black napa leather with executive second row seating and third row bench seating. Are you a previous customer here?"

"I'm a current customer. I bought my other Escalade here, and all the service work's been done here since."

"We certainly want to keep you as a customer."

Dylan sat down with the man in his office, and thirty minutes later, after some back and forth followed by the signing of a large stack of papers, he was the owner of the new Escalade.

"We'll have it detailed, registered, and ready to go in about an hour if you want to take it home today."

"That'll be fine. I have a rental car here I need to return," he replied as a thought came to mind. "Is Cadillac making an electric Escalade yet?"

"Oh, yes. The new Escalade IQ is all-electric and now available. We also have EV models in sedan and smaller SUV formats."

"How much is the electric Escalade?"

"They run about a third higher than a comparably equipped gasoline model."

"How has the demand been so far?"

"We have none in inventory, and a few people have ordered them. Mostly repeat customers that like to have the newest shiny toy."

Dylan grimaced. "What percentage of the Cadillac lineup is now electric?"

The salesman leaned forward and lowered his voice. "You made a good purchase decision today. EVs are the way of the future by mandate. Currently, they're a small percentage of our lineup, but the federal government is requiring that vehicles equipped with an internal combustion engine be limited to sixty-four percent of total production by 2027 and the cap goes down to twenty-nine percent by 2032."

"How is that even possible without a full-scale national charging network?"

"Your guess is as good as mine. I understand GM, our parent company, is losing considerable sums on every EV they sell, including the Cadillac line. It doesn't seem sustainable. The car companies are continuously reaching out to Washington about the feasibility of their mandates, but they're not making much headway, to date, as I understand it."

Dylan shook his head. "Let me tell you something else," the salesman continued, his voice down to barely a whisper. "We installed a bank of courtesy charging stations for our customers in the back. People wait in line all day long just to charge their vehicles. And the kicker is, the charging stations are powered by a huge diesel generator."

Two hours later, Dylan was driving his new vehicle home when his phone rang and Esther's name appeared on the large display screen. "Hello."

"Dylan, it's Esther. I was calling to see how you're doing."

"I'm very well. In fact, I just picked up my new car from the dealership, and I'm on my way home."

"That's nice to hear, but property is always replaceable. I've been concerned about you since you called last week and told me what's been going on. How are you doing really?"

"I'm feeling much better, and my injuries are just about healed. The doctor advised me to avoid perspiring for a week so I haven't been working out, but I may get back to it tomorrow as it's been ten days now."

"That's certainly good news. Have you told your mother about this? Last time we spoke you hadn't said anything."

"I told her I was in a car accident and left out the details about getting shot at. I don't want to worry her or my grandparents."

"I see. Have you heard anything more about the incident?"

"Since I spoke with you, I gave a statement to the detective, and he told me the department would be in touch if there was an arrest. I haven't heard anything yet."

"What about the matter with the construction project?"

"The archeology team completed their investigation and found nothing. They're preparing a report for my attorneys who will be presenting it to the feds with a demand for disclosure of specific evidence of a burial ground or, alternatively, a proposed resolution so we can move forward with the project."

"It sounds like everything is working itself out. Please do me a favor and be careful. I worry about you."

"I will do that. You take care of yourself."

Fanci was lying on her back on Kari Baldwin's bed, naked, except for a pair of knee socks and patent leather Mary Janes. A schoolgirl outfit lay on the floor next to her. Baldwin was pleasuring her with an adult toy, reciprocating for the hours of lecherous pleasure Fanci had performed on her at Baldwin's specific direction.

"See what happens when you're a good girl," Baldwin said.

"Yes, ma'am."

"Are you my bitch?"

"Yes," she moaned.

Baldwin stopped and lay beside her, kissing her passionately. "Tell me about the things the man who flew you to Florida did to you."

Fanci recounted the salacious details while Baldwin pleasured herself. "I may have been wrong about you. You're not a good girl. You're a very dirty bad girl. I'm going to give you a spanking."

When they were through, Baldwin sat up and looked at her. Fanci instinctively diverted her gaze downward to avoid eye contact. "The information you gave me about Mr. Tomassi was helpful, but there's a few more things I need. Have you spoken with your friend in Florida since the visit?"

"Just once. He let me know he's coming back to Connecticut and wants to get together."

"Good. Here's what I need." After giving her specific instructions, she continued. "One more thing. When you do get together, I'll want to hear all the details of what the two of you do to each other. Do you understand?"

"Yes, ma'am."

# CHAPTER TWENTY-TWO

Tuesday was a typical mid-February Florida day. Comfortable temperature, no humidity, and a brilliant blue sky. Dylan decided it was time to get back to his morning workout routine, and he opted for a bike ride. He went down to the garage, retrieved his bike, and began pedaling in the direction of the Pinellas Trail. He proceeded north and was riding along an isolated section adjacent to Azalea Park. Bike and pedestrian traffic were light, and he felt good, clearing his mind and moving along at a sprightly pace.

He became aware of two men, walking in the opposite direction on the right side of the trail, carrying walking sticks. He gave them a wide berth, moving all the way over to the left. He took them in as he approached. Both were large and wore work boots, jean shorts, and sleeveless shirts. As he attempted to pass, the man closest to him moved suddenly in his direction and jammed his stick into Dylan's front wheel. His bike came to a sudden halt, and he was ejected forward, initially landing on his feet before going into a roll and coming to rest on the grassy area adjacent to the trail.

As he struggled to get off the ground, one of the men swung his stick, and Dylan ducked back down just in time to avoid a blow to the side of the head. The other man tackled him, mounted his stomach, and began delivering punches to his head and face. Using his arms to cover up and mitigate the blows, he contemplated his next move. As he peered out from between his forearms, he observed the man had long hair and a beard and smelled of body odor.

Dylan shifted his gaze sideways and saw the second guy approach, winding up to kick him in the head. Dylan timed his movement perfectly, his right hand catching the man's leg just above the ankle, and he pulled hard causing, causing the man to fall to the ground.

As the man on top of him turned toward his companion, Dylan used all his strength to leverage the momentum and push him off. He rolled to his left, scampered to his feet, and looked for an escape route. The two men also got up and were standing between him and his bike, fists raised. Dylan moved toward the closer one, hands up, and swung a roundhouse kick, striking the closer man on the side of the left knee.

"Son of a bitch," the man screeched as his leg buckled.

The other guy threw a punch, landing on the side of Dylan's head. They squared off, both men continuing to land blows until Dylan felt a kick to the groin, doubling him over. He was tackled to the ground and kicked and punched. He covered up the best he could, but he absorbed several upper body blows. The man grabbed him by the hair and began smashing his head against the ground. He fought to remain conscious, peered through blurry vision obscured by blood and perspiration, and saw the image of a cyclist a short distance away, straddling his bike with what looked like a cell phone to his ear.

One of the two assailants looked in the same direction and started to back off. "We need to get outta here," he instructed his partner.

The guy on top of Dylan continued to unleash a barrage of punches to his face before grabbing him by his torn T-shirt. "You messed with the wrong people. We'll be back to finish this, and next time you won't see us coming," he uttered through gritted teeth before shoving him back to the ground.

Dylan managed to painfully lift his head and watched as the two men ran off into a wooded area, one falling behind and limping noticeably as the cyclist approached him. "Are you okay?" he asked.

"I'm not sure," Dylan replied, struggling to get to his feet and wiping blood from his face with the bottom of his shirt.

"I called the police. They should be on their way. Do you know who those guys were?"

"I have no idea. Have you ever seen them before?"

"No, and I'm out here riding most days."

Dylan looked around and located his bike. He picked it up and could see the front rim was bent. He lifted the front end of the bike and attempted to spin the wheel. It barely rotated, rubbing up against the front forks and disc brake housing. A pair of spokes dangled from the wheel. He snapped them off, then repositioned himself with the front tire between his legs, facing the handlebars as he attempted to straighten the rim. He spun it again, and it continued to make a rubbing sound. The wheel was badly damaged, but he decided the rotation was sufficient to make it back home. "Thanks for your help," he said to the cyclist as he turned the bike around and gingerly mounted the seat.

"Are you well enough to ride? It looked like those two guys inflicted a good deal of punishment on you."

"I'll manage. Thanks again."

"What about the police?" he asked.

Dylan ignored the question as he unsteadily pedaled away, writhing in pain and struggling to breathe.

He managed to make it back to the house, dumped his bike, and staggered into the garage, where he collapsed in the elevator and reached up to press the button. The car ascended slowly upward until doors opened to the second level. He looked up to see Shirley standing there, staring down at him aghast "What happened to you?"

"I ran into a couple guys on the trail who apparently harbor considerable disdain for my existence."

"What on earth are you talking about?"

"Two guys jumped me, beat the crap out of me, and as they were leaving, said something like I'm messing with the wrong people, and they'll be back to finish me off."

She helped him to his feet and sat him in a kitchen chair before handing him a bottle of water. She disappeared for a moment and returned with an ice pack and first aid kit. "Put this on your eye. It's just about swollen shut." She twisted some cotton balls and placed them in his nose to stop any residual bleeding before going to work cleaning the cuts and abrasions on his arms and legs. "I'm going to call your doctor. You need to go get checked out."

He nodded but was otherwise silent, as he began to process the latest in a series of aberrant events.

Shirley returned a short time later. "Your doctor said to come over at four o'clock, and he'll fit you in. I'm driving you, and I don't want to hear another word." She stared at him. "Well?"

"Well, what? You told me you didn't want to hear another word."

She shook her head and smiled. "Here, take two of these. They'll help with the pain," she said, handing him two ibuprofen tablets. "You should lie down until it's time to leave for the doctor's office."

He lay down on a living room couch with the ice pack on his head and closed his eyes but couldn't relax, his adrenaline still pumping. He got up slowly and made his way to his office where a stack of mail was sitting. He had begun to sort through it when he came upon an envelope from the Internal Revenue Service. He opened it and read the letter. It stated that his personal and corporate returns for the past three tax years were subject to a full in-person audit.

# CHAPTER TWENTY-THREE

Dylan slept late the next morning, and when he opened his eyes, he felt pain throbbing through every fiber of his body. His head felt heavy and was pounding worse than he'd ever imagined. The slightest movement elicited a piercing electrical shock wave of pain. He managed to stagger to the bathroom, leaned on the countertop, and peered at his image in the mirror. His left eye was swollen shut and his jawline as puffy and tender to the touch as if he'd spent the day in the chair of an endodontist. It hurt to breathe, and the complexion of his arms and hands reminded him of spoiled raw meat.

He started the water in the oversized garden tub. When it was full, he checked the temperature, turned on the jets, and gingerly lowered himself into the bath. He rested his head against the back of the tub, closed his eyes, and let his body soak. Ten minutes later, he got out feeling only minimal relief. He carefully put on a pair of shorts and T-shirt, minimizing his movements. He made his way back to his bed and called down to Shirley's office.

"He's alive," she exclaimed. "How are you feeling?"

"Worse than yesterday."

"The doctor told you that was to be expected. The diagnostic studies revealed swelling on the brain and multiple rib fractures. You need to take the doctor's advice and rest. He's very concerned you've suffered multiple head injuries in a short period of time. Stay in bed, and I'll bring up something for you to eat."

"Thanks," Dylan replied. "Could you also bring my iPad? It should be in my office."

"Of course."

He crawled back into bed and closed his one good eye.

Shirley arrived with the provisions, handing him two ibuprofen pills and a bottle of water, placing the tray containing a soup bowl and the iPad on the nightstand. She observed him for a moment. "Can you see out of your left eye? It's completely shut. You look like a boxer on the losing end of a fight."

"No, I can't, but I'll manage with my one working eye for the time being."

"It's a shame," she commented, shaking her head. "Because your face was healing up nicely from the car incident."

He managed a slight smile. "You know, I was thinking that very thing when I went out for the bike ride yesterday."

Sitting on the edge of the bed, she looked him in the eye with a somber expression. "You need to listen to me. I can take care of everything with the businesses while you recover. I went through yesterday's mail and saw you opened the letter from the IRS. I spoke with Walt Jackman this morning. He and your accountant both received copies. He wants to speak with you."

"Please get him on the phone."

A few minutes later, Shirley put the call through to his cell. Dylan brought his attorney up to date on the recent attacks.

"First things first, we will handle everything with the IRS. We have in-house private investigators who can discretely look into those other matters for you. We also have a relationship with a personal security firm that provides protection for our high-level executive clients and offer those services."

He thought about that. "I gave a statement to the St. Pete police detective that's been assigned to my car case. I think I'd like you to have an investigator dig around, but discretion is key. I want as few people as possible to know about yesterday. I barely told my mother about the car accident."

"That's what you told her? You were in a car *accident*?"

"Yes. I was driving and another car collided with mine. That's the textbook definition of a car accident."

"What about your bullet-riddled car? Is that part of the textbook definition?"

"You have a point there."

"Let me know if you decide to avail yourself to the security services."

"Will do."

After he hung up, Shirley reappeared. "Do you need anything else?"

"No. I think I'm good," he replied, sitting up and leaning his back against a couple of propped-up pillows.

"All right, just call downstairs if you need anything."

"I will. And, Shirley, thanks for everything."

She smiled and left the room quietly. He looked at the soup bowl and leaned over, but it hurt too much to extend all the way to lift up the tray. He moved back to the bed and adjusted to a position that mitigated the pain. He closed his eyes for a few minutes until he heard his cell phone buzzing. He squinted at the screen with his good eye. Esther.

"Good morning," he said with as much energy as he could muster.

"Good morning to you, Dylan. I was calling to see how you were healing up."

"Actually, my face was starting to look normal again yesterday until I suffered a setback." He provided her with a detailed account of the bike trail attack.

Her voice took on a serious air of concern. "Let me see if I have this right. In the course of a little over a two-week period, you receive an anonymous letter in the mail, your car is slammed into, and you're shot at in a drive-by attack, then two men jump you and beat you to an inch of your life and warn you that whoever you got on the wrong side of isn't through with you yet."

"That's pretty much it. Except the federal government shut down one of my construction projects, and I just received notice that the IRS is conducting a complete audit of my personal and business tax returns for the past three years. Of all this unpleasantness, that concerns me the most. I do everything by the book, but the IRS still scares the heck out of me. I feel like the complexity of the tax code and all its ambiguities leaves the government with much leeway to make a case against anyone they target."

There was silence on the other end of the line before she spoke again. This time her tone was lower but just as serious. "Dylan, we've known each other a long time, and we've been through a great deal together, good times and tough ones as well. We'll get through this, but I need you to listen to me carefully. You will receive a package from me tomorrow. When it arrives, call me before you open it. Do you understand?"

"Yes, but—"

"No buts, Dylan. Just do it, okay?"

"Okay. I'll call you as soon as I receive it."

"Good. I'll speak with you tomorrow," she said, and the phone went dead.

Marion Bishop was about to start a meeting in a small conference room. In attendance were the half-dozen interns for the spring semester and a handful of regular staffers. The unintelligible sound of mixed chatter filled the room. Fanci was sitting quietly in the front row when another intern from the University of Pennsylvania sat down next to her and smiled and nodded in her direction. "Hello. What was your name again?"

"Francis Nagle."

"That's right, Francis. You're from Turing, right?"

"Yes."

The woman leaned in and lowered her voice. "It's so nice to have a fellow Ivy Leaguer here. How come I don't see you around much?"

"I've been working on a special project upstairs."

"On the executive floor? I'm so jealous," she said, clutching her chest. "Have you met Kari Baldwin yet?"

"Oh, yes."

"Wow. She's such a powerful woman and an idol of mine. I would love to meet her. How did you get that assignment?"

"I got a call one day and assigned some work. I suppose they were pleased with the results."

"What's Ms. Baldwin like?"

"She's very approachable, but with a definite air of authority about her."

"I've never seen her down here on our floor. She's like a reclusive rock star. We've been told we're all going to have an opportunity to meet her and do a Q&A before the semester is over. I'm really looking forward to it."

Marion Bishop moved to the head of the room, and the chatter began to recede. "Good afternoon, everyone. There are a few items on the agenda. First, interns. Your midsemester reviews are scheduled for the last week in February. You will all be getting emails with the dates and times. Next,

Francis Nagle has been permanently reassigned to work on the executive floor, so we all will miss her down here."

The woman next to Fanci nudged her. "You lucky girl."

Fanci managed a smile and said nothing.

When the meeting concluded she quickly left the room and headed upstairs to Kari Baldwin's office. "Come in, dear, and close the door. How did your meeting go?"

"Fine. My transfer was announced. I need to move out of my cubicle downstairs. Where will I be sitting up here?"

"You won't need a desk. Your new assignment will require a good deal of travel, and when we're in town, you can work remotely, either from your place or mine," she explained with a wicked smile.

"Travel? Where will I be going?"

"We leave Monday for Washington for two days of meetings, and then we'll be flying to Tampa for the national teachers' unions convention. I am the keynote speaker."

"I see. Should I do anything to prepare?"

"No," she managed through a hearty laugh. "Your role is to be my traveling companion. If you're needed for anything else, I'll let you know. We'll enjoy each other's company during downtime, and you'll get to sit in on some of the meetings and events. It'll be a good learning experience." She hesitated for a moment. "There is one thing. We need to update your wardrobe. You and I will go shopping tomorrow afternoon."

"I really can't afford new clothes," she replied with a grimace.

"Not to worry. Everything is covered under the clothing allowance."

"Clothing allowance?"

"It's one of the perks of working with me. Welcome aboard."

# CHAPTER TWENTY-FOUR

THE NEXT MORNING SHIRLEY BROUGHT a package up to Dylan's bedroom. He was sitting up in bed, propped against a stack of pillows and squinting at his iPad through a still-swollen left eye. "Here's the delivery from Esther you wanted right away. How are you feeling?" she asked, handing him an oversized padded envelope.

"A little better, I guess," he replied with a grimace.

"I'm glad you're listening to the doctor and getting some rest."

"I don't have much choice. It hurts to breathe, much less move around."

Shirley nodded. "Is there anything else I can do for you?"

"No, I'm okay at the moment."

"All right, call down if you need anything," she said as she turned and left the room, closing the door gently.

He rested the weighty envelope on his lap and dialed Esther's number. She uncharacteristically picked up. "Good morning, Dylan. I take it you received my package."

"Good morning. Yes, I did."

"Go ahead and open it."

He opened the envelope and removed a laptop computer, two cell phones, and Visa and American Express charge cards. He looked at the names on the cards. They were issued to ICOE, LLC. "What is ICOE?" he asked.

"It's an active LLC that I control."

"Why did you send this stuff?"

"Dylan, you know how I feel about you. I consider you family, and these recent events have left me unsettled. You're always helping others, without any concern for the costs or consequences to yourself. This time

I'm genuinely concerned for your safety and well-being, and you need to hear this and heed my advice. Until we get a better handle on what's going on, I think you should disappear for a while."

"Disappear? Where will I go? I have a life and businesses to run here."

"You can do those things remotely and use the items I sent to communicate with your family, offices, and attorneys, and anyone else for that matter, with complete anonymity. Nothing will be traceable to you, and no one will be able to figure out where you are."

"Why do you think whoever is behind this, if there even is such a person or persons, is that sophisticated and will try to find me if I leave town?"

"I don't know that. I'm assuming the worst. Staying put in Florida and going about your daily routine leaves you a sitting duck, as the expression goes. That's why you need to leave until we get this figured out."

Dylan looked upward in thought, processing what he had just heard while Esther remained silent. "Assuming the worst, and whoever is behind this has the inclination and the resources, wouldn't they be able to track me down from airline passenger lists or the use of my ID to rent lodging and transportation?"

"That's why I sent you those credit cards issued to the LLC. You'll also need a traveling companion. She can book charter flights, lodging, and transportation. Your name will never show up anywhere, except on the charter passenger list, which will not be accessible as public information."

"You said *she*. Sounds like you have someone specifically in mind."

"Of course. I've already spoken with your friend Penel. As you know we had a very nice talk at the dinner party, and we've kept in touch. She mentioned her plans to come down to Florida for a visit. I've already run this by her, and she's completely on board. Her name is included on the LLC charge cards as an authorized user if someone were to check. She'll book everything that requires an ID."

Dylan's stared straight ahead, his mouth agape. "Wow," was all he could muster.

"Expect a call from her and the two of you can figure out where you want to go."

"Okay, Esther. I'll think about it. Just one more thing," he said while staring at the credit cards. "What does ICOE stand for?"

"In Case of Emergency."

That evening Alex and Fanci returned to Alex's Connecticut home after a dinner date. They entered the house hand in hand and headed straight for the master bedroom. "How did you enjoy dinner?" Alex whispered in her ear from behind, his arms wrapped around her waist.

"Dinner was great, but I'm really looking for my next lesson on how to behave like a bad girl."

"You're in luck," he replied, turning her around and placing his face directly against hers, foreheads touching. "Your teacher is here, and class is now in session."

Alex began kissing her passionately, turning up the heat before he began instructing her on the fine art of exotic seduction. An hour later, they lay naked in bed next to each other, fully spent and basking in the afterglow. Fanci moved closer and placed her head on his chest. "How long will you be in Connecticut?"

"Why? Are you ready to schedule your next lesson already?"

"No," she giggled. "It's going to take me a while to process everything you taught me tonight. I was just wondering. I'll be out of town next week with work."

"Where are you going?"

"Monday and Tuesday, I'll be in Washington, DC, and then down to Tampa for a convention."

Alex looked over at her. "Wow, Liz. That's great. I'm planning on being down there next week. I have some business in the Tampa office, and I need to check on my friend Dylan."

"Dylan? That's your friend with the charitable foundation, right? What's going on with him?" she asked innocently.

He shifted himself on the bed slightly, propping against the headboard and placing his arm around her. She moved in a similar fashion, so they were situated side by side. "You wouldn't believe it. The guy gets involved in a collision with a truck and gets shot at, then he gets a threatening letter in the mail, and a week later, he's attacked and nearly beaten to within an inch of his life."

"My gosh, that's horrible," she replied. "What do you think that's all about?"

"I have no idea. I talked with him this morning, and he's been laid up in bed since the attack. I really need to be there for him."

They both became silent in their own thoughts until Alex looked over at her. "But enough about that. There's one last part of tonight's lesson."

"Oh, what's that?"

"Always offer a final parting gift," he commanded, placing her head between his legs. She complied while he closed his eyes and enjoyed the fruits of his pedagogy.

# CHAPTER TWENTY-FIVE

Dylan spent Saturday lounging in bed and thinking about what Esther had said about disappearing for a while. Shirley had already volunteered to run the business for him, and Claire had the foundation operating smoothly. All the current construction projects were moving along nicely, except for Largo Palms, which was now in the capable hands of his attorneys, along with his audit case with the IRS. He continued to think things through and decided he could, in fact, keep in touch with his team remotely and manage his investments from anywhere with the tools Esther had provided. He would need to tell his mother and grandparents something without causing them any concern. That was the only loose end he could think of.

His phone rang, and Penel's name appeared on the screen. "Hello," he answered.

"Hello yourself. How are you feeling?"

"Still in pain, but there is some improvement."

"What you need is a good therapist, and I'm a willing and able volunteer. I understand we'll be traveling together."

"I was recently informed about plans of that nature."

"Your friend Esther is quite a remarkable person."

"She says the same thing about you. I understand you two chat regularly."

"We had a good conversation at her party, and we've kept in touch since. I've been able to clear my schedule sufficiently so that I can appear remotely with clients and court hearings for the foreseeable future. The only question now is where will we go?"

"Do you have any preference?"

"It's been bitterly cold up here. I was looking forward to spending time with you in sunny Florida so some place warm would be nice."

"I don't want to leave the country. How about southern California? We may run into some rain, but otherwise the weather should be to your liking."

"Isn't there a wine region in the southern part of the state?"

"Yes, there is. I'm very familiar with the area. The wine and scenery are excellent. In fact, I enjoy it as much as Napa Valley. It's less well known, but also less crowded, not as pricey, and the weather is better this time of year."

"We can start there. I'll fly down to Florida, and then we can charter a plane out west. How soon can you be ready to go?"

"I've been in bed for the past three days, and it's time for me to get moving. I'll be ready whenever you can get here."

"I'll book a flight for the day after tomorrow. We can hunker down at your house and make plans once I get there."

"That sounds good."

Once the call ended, he sat back, hands behind his head, and stretched his legs. *Leaving some distance between me and Florida may just be the best thing under the circumstances,* he surmised. He thought for a moment about the discussion he would have with his mother and then dialed her number.

"Hello, Dylan. I was just thinking about you. How are you doing?" she inquired.

"I've all but recovered from the auto accident. I'd like to see you if you're available."

"Sure, I'm home now if you want to stop by."

An hour later he was seated on the back porch of his mother's condo, looking out over the waterfront as they sipped coffee.

She kept staring at his face. "Are you sure you're okay? You still look beat up to me."

"I'll be fine. I had a plastic surgeon extract the glass from my face and neck. He said it will all heal in time, and I'll be good as new."

She touched his arm affectionately. "I think you should slow down and take it easy for a while."

"Funny you should mention that. I have a trip scheduled, and I'll be out of town for a while."

"Business or pleasure?"

"I would call it a working vacation. I'm checking on some investments and then spending some down time. Penel's going with me."

"Oh, honey, that's wonderful. You worked so hard to get the youth center started, and now that everything's up and running you certainly deserve a break. How long will you be gone?"

"I'm not sure yet. We'll play it by ear."

They continued their conversation, catching up on things. "Please call your grandparents before you leave. They've been concerned about you since the auto accident."

"I certainly will."

"Love you. Safe travels and keep in touch while you're out there."

"Will do. I love you too."

# CHAPTER TWENTY-SIX

BARRY FILMORE WALKED INTO LYMAN Scott's office at the Department of the Interior building in the Foggy Bottom neighborhood. The two men shook hands. "How was your trip?" Lyman asked.

"Fine. I flew down from Westchester and checked into the AKA hotel. It was a short walk over here. What's up? Why did you want me to come down to DC?"

"Have a seat," Lyman said, directing him to one of the two leather wing chairs in front of his antique mahogany desk before making his way back to his own seat. He leaned forward and folded his hands on the tabletop. "An excellent business opportunity has presented itself. Kari Baldwin is in town for a couple days, and I've been working on a deal with her. Our meeting in Connecticut helped seal it."

"What kind of a deal?" he interrupted, a confused look on his face. "She runs a teachers' union, for Christ sakes."

"Barry, shut up and listen to me. This is a blockbuster for both of us. The New York Metro Area Teachers' Union is the biggest and most powerful in the country and a heavyweight in politics. They are a major campaign donor, and Baldwin controls the purse strings. Here's how things work. She is very tight with key members of the Congressional Appropriations Committee who, each year, spearhead generous annual funding for education-related studies. That money gets funneled back to her through the Department of Education. She then, in turn, contracts with consulting groups to perform the work. Those groups subcontract out a portion of it, including deals with private companies that kickback money to her."

Filmore had been listening intently. "So, what's our involvement in all of this?"

"The union membership is interested in developing a curriculum on climate awareness for the elementary, middle, and high school levels, and that's where you come in. The funding is already in place and the major research contract will be issued to you as an expert on climate change. You'll funnel work to a group of entities, including an LLC that I control and, of course, Baldwin's companies."

Filmore rubbed his hands together. "How much money are we talking?"

"The contract is worth tens of millions over the course of the study. You won't have to do anything of substance except be the conduit through which the money passes, and we'll all profit handsomely."

"What about transparency? It seems Baldwin's self-dealing is the weak link if someone was to dig into this?"

Lyman stood for effect. "The last person you have to worry about is Kari Baldwin. First, she's the mastermind behind all of this and has been engineering these deals for years. We should consider ourselves fortunate we're being brought into her orbit. The timing is perfect for a campaign educating future generations on a pathway to dealing with the threat of climate change. All major players, including the political class, the media, and academia, will be lauding this initiative. We're in the right place at the right time, my friend."

He smiled. "I got to hand it to you, Lyman. You had me confused about why we were spending time with that obnoxious dike. I was really smarting after buying her dinner and picking up her tab at the strip club. Turns out it may have been the best investment I've ever made."

"You'll need to open up your wallet again tonight. She's in town, and we're having dinner at the Blue Duck Tavern at seven to seal the deal."

"Fine. I'll be there."

"By the way, Dylan Tomassi's name came up on my interagency search alert. He's being audited by the IRS. Is that your doing?"

"I don't know anything about it."

"Someone filed a whistleblower claim and stands to earn a fee if the audit results in a recovery of an underpayment. I figured it was you."

"Can't you find out who filed the claim?"

"No. The information is confidential."

"Hmm. I think I'll take credit for it anyway with Kari Baldwin. Can't hurt."

Kari and Fanci had just finished breakfast in their private room on the Amtrak train to Washington, DC. Baldwin waited patiently until the butler removed the dining cart and exited, closing the door behind him. "How did you enjoy your pancakes?"

"They were fine."

"Come sit with me for a moment," Kari commanded, taking a seat on the couch. Fanci complied, and Baldwin snuggled up next to her. "Did you see that man this weekend?" she whispered in her ear.

"Yes, ma'am."

"I want all the details."

Fanci timidly began a summary of her bedroom activities with Alex. Baldwin listened impatiently. "You know, Fanci, you need to be more confident when you speak. Did you enjoy yourself?"

"Yes," she murmured.

"Did you please him?"

"He seemed to like it."

"Did he please you?"

"Yes."

"Do you think you prefer being with a man or a woman?"

"I didn't have much experience before, but I always thought I preferred men. Now I'm beginning to think I'm bisexual."

"Do you like it when I boss you around in bed?"

"Oh, yes."

"And did that man boss you around too?"

"Yes, but not rough the way you do. It was more instructional."

"Then you have something to thank me for. You know my background's in teaching. It's time for a lesson. Get on your knees," she demanded as she stood and pulled down her pants. Fanci dutifully complied, and Baldwin directed her through the session, hands gripped tightly on her head, and raising her voice at times until she was satisfied with the performance. When it was over, she stood and rearranged her pantsuit while Fanci got up off the floor and sat back down beside her in silence, eyes averted downward.

Baldwin sat down. "Shouldn't you thank me for the lesson?"

Fanci nodded meekly.

"Were you able to learn anything more about our subject?" Baldwin asked.

"Yes. He told me his friend's been attacked a few times. One time he was shot at in his car, and then a couple guys beat him up pretty badly."

Baldwin smiled and gave an approving nod but said nothing in reply.

After their train arrived at Union Station, the pair took a cab to the Park Hyatt and checked into their suite.

Penel arrived at Dylan's house around midday. Aengus escorted her upstairs on the elevator and dropped her off at the second level before delivering her luggage to the master suite. Dylan was waiting for her in the kitchen. She hugged and kissed him, causing him to wince.

"What was that look for?" she asked.

"Sorry, my ribs are still painful. How was the trip?"

"No complaints. My flight was on time, and Aengus was waiting for me at arrivals. I like the new car, by the way."

"Thanks."

She stepped back and looked him over closely. "How are you doing, *really*?"

"I'm getting better. I've been moving around a little the past few days."

"You look like you've lost some weight."

"Probably because I haven't eaten much for almost a week. Plus, I haven't left the house the whole time and spent most of it in bed."

"Are you concerned about security here?" she asked with a solemn expression.

"Not at all. We have state-of-the-art surveillance cameras and security systems, and Aengus regularly patrols the grounds. He's a former military policeman and quite capable of responding to any intruders."

"When do you think you'll be ready to travel?"

"Anytime. I've got Shirley and my legal team taking care of things, and I'll be able to keep in touch with them from wherever we are. Esther provided me with a computer and cell phones that won't be traceable, if anyone is trying to find me."

"Where is Shirley? Doesn't she work out of the house?"

"Yeah, but she said something about having work to do at the youth center this afternoon."

"Did she know I was coming to stay with you today?"

"Of course. Why?"

"I get the feeling she doesn't like me."

"Why do you say that?"

"Just the vibe I get from her."

"I don't know anything about that," he replied dismissively. "Why don't you get settled and then we can work on our exit plan?"

"I am settled. Let's leave tomorrow, and then I won't need to unpack. Is there someplace I can sit down and make travel arrangements?"

"You can use Shirley's office. Use Esther's computer and one of the new cell phones. I'll be in my own office wrapping up a few things, and then I'll go pack."

He took her to Shirley's office and got her situated. An hour later, he was in his bedroom when she entered. "We're all set," she announced. "Our flight leaves from the Clearwater Airport tomorrow morning. A Citation VI charter will take us directly to the McClellan-Palomar Airport in San Diego County, about a thirty-five-mile drive to Temecula. I found a house in wine country on five acres and rented it for a week. It's a functioning vineyard, gated and very private. They grow grapes and olives on the property, and it's within walking distance of several wineries."

"That sounds great." He looked at his phone. "It's almost five o'clock. Why don't we go downstairs to the bar and have a drink, and then we can decide what we're going to do for dinner."

"Okay," she said with a smile, taking him by the hand and leading him downstairs. The entertainment room included a bar, lounge area with couches, a billiards table, and several large-screen televisions. An adjacent glass-enclosed, climate-controlled wine room held 500 bottles. She looked around. "I love this room. It's the quintessential man cave," she exclaimed.

The room was decorated with wainscoting walls and a coiffured wood ceiling all finished in dark mahogany. She took a seat on one of the bar stools finished in chestnut leather. Dylan made his way behind the bar and played bartender, beginning to feel like himself.

"What's a girl like you doing in a place like this?" he asked playfully.

"Looking for trouble, I suppose," she replied with a seductive smile.

"You've found the right spot. What can I get you?"

"I'm not that easy. Bring me your premium wine list."

"The list is so exclusive it's unpublished. As the sommelier of this fine establishment, I can recite you the options: white or red?"

"Red, please."

"Tonight, we're featuring a Chateau Trotanoy Bordeaux. We don't get many beautiful women in here, so for you the bottle is complimentary."

"You are so kind, and quite handsome, I might add. Are you trying to seduce me?" she said with a batting of the eyes.

"That is quite possible, although I can neither confirm or deny," he replied as he disappeared into the wine room and came back, presenting her with the bottle.

"Excellent choice. A 2015. Please decant it and allow it to breathe."

"As you wish, ma'am," he said with a nod. Dylan placed the bottle on the bar for a few minutes, allowing the sediment to settle to the bottom. He then uncorked it and poured the contents into a crystal decanter, filtering it through a swath of cheesecloth. "What would you prefer to dine on this evening?"

"I'm famished," she replied. "I haven't eaten all day, and, quite frankly, you look like you can use a good meal. How about some beef?"

"Excellent suggestion. I have some aged filet mignon in the fridge. We'll have to improvise on the sides."

"Perfect. You take care of grilling the steaks, and I'll handle the accoutrements. How long before the wine is ready?"

"Let's give it an hour to aerate. How about a drink to hold you over?"

"What's your poison?"

"I recommend a Soldier Horse," he replied, reaching for a bottle on the top shelf and grabbing two glasses. He poured the drinks and set them on the bar. "To a good dinner with a fine companion." He held up his glass.

She picked up hers and clinked it against his. "And to safe journeys and erotic adventures."

They both took healthy sips of their drinks. "Let's move to the kitchen so we can start working on dinner," he suggested.

He pulled two eight-ounce filets from the Sub-Zero refrigerator, seasoned the meat and placed it on a wooden platter. Penel surveyed the fridge and pantry and selected a box of elbow macaroni, an unopened container of grated Parmesan cheese, a hunk of cheddar, and a head of Romaine lettuce. She began boiling a pot of water, then chopped the lettuce, transferred it to a ceramic bowl, and returned it to the fridge to chill. She then melted butter in a saucepan added flour, salt and pepper and then mixed in the two cheeses. Once the pasta was ready, she drained it and mixed it with the sauce, placing it in a baking pan.

Dylan enjoyed his drink and watched with amusement. "I had no idea you possessed such culinary skills."

"Necessity is the mother of invention," she replied humbly.

He produced a rolling cart from a closet, and they loaded it up and took the elevator down to the covered outdoor living area overlooking the pool and waterfront. The sun had set, but lights from Treasure Island and the bridge illuminated Boca Ciega Bay, creating a stunning backdrop on the cool evening.

Dylan fired up the gas grill and pizza oven in the built-in kitchen. He broiled the steaks while the mac and cheese baked in the oven. Penel mixed the salad with Caesar dressing and balsamic vinegar and topped it with the balance of Parmesan cheese. They sat down at the dining table and dug in.

"Mmm," she moaned, after taking a bite of the steak. "This is outstanding. My compliments to the chef."

"It was a team effort. How do you like the wine?" he asked.

"It's wonderful, as is the view, but I particularly enjoy the company."

"It's good to see you again," he replied with a gesture of his glass." Have you ever been to Temecula?"

"No. I've never even heard of it until now."

"I think you'll enjoy it. And if we need to move on, I have a few other places in mind."

"Do tell."

He flashed a mysterious smile. "I think I'll keep you in suspense. Just let me know when you're ready to leave California."

After dinner, they cleaned up and headed upstairs to the bedroom. Penel snuggled close to him, and they talked for a while. Before long, they were both fast asleep.

## Two Lefts Don't Make a Right

Kari Baldwin and Fanci were seated next to each other across the table from Barry Filmore and Lymon Scott, finishing their dinner in the crowded dining room at the Blue Duck Tavern, located downstairs in the Park Hyatt Hotel. At Kari's direction, Fanci was wearing a Steve Madden velvet lace dress, textured stockings, and stiletto heels, one of the outfits purchased during their shopping spree. She had introduced her as Francis, her personal assistant, and Fanci remained quiet during dinner, deferring to the others and speaking softly only when addressed directly. Filmore had been leering at her all evening, tossing the occasionally overtly crude comment in her direction.

The waiter brought the check and placed it in the center of the table. Baldwin slid it in Filmore's direction.

"Dinner was excellent, gentlemen. Why don't we head upstairs and discuss our business?" she said, glancing around at the groups seated near them. "It's much more private. Meet us upstairs, Suite 1045. And bring a bottle of Hennessy with you."

She rose. Fanci got up and followed her out of the dining room.

After the women left, Filmore ordered a bottle of Hennessy Paradis cognac from the menu, turning his American Express card over to the waiter. "That woman is something else," he whispered to Lymon as the waiter departed. "That bottle is $4,600."

"Cost of doing business," Lyman replied, placing his napkin on the table in front of him. "I'm going to use the restroom. Take care of everything here, and I'll meet you in the lobby."

Kari and Fanci were in the suite's living room area. "I'm going to be discussing some very sensitive business with these men. You can wait for me in the bedroom. If I need you for anything, I'll let you know."

"Yes, ma'am," she replied as she retired to the bedroom and closed the door behind her.

There was a knock on the door, and the two men entered. Filmore displayed the bottle. "Please pour us all a glass," she told him, nodding toward the bar set up in the corner. She and Lyman took seats on couches opposite each other.

Filmore stood there for a moment. "Where's your assistant? Why don't you have her serve us. I enjoy her company."

Kari glared at him. "All right," she finally replied, turning and yelling in the direction of the bedroom. "Francis, come out here, please."

Fanci appeared, and Kari instructed her to pour them each a drink "One for you too, dear, and then come sit with us for a while." She did as she was told and served the drinks from a platter, setting them on the table between the two couches. She then took a seat next to Kari.

They began discussing the details of the climate curriculum contracts, with Kari and Lyman doing the bulk of the talking. Fanci did her best to look away as if she were disinterested.

After consuming two glasses of cognac, Kari motioned for Fanci to sit on her lap. As they continued to discuss business, the two men looked on in astonishment while she nonchalantly rubbed Fanci's leg and slid her hand up her dress, pulling back the material and exposing a matching black garter belt and lace panties.

Filmore was staring, and Kari glared back at him. "Let's talk about our Catholic school systems donor," she said to him. "What's happening with his construction project in Florida?"

"Still shut down and will be indefinitely from what I understand."

"I've been informed he was recently on the receiving end of a couple of attacks, including a beating within an inch of his life. That your doing also?"

Fanci's ears perked up as she observed Filmore shift his gaze and stare off for a moment.

"Well?" Kari finally asked him again.

"Of course, it was," he stated with authority. "I'm a man who gets things done. He's also the subject of a full IRS audit that I initiated with a whistleblower claim. He's been delivered a message loud and clear about his transgressions. He won't be a problem for you going forward."

She nodded with approval. "It's getting late, gentlemen. We're about done here," she said, gently sliding Fanci aside and rising from the couch.

Filmore downed the rest of his glass. "I was beginning to enjoy the show. Can we see a little more?" he asked boldly.

Kari scowled at him before her expression turned to a smile. "Sure, why not?" She turned to Fanci. "Stand up and take off your dress."

Fanci complied and stood there in heels, stockings, panties, and matching bra, her lean build and dark complexion highlighted by the room's lighting. Filmore's jaw dropped.

"You like what you see?" Kari asked.

"Of course. Who wouldn't?"

"The night is young. I'm bushed, gentlemen, but it's Francis's first trip to DC. Take her with you and show her the town."

"Uh, I need to stop by my office and take care of some things before I head home," Lyman interjected, "but I'm sure Barry wouldn't mind."

He smiled. "The pleasure will be all hers. I'll give her an evening she won't soon forget. You probably should put your dress back on, although I won't object if you want to go out like that," he said, slapping his knee and bellowing a hearty laugh.

Baldwin shot him a disdainful look as Fanci slid back into her dress. "Have fun, but get her back here in one piece, or you'll answer to me, understood?"

"Of course. Let's go," he said, jerking her by the arm and leading her out the door.

# CHAPTER TWENTY-SEVEN

Early the next morning, Kari Baldwin was sitting at the dining table in her suite, dressed in one of her signature pantsuits, her short gray hair slicked back. She was drinking coffee and reading the *Washington Post* when Fanci walked through the door. Her face was red, eyes swollen, and hair disheveled. Rug burns on her arms and bare legs were evident through her torn dress.

"Where have you been all night?" Kari mumbled, barely averting her eyes from the newspaper.

Fanci stood in silence as tears began to run down her cheeks.

Kari finally looked up and took her in. "What happened to you?"

She shook her head and broke into a full hysterical cry before rushing into the bedroom and slamming the door behind her. Kari sighed and drank the rest of her coffee while she finished the article she was reading. She finally got up and made her way to the bedroom.

Fanci wasn't in there, but the bathroom door was closed. Kari walked in, and Fanci was seated on the toilet, head in her hands, still crying. "You need to tell me right now what the hell is going on," Kari demanded in a stern tone.

Fanci looked up, crestfallen, and said nothing. Kari grabbed her by the wrist and led her into the living room, setting her down on one couch before taking a seat opposite her. "Enough of this childishness. Right this minute, you're going to tell me what happened." She folded her arms and stared at Fanci, waiting for a reply.

She gritted her teeth and spoke in a quiet tone, disgust in her voice. "What happened was you left me alone with that . . . that animal."

"And? Start at the beginning."

There was a prolonged pause before she took a couple of deep breaths. "We went to a couple of clubs and had some drinks, and then he demanded I go back to his hotel room. I said no, and then he slapped me and told me no one says no to him. He forced me back there and did unthinkably vile and disgusting things. Just look at me," she said, lifting her torn dress to expose raw knees before extending her arms.

"This is from being dragged around on the floor all night. When I finally got out of there, I spent several hours in the hotel lobby bathroom before I could stop all the bleeding and get cleaned up enough to make my way back here. That barbarian should be in a jail cell or worse," she whimpered.

Kari bit her lip in thought before looking at her and making eye contact. "You are weak and selfish," she scolded. "Listen to me very carefully. Despite what happened, the man is useful to me and necessary to accomplish important work for the benefit of our membership. I will make certain you are not placed in that position with him again. Now I'm leaving for meetings at the DOE. I'll be gone most of the morning. You will use that time to get yourself together and pack up your things. We check out of here at noon and head to the airport."

She got up and walked out the door, leaving Fanci stunned and speechless.

Their plane landed at the airport outside San Diego just after noon local time. Dylan waited with the luggage while Penel handled the arrangements with the rental car. She pulled up in a Land Rover Defender, and Dylan loaded everything in the back.

"I'm a city girl. You better drive," she said, switching to the passenger seat. Half an hour later they were on Interstate 15 driving through Old Town. They pulled onto Rancho California Road and arrived in wine country, drove past Calloway, and made some turns off the main drag until coming to an area with residences on one side of the road and wineries on the other. He stopped the car in front of a large single-story house with a gated driveway. The front and sides of the home were surrounded by rows of vineyards. A light mist was trickling from the irrigation system on one side.

"This is it," he said.

Penel got out and pressed some buttons on the keypad adjacent to the gates, and they slid open. She jumped back in, and he drove slowly up the long drive until they got to the house. "This is beautiful," she exclaimed, taking in the property with mountains set in the background of a brilliant clear blue sky. "I can see why you like it here."

They unpacked and got situated in the master bedroom. "I'm starving," she said. "What do you want to do for lunch?"

"We can go over to Leoness. The wine and food there are excellent, and it's within walking distance. I really need to stretch my legs."

"Sounds good."

"I don't think I mentioned this, but all the wineries typically close around six o'clock. It's truly an early town. I find it best to eat one big meal around midday."

"Let me change into some tennis shoes, and I'll be ready to go."

They left the property and walked hand in hand. The weather was cool and dry and comfortable for walking. They hiked their way up the long driveway and got a table in the restaurant. They ordered a bottle of Syrah and shared an order of the famous hand-cut fries as an appetizer. For dinner, Penel decided on the swordfish and Dylan opted for the wild mushroom risotto.

"That was excellent," she exclaimed as she took care of the check, using the company credit card.

"I can get used to your taking charge and paying for everything. It's very high-powered and quite the turn-on," he commented with a smile.

She glanced around the dining room and leaned forward, lowering her voice. "I'm excited to see you're starting to return to your old self."

"You have that effect on me. Before we settle in for the evening, we should run out to the store and pick up some provisions. How did you enjoy the wine?"

"It was excellent."

"They're known for their Syrahs. Let's grab a few bottles on the way out. I prefer to drink the local wines, and most of them are only available at the wineries."

Two hours later they were back at the house, and the groceries were put away. "Let's sit out front and have a glass of wine," he suggested.

She smiled and nodded with approval. He opened a bottle, grabbed two glasses, and led her out to the covered front porch. They sat down in wooden lounge chairs, and he poured two glasses of wine. They sat silently, taking in the breathtaking views. "I could really get used to this place," she commented.

"I'm glad you like it. There's a lot more to explore."

After they finished their wine, they showered together and made love gently, Penel taking charge and handling the bulk of the workload, much to Dylan's delight.

# CHAPTER TWENTY-EIGHT

THE NEXT MORNING, DYLAN AND Penel were sitting outside in the backyard drinking coffee and enjoying the view of the endless hilly rows of plantings. Suddenly, three hot air balloons appeared on the horizon against the backdrop of the gray sky.

"Oh, my gosh, look at that!" she exclaimed.

"You'll see them just about every day around this time," he replied.

She continued to stare in awe. "The balloons are so colorful, and they're flying so low it seems like we'll be able to reach out and touch the baskets when they fly overhead."

"They take off not far from here," he explained. "They increase their altitude pretty quickly as they move along."

"Look, there's two more," she said, pointing in another direction. "That is so cool. I've never seen one before." She continued to look skyward, straining her neck, completely consumed with fascination.

Dylan remained silent and allowed her to enjoy the scene. Eventually, she turned and looked back at him, a broad smile on her face. "I'm glad we came here. It's absolutely beautiful."

"And I'm glad you're enjoying yourself. It's about ten o'clock in the east," he said, consulting his phone. "Why don't we go for a walk, and then we can set up offices on the other side of the house and take care of some business back home before it gets too late?"

"That sounds good. Give me a minute to change, and I'll be ready."

Dylan was waiting for her in the living room when she appeared. She looked stunning in a pair of yoga pants with her hair pulled back. They walked down the driveway and turned right, continuing along the narrow road past the Oak Mountain Winery situated on top of a hill. They came upon a newer development with a portion of the houses completed, others under various phases of construction. All were situated on multiacre lots and had grapevines planted in rows on trellis systems.

"Look at those houses," Penel said, indicating with an index finger. "Why do you think all the lots have grape plantings? I can't imagine every homeowner would care for that look or want to deal with all the work involved."

"I can venture a guess. It's probably so the land can be zoned agriculture. Just eyeballing, I'd say each lot is three acres. Typically, the land is leased to growers who handle all the work. In turn, the owners receive a significant property tax break. With California tax rates, that could be significant."

"How do you know all this stuff?" she asked with a pinched brow.

"I don't for sure, but I own farm and ranch land, so I'm familiar with how it works."

She stopped walking and looked him in the eye. "Where are these properties?"

"I own farmland in Nebraska and a cattle ranch in South Dakota."

"Ha! You, a farmer?"

He laughed. "I'm a gentleman farmer at best. I just own the land. It's leased out to actual farmers and ranchers who work the land. I've never even seen the properties. They just send me a check every year."

Penel shook her head and smiled. "You are full of surprises."

When they returned to the house, they each set up an office. Dylan used the computer and phone Esther had provided. He checked in with Shirley, who assured him everything was fine. Next, he called his attorney's office and got Walt Jackman on the phone.

"How are you, Dylan?"

"Fine. I'm settled in California for the time being. What's happening with the audit?"

"I've had several conversations with the examining agent regarding your in-person examination. He wants to do it as soon as possible."

"Is it voluntary?"

"Technically, yes. But he has made it clear that if you don't agree he's prepared to issue a subpoena to compel your presence."

"I just got out here. What exactly does 'as soon as possible' mean to a government agent?"

"As soon as you can at your convenience."

Dylan thought about that for a moment. "I'll fly back tonight and be at your office first thing in the morning. Allow time for us to prepare and schedule him right after that. I'll head straight back to the airport and return the same day."

"All right, I'll schedule the meeting. Just so you know, I did learn that the audit was generated by a whistleblower claim."

"What exactly does that mean?"

"Someone submitted IRS Form 211 with enough information alleging tax noncompliance that the service determined the claim warranted further consideration, and thus, the audit."

"Why would someone do that?" he asked, perturbed by the news.

"Any number of reasons, from retaliation to financial incentive."

"Financial incentive?"

"A tax whistleblower can receive an award of fifteen to thirty percent of the proceeds of any recovery for fraud or underpayment."

He stood and began pacing the room. "Can you find out the whistleblower's identity?"

"I've inquired, and the service is protecting the person's identity."

"Do they have to disclose it?"

"The IRS has discretion, and there are several instances where mandatory disclosure is required, but it's not unusual for them to decline. Look, Dylan, I sense your frustration, so allow me to say this. You have very complicated returns between your personal and business interests, and now there's your 501(c)3. Someone could submit a claim with very general allegations and the complexity of your returns could trigger the IRS's interest. You're a big fish, so to speak."

"I see."

"The good news is all your returns are prepared by your CPA and reviewed by me prior to filing, and I'm confident everything is in order, and you will come out fine. That being said, even when you come out clean from an audit, the process is the punishment. As we bean-counter types often say, it's not the destination but the ride."

He stopped pacing and ran his hand through his hair. "I understand what you're saying. I want you to fight this tooth and nail. No holds barred and no settlement. Do you understand?"

"Loud and clear. Oh, one last thing. Not sure if you heard, but snow is forecast for Tampa tomorrow."

"Really? I hadn't heard, and I just got off the phone with Shirley."

"I'm surprised she didn't say anything. It's the talk of the town. First time in nearly fifty years."

He hung up and went into the kitchen where he grabbed a bottled water from the fridge. He checked the time and knocked gently on Penel's door. She had her back to him, typing away on her laptop. "How's it going in here?"

She turned around and smiled. "I've made all my phone calls, and I'm just finishing up this last letter for my secretary to print and mail."

"Slight variation in our plans." He explained his phone call with Walt.

"No problem," she replied. "I'll find you a plane, and you can leave late tonight. With the time change, you'll land in Tampa early in the morning. You can take care of your business and fly back the same day. I'll get to work right now."

Dylan was in the living room when Penel walked in, a smile on her face and a notepad in hand. "I found you a plane with a bedroom and shower. It will be here at the Temecula Valley Airport tonight. Flying time is about five hours. You can leave around midnight, sleep on the flight, shower and change, and be ready to go in the morning. The plane will wait for you at Tampa Airport until you're ready to leave. You should be back here in time for dinner."

He looked at her in amazement. "You are incredible and truly awesome."

"Thank you. Compliments are graciously accepted."

He glanced at his phone. "It's two thirty now. How about we go to Europa for dinner? I'm a member of the wine club, and they have an amazing Spanish restaurant. Plus, they recently opened their Italian village, so we'll have our choice of cuisine."

"That sounds great."

An hour and a half later, they were seated in the hospitality room enjoying complimentary wine. Dylan had arranged for a table in Bolero, the Spanish restaurant, but he wanted Penel to sample some of their wines. A slim attractive blonde was working the wine bar and attending to them.

They tried several varietals and were tasting the Aleatico Rosé when she brought over another bottle and two more glasses. "This is our Rioja Reserve. It's aged for two years in oak barrels and then another year in the bottle," she explained as she poured the glasses.

They both tasted the wine. "This has a fine finish with hints of plum," Penel commented as she held up her glass and inspected the color.

"You have a very good palate," the server replied.

"Thank you."

Dylan looked around the room. "Is Shane here?"

"No. Today's his day off. I've been here for a year now, and everyone asks for him. He's legendary."

"I first met Shane when I visited about twelve years ago, and they were just breaking ground on the development," Dylan said. "The tasting room was a temporary structure that could only fit about a dozen people."

The server smiled and nodded. "I've heard about those early days."

He was relieved Shane was not working. Dylan had been there six months ago with another woman, and Shane had taken care of them. He did not want to be in the awkward position of explaining the disastrous ending of that relationship to Penel had the issue come up.

"I really like this wine," Penel said. "We should have this with dinner."

"It's about that time. We can order a bottle in the restaurant." He left a twenty-dollar bill on the bar and led Penel into the dining room.

"What do you recommend?" Penel asked as they enjoyed their wine and looked over menus.

"I usually get the paella. It's outstanding. We can share, or you can try something else, and I'll take the leftovers back to the house. I can't finish it by myself."

"That sounds good. Let's share."

They enjoyed dinner, and Dylan began to feel like himself for the first time since the attack. That night in bed he did not hold back. She immediately picked up on his increased vigor from the previous evening and matched his enthusiasm, building to a rhythmic crescendo until they both shuddered in ecstasy. Afterward, they gently kissed and caressed until she fell asleep in his arms. He gently extracted himself, tucked her in, and changed clothes before using the app on the phone Esther had given him to arrange for a ride to the airport.

# CHAPTER TWENTY-NINE

THE PLANE WAS ABOUT A half hour from Tampa Airport when the flight attendant rustled Dylan from a deep sleep. "Mr. Tomassi. We have about thirty minutes before we land in Tampa if you want to shower."

"Thank you," he replied groggily.

The water pressure was surprisingly strong, and he felt refreshed and alert as he dressed in gray slacks, a white shirt, and a blue blazer. He also had his puffer jacket handy, having checked the weather and confirmed the forecast for unusually frigid temperatures accompanied by a light snow.

He sat in one of the wide leather chairs and strapped on his seat belt as the plane began its descent into Tampa. He checked his phone. It was almost eight o'clock. Using his ICOE cell phone, he texted Aengus, who confirmed he was parked and waiting at the Executive Jet terminal.

Once the plane had landed, Dylan exited the staircase and found Aengus standing close by, next to the Escalade. He walked over and hopped in the front seat.

"How was your flight, sir?"

"Wonderful. I slept most of the way, showered and dressed, and found you here waiting for me when I came down the stairwell. I got a glimpse into the lifestyle of the jet-setting one percenters."

"Very good, sir. How long will you be at your attorney's office?"

"I'm not sure exactly. Several hours, I would imagine, and then I'll need a ride back to the plane."

"I'll be close by. Just text me when you're ready, and I'll pick you up in front of the building."

Dylan was seated in Walt Jackman's office shortly after nine o'clock.

They were drinking coffee while Walt prepared him for his statement. "Do you have any questions?"

"No."

"Per your instructions, I arranged for a court reporter to record the examination, and I notified the agent as is required. He advised that his supervisor will be present."

"Is that typical?"

"No. But it's also atypical to request to record the meeting. Usually, the agent asks questions and takes notes."

"If I can be held criminally liable for providing false information to a federal agent, I don't want to rely on their word without an official record of what was said."

Walt nodded. "It's about time," he replied after consulting his watch.

Dylan followed his attorney into the conference room, where an older man and younger-looking woman were seated on one side of the table. Introductions were made, and it turned out the man was the agent in charge and would be conducting the interview while his female supervisor observed.

"Please state your name and address for the record," he began. Following Dylan's reply, he continued, "I am the agent in charge of a full audit being conducted by the Internal Revenue Service regarding your personal and business returns for tax years 2021 through 2023. Each of my questions will pertain to that time period. Do you understand?"

"Yes, sir."

"How were you employed during that time frame?"

"I was self employed."

"Did you own any companies?"

"Yes."

"How many?"

"I'm not sure."

"Do you have any type of medical condition or other issue that affects your ability to answer questions here today?" the agent asked with a hint of sarcasm.

"No."

"Why are you unable to tell me the number of companies you own?"

"I can't be certain, and I don't want to guess."

"Why can't you be certain?"

"I just can't, but what I can tell you with certainty is that each of them is listed on my tax returns."

"Please provide me a summary of your business dealings."

"Generally, I own an investment company and a real estate development company."

"Are those incorporated?"

"Yes."

"How many separate corporations?"

Dylan glanced at his lawyer, who took the cue and replied, "You've already asked that question, and Mr. Tomassi advised he doesn't know."

The agent exhaled in obvious frustration. Dylan looked at the supervisor, who averted her eyes, looking down at her note tablet.

The exchange continued in a similar fashion for more than an hour. The agent changed direction and began placing documents in front of Dylan and questioning him about each. Dylan continued to provide short direct answers, peppered with "I'm not sure," "I don't recall," "I don't know," or "All that information is contained within my tax returns."

After two more hours, the agent requested a break and consulted with his supervisor. Dylan and Walt headed back to his office during the recess.

"How do you think it's going?"

"You're doing a good job, and the agent is obviously frustrated. I'm your tax attorney, and I wouldn't know the answers to most of his questions without consulting your returns. For example, you own dozens of warehouses, convenience stores, and hotel properties in addition to multiple development projects going on at any one time, and an LLC was established for each of those. It's unreasonable to know that number offhand, and either he's trying to trip you up or he's simply inexperienced."

When they returned to the conference room, the agent advised that he had no further questions, and he and his supervisor abruptly left the office.

Dylan looked over at Walt, who had an amused look on his face. "I guess he had enough of you for one day. Where are you headed now?"

"Back to the airport and out west again. Where does this leave us?"

"They've taken your statement, and I don't expect they'll be requesting an update, so I'll handle things from here. Go enjoy yourself, and I'll be in touch."

Dylan thanked him and headed to the lobby, where he texted Aengus. A moment later he received a reply. "I'm parked on the street near the Fort Brooke parking garage."

"Stay there. I'll walk over," Dylan texted back.

He left the Bank of America tower, zipped his jacket up to the neck, and stuffed his hands in his pockets. The weather app on his phone said the temperature was 38 degrees, but it felt colder with the wind chill. As he proceeded east on the sidewalk he observed two people walking side by side directly toward him. One was small in stature and well dressed in a full-length cashmere overcoat, wool hat, and a scarf that covered the lower part of his face. The other person was tall and wide, dressed in a long overcoat and a Russian-style fur hat. The androgynous face under the hat was fleshy and flushed.

As they approached, Dylan made eye contact with the smaller man, who appeared ready to walk right into him. He stopped just short, and Dylan began veering around him. The man leaned in and uttered through the scarf, "You're a dead man" before he continued on.

"What the hell was that?" Kari asked, after she and Barry Filmore almost collided with another man on the sidewalk.

"*That* was Dylan Tomassi, the private school donor you asked me to take care of."

She glared back at him. "Do you plan on keeping the promise you just made him?"

He smiled wickedly. "Just wait and see."

Fanci had been in Tampa for two days and was relegated to hanging around the hotel suite while Kari attended meetings and events at the nearby Tampa Convention Center. The temperature had dropped more than thirty degrees overnight, and snow flurries were falling from a gray sky. The roadways were wet, and a light dusting of snow covered the grassy areas.

Kari returned to the hotel room. "Brrrr, it's cold out there," she commented, shedding her overcoat and removing her hat. "Especially with that wind coming off the waterfront. Good thing we packed heavy clothes. Be a dear and make me a cup of coffee," she demanded as she plopped down on the couch.

Fanci produced a steaming mug and handed it to her. "Come sit down and talk with me for a moment," Kari demanded.

Fanci complied and sat demurely, hands folded on her lap. Fanci had been even quieter than usual since they left Washington, and, mercifully, Kari had not demanded sexual favors since Fanci's night out with Barry Filmore. She expected the reprieve to be over, as this was Kari's usual modus operandi.

Kari placed her hand gently on Fanci's thigh. "We need to have a discussion. Since our meeting in DC, I invited Barry Filmore to speak at the conference and discuss the new climate educational awareness program we're developing. He flew into town today, and he's been doing press all morning, providing commentary on the threats of climate change after the snowfall. Your paths will cross again, and I fully expect you to be nice to him. Is that understood?"

She nodded ever so slightly, head bowed, and eyes averted downward.

"Good. I'm glad that's out of the way. I'll be gone the rest of the afternoon, and we're having dinner with him tonight. I want you to wear than mint sweater dress I bought you and the white lace bra and panty set."

Fanci sat silently for a moment and then looked over at her. "I've been holed up in this hotel room for two days. I think I'll spend the afternoon exploring the city if that's okay."

"Fine, just be back here and ready to go by six thirty. Dinner's at seven."

After Kari left for another meeting, Fanci changed into jeans and a turtleneck sweater and took the trolley to Ybor City.

Later that evening, Fanci and Kari arrived at Bern's Steak House and had a seat in the lobby. The red-and-gold decor with ornate furniture and framed artwork reminded Fanci of a bygone era. The dining room style was an extension of the lobby. Barry Filmore appeared with two women, one on each arm, one an obviously bleached blonde and the other a faux redhead. Both were heavily made up and wore low-cut dresses that revealed substantial cleavage and leg. Several of the other male patrons stole glances.

"Kari, Francis," he bellowed, breaking away from the two women. He shook Kari's hand and then bearhugged Fanci as she stiffened up and shuddered, arms at her side. "Nice to see you again," he whispered in her ear, flicking his tongue for good measure. "Ladies, these are Leah and Aerial."

They were seated at the end of one of the small rooms in the choppy layout of the restaurant, Kari and Fanci on one side and Filmore on the other, bookended by his two dates. "Have any of you ladies been here before?" he asked.

All four indicated in the negative. "You're in for a treat. It's quite a unique experience. The wine cellar is one of the most exclusive in the country. I've arranged for a tour after dinner before we head upstairs to the dessert room."

During the meal the conversation was limited to small talk, with Filmore handling the bulk of the dialogue, often in a boorish manner. Fanci said little, only responding briefly when addressed directly. Kari seemed uninterested, consuming her usual hearty portions of food and drink. Fanci noted two bottles of champagne and two magnums of wine were consumed by the time Filmore handled the check and everyone followed an assistant sommelier who guided them through the wine tour.

Afterward, he led them up a narrow staircase to rows of booths with old-fashioned telephones and mini jukeboxes mounted on the wall. The group squeezed in with identical seating arrangements to downstairs, Filmore nestled in between the two women. Fanci passed on dessert while the other four indulged in a variety of decadent homemade cakes and ice cream sundaes, washing them down with a bottle of Yalumba twenty-one-year-old Tawny port.

As the group was on coffee, Filmore's two guests excused themselves to use the restroom. Kari stared at their backsides as they sashayed down the narrow walkway. "You like what you see?" Filmore asked her.

"Of course."

"They're yours for the evening. It's my gift to you."

Fanci looked on, attempting to conceal any expression of her feelings of disdain.

Baldwin leaned in across the table. "How is this going to work?"

"As I said, everything's been arranged. They work for a high-end agency with a very discreet clientele. Take them back to your hotel, and when your visit is concluded, they'll find their way out."

"What about Francis?"

"Your choice, but if it's all the same to you, I'll be happy to take her for the night."

Kari looked over at her, and Fanci gave her a sideways glance, eyes narrowed. "Francis will be happy to spend the evening with you. Just bring her back in one piece."

"She hasn't been broken yet, although I may have broken her *in* last time," he guffawed, slapping the tabletop with an open palm, causing dishes and glasses to rattle.

The two women returned, and Filmore remained seated. "No need to sit, ladies. You're done here and leaving with Ms. Baldwin. Enjoy your evening."

Fanci watched with helpless trepidation as the three ladies left, leaving her alone with the lecherous brute. She was horrified and frozen in place as she began the process of blocking out of her mind what was about to happen.

# CHAPTER THIRTY

Dylan and Penel had fallen into a comfortable daily routine. Breakfast outside followed by a long walk, a few hours of work in the office, and then wine tastings and an early dinner. Evenings were capped off in bed, where they made love and continued to explore and satisfy the outer limits of each other's desires.

Since it was a Saturday, Dylan was in his makeshift office catching up on his reading when Esther called. "How are you feeling?" she asked.

"I'm just about back to normal, although my ribs regularly remind me why I left town."

"We haven't spoken since you left. Where are you?"

"In Temecula, California. We rented a house in wine country."

"That sounds nice. How is Penel?"

"She's well. We've been here almost a week, and we're enjoying every moment. The weather's been just what you'd expect this time of year. Warm days and cool mornings and evenings. We've had some rain, but it doesn't last long. How are things with you?"

"I'm doing well. The extreme cold snap is over, and I've been getting outside to do my walking, which I prefer. I heard it snowed in Tampa recently."

"I know. I was there."

"Really?" Esther replied, surprise in her voice. "Why?"

"I had to give the IRS agent an in-person statement, and I decided to fly back and get it done." He provided a summary of the day and the strange encounter with the guy on the sidewalk.

"Have you ever seen these people before?"

"The larger one, definitely not. The smaller man, I don't think so. He had his hat pulled down and his face partially covered with a scarf. His voice was muffled when he spoke."

"That's very concerning. Have you used any of your own electronic devices or credit cards since you left?"

"No. And Penel has made every reservation in her name."

"Have you seen anything suspicious since you got back to California?"

"No."

"Well, I still worry."

"I wish you wouldn't," Dylan replied. "Getting back to the weather, we've been experiencing unusual patterns across the country. Seasonal in the Northeast and West, yet it snowed in Florida recently, and there's a warming trend across the Midwest. It's going to be seventy degrees in South Dakota tomorrow."

"I did see the pictures of Tampa on the news, but that was hardly what we would call a snowstorm around here."

"You know what else I've noticed since I've been out here? California really embraces its green energy policy."

"Are you still in your climate change compulsion phase?"

"Compulsion's too strong a word. I would say awareness."

"Fair enough. There's no question California is the leader in the green movement."

"I've never seen so many Tesla cars and trucks, and we have our share in Florida. But it's more than that. There are EV cars, trucks, buses, and vans from pretty much every manufacturer. I find myself looking for tailpipes to see if a vehicle is gas or electric."

She laughed. "I would call that compulsion."

"And solar panels are everywhere, not just on homes and buildings. Even the streetlights and traffic signals are solar."

"California has by far the most homes with solar panels in the country, but they also have the most expensive and unreliable electricity service. There are regular blackouts during times of peak demand. Why do you think that is?"

"I'm not sure."

"Because they went all-in on solar energy without consideration of a well-thought-out, comprehensive plan. The fundamental problem with solar is electricity's only generated when the sun is out, and it's prohibitively expensive to store the excess power. The large number of solar homes have created a glut the state is unable to manage because its grid and transmission systems are inadequate. It's the result of leadership promoting a 'drop-everything sense of urgency' and rushing to adopt an energy policy without scientifically proven and economically feasible solutions. Are you driving an EV?"

"No."

"How much does gasoline cost?"

"About twice what I pay in Florida."

"How much longer are you planning on staying where you are?"

"I'm playing it by ear."

"Have you heard anything from the police investigation?"

"Not yet. I did speak with the chief of police, who's a friend, and my attorneys have a private investigator looking into the attacks while they handle the other matters."

There was a moment of silence on the other end before Esther continued. "I'm pleased to hear you're safe and feeling better and enjoying your time with Penel, but it wouldn't be a bad idea to keep moving and go somewhere else. I don't think you should stay in one place too long. Please give Penel my regards and keep in touch."

"I'll pass that on. And, Esther, thanks for everything."

"You are certainly welcome."

He hung up the phone and sat quietly in thought before he walked down the hall, where he found Penel seated at a small desk looking at her computer screen. He knocked gently on the door frame. "Are you busy?"

She craned her neck and smiled. "Not really. Just catching up on some work files. What's up?"

He approached her from behind and caressed her around the shoulders before he began kissing her on the neck.

"I think I know what you have in mind," she breathed.

"That's regularly on my mind when you're around, but I had another idea."

"Oh," she remarked, breaking away and turning around in her chair.

"How do you feel about moving on to somewhere new?"

She narrowed her eyes. "Are you getting tired of drinking wine all day and having wild, passionate sex all night?"

"Hardly. We can continue to do those things. I was just thinking about a change of scenery."

"Where would you like to go? I'm enjoying the warm weather, and it's the last week of February. Our options are limited."

"It's seventy degrees in South Dakota, and the forecast calls for temperatures in the upper sixties all next week. I thought we would go check out that part of the world."

"What will we do there?"

"You mean besides drink wine and make love?"

She laughed. "Exactly."

"I thought we'd fly into Nebraska and drive up from there. That way we can see my farmland and check out the countryside. We can stop wherever we see something interesting, and when we get to South Dakota, we can visit my ranch. Plus, there's Mount Rushmore and the Badlands."

"Can we go horseback riding?" she asked enthusiastically. "I used to ride out in the Hamptons when I was a girl."

He smiled broadly. "I'm pretty sure they have horses there."

She jumped up and hugged him. "That's a wonderful idea. It'll give us both an opportunity to see that part of the country. I'll get started on the travel plans."

An hour later, Dylan was sitting outside in the backyard when Penel came and sat down next to him with her laptop in hand. She set it down on the table and opened it up. "I booked a charter flight out of John Wayne airport. It's a Citation CJ2," she said, reading from her computer screen. "It's about a two-and-a-half-hour flight to Western Nebraska Regional Airport, which is only about twenty miles from your farmland. I found a decent hotel in Gering, which is close by."

Dylan stared at her intensely. "You're really embracing this travel-planning thing."

"It is kinda fun, actually. When we're ready to leave, we can drive up to Rapid City. That'll take us about a half a day, but it's only an hour from your ranch in Interior."

"When do we leave?"

"We have a two-hour takeoff window tomorrow morning between ten and noon, and we can drop the rental car at the airport."

"Why don't we get packed and then have an early dinner?"

"That sounds like a plan. Where would you like to dine?" she asked.

"I've taken you to all my favorite places. Utilize those excellent research skills and pick a place for our last night."

"I'll get right on that," she replied with a smile, clicking away at the computer keys.

# CHAPTER THIRTY-ONE

Dylan stared out the window of the light jet as it began its descent into the airport. The midafternoon sky was a brilliant blue, and the sun glistened off the snow-covered grounds. Penel was seated next to him.

"Why is there snow on the ground?" she asked. "My weather app says the temperature is sixty-eight in Gering."

"Probably because they had a good amount of snow before the recent warming trend. It takes time for it to disappear after the temperature warm-up."

"I know that," she replied, nudging his arm. "I live in New York, remember?"

"I'm surprised the land is so hilly," he said. "I thought Nebraska would be flatter than this."

The plane landed smoothly and taxied over to Classic Aircraft Service, the airport's fixed-base operator. Dylan thanked the flight crew, and as they departed, a lineman was unloading their luggage onto a cart. He tipped the man and asked him to deliver their bags to the rental car desk. Once inside, he hung back while Penel arranged for the rental car using the ICOE credit card.

She walked over to him, a slight frown on her face. "All they have available in a large SUV is a Suburban. I asked if it was all-wheel drive, and the guy looked at me funny and said, 'Ma'am, every vehicle we have is all-wheel drive.'"

After their bags were loaded, Dylan drove to their hotel while Penel navigated. "It's on this road, another mile and a half on the left."

"The terrain is definitely flatter on the ground than it looked from the sky," he commented before glancing in her direction. "How'd you find this place?"

"It was close to the airport and looked nice for the area. The pickings were slim."

"I was wondering because we're getting close, and we just passed an auto parts store, a junkyard, and a motel that looks like they rent rooms by the hour. And look," he said pointing ahead. "There's a steel company."

"There it is," she said.

"What have we gotten ourselves into," he mumbled to himself as he pulled into the parking lot of the Hotel 21. "Let's take a look around before we check in."

"Whatever you say."

Dylan was pleasantly surprised as they walked into the marble-appointed lobby. To the left was a spacious area with quality furnishings and a full-service bar finished in resplendent wood. A small reception area was situated on the opposite side.

She flashed an 'I told you so' smile and marched over to the front desk. A well-dressed woman appeared from a rear office. "Good afternoon. How may I help you?"

"Good afternoon. I have a reservation. My name is Penelope Stanhill."

The woman tapped her keyboard, "Ah, yes, Ms. Stanhill, we have you staying with us for two nights. Your room is ready, a single king-size bed as you requested."

She nodded approvingly as she handed over her credit card and ID. The clerk examined both before processing the card. "What brings you to Gering?"

"Business."

"Oh," the woman replied with a raised eyebrow and a quick glance in Dylan's direction. "What business are you in?"

"Agriculture. We're looking to expand our holdings," she fibbed.

"Well, enjoy your stay," she said, handing her the key cards. "Your room number is written on the case. Let me know if there's anything I can do to make your stay more enjoyable."

"Do you have any recommendations for a restaurant for dinner?"

"If you're looking for a steak joint, I would recommend the Steel Grill. It's just up the road."

"Thank you," she replied, turning toward Dylan, who had commandeered one of the hotel's luggage carts. While they were outside loading their bags from the car, she said to him, "You know that desk clerk has me pegged for some high-level executive and you as my boy toy."

"Why do you say that?"

"You couldn't tell?"

"I wasn't really paying that much attention."

"Come on, Dylan. I'm checking into a hotel with a corporate credit card while my handsome paramour hangs back. I rent a room with a single king-size bed and mention I'm here on business. What would you think?"

"Either that, or I'm on the run and I don't want anyone to know where I am."

She smiled and shook her head. "I'm sure that's exactly what she was thinking."

By the time they got settled into their room, showered, and changed, it was approaching the dinner hour. "Why don't we go down to the bar, have a drink, and get a second opinion on where to eat?" he suggested.

"How do you know it's open? The bar was abandoned when we checked in."

"It's five o'clock. Isn't that the universal time for drinks? You know the old Jimmy Buffet song, 'It's Five O'Clock Somewhere'. That means there must be a bartender on duty."

"I'm ready. Let's go down and check it out."

They took the elevator downstairs and made their way to the lobby. It was empty except for a man standing behind the reception desk. Dylan approached him. "Good afternoon, sir. What time does the bar open?"

"It's open now," the man said with a smile. "I'll be right with you. We all do double duty around here. Go have a seat and make yourselves comfortable."

They sat down on two of the matching stools, and Dylan scanned over the selection of wine and spirits bottles set up behind the bar. "What do you think?" he asked Penel.

"We probably should stick with liquor. The wine in Temecula has spoiled me."

"The wine selection does look a little on the light side," he whispered in her ear as the man approached and slid behind the bar.

"What can I get you?" he asked.

"Can you make a vodka tonic?" Penel asked.

"Sure thing. And for you, sir?"

"I'll have a Maker's Mark."

"Coming right up."

After serving the drinks, the bartender asked, "Where you folks from?"

"New York," Penel responded.

He smiled. "I'll bet you find our part of the world a bit different from the big city."

"We just got into town. I'll have to get back to you on that."

Dylan sat silently and sipped his drink. "What about your friend here?" the bartender inquired.

"He's with me," Penel added.

"I see," the man replied. "Can I get you anything else?"

"I think we're all set, although we're beginning to think about dinner. Do you have any recommendations?"

"Best place in town is the Steel Grill. Try the steak nachos and the prime rib. That's what they're known for."

"Thank you," she said with a smile.

"I'll be over at the front desk if you need anything else. Just give me a holler."

After he left, she nudged Dylan. "If we stay here much longer, you're going to forge a reputation."

"I'm okay with that. It's not a bad gig. They'll never suspect I'm on the run and checking on the thirty-five thousand acres of farmland I own in their county."

They finished their drinks and headed out for dinner. The Steel Grill was a dark, windowless establishment full of patrons and staff wearing the ubiquitous uniform of jeans, flannel shirt, boots, and cowboy hat. They were seated at a table and looking over the menus left on the table when a waitress approached. "What can I get you folks to drink?"

"Do you have a wine list?" Penel asked.

The woman looked perplexed. "I'll have to look around and see if I can find one."

Dylan could barely contain himself. "Just bring us two beers, please."

She nodded, pulled a pencil from the considerable nest of hair on her head, and wrote down the information before heading in the direction of the bar.

"What?" Penel asked after she had departed.

"Remember: when in Rome."

"I guess we're dining on the steak nachos."

"With a side of prime rib."

The food was surprisingly good, and they washed down their meals with second glasses of beer. After dinner, they headed outside, where the temperature had dropped dramatically. Dylan turned on the car and pressed the buttons for the heated seat and steering wheel. "I think we should look for a clothing store in the morning and get some boots and warm-weather gear."

"What's the matter, Dylan? Afraid you're not fitting in with the locals?"

He shot her a quizzical glance. "Me? I'm perfectly comfortable in my jeans and puffer jacket. I was concerned about you. With your sense of high fashion, you stick out here in flyover country."

She laughed. "Fine. I plead guilty, and I could use a pair of boots. You should get some too. Your sugar momma wants you to fit in as well."

# CHAPTER THIRTY-TWO

Dylan awoke early the next morning and quietly slipped out of the room so Penel could sleep in. He went downstairs to the fitness center and was pleasantly surprised to find a quality assortment of exercise equipment. He put himself through an hour-long weight training circuit followed by half an hour running on the treadmill.

Afterward, he grabbed two coffees and bottled waters from the lobby and took them upstairs to the room. Penel was just beginning to stir. She sat up in bed, her tousled chestnut hair framing her pulchritudinous features.

"Good morning," she moaned while stretching her arms. "Where have you been?"

"Downstairs in the fitness center. I brought you some coffee," he said, handing her one of the cups from the tray.

"You are a sweetheart." She took a sip. "Not bad. What's on the agenda for today?"

"We're on mountain time here, so I'm going to take a shower and do some work. I found a business center downstairs, so I'll go down there, and you can use the room. We'll head out before noon, do some shopping, and grab lunch, then check out my property. How's that sound?"

"That works for me." She looked at her watch. "I should be ready to leave by eleven."

Dylan was alone in the business center, checking the financial markets on his laptop, when his phone rang. The screen read Driscoll Williams. He stood and closed the door. "Dylan Tomassi," he answered.

"Hello, Dylan. Tina Fischer. Walt Jackman told me you were out of town. Do you have time to talk?"

"Sure, Tina. What's up?" he asked, returning to his chair.

"I want to bring you up to date. The archeology group concluded their study and provided me with a report. Bottom line: there is no physical evidence to suggest the property was ever utilized as a burial ground. At the same time, my department conducted comprehensive research on the property going back to pre-European settlement times. The Largo area was first inhabited by the Tocobaga Indians, but most of their major settlements were situated north of there in what is now Safety Harbor. I just got back from Washington, where I met with Department of the Interior officials. The strange thing is they insisted there is no record of evidence of a Native American burial ground on the property or the issuance of a cease-work order on your project."

After taking in the information, Dylan shot out of his chair and began pacing the small room. "How is that possible? The order was printed on their official letterhead. And what about their guy from their Atlanta field office who showed up on the site?"

"I provided all that information to my contacts, including the name of their man and the FBI agent who accompanied him. I got back to town on Thursday, and on Friday, I received word that the department's official position is the order was issued in error. I demanded a letter to that effect and just now received it. You can get back to work on the project."

"Thanks, Tina, for letting me know. We've lost a month on this project over what turned out to be nothing."

"You're welcome, Dylan. Have a good day."

"It's just gotten better. I've got some calls to make. Thank you for all your hard work."

"Glad to be of service."

He hung up and called Rock Wright, who assured him everything was in place to be back up and working by the middle of the week. Next, he dialed Madison James. His call was promptly put through to the mayor. "Dylan, how are you?"

"I'm well, Madison. How about you?"

"I'm doing fine. Have you recovered from your accident?"

"Yes. I'm out of town, but I just received news on the Largo Palms project and wanted to let you know right away. Everything's been resolved, and construction will be back up and running next week."

"Oh, Dylan, that is good news indeed. I am so relieved. You promised me you would take care of it, and you did. You are truly a man of your word. It's my turn to buy *you* dinner. When will you be back in town?"

He took a deep breath while he gathered his thoughts. "I'm not certain. I'm looking at some business investments, and it could take a while. I'll be in touch after I get back home."

"Okay, I'll wait to hear from you. Take care of yourself. And thanks for letting me know about the project."

He returned to the room and found Penel dressed and ready to go. They stepped outside to gray skies and crisp, cool air. "I found an old-fashioned general store not far from here. The website says they sell clothing and footwear. I thought we'd check it out."

"All right, I'll drive, and you navigate," he replied as he held the passenger door open for her.

The store was in the heart of the city's downtown, a short strip of four-lane road with a series of single- and double-story brick buildings. They walked into the well-stocked clothing department in front of the store. There were a good number of customers for the middle of a winter weekday. Beyond the clothing section, there were toys, games, candy, and assorted confections in the rear. An upstairs loft held home decor, furniture, and pottery, and a downstairs area outdoor gear, including light farming equipment, camping supplies, cooking accessories, and a wide assortment of knives.

"May I help you?" a pleasant woman inquired.

"I'm looking for some jeans, sweaters, and a pair of boots," Penel replied.

The clerk gave Penel a quick up and down. "You'll find items in this section. There's a shoe department on the opposite side through that small opening," the clerk said, indicating with a pointed finger. "There're also more boots downstairs, and the fitting rooms are right behind you."

Penel smiled. "Thank you."

Dylan looked on with amusement as he stared at two rooms the size of phone booths with folding chairs and tattered curtains hanging from a rod. "Not exactly like shopping on Fifth Avenue," he whispered.

"Stop," she said with a grin. "I think it's very charming, and they have some nice things in here."

An hour later, they left the store with two oversized shopping bags filled with blue jeans, sweaters, sweatshirts, a riding jacket, and two pairs of boots for Penel, and a pair of cowboy boots for Dylan. "Why didn't you let me use the credit card to pay? she asked while he was loading their haul into the rear of the Suburban.

"You've used that card for most of the trip. I plan on paying Esther back, but I brought cash with me too. I thought I'd use some of it."

She shrugged. "All that shopping has made me hungry. Where would you like to eat lunch?"

"There's a diner across the street. Wanna try that?"

"Why not? I'm up for an adventure."

After they ate, Dylan had started to leave cash on the table when the waitress came by, handing him a slip she tore off an old-fashioned, green-lined guest check pad. "You have to pay at the register, darlin'."

"Thanks. I'll do that," he replied with a smile, handing her a ten-dollar bill.

"Thank *you*. You all have a blessed day," she said with an appreciative grin.

About fifteen minutes later, Dylan stopped the SUV on the side of a narrow two-lane road with rows of brown corn stalks separated by lanes of snow-covered pathways on either side. "This is it," Penel commented, consulting her phone's GPS. "There's no signs or anything, but according to my navigation app, we're in the middle of your property."

He proceeded for several miles with no other cars or signs of human life in sight, the scenery unchanged. They came upon a crossroad, and he took a right turn. After driving a few more miles, he stopped and looked over at Penel. She began to laugh. "You really know how to show a girl an exciting time."

He laughed too. "You mean you're not impressed?"

"Honestly, this may be the most boring, mundane sight I've ever seen."

"Hey, I'm just doing my part to help feed America."

"Did you call anyone to let them know we're coming?"

"Honestly, I've only ever dealt with one person, and I'm not even sure he lives around here or works the land himself. Since I bought the property several years ago, I receive my check every year, and that's the extent of our interaction. I've spoken with the guy maybe three times."

"We still have a few hours of daylight. I read about the Scotts Bluff

National Monument in one of the tourism books at the hotel. It's not far from here. Let's go check it out."

"Lead the way, my fair copilot."

After a short drive, they came to a small reception building. The parking lot was virtually empty, and a covered wagon was parked off to one side. Rock formations jutted out from snow-covered terrain, and a single road ran through a tunnel in one of the bluffs. "The place looks abandoned," Dylan observed. "How are we going to hike? Everything's covered in snow."

"Let's go inside. I want to change into my new jeans and hiking boots."

They walked into the reception area to find a man seated behind a glass display case. "Good afternoon, folks. How are you all doing today?"

"Fine, thanks. We were passing through and decided to check out the park. And my friend here would like to change her clothes."

"Ma'am," he replied with a tip of his Stetson. "Ladies' room is back that way," he said, indicating the opposite end of the room. Penel disappeared into the restroom with a shopping bag in hand.

"Not many people around," Dylan commented.

"Not unusual for this time of year. Especially when the trails are covered with snow. Makes hiking difficult even with the fine weather we're currently enjoying. Summit Road is open. You can drive up to the top of Scotts Bluff."

Dylan walked down a hallway, admiring the photographs on the walls. "What can you tell me about this artist?" he asked the man.

"William Henry Jackson was the first person to photograph Yellowstone. He was also an accomplished artist. The drawings and watercolors on display are his."

Dylan was looking over a series of Native American paintings when Penel emerged from the restroom, wearing skintight jeans and hiking boots. "I'm all set."

They thanked the man and walked back to the car, Dylan trailing Penel with a view of her backside. He caught up and caressed her derriere. "You look outstanding in those jeans," he commented.

"I do, don't I?" she replied with a smile. "If you're a good boy, I'll let you peel them off when we get back to the hotel."

"That certainly provides me with an incentive to behave."

He drove up Summit Road to Scotts Bluff and parked in the lot. They followed the footprints in the snow-covered trail to the top of the bluff. The wind had picked up considerably, and Penel shivered. Dylan put his arm around her.

"What a beautiful view," she commented as she snuggled up to him.

"It certainly is," a husky voice replied from behind them.

Dylan turned around and observed a large man with a long gray beard and ruddy complexion. He wore layers of tattered clothing, and a coonskin cap sat upon his head. He carried a walking stick, and a good-size knife in a sheath was attached to his belt. Dylan instinctively shielded Penel, who huddled close behind him, as a single thought permeated his mind. *You're a dead man.*

# CHAPTER THIRTY-THREE

"No need to be alarmed," the man said. "Name's Abel. What brings you folks out here today?"

Dylan continued to assess the man while Penel wrapped her arms around his waist. The man's voice was raspy, but his words were delivered in a friendly tone with a midwestern dialect. He sensed the casualness in the man's voice and unclenched his fists as the pounding of his heart against his chest decreased. "We came to check out the Bluff. You from around here?" Dylan replied cautiously.

"Born and raised in Scotts Bluff. I hike up here just about every day. Be happy to show you folks around."

The man reminded Dylan more of a character out of a Mark Twain novel than a hired assassin. "Sure, why not? It's tough to walk the trails when they're covered in snow."

"Where you folks from?"

"I'm Dylan, and this is Penelope. I live in Florida, and she's from New York."

"The city?"

She moved out from behind Dylan and stood next to him. "Yes, sir. I live in Manhattan."

"It's nice to meet you both, and it's always a pleasure to cross paths with such a fine-looking woman," he said with a smile and slight bow.

Dylan smiled, now confident the man posed no threat.

"We're standing on Scotts Bluff," he continued, "which was named after Hiram Scott. He was a fur trader whose party abandoned him during an expedition after he took ill. His body was later found right around here. This bluff was a landmark for travelers on the Oregon Trail. The vantage point provided excellent visibility to ascertain any dangers ahead. Over yonder is the North Platte River, and the area in between is known as the Badlands."

"What about all those other rock formations?" Penel asked.

"The one behind us is called South Bluff, and most of the major formations have names," he explained. "If you follow me, we can walk this way."

They spent the next hour hiking the trails with Abel, who acted as a guide and illustrated the history and geography of the area. When they returned to the parking lot, Dylan shook the man's hand. "It was a pleasure meeting you, and thank you for being so generous with your time. You are a wealth of information."

"You're most certainly welcome," he said, turning to Penel. "It was a pleasure spending time in the company of such a beautiful woman. You certainly made an old man's day."

The sun was setting as they made their way back to the hotel. "That was fun," Penel commented. "And Abel was adorable. I'm glad we ran into him."

"He was certainly thrilled to meet you."

"What's the matter? Are you jealous?"

"Of course," he replied with a smile. "He may be older, but that guy was a real man, right out of an old spaghetti western."

"Don't sell yourself short, cowboy. You'll do just fine."

# CHAPTER THIRTY-FOUR

ALEX WAS WORKING LATE IN his Tampa office and feeling melancholy. Dylan was out of town, and he was lacking female companionship. Ann Hefner, Dylan's lawyer, had been dodging his calls, and he hadn't been with a woman since his date with Liz in Connecticut. He thought about her, fondly recalling her submissive nature and willingness to please him. He decided to give her a call, and it went straight to voicemail.

"Liz, how are you? It's Alex. I've been thinking about you. I'm down here in Florida working, and I'll be here through next week. My son is with his mother, and I could use some company this weekend if you're available."

He returned to his work, reviewing the draft of an appellate brief written by an associate. An hour later, his cell phone buzzed.

"Alex, it's Liz."

"How are you?"

"I'm well. I got your message. It was nice to hear from you, and I'd love to visit again."

"Great. I'll be free all weekend. What would you like to do?"

"Can we go to the beach?"

"Sure. Whatever you want. We can even get a place out there if you'd like."

"That would be wonderful. Where would we stay?"

"Let me worry about that. Can you fly in early Saturday morning and leave Sunday evening?"

"Yes, as long as I'm back in time for work on Monday."

"No problem. I'll have my secretary book your flight, and I'll pick you up at the airport."

"Don't worry about the plane ticket. I'll take care of that."

"Okay, if you insist. Text me your flight information, and I'll see you at the airport."

"I'm looking forward to it. See you then."

He spent the next half hour calling around to the beach resorts, starting with the Don Cesar on St. Pete Beach. The responses were the same: it's the height of tourist season, and everything is booked. Frustrated, he called Dylan, and it went to voicemail. Then he remembered he was out of town. He went into his contacts and dialed the alternate number Dylan had given him.

"Hello."

"Dylan. It's me, Alex. What's going on?"

"Oh, Alex. It didn't sound like you."

"That's what happens when you don't talk to me for a week. Where are you?"

"I'm with Penel. We're in South Dakota."

"What are you doing up there? Isn't it cold and desolate this time of year?"

"Hardly, it was in the sixties today. We're staying in a cabin in Custer. We drove up to Sturgis today and spent the day."

"Isn't that the place where they have the huge motorcycle rallies in the summer?"

"That's it. Even though it's the middle of winter, there are signs everywhere that it's their biggest event of the year. They even have a motorcycle museum and hall of fame."

"So, what are your plans? When are you coming back?"

"I'm not sure. I came up here to check on some land I own. We're taking our time and stopping off at places along the way that interest us."

"How are things going with Penel?"

"We're getting along great and really enjoying each other's company."

"Would she agree with that statement?"

Dylan laughed. "I hope so. We've never spent this much time together, but I feel we've really connected."

"Uh-oh."

"What?"

"I'm concerned there's a nonzero chance you're going to run off and get married on me. How far are you from Vegas?"

"Don't be ridiculous."

Alex cleared his throat. "While we're on the discussion of women, I need a favor."

"I do favors."

"I'm in Tampa through next week and quite lonely for companionship, so I have a guest coming into town for the weekend. I was planning on staying at the beach, but all the resort hotels are booked. Can I use your guest house?"

"Who's the young lady?"

"It's the college student from the University of Bridgeport."

"How many times have you been out with this woman?"

"Once in Connecticut and the one time down here. She said she'd never been to Florida before. I think she likes it."

"Is she coming to Florida to see you or for the weather?"

"Probably a combination of both. Can I use the guest house?"

"Sure. I speak with Shirley daily, so I'll let her know. The main house is locked down, and the alarm's on whenever she's gone, so ask Aengus if you need anything from there."

Alex rubbed his eyes with his thumb and index finger. "Have you heard anything about the investigations?"

"Nothing. Except that the issue with the Largo construction project's been resolved, and it's back up and running." He reiterated what Tina Fischer had told him.

"Sounds like you're making progress. Keep in touch, and thanks for the use of your place."

Barry Filmore was at home when Lyman Scott called. "Good evening, Ly. What's up?"

"Hello, Barry. I received word things are moving quickly on the education appropriations. You should receive the first installment within the next couple weeks. I want to make sure everything is ready to go on your end."

"The LLCs and bank accounts are set up, and I've received all the information from the contractors. I'm still waiting on our union friend. I haven't spoken with her since we were in Tampa."

"You won't. This is how it works. Once you receive the funds and pay the contractors, you'll pay her in cash and deliver it personally. She can't have a paper trail that leads back to her."

He stood and paced the room. "How am I supposed to convert that much cash? It's a small fortune!"

"That's up to you to figure out. It's part of the reason you were brought into this deal. Sounds like you have some work to do, so you better get a move on."

# CHAPTER THIRTY-FIVE

Dylan and Penel were finishing breakfast in their cabin. "I spoke to the ranch manager earlier. He's going to show us around the property on Friday. It's about 120 miles from here, so we're going to have to leave early in the morning."

"Did you ask about horseback riding?" she asked excitedly.

"I did. He told me most of the horses are broodmares, but they have several general riding horses the staff uses for herding cattle and hunting on the property. We can ride those."

"Is this one of those ranches where tourists go and pretend to be cowboys and cowgirls?"

He laughed. "No. It's strictly a working ranch. They do have some groups come in to hunt, and there's a lodge on the property, but apparently, it's very exclusive. He's invited us to stay the night."

"Please tell me we're not going to hunt."

"We're not going to hunt. I've never fired a gun in my life."

"Me neither. What do they hunt anyway?"

"I have no idea."

She looked at him with raised eyebrows. "You don't know much about what goes on on your property, do you?"

He grimaced. "Honestly, no."

"How did you end up owning a ranch?"

"I bought it about ten years ago from a family that had owned it for three generations. The couple was retiring, and their children had all gone into different careers. They were raising cattle and said their foreman was a good man who was interested in running it but didn't have the ability to buy the property outright. The owners were moving to Arizona and wanted a clean deal with full payment up front so they could move on without any worries. I did some research, hired a consultant to look over the property, review the operations, and examine the books. My attorneys worked with a local law firm and handled the purchase and closing. The foreman and his partners formed a new company, and I leased the property to them. They've paid the rent every year since without an issue."

She shook her head, grinning. "You are amazing. A Connecticut Yankee moves to Florida, buys a farm in Nebraska, a ranch in South Dakota, and never even visits his properties. What are you going to do for an encore?"

He narrowed his eyes, a contemplative expression on his face. "Who knows? I might sell everything and buy a winery in California or possibly Oregon."

"Really?" she asked, giving him a playful shove in the arm. "Are you serious?"

"Maybe. But I can tell you what I do know for sure."

"What's that?"

"I'm taking you to see Mount Rushmore today."

"That sounds like fun. How far is it?"

"It's about twenty miles, and there's other stuff to see in the area, so we can make a day of it."

They were driving north on State Road 244 when Dylan exited the highway. "Where are we going?" she asked. "My app says we have another ten miles to Mount Rushmore."

"You'll see," he replied with a smile. Soon the entrance to a large property in the Black Hills came into sight. They were greeted by the silhouette of an Indian warrior forged in iron. He was mounted on a horse, his left arm extended and index finger pointing forward. It sat above an engraved sign that read Crazy Horse. "I've heard of Crazy Horse, but I didn't know about this," she said.

"Crazy Horse was a Native American war leader of the Lakota tribe. He led battles against the federal government over its attempts to take over their land. The most notable was the Battle of Little Big Horn, which was Custer's last stand, where his entire battalion perished."

"That's right. So, what is this place exactly? she asked as they drove along the entrance road.

"It's the Crazy Horse Memorial. They've been working on the monument for decades. One of the sculptors from Mount Rushmore was commissioned to work on the project, and when he died, his family took over. When it's finished, it'll look like the image at the entrance. So far, the only thing that's been completed is Crazy Horse's face. They still have to finish his upper body and horse."

They parked the car and entered the village. It was a conglomeration of historical artwork and exhibits, cultural performances, theaters, gift shops, and restaurants. They walked around before heading outside to check out the monument. Several people were standing along a walkway that jutted out from the face carved into the mountainside.

"Wow. They do have a long way to go," Penel observed, straining her neck to look upward and shielding her eyes from the bright late morning sunshine. "What do you think that hole is for below the walkway?"

"My guess is it's the beginning of the gap between Crazy Horse's arm and his horse."

"That makes sense."

"Did you know that Crazy Horse was never photographed? He believed that taking his picture would diminish his spirit, so the sculpture is based on various reports of what he looked like."

She looked him in the eye. "Is that true?"

"I'm pretty sure it is. I read it on one of those plaques in the cultural center."

They browsed around for a while before returning to the car. They were driving on Iron Mountain Road, a two-lane winding thruway, when they came upon the Doane Robinson Tunnel, a narrow one-way passage carved through the mountainside. As they approached the other side, he stopped the car.

"OMG!" Penel shouted. "Look at that." The outline of the tunnel exit perfectly captured the image of Mount Rushmore, the brilliant sunshine serving as a glowing frame around the spectacular sight. She snapped several pictures with her iPhone.

They continued along the roadway until they caught up to a tour bus. As the road wound around a bend, another tunnel came into sight, and the bus stopped. Dylan pulled up behind it. "How in the world is that bus going to make it through the tunnel? It doesn't look like it's going to fit," Penel observed.

The tunnel turned dark as the bus began to crawl through, its body filling the entire space. Occasionally, sparks flew along the sides as the mirrors scraped against rock. After a few tense moments, light shone through from the opposite end as the bus safely exited.

"That was crazy," Dylan remarked.

When they entered the park, Dylan and Penel walked hand in hand along the Avenue of the Americas, the main thoroughfare decorated with flags from all fifty states and the US territories. The walkway dead-ended into a wide observation area enclosed by a waist-high granite wall that provided a perfect view of the Mount Rushmore monument carved into the hills. They stood and observed the magnificent landmark. "Which one is your favorite?"

She stared ahead in thought. "I'd have to say George Washington. He's the father of our country. What about you?"

"I'm partial to Theodore Roosevelt. Some say he didn't warrant being included with others, but I disagree. He was a fascinating man. Most people aren't aware he was born and raised in New York City and received an Ivy League education. He's usually remembered as an adventurer and rugged outdoorsman, but he was quite the Renaissance man—a war hero, reformist, and conservationist."

Penel placed her arm around him. "Bring it in closer," she said, extending her other arm, phone in hand, as she snapped a photo.

"Would you like me to take a picture of the two of you?" an older man asked.

"Yes, please," Penel answered, handing him her phone.

The man took several photos with the monument in the background as his wife looked on. "What a beautiful woman," she remarked to Penel. "And your husband is so handsome. You are quite the couple."

"Thank you," Penel replied with a smile, "but we're not married."

"What a shame," she said, pursing her lips and gently shaking her head. "Two people as tall and good looking as you should get married and have children."

"Pay no attention to her," the man said, handing back her phone. "She gets carried away sometimes."

"No, I don't, Lester. You tell me those two don't look like movie stars."

Dylan and Penel laughed as they thanked the couple and made their exit.

"That was something," Penel said after they had broken away. "What do you want to do now?"

"Let's head back to the car. I've got another surprise for you."

It was early afternoon, and the sun was creeping toward the horizon when they pulled into a dusty parking lot. An idle modern roller coaster sat next to a series of old-western-style wooden buildings. "Here we are," he announced.

"What is this place?"

"This is where we're having dinner."

"At three forty-five in the afternoon?"

"Actually, it's more than dinner. It's dinner and a show. This is the famous Fort Hays Cowboy Music Show and Supper Club and the movie set for *Dances with Wolves*."

"Oh, my gosh! I love that movie."

"Some of it was filmed right here. We've got plenty of time to look around before the show starts."

After they checked into the office and purchased dinner tickets, they strolled along the strip of buildings. "Let's go in here," Dylan said, leading Penel into a long, narrow space with a desk set back at the end of the room surrounded by colonial-style windows. "Do you recognize this place?"

"Is that the desk where Major Fambrough sat and gave Lieutenant Dunbar his orders to report to the frontier outpost right before he shot himself?"

"That's it."

She sat in the chair and placed her folded hands on the desk. "Take my picture."

He snapped off several photos. "Come on. There's a lot more to see."

They spent half an hour touring the rest of the old movie set before heading over to the supper club. They approached the reception desk, and a young woman dressed in a red checkered dress and cowboy boots and hat greeted them. "Good afternoon, how may I help y'all?"

"We have reservations for dinner. It's under Penelope Stanhill."

She scanned a hand-written chart. "Yes, ma'am. Party of two. If you'll follow me, I can seat you now, but table service won't start for another fifteen minutes. You're welcome to have a drink at the bar."

"Thanks, we'll do that."

As they followed the woman to their table, she said, "If you're here in morning, you should try our ninety-nine-cent, all-you-can-eat pancake breakfast."

"Thanks, but we're staying in Custer, so we'll have to pass on that," Dylan replied, glancing in Penel's direction.

They were seated at a table just in front of the stage, and Penel watched as the woman walked back to her station. "I saw the sign out front. Ninety-nine cents for all-you-can-eat pancakes, sausage, and biscuits and gravy. Can you imagine? How can they possibly make any money doing that?"

"It's one of the great wonders of the world. Can I interest you in a cocktail?"

"You most certainly can."

There were a few people at the bar, and they found two seats at one end. Penel ordered a vodka tonic, and Dylan stuck with Maker's Mark, his drink of choice since they had arrived in the Midwest. "Where y'all from?" the bartender asked as he served their drinks. He was dressed in blue jeans, cowboy shirt, and boots, a kerchief wrapped around his neck.

"I'm from Florida."

"And I'm from New York."

"The big city?"

"Yes, sir," she replied with a smile.

"Well, welcome. What brings you to our part of the world this time of year?"

"I'm checking on some property I own," he replied.

Handing them a silver bucket of peanuts, "Where's your property, if you don't mind my asking?"

"I own ranch land in Interior. What type of crowds do you draw this time of year?"

"A fraction of what we get in season."

"When does that start?"

"Beginning of May. That's when the bus tours that run out of here begin, and then we're full every day. The show's still the same, and in my opinion, it's better this time of year with the smaller audiences. Enjoy the performance," he said as he turned to serve another customer.

The variety show was anchored by a country-western band, with appearances from an Elvis impersonator and a series of comedic performers. Even the wait staff got in on the act. Their waiter, a strapping young lad, took Penel by the hand and led her to the stage, where the pair performed an impromptu high-intensity square dance. They received a standing ovation from the small but vocal group. Dinner of fried chicken, barbeque ribs, cornbread, macaroni and cheese, and coleslaw was served family style. They arrived home late, tired, and sated, and showered together before falling fast asleep.

# CHAPTER THIRTY-SIX

THE CARBON CREDIT SYSTEM IS a program that evolved from the battle against climate change. It was developed as a financial incentive for companies to reduce greenhouse gas emissions from their operations through investment in research and other innovative reduction strategies. Those companies that successfully lower their emissions through more sustainable operations receive carbon credits. The standard unit of measure is one carbon credit for each metric ton of carbon dioxide or its equivalent in another greenhouse gas.

Companies that are unable to sufficiently lower emissions or elect not to invest in greener practices often buy excess credits to meet government mandates or stakeholder initiatives. The carbon trading market currently operates under a patchwork of various governmental regulations, international agreements, and independent third parties born out of the private sector.

Barry Filmore had spent the night at the Four Seasons Hotel near the financial district in Manhattan and was attending an early morning meeting with the board of directors of a financial services company. The board had recently come under attack when an activist investor called for a shareholder vote of no confidence in the board after the investor's efforts to force the company to divest itself of all holdings in the oil and gas sector barely failed to pass.

The chairman started in. "There's no way this firm can divest itself of its positions in fossil fuels. Those companies' performance is instrumental in creating the stellar returns we provide our clients year in and year out.

And, assuming we were to sell, any plan would come under public scrutiny, and we would end up with significant losses on the transactions. You come highly recommended, Mr. Filmore, and we've asked you here today to hear your thoughts on the matter."

Filmore adjusted himself in the high-back leather chair and folded his hands on the table. The sleeves of his three-thousand-dollar bespoke suit and starched white dress shirt crept past his wrist, revealing a stainless steel Hublot chronograph watch. There was a smug look on his face. "Good morning, gentlemen, ladies," he began. "I can sum up the solution to your problem in two words: carbon credits."

He scanned the room as the heads of the seven men and two women seated around the table bobbed in various degrees, accompanied by a chorus of murmurs. Filmore, a seasoned salesman, had just executed an assumptive close and remained silent, waiting for the buying signals to commence.

"How exactly would that work?" the chairman finally asked.

"It's a turnkey solution. As a certified carbon credit dealer, my firm is uniquely qualified to handle the entire project. First, my team will conduct an in-depth analysis of the firm's holdings. Since the focus of this recent shareholder action involves fossil fuels, we'll start there. We calculate the carbon footprint of those holdings with setoffs for shares you own in companies that have implemented certified emission reduction plans. We then develop your own voluntary emission reduction plan and purchase the necessary credits to meet your sustainability target. As a publicly traded company with headquarters in New York, we will ensure that the plan meets the standards set forth in the Regional Greenhouse Gas Initiative before it is verified by an independent third party accredited by ACR, the American Carbon Registry. You then incorporate a summary of the plan into your prospectus and have your PR firm promote the reduction program. You not only extinguish the current threat, but you now are out in front of the sustainability movement, and management can continue to invest freely in those companies it believes best meet your objectives."

Filmore stopped speaking and looked around the room, his gaze landing on the chairman, with whom he maintained eye contact. "I took the liberty of preparing an Agreement in Principle. With your authorization, we can begin work immediately."

"I have some questions," a woman shouted. Filmore looked at her. She appeared to be in her sixties, with short gray hair and glasses. He found her off-putting and sensed she presented a threat to closing the deal.

"Yes, ma'am. I'm here to address any questions or concerns."

"First, how standardized are these processes? It appears to me that these carbon emissions calculations are all over the map. And where do the credits come from? How are those companies earning excess credits they're able to sell?"

He flashed his best disarming smile. "Those are very salient questions. Allow me to use an example that will best illustrate how the program works in practice, and that should address your concerns. The federal government publishes emissions standards that all auto companies doing business in the US must comply with. As you are all aware, Paradise Automotive is a relatively new electric car company. In its short history, it has lost money every year on its manufacturing operations. So how is it that a company that has never made money selling cars has a market capitalization of nearly a half a trillion dollars?"

He scanned the room to confirm he had everyone's attention. "Again, we return to the same place, carbon credits. The auto industry utilizes a cap-and-trade model based upon emissions standards. Paradise captures a significant number of excess carbon credits because it builds EVs exclusively, compared with its competitors that still rely heavily on producing cars and trucks with internal combustion engines. Paradise is profitable primarily from selling those credits to its competitors so they are able to meet the standards."

Most heads were nodding in unison when the woman spoke up again. "But how does that apply to our situation where there may or may not be published standards for every industry we hold investments in?"

"That's why you're hiring us."

"Not yet," she interrupted.

Filmore took a deep breath as he fought the urge to snap back at the woman. "I believe I understand your point. These are complex calculations that vary greatly from industry to industry. In your case, the situation is compounded by the fact that the firm holds ownership interests in every major business sector. As I mentioned, after my team completes its work and before the plan is implemented, it goes through the carbon credit verification process by an ACR-accredited third party. Think of it as an audit of your financials by one of the Big Four accounting firms. Once it's complete, you can move forward with confidence the plan has been fully investigated and vetted utilizing the gold-standard verification process."

"How much does all this cost?" she asked, a frown on her face.

"It's a significant financial investment that, I believe, the company cannot afford *not to make*. Your management team is currently under siege, and the climate activists are not going away. This will get you out ahead of the issue and put an end to the attacks once and for all."

The woman started to speak again, but she was interrupted by the chairman. "Thank you, Mr. Filmore, for clearing up those issues. If you will excuse us, the board is going to hold a vote on the matter."

"Certainly," he replied, rising from his chair and exiting the boardroom, closing the double doors behind him. He took a seat in the lobby and checked his phone. There was a text message from Lyman Scott. "How's it going with the presentation?"

He returned the text. "I'm here now. Just about to close the deal. I'll call when I'm done."

He was checking his email when the chairman came through the doors, a smile on his face. He extended his right hand. "Congratulations, Mr. Filmore. The board has voted eight to one to accept your proposal. I'll have legal promptly review your preliminary agreement so we can move forward on this."

"Thank you, sir. My team and I look forward to working with you." He handed him the paperwork and quickly turned and left the office, flawlessly executing another trick of the salesman's trade: close the deal and promptly leave the room before buyer's remorse can set in and he has a chance to change his mind.

He was in the back of his chauffeur-driven car when he dialed Lyman's number.

"So, how did it go?" Lyman asked.

"It's a done deal. They don't call me the closer for nothing."

"Barry, this one needs to be done by the book. The referral came down from the director himself, and we can't have any problems."

"What book are you talking about?"

"This needs to be legit. Not one of your bogus deals."

"Ly, you know better than that. All my deals are legit."

"Come on now, Barry, it's me you're talking to. I'm fully aware of how you operate. You type a few details into a template, call it a carbon reduction plan, and sell the client credits that may or may not exist."

Filmore glanced up at his driver and lowered his voice. "You know damn well I may fudge the numbers on the genuine carbon credits, but my program is foolproof. All my deals are verified through my guy at the GreenThumb Foundation. I haven't had a problem yet."

"I'm being real here. These are serious people. If you're not capable of doing this one the right way, you need to pass on the deal."

"Are you crazy? We're talking about a seven-figure fee and a substantial commission for you."

"You can keep my commission. I don't want my name anywhere near this."

"What aren't you telling me about these guys?"

"Nothing I haven't already told you. If you're going forward, you best keep that perfect record of yours intact. I'll put it like this. People who play fast and dirty have significant investments with this company. If anything goes wrong, it could get dangerous, and I won't be able to provide you with cover."

Kari Baldwin was in her office, dressed in one of her signature pantsuits with matching high-top sneakers, when Cindy Seravisi buzzed her on the intercom. "Ms. Baldwin, your ten o'clock appointment is here."

"Let her know I'll be out shortly."

The appointment had been scheduled with the US Secretary of Education a week ago at the secretary's request. When Cindy had inquired about the matter to be discussed, she was informed that everything would be revealed during the meeting. Kari had met the secretary on a few occasions but, in her typical fashion, waited five minutes before she left her office and walked out to the reception area.

Upon arrival, she was surprised to see two women seated next to each other, neither of which was the secretary. An older woman sat next to another who was considerably younger. Kari waited for one of them to speak. The older woman stood, and Kari took her in. She was attractive and well-coiffed, perhaps in her late forties. Her expensively cut auburn hair touched her shoulders, and the tailored skirt of her custom suit accentuated shapely legs, clearly the result of daily workouts. She took a few steps toward Kari and smiled, extending her right hand. "Good morning, I'm Wolinka Wivell, chief of staff to the education secretary."

She found the woman's smile warm and disarming. "Kari Baldwin," she replied, accepting the hand and shaking it firmly while maintaining eye contact.

"Please, call me Linka." She turned and waited for the younger woman to stand. "This is my assistant, Yvonne Tucker."

"Nice to meet you, ma'am," the young woman said.

"Same here," Kari replied before directing her attention back to Linka. "Please follow me. We can meet in my office."

"Wait here, Yvonne," Linka directed.

"Yes, ma'am."

Kari led her to the section of the office that was set up as a conference room and directed her to a chair at one end of the table before taking a seat directly opposite.

"How was your trip up from DC?" she asked in as sincere a voice as she could muster.

"Fine. We left early this morning and took the train into Bridgeport. We're headed right back as soon as we're finished here."

"Can I have my assistant get you anything?"

"No. We had breakfast on the train."

"I was surprised by the secretary's absence. It was my understanding when the meeting was scheduled that she would be here."

Linka straightened herself in her seat and reproduced her warm smile. "The secretary sends her regards and regrets she was unable to attend today. That was originally the plan, but a last-minute cabinet meeting was called, so she sent me."

"I see. To what do I owe the privilege of a visit from the department?"

"I'll get right to the point. Consider this a preliminary introduction to discuss a high-priority matter for the department. As you are aware, we are strong advocates for the public education system as well as the teachers' unions. Our department maintains detailed statistics on every school district, a report card if you will, and the recent trend toward state legislative-mandated school choice is of great concern. Many districts are reducing the number of teaching and administrative positions to conform with shrinking budgets."

Kari nodded in agreement. "I share those concerns. School choice, charter schools, and private education are serious threats. It's essentially a movement to defund public education."

"That's why we called this meeting. The administration, from the president on down, feels there needs to be a change at the top of the national union leadership. Your district is now the third largest in the nation, after Los Angeles and Miami. While we appreciate the unions' support, we simply don't feel current leadership is effectively providing a good return on our sizeable investment. The administration is impressed with the job you've done and wants to gauge your interest in moving into a leadership role at the national level."

She raised her eyes to the ceiling and sat silently in thought, taking in what she had just heard. She then leaned forward and folded her hands on the table until Linka's body language conformed. "May I speak frankly and in confidence?"

"Of course. I'm sitting in for the secretary, so anything we discuss is confidential, and she will be fully briefed on our meeting."

"Very well. I'm sure you're aware of the arrangements I have with Washington."

"Yes."

"And that I have similar consulting deals at the state and local levels, all of which must continue."

"I understand, and we support the continuation of those relationships. In fact, the administration would like to see those deals extended to all the major districts nationwide, and you would benefit personally as the leader of the movement. With the right personnel in place, we would be in a position to increase our investment, but naturally, we're looking for something more in exchange."

"And what is that?"

"In addition to stemming the decline in public school enrollment, we want to roll out a new state-of-the-art recruitment program to hire and train teachers who share our worldview and will promote our national curriculum blueprint."

"Can you provide more specifics?"

"I can speak in general terms. We're looking for someone to oversee an increase in the recruitment of teacher membership that conforms to promoting our agenda. We've had great success at the post-secondary university level and believe we can accelerate our program more effectively if we reach students earlier during their formative K through twelve years."

"I see."

"Is this something you are interested in?"

She maintained a stoic comportment and locked eyes with Wolinka. "It's something I'm willing to consider, but there's much to think about."

Wolinka paused for a moment, appearing to be deep in thought. "I'm also authorized to mention that the position comes with a premier benefits package, including membership in the coterie. Are you familiar with that?" she asked in a hushed tone.

"I've heard of it."

"Here's what I'm going to do. I'll report back to the secretary that you are interested in our proposal, and we'll be in touch to discuss further details and chart a path to move forward." She stood and extended her hand across the table. "It was nice meeting you. I can find my way out, and we'll talk soon."

Kari felt a warmth permeate her body at the softness of the touch of her hand. "I look forward to seeing you again." She watched with pleasure as Wolinka gracefully traversed the considerable square footage of her office on the way out.

# CHAPTER THIRTY-SEVEN

THE EARLY MORNING SUN CREPT above the horizon as Dylan and Penel drove along the narrow two-lane road. She was staring out the window. "It sure is quiet out here. I can't remember the last time we saw another car."

"Not since we were on 44, and even then, we only passed a few trucks," he replied. Ten minutes later, he slowed the SUV as they reached the entrance to the Circle T Ranch. A large sign set high above the open gate announced the name. Cedar split-rail fencing enclosed the vast acreage that ran along the roadway.

Penel looked at him with amusement. "Come on, Dylan, really? Circle T? Couldn't you come up with something more original?"

He pulled onto the property and glanced over at her as he proceeded along the paved driveway. "What are you talking about?"

"Circle T. As in Tomassi."

He laughed. "That went right over my head. I never even thought about it. Circle T was the name of the ranch when I bought it. Besides, I've heard it's bad luck to change the name of a property."

"I thought it was bad luck to change the name of a boat."

"That too."

The driveway ended at a large single-level house with a parking lot in front. Next to the home was a separate garage with four oversized rollaway doors. He parked the SUV next to a pair of pickup trucks and knocked on the front door. A rugged-looking guy with a well-trimmed beard who could have passed for the Marlboro man's stunt double answered.

"Good morning. I'm looking for Buck Larson."

The man stepped outside. "I'm Buck. You must be Dylan," he replied, extending a beefy paw. "It's a pleasure to meet you, sir."

He shook the man's hand and turned toward Penel. "This is my friend, Penelope Stanhill. Thank you for allowing us to visit."

He extended his arms and belched out a deep, throaty guffaw. "Come on now, Boss, this is your land. We're grateful for the opportunity to work it. You folks are welcome here anytime."

Dylan shot a quick glance at Penel, who cast her eyes downward. "Thank you. We appreciate the hospitality," he replied.

"Have you folks had breakfast?"

"We had coffee and a snack on the ride over."

He reproduced the same laugh. "You call that breakfast? That's okay. You can save your appetite for dinner. We have a real treat in store for you." Dylan snuck another look at Penel, who appeared to be staring at her boots. "How 'bout I show you around the property, and then we'll get you settled in the lodge?"

"Sounds good."

They stood by while Buck retrieved a Gator utility vehicle from the garage. The four-seat UTV (utility task vehicle) was finished in camouflage with a small bed in the rear. Another man followed behind him in a similar vehicle, except it was a two-seater with a much larger bed. "This here's Trevor. He's one of the ranch hands. He'll take your bags out to the lodge." Trevor was tall with broad shoulders and a weather-worn face. He tipped his hat but said nothing.

Dylan led him over to the SUV. "We just have these two bags," he said, handing them to the man from the back. Trevor secured them to the bed of his UTV and sped off down a trail that led behind the house.

"Saddle up," Buck announced. Dylan hopped in front while Penel climbed in the back and fastened her lap belt. "This here was the main house where the previous owners lived. I stay here now, but we also use it as our office."

"Do you get many visitors?" Penel asked.

He turned and looked back at her as he drove slowly behind the house. "We get buyers and vendors out here mainly, along with some hunters. The building at the back of the property was shuttered when we took over. I knew some guys who were interested in hunting, bigwig politicking types who are farming friendly, so we decided to re-open it as a hunting lodge. We formed a club of sorts. It's a close-knit group. We only allow new folks through word of mouth and only after another member vouches for them."

"What do they hunt?" Penel asked in a raised voice above the noise in the open-air UTV.

"Game, antelope, deer, and turkey mostly. The ranch hands will also hunt coyotes and prairie dogs if they pose a threat to the livestock."

Dylan was sitting sideways, holding onto the handle that secured the roof bar, and caught Penel scrunching her face. He smiled and shook his head as Buck slowly moved the vehicle along. "These are our two barns. We raised beef cattle and horses. Over yonder are the badland formations," he explained, indicating the direction of large rock formations jutting out of the hilly terrain. "The property sits not far from Badlands National Park."

"I've never seen anything like that," Dylan said. "How did they come about?"

"Mostly from different types of rocks slowly stacking up on each other from rivers and wind over millions of years. We have, or I should say you have, thirty-two thousand acres out here, and the land is quite diverse. There's forests, river valleys, and, of course, several grazing pastures. We utilize rotational grazing. By moving the herds around, it allows the pastures to rest and recover. We're going to head out toward the back of the property, so hang on," he said as he pushed the gas pedal to the floor.

The UTV bounced along the rugged landscape until they came to a tree-lined area. He slowed down and pulled the vehicle along a dirt path until they came upon a herd of cattle in a large grassy area surrounded by hardwood trees. "This is one of our grazing areas. We utilize the natural geography where we can. The fenced-in pens we passed are also for grazing."

He pulled up slowly, closer to the herd. "We cross-breed Akaushi bulls with Angus cows to produce the best beef. Cattle are born out in pasture from May to July, which minimizes stress for the cows and their calves. The calves stay with their mothers until they're between five and six hundred pounds. None of our cattle are ever administered hormones or antibiotics to enhance growth."

"How many are on the property?" Dylan asked.

"About six thousand at any one time."

"What about the horses?" Penel chimed in.

"We raise quarter horses. They have good cow sense, and we use them to manage the herds, but the majority we sell to rodeos and stables for recreational riding."

They continued along a dirt trail surrounded by thick forest until a large wooden structure appeared in an opening. "This is the lodge. Come on, I'll show you around."

The front entrance led to a large, spacious room. The floors, walls, and ceilings were all wood. Large windows on either side of a fireplace provided a view of Badlands. A masonry fireplace mantle ran up to the high ceiling. Animal trophy heads and skins were mounted along the walls. The room was furnished with a large assortment of leather couches and chairs, and a beautifully varnished wood bar was built into one side of the room. The space reminded Dylan of something out of an old-time men's club.

"Do any women ever use the lodge?" Penel asked.

Buck placed his hand on his chin and rubbed the bottom portion of his beard. "Not that I can recall. They're certainly welcome, but since we reopened, it's been all men to the best of my knowledge."

She shot Dylan a cold stare. They followed Buck into the gun room. A wall of shelving was filled with racks of rifles, compound bows, accessories, and hunting gear. Wooden benches were set up in the center of the space. Next, they walked through the dining room and into the kitchen. A butcher block island sat in the center, surrounded by stainless steel commercial ovens and appliances, including two large steak refrigerators filled with beef. "This is our commercial kitchen," he explained. "All the steaks are sourced from our own livestock. We have a chef who comes out when we have guests. He'll be here around noon to prepare dinner, but if you're hungry in the meantime, just ask, and he can rustle up something to hold you over."

They exited and continued along past the dining room and a small glass-enclosed cigar room before walking down a hallway to the bedrooms. "These are the sleeping quarters. There are six suites, each with its own bathroom. We put you up in the largest one." He pointed it out, and their suitcases were sitting on folding luggage racks next to a closet.

After leaving the lodge, Buck spent the next hour showing them every corner of the property, pointing out details along the way. He stopped on a hill above a roaring river. "That's pretty much everything there is to see," he said. "Do you think you're comfortable finding your way around on your own?"

Dylan looked at Penel. "I think we'll manage. Penel has been copiloting us across the country. This should be an easy day for her."

"Cool beans. Then I'm going to take you over to the horse stables and get you situated for riding. When you're done, take the UTV back to the lodge and get settled. I'll meet you for drinks in the bar at five thirty if that works for you all?"

"That will be fine," Dylan responded.

Buck nodded. "Some folks prefer to eat later, but around here, we work hard all day, eat dinner early, go to bed and rise early."

Dylan sensed Penel's excitement as they arrived at the horse barn. Buck led them into a section of stalls where a stable hand was equipping two of the horses. He approached a brown horse and petted its mane before moving his hand along the animal's body and patting its hindquarters. "This here is Autumn. She's a five-year-old mare. You're rather tall, Penelope, so she'll be a good fit for you."

Penel approached the horse confidently and spent a few minutes caressing her while she got acquainted. Buck took Dylan over to a black stallion. "Have you ever ridden before?"

"No. This will be my first time."

"This here is Jay. He's a nine-year-old gelding. Excellent temperament and a good horse for a beginning rider." He handed Dylan and Penel riding helmets, looking over Dylan before giving Penel a once over. "You're well dressed for riding," he said to Penel, who was layered in a turtleneck, sweater, and low-cropped leather jacket. Blue jeans and boots completed her ensemble. He turned to Dylan, who was wearing jeans and work boots. "What size shoe do you wear?"

"Eleven."

"I could lend you a pair of riding boots if you prefer."

"I'm comfortable in these, thanks."

"Suit yourself," he replied as he led Jay outside by the bridle. The ranch hand followed behind with Autumn.

Once outside the stable, the hand turned the reins over to Penel, and Dylan observed as she impressively mounted the mare, placing her foot in the stirrup, pulling herself up into a standing position and then smoothly gliding her other leg over the horse before gently landing in the saddle. She leaned over and caressed the horse again, speaking to her in a soft voice.

"Your turn, Dylan," Buck said, handing him the reins. "You'll want to relax as much as possible. Horses are sensitive to a rider who appears unsure of himself. Repeat what Penelope did; place your left foot in the stirrup and pull yourself over the top of the horse in a standing position while you slide your right foot into the other stirrup. Then slowly seat yourself in the saddle, relaxing your muscles as much as possible."

He glanced over at Penel, who was walking her horse in small circles before she pulled the reins firmly, stopping the horse in a position that faced him, a look of amusement on her face. Dylan clumsily attempted to slide his foot into the stirrup while lunging for the saddle horn, and his weight caused him to fall back to his left. He awkwardly landed on the ground and instantly tried again, this time facing directly toward the saddle. The horse began to stir and let out a whine as its hindleg swung forward and just missed catching Dylan in the right thigh with its hoof.

"Hold the mount," Buck yelled to the ranch hand. He ran into the stable and came back with a small footstool. "Try this," he said, placing it on the side of the horse. Dylan managed to land in the saddle. "Now take hold of the reins and pull them firmly," Buck instructed. He looked over at Penel. "How often have you ridden?"

"Quite a bit as a child, but I haven't been on a horse in probably twenty-five years."

"You certainly look right at home. Do you think you can help Dylan out?"

"I think I can manage that." She turned toward him. "Sit tall and relaxed in the saddle, follow behind me, and do what I do."

He watched as she pulled the reins to her right before loosening them. She then squeezed the animal with her legs, and it began to walk. He duplicated her movements, but his horse remained motionless. "He won't move."

"Give him a few soft kicks with your heels."

Dylan did so, and the horse began to walk. "Hold the reins loosely and try and move in rhythm with the horse's gait."

They walked slowly for a while. "Isn't it beautiful out here?" she asked.

"I wish I could enjoy the scenery, but I'm extremely nervous up here."

"You're doing fine. Remember to relax. Next, we're going to move into a trot. It's the same as getting the horse to walk. Try squeezing its midsection with your legs. Once you get moving, rise slightly out of the saddle and bounce gently in rhythm, but remember to look ahead between the horse's ears. If you need to slow down or stop, pull in a gradual motion evenly on both sides of the reins."

They had been riding for about an hour when they came upon a wooded area. "Do you think you're ready to step it up, cowboy?"

"Ready as I'll ever be."

"We came through this trail with Buck. It runs through the forest. Let's take it up a notch. It's the same procedure as before. After they go into a trot, squeeze the horse again with your legs and stay balanced in the center of the saddle. Think of the reins as brakes on a car if you need to slow down."

Dylan was following behind her at a good pace when they came upon some tree branches hanging across the trail at about eight feet. He watched as Penel and her horse lowered their heads in unison as they passed under. He dropped his head just in time as his horse dropped its head without slowing down. "Shit," he yelled as he pulled on the reins, and his horse came to a sudden stop. Penel stopped and turned back. "What's wrong?"

"I almost got decapitated by those branches."

"You have to stay as low as the horse's head. He knows what clearance is required for him, but he doesn't factor in his rider."

"You tell me that now."

"Do you want to stop and give the horses a break for a while?"

"No. If I get off, I'm not sure I'll be able to get back on out here."

She laughed. "You're doing fine. But it is cute to see you vulnerable for a change. You're always so sure of yourself. It's good to get out of your comfort zone once in a while."

"Oh, I'm definitely out of my comfort zone."

They rode along at a good clip until they came upon a creek, and Penel slowed down. "Can we cross here?" he asked.

"We'll let the horses decide. They know how to handle water." Penel went first, and her horse led her through a shallow area where there were no rocks. She stopped and watched as Dylan's horse entered the water. Suddenly, it stopped halfway across and dropped its hind legs, allowing its back half to submerge in the water. "Oh, shit!" he yelled again.

"Grab onto the saddle horn and lean forward," she instructed. He did so, holding on for dear life until his horse stood straight up on all four legs, shook out its coat, and crossed to the other side.

Penel was laughing hysterically. "I so wish I had a video of that."

Catching his breath, "I'm so glad you don't. I think I've had enough riding for one day. Are you ready to head back?"

"I guess so. It's a good ways back to the stable."

They were showered and dressed in their room at the lodge when Penel came up from behind and put her arms around him, kissing his neck. "How are you feeling?"

"I don't think my butt has ever been this sore."

"I'll be happy to massage it along with other parts of your anatomy," she whispered as she continued to work her way up to his lips, kissing him passionately on the mouth.

"Whoa, it's almost time for dinner. We're gonna have to wait until tonight," he said, battling the urge of the sensation stirring in his loins.

She faced him and utilized her hands to work her way down his body. "All that riding has made me incredibly horny."

"Lie down on the bed," he commanded, finally relenting. She was on her back with her legs hanging over the side. He got down on his knees and worked his way up, lifting her dress to find she was not wearing underwear. "You are a very bad girl."

"I told you I was horny," she panted.

"Let's take care of that," he breathed as he went to work gratifying her desires.

# CHAPTER THIRTY-EIGHT

When Dylan and Penel came out for dinner, they found Buck seated at the bar with a drink in his hand. He appeared recently scrubbed, his hair slicked back, wearing freshly pressed jeans and a western-style jacket with fringes across the chest and down the sleeves. "Good evening," he said. "How did you enjoy riding?"

"It was wonderful," Penel replied. "It reminded me of my childhood."

"I watched you. You're a natural, the way you sit up high in the saddle and move gracefully with the horse."

She tilted her head slightly and smiled. "Thank you, Buck. I guess it's like riding a bike."

"How did you find it, Dylan?"

"I survived, but I think my sore butt will remind me of the experience for some time."

He laughed heartily. "Nothing a couple of drinks won't soothe. What's your pleasure?"

"What's the house specialty?"

"We're mostly bourbon drinkers around here, but we have a respectable American wine collection. I picked out a few bottles of Monticello cabernet for dinner. I'm drinking Maker's Mark," he indicated with a raised glass.

"I'll have one of those," Dylan said. "I've been drinking that since we came out west, and I've become quite fond of it."

"How about you, Penelope?" he asked as he stood and made his way behind the bar.

"If you'll open a bottle of the wine now, I'll stick with that."

"Sure thing, darling." He opened one of the bottles and let it breathe while he served Dylan's drink. He then poured a small sample into a wine glass and handed it to Penel. "It's a 2019 Estate cabernet. Tell me what you think?"

She swirled the glass and then held it to her nose, breathing in the aroma before taking a sip. "It's wonderful."

He filled her glass and lifted his own drink. "Thank you for visiting and for all you do to support cattle ranching. My partners and I appreciate the opportunity to be in business with you."

"You've been a great business partner and a gracious host. Thank you again for having us."

They all clinked glasses and indulged in their drinks. A man appeared from the kitchen in a white chef's jacket and houndstooth pants, holding a platter of thinly sliced raw meat resting in a bed of garnishes. Buck made the introduction. "This is Chef Randall."

"Good evening, Mr. Tomassi. It's a pleasure to serve you and your guest this evening."

"Thank you, Chef. Please, call me Dylan. This is my friend, Penelope."

"Nice to meet you, ma'am. Tonight, for dinner, I will be serving the steak of your choice, broiled to order. For sides, we have Parmesan truffle fries; maitake mushrooms with garlic and cognac; grilled twice-baked potatoes with bacon, garlic, and herbs; and roasted corn with piquillo butter. I've brought you out an appetizer of steak tartare with arugula, pickled onions, Parmesan, and truffle oil," he concluded, placing the tray on the bar.

"Thank you, Chef," Buck said.

"What type of beef would you all like for dinner? I recommend the dry-aged cowboy. It's a twenty-ounce bone-in Wagyu ribeye, sourced from our own ranch and aged forty-five days." He looked in Penel's direction. "Ma'am?"

"That sounds good to me. Thank you, Chef."

"Mr. Tomassi?"

"I'll have the same."

"Make it three," Buck chimed in.

"Very well. Enjoy the tartare, and I'll serve a Caesar salad in the dining room shortly." He nodded and made his way back in the direction of the kitchen.

"That's quite a meal he's preparing," Penel commented. "I'm famished."

Dylan looked at her. "Me too. I just realized we haven't eaten all day."

"Then you'll all be good and hungry," Buck said, finishing the last of his drink and pouring himself another. "Can I get anyone else a refill?"

"I'll have a little more wine."

Dylan was feeling the effects of the drink on his empty stomach. "I'm good for now."

He poured Penel another healthy glass, and she took a sip. "So, Buck, is there a Mrs. Buck?"

He laughed heartily. "No, ma'am. Running this place takes up all my time, and there's not much chance to meet young ladies out here."

"I'm surprised some woman hasn't snatched you up. You're a real man's man and quite the catch. That's hard to find these days."

Dylan studied her face and noticed she was flushed. *The wine must have gone straight to her head, and now it's talking.*

"Thanks for the kind words," he replied with a wide grin.

"That's a high compliment coming from Penel. She's a divorce attorney and uniquely qualified to evaluate us menfolk," Dylan chimed in.

Penel burst out laughing. "Hah. Menfolk? I never heard you use that word before."

Dylan felt a surge of heat across his forehead. "So, Buck, how is the ranching business these days?" attempting to redirect the conversation.

He took a deliberate sip of his drink. "It's hard work but a true labor of love. Battling the forces of nature comes with the territory, but I've learned a lot about the business and politics sides I wasn't aware of until I started running the place myself."

"How so?"

"Our industry is under tremendous pressure from the climate crowd. We're a popular target, the whole 'eat-less-meat-and-save-the-environment' thing." He took a thoughtful sip of his drink. "It's a bunch of bull cocky. Excuse my language, Miss Penelope."

"I've heard people say that about cow farts," she commented, faintly slurring her speech.

"And many of the people leading those attacks fly around in private jets. That's one of the reasons we reopened the lodge. A lot of our members are politicians and lobbyist types who fight for our industry, and they're working to expose the flaws in the climate crowd's messaging." He paused to empty his glass before placing it down on the varnished bar top with a thud. "There's people out there saying we're worse offenders than cars, that half the global emissions come from raising livestock. But the studies they rely on are flawed, just like when they go after the automobile industry, then they change the rules against them."

Dylan placed his hand under his chin and narrowed his eyes. "What do you mean by changing the rules?"

"Here's what's wrong. The unfavorable studies they use against cattle are dishonest. They don't just count cow farts," he said, glancing at Penel. "They add in anything even remotely associated with meat production like feed farming, fertilizer manufacturing, ranch equipment, and meat production facilities. But when they compare us to cars, all they count are tailpipe emissions. They leave out things like manufacturing parts and materials, vehicle assembly, gasoline production, tire wear, and maintaining roads. It's hardly an apples-to-apples comparison. And the nuts-and-berries crowd completely ignore legitimate studies like the one done by our own government that found animal agriculture produces less than four percent of greenhouse gas emissions."

Penel giggled. "I take it you've never been to California."

He pounded his fist on the table, catching himself just in time to diminish the blow. "If those communists had their way, meat would be outlawed." He took a deep breath. "Sorry, folks. This nonsense gets me fired up, but it's a real threat to our way of life out here."

Dylan was rapt. "How do you know so much about this stuff?"

He took a deep breath. "I initially started talking with the guys I hunt with out here 'cause it affects our livelihoods. But then I started studying the subject on my own. I read a lot from people like Dr. Judith Curry and Bjorn Lomborg. And I pay no attention to those unqualified clowns always hollering climate doom and gloom for personal gain, like that former vice president or the little lady from Europe, or God forbid, that charlatan, Barry Filmore."

Dylan almost came off his stool. "Barry Filmore?"

Buck looked at him. "You know the man?"

"I've met him." He briefly explained their interaction.

"So what did you do?"

"I sent him packing, in so many words."

He let out a holler and slapped him on the shoulder. "Good for you. You're my kinda guy. You and your friends are welcome here anytime. If you ever want to go hunting, just let me know."

"Thank you, Buck."

The chef approached. "If you all are ready to move to the dining room, I'll serve the salad now." He grabbed the wine bottles and led them to the table. Three full settings were placed at one end. They were seated, and the chef prepared the Caesar salad table side before filling their wine glasses. "How would you like your steaks prepared?"

"Medium rare, please, with a pink center," Penel answered. The two men nodded in agreement.

"Very well. I'll put those on, and dinner will be served shortly."

During dinner, the conversation was light, with Buck providing entertaining stories of life on the ranch. As they were finishing dinner, he continued. "One time, Trevor got so drunk after a cattle drive we found him asleep in the morning with his arm around one of the calves. One of the guys snapped a picture of the happy couple, and we had T-shirts made up that said 'Cowboys ain't easy to love and they're harder to hold.'"

"Buck, you are *sooo* funny!" Penel roared with laughter, her body writhing in spasms that caused her to barely remain in her chair.

Dylan gave her a sideways glance. "That's a line from the song 'Mammas, Don't Let Your Babies Grow Up to Be Cowboys'."

"I know that," she replied, her eyes welling up with tears of merriment.

Buck looked on with amusement. "Looks like we're about finished here. Chef Randall will clear the dishes. Come with me. I want to show you something."

He led them into the cigar room. It was furnished with burgundy leather couches and chairs surrounding a large oak table. A liquor cabinet was built into one wall, which displayed an assortment of dessert wines, cognacs, and other cordials. Adjacent to the cabinet was a glass humidor filled with cigars. A large ventilation system was installed in the center of the coiffured wood ceiling. Several smaller trophy heads were mounted along the walls.

"Please sit down. We'll have dessert served in here. Can I get anyone an after-dinner drink?"

"What do you have in a port?" Dylan inquired.

Buck went over to the cabinets and looked around. "We have a Graham's Reserve and a Yalumba twenty-one-year-old Tawny. Either one will go well with our dessert."

"I'll have a glass of the Yalumba," Dylan said.

"Me too, please." Penel chimed in.

Buck served the drinks as Chef Randall brought in a tray of confections and placed them on the table, along with sets of silverware and cloth napkins. "Tonight, for dessert, I'm serving a flourless chocolate torte with mixed berries. Please enjoy," he concluded as he exited the room.

The group was finishing off dessert when Buck stood. "If you don't mind, I'm going to enjoy a cigar. Would anyone like to join me?"

Dylan was feeling good, having consumed the right mix of beef, wine, and dessert. "I'll pass on the cigar, but you go ahead. I'll finish the rest of my port."

"How about you, Penel?"

"Sure, put me down for a stogie and another glass of port."

Buck stood and made his way over to the humidor. He pressed a button on the wall, and the overhead ventilation system came to life. He returned with two cigars and a sterling silver lighter. He handed one to Penel, who placed it in her mouth. He lit it for her while she puffed and rotated the cigar until the end burned a brilliant orange. Dylan narrowed his eyes and glared in her direction. "What?" she proclaimed in a tone of forced innocence.

"Nothing, nothing at all," he replied, shaking his head, an amused smile on his face.

"Not a cigar smoker, Dylan?" Buck chimed in.

"No. I can honestly say I'm not."

"Your friend Penel seems a bit more adventurous."

Both men looked over at her simultaneously. Dylan observed as her complexion began to take on a greenish-pink hew. "I think the room's starting to spin," she grumbled as she leaned forward and placed her cigar in the ashtray set before her.

"Who saw this coming?" Dylan mumbled under his breath. "I think it's time for us to call it a night."

"I don't feel too good," she complained as she stood unsteadily on her feet and clutched her belly.

"Come on. Let's get you to bed," Dylan said as he steadied her. "Buck, thanks again for a wonderful everything. Sorry to cut it short, but as you can see, Penel is not feeling well."

He stood and managed to curtail a delightful smile. "Understood. It was my pleasure. Enjoy the rest of your evening."

"Bye-bye, Bucky," she slurred. "You're such a good guy. Thanks for everything."

"You can thank him by not throwing up in his lodge," Dylan whispered in her ear.

"I think I can make it to the bathroom."

Dylan led her back to their room, carrying her the last several steps. He got her situated in the bathroom. "Thank you, Dylan. You're a good guy too. I don't think I should have smoked that cigar."

"Really?" he remarked with a roll of his eyes as he gently closed the door behind him.

# CHAPTER THIRTY-NINE

Alex and Fanci were driving over the Howard Frankland Bridge toward St. Petersburg. "Where are we staying?" she asked.

"My friend Dylan has a guest house at his waterfront estate. There's a pool and a private beach. He also has a boat and WaveRunners if you're up for going out on the water."

"Really," she said with a raised eyebrow. "Am I finally going to meet him?"

"No, unfortunately, he's out of town. The good news is we have the place to ourselves," he replied with a smile.

"How long have the two of you known each other?"

He glanced over at her. "Since we were kids."

"And you've remained friends all this time?"

"Yes. Through college, my marriage and divorce, and living twelve hundred miles apart at times."

"That's pretty impressive," she commented. "A person's lucky to have one good friend in their life like that."

"What about you?" he asked.

"What about me?"

"Do you have a best friend?"

"I do. My mother. We're extremely close. She raised me as a single mom and worked two jobs at a junior high school to support us."

Alex stared thoughtfully ahead as he weaved his way through traffic on Interstate 275. "You know, you and Dylan have a lot in common. It's too bad you won't get to meet him on this trip."

"Oh. How's that?"

He looked over at her again. "For starters, you were both raised by single mothers. Was your mom a teacher?"

"Hardly," she snickered. "She worked in the cafeteria during the day and was a custodian at night."

"Dylan's mom taught at the school where you and I met, and he got to attend there as a benefit of his mother's position. Otherwise, they never would have been able to afford it. He grew up poor and has been working as long as I've known him. He had a paper route as a kid that he kept right up until he left for college."

"Hmm," she mumbled as she turned and stared out the window.

They drove in silence for a while until they exited the highway. "Is everything okay?" Alex asked.

"Yeah, why?"

"You've hardly said a word since we got off the bridge."

"I was just thinking about what you told me about Dylan. How did he make all his money?"

"After college, he moved down here and worked for a brokerage house for a few years before he struck out on his own. He started several businesses and became an old-fashioned, self-made American success story. He bought houses for his mother and grandparents, and he started a foundation to help underprivileged kids. He just opened a youth center right around here."

"Really?" she turned and looked at him, nudging his arm. "Can we stop by and see it?"

He narrowed his eyes. "Why do you want to do that with all the fun we have waiting for us at the house?"

"Just curious, that's all," she replied with a grin.

"Sure, why not," he shrugged.

He made a couple of turns and drove by Tropicana Field, home of the Tampa Bay Rays baseball team. He proceeded down the road until he came to a large property enclosed by a high landscaped wall, pulled up to the guard house, and rolled down his window. A security officer emerged and leaned over to peer into their car. "How may I help you, sir?"

"I'm Alex Malloy. I'm a Tomassi Foundation board member."

"Do you have some identification?"

"Sure," he replied, digging into his wallet and producing his driver's license.

The guard retreated inside and typed into a computer before lifting the security gate arm and handing back the license. "Here you are, Mr. Malloy."

"Thank you, kind sir," he said with a grin. "You have a good day."

Alex pulled into a parking spot in front of the administration building. The lot was empty except for cars and a bus bearing the Tomassi Foundation name parked near the baseball field at the back of the property. The field buzzed with activity from a practice taking place.

They got out of the car and Alex tried the front doors, but they were locked. "I don't have a key, but this is the admin building. It houses offices, a cafeteria, and tutoring centers," he explained. He pointed to his left. "That building over there is the athletic center. It has basketball courts, a fitness center, and locker rooms." Fanci nodded approvingly.

They walked over to the baseball field and stood by, watching the practice. Alex recognized one of the coaches and moved closer to the fence. "Parker," he yelled out.

Parker Gough looked over. "It's me, Alex Malloy," he shouted with a wave as he moved toward the fence that surrounded the field.

Parker walked over in his direction, displaying a warm smile. "Alex, it's nice to see you again. What brings you out here?"

He turned and indicated to Fanci, putting his arm around her as she reached the fence. "This is my friend Liz. She's visiting from up north, and I was just showing her around."

"Nice to meet you, Liz," he replied with a nod and a big smile.

"Same here," she said, batting her eyes.

"Are you coaching the baseball team?" Alex asked.

"Yeah, I volunteered to help. That's Evan and Junior. I'm helping them out."

Suddenly, Alex ran excitedly onto the field, leaving Parker and Fanci standing there in stunned silence.

"Coach Fedorko!" Alex yelled out. The old man slid his sunglasses down his nose and stared. "Take five," he told the players, who immediately began jogging toward the dugouts. Alex ran up and embraced him with a bear hug.

"Alex Malloy, how the hell are you?"

"I'm doing great, Coach. It's good to see you. Dylan told me you'd be helping out."

"You remember my son, Junior."

He shook his hand. "Of course."

"What brings you out here?"

He turned toward Fanci. "I was just showing my friend around the facility." He waived her over and made the introductions.

"Dylan and I played for Coach Fedorko back in the day," he explained.

The old man let out a hearty laugh. "As I recall, Dylan played, and you sat next to me on the bench. You always had a mind for the game. I figured you'd end up coaching someday."

Parker joined them, and the group engaged in small talk until Evan glanced over at the dugouts. "We need to get these boys back to work. It was nice seeing you, Alex, and a pleasure to meet you, young lady."

They all said their goodbyes, and Alex and Fanci got back in the car and headed to Dylan's.

"That was interesting. Thanks for stopping and showing me around," she said.

Alex looked over at her and smiled. "My pleasure. Now the fun part begins. Sun, surf, and the full Alex Malloy experience."

# CHAPTER FORTY

On Monday morning, Dylan was on the phone with Shirley, listening as she gave him a report on the status of the business and household activities. "I'm glad to hear everything is running smoothly. Any fallout from Alex's visit over the weekend?"

"No news is good news when it comes to Alex. I checked the guesthouse and didn't find any dead bodies, so that's positive. Honestly, it's like he was never here. Everything was neat and tidy. The bed was stripped, and all the dirty linens and towels were piled in the bathtub."

"That's good. Maybe the boy is maturing and found a nice girl to settle down with or at least to settle him down."

She laughed. "Let's not get carried away. Have you spoken with him?"

"Not since he asked about using the guest house."

"It's almost ten o'clock here. You have a Zoom meeting with Walt Jackman. I emailed you the link."

"Thanks. I got it."

"Any idea when you'll be coming back?"

"I'm playing it by ear. I haven't heard anything from the police on the investigations, and I'll get an update from Walt."

"He's contacted me a few times, and I sent them everything he asked for right away."

"Excellent. I need to log on for the meeting. Have a good week."

"You do the same, Dylan."

After the call disconnected, he looked at his phone screen. It read 7:59. He fired up his computer, logged into his email, and clicked on the link. Walt Jackman appeared, a solemn expression on his face.

"Good morning, Walt."

"Good morning, Dylan. How are things out there?"

"The temperatures are returning to normal, so it's a bit colder than I'm used to, but we're enjoying ourselves. I spent some time at the ranch property. It's quite impressive. Buck Larson is a good man, very hospitable, and a competent manager. I was impressed with his knowledge and forward-thinking ideas about the ranching business."

"They've never missed a rent payment, and that assessment bodes well for it to continue," Walt commented.

"What's going on with the audit?" Dylan asked.

"This is where we're at. Since you provided your statement, the service has buried us with document disclosure requests, and we've submitted everything in a timely fashion. I've maintained a firm, nonadversarial posture, but things are deteriorating on that front. I've demanded disclosure of evidence of any suspicious filings, and they've provided nothing. However, they've stopped short of admitting this is simply a verification audit."

"If that's the case, then why not push for a dismissal?"

"My read on that is the agent-in-charge has orders from above to continue his fishing expedition. I just received a formal offer of settlement." He read the number directly from the letter.

Dylan ran his hand through his hair. "That's a big number without any justification from what I'm hearing."

"I agree. It's unsupported by the findings and completely unreasonable. I've already made our position clear that we're prepared to litigate the case through the tax court. My recommendation is to go back with a counterdemand to the government for them to pay *you* double that amount to settle the claim, and, in the event it's not accepted, I'll make it clear that we'll pursue attorneys' fees, costs, and sanctions against them in court."

"Go ahead. You have my authority."

"All right. Dylan, I want to reiterate that while I believe we have a strong case nothing further is owed, recovering fees against the IRS in court is uncertain at best. You know the old saying about these audits. You could easily spend the amount of their settlement offer, or more, on attorneys' fees if this ends up in court."

"I understand. Is there anything else to discuss?"

"Yes. I received a report from our investigator. I can send you a copy, but to summarize, he hasn't been able to come up with much. He's spoken to the business owners on the trail near the location of the attack and canvassed the area for about a week, talking with people who use the trail regularly. No one claims be familiar with two men fitting the description of the assailants."

"I see."

"He also investigated the scene of the vehicle shooting. The gas station across the street has a surveillance camera that covers the intersection. They told our guy the police have a copy of the video that captured the incident. He asked for one, and the owner told him he would need to get a court order. The police won't share any information because there's an ongoing investigation. I can have him continue, or I can pull him off the assignment."

"Go ahead and terminate him. I don't see what else he can do."

After he ended the call, Dylan stood and paced the room. He was thinking about what Walt had told him when he heard Penel stirring. She approached from behind, putting her arms around his shoulders and kissing him on the cheek. "Good morning. What's on the agenda for today?"

He chuckled. "You always make me feel better. I've been reading a biography on Teddy Roosevelt. He spent a lot of time up in North Dakota. I thought we would head up there and check it out."

"Sounds good to me. It's beautiful around here, but I feel like we've seen and done everything there is to do."

"Agreed. I already made a hotel reservation in Medora. We're staying at the Theodore Roosevelt Rough Riders Hotel."

"How far is it from here?"

"It's about a four-hour drive. If we get packed and head out by noon, we'll be there in time to check in and have dinner."

She held him tighter and continued to kiss his neck, working her hands down his body. "Perfect," she purred. "That gives us time to give the cabin a proper send-off."

He turned and stood, embracing her and kissing her on the mouth. "You ready to get back on that horse? All that wine and the cigar put you down for a few days."

"The cigar was a poor choice, but if you're the horse in that metaphor, it's time to saddle up. I'm ready to ride again." He took her by the hand and led her to the bedroom. She spent a few moments arousing him, then mounted and rode him passionately. He felicitously allowed her to take control. After they both collapsed in exhilarated exhaustion, she extracted herself and lay down beside him.

"That was nice," he exclaimed.

"That was my thank you for taking care of me when I went down with the stogie flu."

"You're welcome. And please know I'm highly motivated to take care of you anytime you find yourself under the weather."

Barry Filmore was finishing up work in his home office for the day. The contracts with the financial services company had been signed, sealed, and delivered, and he was reviewing the boilerplate assessment of their carbon credit requirements. His final task for the day involved emailing documents to their office along with invoices for his retainer and a separate deposit for procurement of the initial credits. The documents stated the credits would be purchased from a domestic paper companies' forest regeneration program.

The sun had recently set when Dylan maneuvered the Suburban down the two-lane road of the main drag in Medora. He spotted the hotel and pulled off onto the side street, locating a parking spot directly in front of the covered porch that served as the lobby entrance. They walked in together. The front desk was constructed of coffered dark wood, and there was a large open library off to the right. To the left was the entrance to the hotel restaurant. An adjacent staircase led to the second floor of rooms and suites.

Dylan stood back as Penel approached the young woman, who was dressed in a jeans skirt, plaid shirt, and cowboy boots. "Good evening, or should I say afternoon? I'm Penelope Stanhill. I have a reservation."

The woman clicked some keys on the keyboard before looking up with a broad smile. "Yes, Ms. Stanhill. Your assistant called yesterday. I spoke with him myself, and we have you booked in the Teddy Roosevelt suite."

Dylan was standing off to the side, wearing an impish smile, and he caught her eye as she turned and looked at him. "I understand that's the suite where President Roosevelt stayed," he interjected.

"Yes, sir. That's correct. The hotel has undergone a major renovation since that time, but back in 1885 when the hotel was known as the Metropolitan, President Roosevelt stayed in that room when he was in Medora, going back and forth between the ranches he owned in the Badlands. There's a small desk in the room, and it is believed that he sat at that very same desk to work on some of the books he wrote."

He smiled and nodded.

Penel completed the transaction with the corporate credit card. "Welcome again, Ms. Stanhill," the clerk replied, handing back her card and ID. "How many room keys do you need?"

"Two, please."

"Yes, ma'am," she replied, glancing in Dylan's direction. "Your suite is on the second floor at the end of the hallway. It's quicker to take the stairwell, but if you want to use the elevator, it's just past the library."

After they got to their room, Dylan stood in the doorway admiring the space. The small desk sat along the far edge of the room with a framed poster on the adjacent wall entitled *Theodore Roosevelt Stayed in This Room*. The poster included a picture of the original Rough Rider's Hotel. He looked it over. "How cool is this?"

"I admit, Dylan. I'm very impressed. It was a nice surprise. You would make an excellent personal assistant."

"Maybe so, but I would have to sue you for sexual harassment."

"I would have an absolute defense."

"What's that?"

"You exploited me as a teenager."

"That summer weekend we spent in the Hamptons? As I recall, you were in college, and I was still in high school. Plus, you invited me to your house and snuck into my room in the middle of the night."

She came over and put her arms around his neck. "Yeah, you're right. I would definitely lose that case."

"How about we put away our things and have dinner downstairs in the restaurant? I heard it's excellent."

"You really do your research. You would make a great assistant. It's a shame my exploiting you prevents me from pulling the trigger on the hire."

# CHAPTER FORTY-ONE

By the beginning of the following week, Dylan and Penel had fallen into another comfortable routine. Mornings were spent working remotely, which coincided nicely with the time zone difference back east. Afternoons were spent reading, hiking, and discovering the town, usually ending with dinner at Theodore's, the hotel restaurant. The food was excellent, the restaurant had a varied menu, and the bar was open late, so most nights, they ended up there.

Dylan was sitting at Teddy Roosevelt's old desk, wrapping up his morning work, when the burner phone rang. He looked at the screen. Esther.

After the usual pleasantries had been exchanged, she asked about Penel. He glanced around the room and saw her sitting some distance away in the bedroom with her computer across her lap. "She's doing wonderful. I don't think she's tired of me yet," he said in a raised voice that caused her to look over in his direction.

"If that's Esther, please pass on my regards and let her know I'm still tolerating you for the moment," she yelled back.

He smiled and waved in her direction before turning his chair back and resuming a normal phone voice volume. "Penel says hello and confirmed she's not quite ready to kick me to the curb just yet."

"It sounds like you two are getting along like an old married couple."

"I wouldn't quite put it that way."

"Anyway, what's going on with the matters responsible for your prolonged trip?"

He provided an update on the tax audit proceedings and the lack of progress from the private investigator. "I haven't heard anything from the police, and it's been over a month now. The truth is we're having a good time, so I'm in no hurry to come out of hiding and go home, but I'm also not going to run forever. I'll know when I'm ready to go back, and that's when I'll return."

"I think that's a healthy attitude."

"I've really enjoyed spending time in the heartland. The people are so genuine, and the scenery is beautiful everywhere we've been. It's so different from the east coast. I don't know if I would have ever come out here if it wasn't for the current situation back home."

"It sounds like the trip has served you well, and it's given you the opportunity to reunite with Penelope. She's a keeper."

"She says the same thing about you, and I wholeheartedly agree."

"Okay, this conversation is getting a bit too sentimental for me, so I'll bid you a good day. Be safe and stay in touch."

After he hung up, he went looking for Penel. "What would you like to do this afternoon?"

"We've been eating a little too well since we got here. How about we go for a nice long hike?"

"That sounds good. The weather is clear and sunny. Let's go back over to Theodore Roosevelt National Park. It's about a four-mile walk to the entrance, and the hilly terrain makes for a good workout."

Half an hour later, they were dressed and walking down Third Avenue toward the park when they came upon the tiniest church he had ever seen. The wooden sign out front read St. Mary's Catholic Church.

"Will you look at that? St. Mary's," Penel exclaimed. "Same name as your church and school in Connecticut. Stand in front, and I'll take a picture you can send to everyone back home."

He dutifully complied and stood in front of the small structure just off to the side of the sign while Penel gleefully clicked several photos with her phone.

They continued to the park and entered past the South Unit Visitor's Center. "Let's hike the Vien trail and then work our way to Boicourt," Dylan suggested as he consulted his map. "By then, the sun will be setting over the Badlands, and the view is supposed to be beautiful."

"How long are the trails?"

"Coal Vein is just under a mile, and Boicourt about a fifteen-minute walk to the overlook."

"How far is it between the two?"

"That I'm not sure."

"Are you trying to hurt me? My phone says we already walked five and a half miles," she replied with a frown.

"I thought you wanted a vigorous workout?"

"I do. I'm not a fitness fanatic like you, but I do a lot of walking in the city. The difference is the city streets are mostly flat. These hills are killing me."

"How about this? We hit those two trails and then dinner and drinks at Theodore's followed by a full-body massage."

"Now that sounds like an offer that's too good to pass up."

By the time they finished the first trail Penel was beginning to slow down, so Dylan got her seated on a large rock and handed her a bottle of water from his backpack. She accepted the water gratefully. "Ahh, it feels good to get off my feet."

"Take a break, but then we must hasten forward quickly if we want to catch the sunset and get back in time for dinner."

She looked at him with narrowed eyes. "Hasten forward quickly? What the heck does that mean?"

"When Teddy Roosevelt first arrived out here, in his tailored suits and weird eyeglasses with his Ivy League lexicon, he didn't fit in and wasn't well received by the locals. They originally made fun of him and called him four eyes because of the glasses. But he proved to be a tough and fearless frontiersman, and he eventually earned their respect. It probably didn't hurt that he owned several ranches and people realized he was a man of power and influence. Anyway, he didn't like foul language, and they continued to make fun of the way he spoke. On his first roundup, he told the other cowboys to 'hasten forward quickly.' The locals adopted it as a phrase in his honor, and it became a command to bartenders to hurry up with their drinks."

"Where did you come up with that?"

"It's in the biography I just finished reading."

"If Jack is working the bar tonight, you should drop that line on him and see what his reaction is."

"Do you think he'll know?"

"Wanna know what I think? He'll think you're being a pompous ass."

"Care to wager on that?"

"Why? You think he'll know it's a Teddy Roosevelt reference?"

"Yes, I do."

She flashed a libidinous smile. "What would you like to bet?"

"Exactly what you're thinking. Loser gives the winner that full-body massage."

"That's not fair. You already promised me that."

"You make a good point. I did promise, and I'm not one to go back on my word. How about we just call it a friendly wager?"

"Did Teddy say that too?"

"No, but he did say he didn't think he would ever have become president had he not come to North Dakota."

"Why did he come here?"

"He was a sophisticated New Yorker, like you. But then, after his first wife died, he left the city and came out here to get away and grieve. He was enamored with the cowboy lifestyle, and it's the reason he became a great conservationist."

She stood and stretched. "You are truly a wealth of information. And all this time I thought you were just another pretty face."

He smiled and took her by the hand. "Come on. If we don't hasten forward quickly, we'll miss the sunset view."

Fanci was working from Kari Baldwin's house in the late afternoon when Kari walked in the door. "Hello, dear. Please pour me a drink and get one for yourself. I need to speak with you."

Fanci prepared the drinks at the bar and brought them over to the living room couch where Kari had kicked off her tennis shoes and was leaning back with her feet up on the coffee table. Fanci set the two glasses of straight vodka on ice down and sat next to her. Kari repositioned herself and raised her glass, waiting for Fanci to pick up hers. She clinked glasses and took a healthy gulp. "Ahh, that's good. I have a meeting here on Friday night, and I want you with me. Because I'm a considerate person, I'm telling you in advance that the meeting's with Barry Filmore, and you need to be polite and accommodating. Is that understood?"

She bowed her head and gently murmured, "Yes, ma'am."

"Good. Now that we have that out of the way, you are to wear something sexy. We will have a lot to celebrate. Plan on spending the night. Are you hungry?"

"Not really."

"You don't eat much. I guess that's how you maintain that incredible figure of yours. I'm starving. Do you want to go out to eat or order in?"

"Whatever you decide."

She smiled and placed her hand on her upper thigh. "That's what I like about you, Fanci. You're very accommodating."

# CHAPTER FORTY-TWO

THE NEXT MORNING, PENEL WAS at Teddy's desk conducting a Zoom meeting with a client. Dylan was sitting on the bed, reading the *Wall Street Journal* on his iPad, when he came across an article entitled "Carbon Copy: How a Counterfeit Carbon Credits Scandal Threatens to Undermine the Battle Against Climate Change." He was reading with great interest when a name stopped him in his tracks: Barry Filmore. He was finishing the article just as his phone rang. The screen read Alex.

"Good morning, Dylan. How goes it?"

"Fine, Alex. What are you up to?"

"I'm back in my New York office. I apologize for not calling sooner, but I wanted to thank you for letting me use your guest house the other weekend. I can assure you a good time was had by all."

"Would your female guest concur with that statement?"

"Based on the sounds she was making and the way her body was shuddering in delight, I can say with confidence that she would."

"You do realize I'm talking about the weekend in general and not the time you spent in bed."

"I'm aware. Although I choose to emphasize the highlights, I would say she enjoyed the entire experience. I think she was particularly impressed with you."

"Me?" he replied with a raised eyebrow. "I find it hard to believe you spent a weekend alone with a woman and talked about anyone but yourself."

"That hurts," Alex said, his voice cracking in feigned disappointment. "You should know I spend at least half the time talking about a woman when I'm with her. Anyway, she was asking about you on the way to your house, and I took her by the youth center and gave her the nickel tour. Coach Fedorko was there with Junior and Parker, holding a baseball practice. What part of the country are you in these days?"

"We're in North Dakota at the moment."

"How's the weather? It's getting cold up here again, just when spring is right around the corner."

"It's colder than I'm used to, but we're getting along."

"If you wanted to hide out, why not just go someplace like Little Palm Island?"

"Where's that?"

"It's a secluded resort in the Florida Keys. The weather is perfect this time of the year, and it's super exclusive. Celebrities and the one percenters go there for peace and quiet where they're not bothered by the paparazzi or the unwashed masses. And there's no security issues. By the way, when are you going to come out of hiding and head home?"

"I'm not sure yet. Have you read the *Journal* today?"

"No. Why?"

He scrolled through the pages on his iPad. "There's an article about a carbon credit scandal that's just been exposed, and Barry Filmore is implicated. He's the so-called environmental activist who paid me a visit just before all the stuff started happening. Turns out the deals he brokers with companies to purchase carbon credits involve the legitimate purchase of only a small fraction of the actual credits he's selling. The rest, he just fabricates."

"How was he getting away with that?"

"According to the article, he recently submitted a proposal to a financial services company based on the net carbon footprint of their investment holdings. He then purchased a few legitimate credits from a forestry company, forged the rest, and pocketed the money. He uses the same verification company to audit his transactions and pays them off. It sounds like he would have never gotten caught, but an activist investor in the company dug into Filmore's business dealings and made the discovery. I'm sure that was the same scam he was trying to pull on me."

"That's crazy. If he is that corrupt, there's a good chance he was behind the things that happened to you after you blew him off. It sounds like he's now got bigger issues to concern himself with besides you."

Dylan stood up and began pacing the room in thought. "You're probably right. The article stated that the federal authorities have begun an investigation."

"Maybe it's safe to come home."

"I spoke with Esther about that the other day. I'm through running. I'm enjoying myself, and Penel hasn't gotten tired of me yet. I've decided that when the time feels right, I'll head home."

"That sounds like a good plan. I've got a meeting to attend. Please tell Penel I said hello, and we'll talk soon."

Barry Filmore placed a call to Lyman Scott. "Listen to me," Lyman started in before Filmore had a chance to speak. "I warned you, and you chose to ignore my advice."

"I take it you're referring to the article in the *Journal*."

"I told you before, the deal had better be legitimate, but you just couldn't help yourself. You're on your own now. Don't call me again." The phone went dead.

Filmore threw his phone in disgust. It bounced off his desk before hitting the floor. He bent over awkwardly and retrieved it to find he had shattered the glass facing. He peered through the distorted screen, found the number for his attorney, and hit Send. "Barry Filmore calling. Is he in?" he blurted to the receptionist who answered the phone at the New York Law Offices of Spencer Roth.

"Let me check for you, Mr. Filmore."

"Don't check, honey. Find him and get him on the line."

He heard a clicking sound, followed by elevator music. Filmore paced the floor of his home office until Spencer Roth, Esquire, came on the line. The bio on his website stated he specialized in white-collar criminal defense, but among his clients, it was well known that his true expertise involved strategic preemptive criminal activity detection avoidance.

"Have you heard?" Filmore asked.

"Yes."

"How bad is it?"

"I've just begun looking into the matter. The feds are now involved, and they've already turned several key players at the GreenThumb Foundation who are willing to testify. The feds want the big fish, and apparently, they see you as the white whale."

"What are you doing about it?"

"I'm working on seeing whether the witnesses can be bought or threatened, but you have another problem."

"What's that?" he asked as beads of perspiration formed on his considerable forehead.

"I've heard your client mentioned in the article is livid and could very well be a bigger threat to your liberty than the feds. I can arrange some extra security if you want."

"Nah, I'll handle that. You worry about the criminal charges, and let me know when you figure out a solution." He hit the End button and dropped his phone on the desk. He grabbed a bottle of Scotch from the credenza and poured a stiff drink. He drained the glass in one motion and refilled it while he thought about a temporary stress relief distraction to his problem. He was looking forward to another session with the submissive assistant who worked for Kari Baldwin, but that was four days away. Too long to wait. He texted the number of one of his local girls. "RU available for a full-body massage?"

He waited a few minutes while he finished off his second drink, then checked his phone. No reply. He texted another number. This time, the response was instantaneous. "Will be there in 15."

He called down to Max. "A young lady with a massage table will be here shortly. Please send her up to my bedroom. Also, call the security company and have them put a couple of men on me 24-7 until further notice, effective immediately."

"Yes, sir, boss."

# CHAPTER FORTY-THREE

Kari Baldwin had spent the night at the Hyatt Hotel at the National Mall and was in a cab for the short ride to the Lyndon B. Johnson Department of Education building for her meeting with the secretary. She arrived at the building shortly before her nine o'clock appointment and made her way up to the fifth floor. She was seated in the lobby when Wolinka Wivell appeared.

"Good morning, Kari, it's nice to see you again," she said with her familiar smile.

"Nice to see you as well."

"The secretary is ready for you. Please follow me." Wolinka led her to a large corner office with a view of the Capitol building in the background. The secretary was looking down at her computer and stood when they entered but made no effort to come around from behind her large executive desk. She appeared as Kari had recalled from their last interaction, with her signature short white hair and grandmotherly appearance in both looks and attire. "Good morning, Kari. It's so good to see you again."

Kari recalled she was somewhat aloof and had a reputation as a germaphobe. "Madam Secretary," she replied with a nod. "How are you?"

"I'm doing well, thank you for asking. My apologies for being unable to meet with you last week, but Linka has briefed me, and she'll be joining us this morning."

Kari sat in one of the two chairs in front of the desk, and Linka took the seat to her left. "How was your trip down from Connecticut?"

"Very comfortable. I prefer a private car on the train to flying."

"That's understandable, particularly when dealing with airports and commercial flights. And how was your stay at the Hyatt?"

"Fine, thanks."

"Excellent. Then let's get down to the matter at hand. First, I wish to commend you on the work you are doing with the school districts in the tristate area."

"Thank you."

"Your efforts have not gone unnoticed by the department, as Linka expressed last week, and we are pleased you're interested in discussing a union leadership position at the national level."

Kari took the opportunity to glance over at Linka, who had a small portable computer set up across her lap. Her skirt had hiked up, revealing a fair amount of leg. Kari fought the urge to stare and forced herself to redirect her focus on the secretary. "I appreciate the kind words, and as I expressed to Linka, I'm certainly willing to listen to your proposal."

"Good. Are you aware of your standing in our rankings metric?"

"It is my understanding that we are now the third largest school system in the nation by enrollment."

"That is correct. And it's particularly impressive considering all three of your states have a net outflow of population, including families with school-age children. You are also number one in the nation in per-student spending at twenty-nine thousand annually. Again, quite impressive. We've completed a deep vetting on you," she explained, producing a thick file, "and wish to offer you the soon-to-be-announced newly created position of National Teachers' Unions President. In short, the position would place you at the top of the chain of command over a newly united organization comprising the various unions that represent public school teachers and administrators across the country. One primary job description is to coordinate a standardized curriculum as developed by the DOE and oversee the recruitment and training of personnel with the appropriate backgrounds necessary to implement the program. You have also been successful in developing strategies to defeat the school choice movement, and that is an equally important objective. The unions have had varying degrees of success in this area across the country, and you would be responsible for duplicating your program on a national level."

She spent the next half hour discussing the position in more detail with little discourse from Kari. The department would use its influence and control of its purse strings to bring all teachers' unions across the country on board under one umbrella, including the powerful American Federation of Teachers and the National Education Association, with the common mission as dictated by the DOE under the governance of Kari Baldwin. The position included a generous benefits package and would allow her to continue and expand her extracurricular activities. Emboldened by the course of the meeting, she decided to inquire further.

"I do have some questions. First, there's a lot of discussion about the department being eliminated. Should that happen, where would that leave us?"

The secretary returned an icy stare, and Kari held her gaze until she relented with a tight-lipped smile that tilted the edges of her mouth upward. "I wouldn't concern myself with that. Reports of our demise have been greatly exaggerated," she replied bluntly. "In any event, we are prepared for all contingencies. Were such efforts to occur, we have set aside a war chest sufficient to wage a long-term court battle that will outlast those who wish to do us harm. We have also established a nonprofit organization that, at present, clandestinely operates parallel to the department. In the unlikely event of a shutdown, we are prepared to pivot and run a shadow nongovernmental organization by transferring our power, money, and influence to the NGO. Either way, we will continue with our business as usual."

Kari nodded admiringly. "I see." She glanced over at Wolinka before leaning forward and lowering her voice. "What can you tell me about a membership in the coterie? I've heard—"

"Please," the secretary interrupted, slapping the palm of her hand against the top of her desk. "Will you excuse us, Wolinka?"

"Yes, ma'am," she replied, shutting her laptop and quietly exiting the office and closing the door behind her.

Her icy stare once again was focused on Kari. "Now, what questions do you have that I have not already answered?"

She hesitated for a beat to maintain control of her breathing before forging ahead. "I understand one benefit of membership includes cover from any federal investigation, but you're asking me to oversee every organization in the country. What happens if some aggressive local law enforcement agency or state prosecutor delves into my affairs?"

She stared back at her with narrowed eyes. "I will say this. Membership does not come with an absolute 'get out of jail free' card. You have managed to conduct your business to this point without drawing scrutiny. That is another quality we admire. We expect you to continue to conduct your affairs in the same judicious manner as you have in the past. In the unlikely event of such an incident, we'll rely on our relationships across the country with key figures in law enforcement, politics, and the media, and we will tap those resources as necessary. In other cases, we have ways of, uh, attacking the root of the problem. A colleague who finds herself in such a situation may take a hit in the court of public opinion, but immunity is assured in order to efficiently carry out our objectives."

"I see."

The secretary stood. "I trust that answers your question." She stared at her again for an uncomfortable moment. "There is one other thing. Don't ever neglect your mission; this is a business of codes. Never violate the code. People occasionally have, and it never ended well for them. I share all this highly confidential information with the understanding you've agreed to accept the position. My office will set things in motion, and we'll be in touch. Good day, and safe travels back home."

"Thank you, Madam Secretary," Kari said as she stood and quickly exited the office.

An hour later, she was in her private car on the train back to Bridgeport. She thought about Fanci and dialed her cell number. "Where are you, sweetheart?" she asked when she picked up.

"I'm working remotely from your house."

"Perfect. I'm on the train and scheduled to arrive in Bridgeport by four thirty. I'll take an Uber to the house and should be home by five. I'm in the mood to celebrate."

"It's only Tuesday. I thought we were celebrating on Friday."

"Order sushi and make sure it's delivered by then," she commanded, ignoring her comment. "Also, take a bath and wear the schoolgirl outfit I bought you. Don't forget the knee socks, and make sure your hair is in pigtails."

"Yes, ma'am," she mumbled submissively.

That same morning, a meeting was wrapping up in the office of the CEO of a financial services company in midtown Manhattan. Among the select group present was the chief security officer. "That's all, gentlemen," the boss said, and the CSO headed back to his own office. He pulled out a flip phone from his desk drawer that was used for special assignments and dialed a familiar number. A man on the other end answered. "Yeah."

"I've got a job for you."

# CHAPTER FORTY-FOUR

THE FOLLOWING EVENING, AFTER ANOTHER delectable dinner at Theodore's, Dylan and Penel were lying in bed together, contentedly spent. Their clothes were strewn across the floor, and she rested her head on his chest. "That was nice," she commented.

"The dinner or the dessert?"

"Both. But I was specifically referring to the dessert," she replied, kissing him on the stomach before working her way up to his lips.

"Are you getting tired of eating at Theodore's?" he asked.

"Not at all. The food is great, and there's an excellent selection."

"We have tickets to *Hello, Dolly!* for tomorrow night at the Old Town Hall Theater, and after that, I'm thinking it may be time to move on. Is there any place else you'd like to visit?"

She sat up and snuggled next to him, taking his hand in hers. "Honestly? I've really enjoyed our adventure together, but I think it may be time for me to head back to New York."

He let out an involuntary chuckle. "Really?"

"Yeah." She glanced sideways at him. "What's so funny? We've been on the road for over a month."

"Nothing, just a reflex. In fact, I was thinking the same thing."

"What about your issues back home?"

"I've considered that. I spoke with my attorneys, and I'm satisfied, under the circumstances, with the progress of the audit. Things are running smoothly with the businesses since the issue with the feds shutting down my construction project was resolved, and, as far as the attacks go, I'm not going to let that dictate my life. I took this trip to spend time with you and get away from everything for a while, but it's time to head home and deal with whatever lies ahead."

"It sounds like you broke it all down and came to a rational decision."

"That's pretty much what Esther said when I ran it by her. I think she used the word *healthy*, though."

"Have you thought about travel plans to get home?"

"I've looked into it. Unfortunately, there's no airport within a hundred miles of here, and the closest ones are small. Bismark is a two-hour drive, and Delta has a connection to Minneapolis. We can fly back to our respective homes from there."

She started laughing hysterically. "How did we end up in Medora, North Dakota?"

"I promise you there was no grand plan."

"Don't get me wrong. It's beautiful and unspoiled. I'm glad we came. It's just so remote and a far cry from New York. Are you through flying private?"

"For now. It's nice, but we did it mainly so I could travel in relative anonymity. I'm over that."

"Does this mean I need to return Esther's credit cards?"

"Uh, yeah."

Barry Filmore was pleased with himself. He sat alone at a table in an intimate fine dining establishment in Pound Ridge enjoying his second drink and perusing the menu while he privately lauded his adroitness. His two security guards, both dressed in cheap dark suits with bulges in their jackets, were present. One sat at the bar drinking bottled water while the other waited outside, screening each person who entered the restaurant with an intimidating stare while simultaneously keeping an eye on the rental car used to transport Filmore around.

He utilized several different banks for his various business activities. They were all pleased to have a prominent environmental activist as a client, but he had developed a unique relationship with one of the two community banks he used. He had identified one of the branch managers as someone willing to look the other way at his questionable transactions, and he had made it a point to funnel his most suspect business in the man's direction.

Filmore had taken him to the city on occasion for evenings that involved good food, heavy drinking, and companionship with women of questionable virtue. After finalizing his latest business deal, he approached the man about handling the accounts and providing him with the substantial cash he needed to pay Kari Baldwin. He had agreed to the arrangement in exchange for 3 percent. They had a ten o'clock appointment the following morning, when he would pick up the funds for his meeting with Kari the following evening.

He looked around the restaurant and briefly made eye contact with his man at the bar, who nodded slightly. It had been a full week since the "Carbon Copy" article was published. He'd read it several times and was convinced that the reporting focused on the large corporations discussed in the story. Each of the companies had demonstrated no initiative to reduce their carbon footprint and used their relationship with the GreenThumb Foundation to carry out a scheme to manufacture a bogus neutral footprint. It appeared to him his name was mentioned almost as an afterthought. He was confident his lawyer would come up with a way to wrangle him out of any legal consequences, and he was fully capable of handling the negative publicity himself.

He had called Lyman three times since the story broke, and each time, the call went straight to voicemail, leading him to believe Lyman had blocked his number. They went back decades to their college days, and he was confident things would blow over. Once Lyman relented, he would get with him about patching things up with the financial services company, and he was certain Lyman had exaggerated the danger of crossing them. He decided he would dismiss his security detail first thing in the morning. They did not come cheap.

# CHAPTER FORTY-FIVE

ON FRIDAY AFTERNOON, DYLAN AND Penel were seated at a quiet corner table, enjoying a buffet lunch in Delta's new Sky Club in Concourse G at the Minneapolis airport. She looked at her watch. "Well, my flight is getting ready to board. I guess this is goodbye," she remarked as moisture accumulated in her eyes.

Dylan stood and slid back her chair. She stood, turned, and hugged him tightly, kissing him passionately on the mouth. "Safe travels, and I'll talk to you soon," she said, her voice cracking slightly.

"Take care of yourself. I'll miss you." He watched as she grabbed her oversized handbag and quickly left the club.

His own flight back to Tampa landed just before five o'clock. As the plane was taxiing to its gate his phone rang. "Hey, Dylan, where are you?"

"Hi, Shirley. We just landed in Tampa."

"Good. I'm glad you picked up. Chief Thompson called. He has some news for you about the investigation. He asked if you could meet him at Ferg's for lunch tomorrow at noon."

"Anything else pressing that can't wait until Monday?"

"I don't think so. You have a stack of documents and checks on your desk I left for you to sign. Anything you have questions on can wait until I see you on Monday. Aengus left for the airport about an hour ago, so he should be waiting to pick you up."

"Great. Please let the chief know I'll meet him tomorrow, and I'll see you on Monday. Enjoy your weekend."

"You do the same."

Dylan exited the plane and made his way through the crowd of road warriors and snowbirds gathered in Concourse E. He took the tram to the main terminal and found Aengus there waiting. "Welcome home, sir," he said, a hint of wistfulness in his tone.

"Good to be home, Aengus. Thanks for meeting me."

"Of course. I parked in the short-term lot so I could help with your bags."

The pair made their way down the escalator to baggage claim, and an hour later, they were driving over the Howard Frankland Bridge with the sun inching down on the horizon. Dylan was riding shotgun, and he looked over at Aengus, who was his characteristically quiet self. "How have things been at the house?"

He glanced over. "Fine, sir. I suspect you will find everything just as it was when you left." He cleared his throat. "How does it feel to be home?"

"It feels great. As soon as we walked outside and I felt the familiarity of the cool March air, it reminded me why the population swells with northerners escaping the cold this time of year."

Aengus nodded in agreement but said nothing further.

They had just crossed the bridge when Dylan's phone rang. It was his mother. "Hi, Mom," he answered.

"Hello, Dylan. I'm checking in. Aren't you due home today?"

"I'm in the car as we speak, heading back from the airport."

"How are you? I've missed you, and we haven't spoken much since you left town."

"I'm doing well. Why don't you call Grandma and Grandpa, and the five of us can have dinner tomorrow night at Villa Gallace? We can all catch up then."

"That sounds wonderful. I'll let everyone know."

"I'll call Luigi right now and make a reservation. Why don't we meet at Grandma's at five? We can all have a drink and watch the sunset before dinner."

Dylan had purchased a condominium for his grandparents in Indian Rocks Beach that sat directly on the Gulf of Mexico, and the complex was across the street from the restaurant.

"What a wonderful plan. I'm looking forward to seeing you, and I know your grandparents feel the same. We want to hear all about your travels."

"I love you, Mom, and I'll see you tomorrow."

He hung up and made the reservation with the woman who answered the phone.

He looked over again at Aengus, who caught his eye. "Are you hungry, sir? I can stop so you can pick something up."

"No, thanks. I had a big lunch at the airport. Let's just head home."

"As you wish, sir."

Soon, they were traveling down the familiar brick-paved road, and Aengus pulled into the driveway and stopped while he waited for the security gate to open. He pulled up under the portico and raised one of the garage doors. The two men loaded Dylan's bags onto the elevator. "Thanks, Aengus. I can take it from here."

"Okay. Good night, sir."

"Good night, Aengus. And thank you for taking care of everything in my absence."

"Of course."

Dylan took the elevator straight to the top floor. He turned on the lights and took in the familiar sight and smell of his house. He wheeled his two bags into the master bedroom with his backpack strapped across his shoulders. His bed was neatly made, and everything was in its place as he had left it. The bathroom shined with the scent of freshly mopped floors.

He raised the blinds and walked out onto the balcony. He felt the cool breeze as he took in the view of the houses across the water whose lights glistened off the waters of Boca Ciega Bay. He watched with amusement as a large cabin cruiser passed by, appearing to squeeze under the highest span of the Treasure Island Bridge. Everything looked and felt familiar, as if he had never left. He was tired and ready for an early bedtime. Tomorrow, he would begin the process of dealing with the matters that had caused him to leave.

# CHAPTER FORTY-SIX

B ARRY FILMORE TOOK THE ELEVATOR down to the six-car garage of his home, carrying two large duffel bags. He was dressed in a bespoke gray suit over a blue open-collar shirt. He lugged the bags to the back of his black Mercedes Benz S63 AMG and dropped them to the floor. He rubbed his narrow shoulders to relieve the burn from carrying the duffels full of cash—twenties, fifties, and hundred-dollar bills banded together. He hesitated for a moment before going back upstairs to the saloon and grabbing a bottle of Duval-Leroy Brut champagne, a small gesture to thank Kari Baldwin for doing business with him.

He got behind the wheel of the sport sedan and set the navigation system for Kari's address in Greenwich. The screen indicated the trip time was forty-one minutes. *Not bad for the tail end of rush hour on a Friday evening.* He was scheduled to arrive fashionably late at seven fourteen.

Filmore set the satellite radio to the classic jazz channel and settled into the contours of the soft napa leather sport seat. As he sped along the inside lane of the Merritt Parkway, he began to experience competing sensations of pangs in his stomach and a stirring in his groin. He intentionally hadn't eaten much during the day but had popped two Viagra pills just before he left. Once he delivered the money, he planned on having a couple drinks to get a nice buzz going before having his way with Fanci, even if he had to share her with Kari.

He arrived at the house precisely at quarter past seven and pushed the button to release the trunk. He clumsily carried the two bags to the door with the bottle of champagne tucked under his right arm. He dropped the bags and pressed the doorbell as the chimes echoed from inside the house.

A gruff voice shrieked through the speaker attached to the doorbell camera. "Yeah?"

"Kari, it's Barry Filmore."

"Wait there. Someone will be with you."

He looked around the neighborhood. Each multilevel house was stately and set back on a wide, well-manicured lawn. Night-scaping lights illuminated the work of meticulous gardening crews. Finally, the door began to open, and Filmore turned back. It was Fanci, outfitted in a gray lace dress with spaghetti straps. She wore black fishnet stockings held up by a garter belt that was visible below the short dress line. He smiled lecherously while he looked her up and down. He estimated her patent leather pumps were at least six inches. He made eye contact, and she immediately averted her gaze downward.

"Fanci, it's very nice to see you again. Please take this," he instructed, jamming the bottle of champagne into her hands.

He picked up the bags and made his way through the foyer and over to a formal living room. A wood fire crackled in the fireplace. He placed the bags at his feet and took a seat on one of the couches with a view of the grand staircase that led to the second level. "Please bring the champagne over here and have a seat next to me," he commanded.

Fanci walked over and sat next to him as instructed, placing the bottle on the Italian marble coffee table in front of them. He leaned over and took in her clean, soapy smell before playing with her hair. He inhaled deeply, catching a whiff of the scent of her apricot shampoo. He became extremely aroused and began rubbing her back.

"How've you been, sweetheart?"

"Okay," she replied, turning her head away from him.

"Come on now," he said, twisting her head back in his direction before taking her face in his hands. "That's no way to treat an old friend."

"No, sir, I apologize. But I'm here with Kari this evening."

He moved his hand to her leg and rubbed her textured stocking, working his way up underneath the short dress where he began massaging her upper thigh. "We have all night, so we'll see about that."

Kari emerged from the top of the staircase, traversing her way down the right side. She wore a full-length taupe evening robe with matching camisole. She had fuzzy slide slippers on her feet. Filmore stood and grabbed the champagne bottle before moving toward the staircase. "Good evening, Kari. It's nice to see you. I brought you this to formally christen our new business venture."

She took the bottle and stared at the label. "Hmm. Take this, honey," she instructed, thrusting it in Fanci's direction, "Open it and pour three glasses. The flutes are in the bar."

Fanci dutifully took the bottle and made her way to the bar area with her back to them. "Now, where's my money?"

"Right here," he replied, retrieving the two bags and placing them at her feet. She picked one up, unzipped it, and rifled through, before zipping it shut. She then repeated the act with the second bag. She grabbed both bulky bags with relative ease and placed them on a counter just as Fanci returned with a tray containing three glasses of bubbly.

"Come, let's sit for a moment," Kari said, making her way to the couch across from where Filmore had sat. Fanci followed behind her and placed the tray on the coffee table between them. She handed Kari a glass, then Filmore, before taking the third one and sitting close to Kari.

"Let me propose a toast," Filmore said, rising. "To the beginning of a long and prosperous business relationship." He held out his glass and strained to clink the other two as the women remained seated. He took a healthy gulp of the sparkling wine and almost immediately felt the effects. "I've got some other news for you as well, Kari."

"Oh. What's that?"

"I've found someone to make good on the promise I made to our private school donor that day in Tampa. I'm flying down to meet with him on Monday."

She glared back at him. "How many times do I have to tell you? I don't need to hear the details about what you're *going* to do, particularly when it involves such a sordid affair. Let me know when it's done."

They sat in silence for a moment, sipping their drinks. He stared over at Fanci, feeling simultaneously buzzed and concupiscent. "Well, now that we've taken care of business, what say we all enjoy some pleasure?"

"Slow down there, tiger," Kari commanded. "Here's how this is gonna go. We're going to finish our drinks, and then Fanci and I are going to go upstairs and make a movie, and you are going to be our cameraman. Afterward, if you do a good job, I may let you have seconds with her."

He smiled, barely able to contain himself. "That works for me."

Suddenly, Filmore heard what sounded like an explosion behind him. He turned to find two men dressed in all black with ski masks covering their faces burst through the front door.

"Everyone on the floor! Get on the fucking floor now!" he heard one of the men yell. His eyesight began to blur, but he was able to discern that both men were carrying handguns.

"Face down, bitches!" he heard the other one scream, and he immediately complied, lying on his stomach parallel to the couch and directly in front of the coffee table. He turned his head and saw the two men manhandling the women and placing them prone on the floor away from the furniture. He fought to maintain control of his bladder as he focused on the women. Kari appeared calm and emotionless, but Fanci was crying and screaming hysterically.

"Shut up! Shut the fuck up!" one of the men shouted before squeezing both sides of her mouth with the fingers and thumb of one hand and thrusting the barrel of his gun down her throat. "Quiet down now, or I'll pull the trigger, bitch," he demanded dispassionately without a trace of emotion. She stopped making noise but appeared to be silently hyperventilating.

One of the two made his way over to him. "What the fuck you looking at, pussy?" he asked, kicking him in the head with the toe of his boot. "Face down, or I'll crush your skull."

Filmore complied as he felt a warm liquid stream down the side of his face. The guy manhandled him as he bound his hands behind his back with duct tape before doing the same with his ankles.

"Whose house is this?" he heard the other man say.

"Mine," Kari replied.

"On your feet. We're going upstairs."

His partner had finished binding Filmore, and he heard him shout from across the room. "Look at this! Two bags full of cash."

"Stay here while I take the big girl upstairs," the other guy replied. Fanci was crying again. "Blindfold both of them and find something to gag her with."

Filmore's head was jerked violently off the floor while duct tape was wrapped around his head several times until everything went black. He felt wetness accumulating in his crotch area and finally just relented. After what seemed like an eternity, his legs were freed, and he was lifted off the ground and dragged outside. He was thrown into the back of a car and could tell by the scent that it was his own Mercedes. He could still feel and taste the blood flowing from the side of his head. For some strange reason, his mind was singularly focused on a concern for the stains on the leather upholstery until he felt a crushing blow to the head, and everything went dark.

# CHAPTER FORTY-SEVEN

Fanci was lying on her back, her bound hands off to her side. Her eyes and mouth were dry and crusty as she focused on breathing through her nose. The strips of duct tape over her eyes extended to her temples, but she could sense it was now daylight. Suddenly, she heard a loud rumble followed by a crash. She tried to yell, but her mouth was stuffed with some kind of cloth material and covered in strips of tape. "Fanci, is that you?" It was Kari's voice.

She tried yelling again, but the most she could manage was muffled sounds.

"Okay. I can hear you, and I know you've been gagged. Listen carefully. Stay where you are and remain quiet until I say so."

Fanci did as she was told and concentrated on the sounds coming from an adjacent area. She heard a lot of rattling, like someone fumbling around in the dark at night in search of something, followed by a crash. "Fanci, I have a knife in my hands. I'm going to come over to you. Get up off the floor if you can and yell so I can find you."

She bent her knees and got her feet under her as she pushed off the ground with her hands. She fell back on her first attempt, but on the second effort, she pushed harder and fell forward into what felt like the side of the couch. She was able to maintain her balance and stand up. She turned around and yelled her muffled screams as the sound of Kari hopping in her direction closed in on her. As Kari came in contact with her, she sensed the wetness of her perspiration and the scent of her body odor. "Grunt once if your hands are bound behind your back."

She grunted once.

"Okay. My hands are also taped behind my back, and I have a steak knife in my hands. Turn around so we're back-to-back, and I'll cut through your tape."

Fanci complied and felt the object land on the tape covering her hands. She moved it over and pulled as tightly as she could to separate her wrists. "Grunt once if the knife is sitting between your hands."

Again, one grunt.

"Good. Now I'm gonna cut."

She could hear and feel the knife slicing through the tape as she continued to pull her wrists apart until she finally experienced the liberating feeling of being unshackled. She dug her fingernails under the lowest piece of tape covering her eyes and tore off the multiple strips in one quick motion. She did the same with the tape across her mouth and spit out the small dish rag the intruder had stuffed in her mouth. She then grabbed the knife from Kari and cut her ankles free.

Next, she bent down and cut Kari's hands free and watched while she tore off her blindfold. She handed back the knife, and Kari cut her ankles loose. She looked at her in a way Fanci had not previously perceived before embracing her with those huge arms and hugging her firmly. She bent down to Fanci's height, nestled her face against hers, and sobbed. Fanci felt the softness of a genuine nonsexual embrace from her for the first time. She finally pulled back with her hands still on Fanci's shoulders and smiled as tears streamed down her face. "Please tell me you're okay and they didn't hurt you."

"I'm all right. What about you?"

She let out a nervous laugh. "Are you kidding? I'm a tough old broad. I did more damage to myself sliding down the staircase."

"Who were those men?" Fanci asked.

"I have no idea."

"What did they want?"

"Money, apparently. The one who took me upstairs didn't say much. He took my jewelry and then told me to open the safe." She looked at her lovingly before continuing. "I told him I didn't have a safe, and then he called me a liar and said he was going to stick that gun back in your mouth and pull the trigger if I lied again. I took him to the safe and opened it. I couldn't let them hurt you. What happened to Barry?"

"I'm not sure, but it sounded like they dragged him out of the house when they left."

"Let's check the garage," Kari said as she hurried off in that direction with Fanci close behind. Her car was there, and everything else appeared untouched. They both went outside. No cars were in the driveway. "It looks like they took Filmore and his car when they left. There were two of them, so my guess is one drove off with his car, and he was with them."

"Do you think he was involved in this?" Fanci asked.

"I doubt it," she replied, maintaining a somber demeanor. "That would be both foolish and shortsighted on his part."

"Should we call the police?"

Fanci observed as Kari's demeanor remained resolute. "No," she answered before turning to her with an expression of concern. "Are you sure you're all right?"

"I'll be okay."

"Then let's not involve the police. I'll handle it. Can I count on you to keep this between us?"

"Of course, Kari. Whatever you want."

She took her in her arms again and hugged her tenderly. Fanci returned the gesture.

# CHAPTER FORTY-EIGHT

Dylan woke up with the familiar feeling of being alone in his own bed. It was just before sunrise, and he went downstairs to the gym for a workout. An hour and a half later, he stood in the kitchen mixing a protein shake from bags of frozen strawberries, bananas, and blueberries he found in the freezer. He sat at the kitchen island and drank the concoction, pleased with himself that he had jumped right back into his routine.

He looked at his phone for the first time that morning and saw a text message from Penel. "Arrived home safely last night. Thank you again for including me on your amazing and memorable adventure. You are a wonderful man and traveling partner. Miss you already. XOXO."

He smiled to himself before finishing up in the kitchen and heading upstairs to shave and shower. He got dressed for the day before making his way to his office. Shirley had stacked several neat piles of paperwork on his desk, each with a sticky note on top, replete with instructions. He worked on the piles until it was time to head to midtown for his lunch meeting.

He arrived at Ferg's shortly before noon and fortunately found a parking spot on the sports bar's property. It was mid-March, and the NCAA men's basketball tournament was underway. The place was packed with fans, many of whom were displaying the garb of their favorite team. He made his way into one of the more intimate interior rooms where Chief Thompson kept a reserved table. The new police station was directly across the street, and the chief and other top brass were regulars.

Dylan sat at the table as a waitress came over, a stern expression on her face. He preempted the situation with a warm smile. "Good afternoon. I'm meeting Chief Thompson for lunch."

She returned the smile with a hand on her hip. "Come on now. You don't look like a cop."

"You are correct. I'm not. Just a grateful citizen, buying lunch for the leader of the men in blue."

"Can I get you something to drink while you wait?"

"A glass of water and a Diet Coke, please."

"As you wish," she replied before turning and heading off.

Dylan focused on the television in front of him where the University of Kentucky was beating a team, whose identity he could not discern, badly early in the first half. His drinks arrived a short time before he observed Leroy Thompson's approach. He was dressed in dark casual slacks and a green golf shirt embroidered with the police logo and his name and rank.

Dylan stood and shook his hand. "Good afternoon, Chief."

"Good afternoon, Dylan. Nice to see you again."

The waitress quickly appeared. "The usual to drink, Chief?" she asked as she handed out old school menus sealed in plastic.

"Yes, please. Seltzer water with a lime twist."

"So, Dylan, how have you been?" he inquired after the server had left.

"Doing well, sir. How's the crime-fighting business?"

"One thing I can say for sure: we'll never run out of work. Our Police Athletic League team scrimmaged against your baseball team last week. I expected to run into you, but your coaching staff said you weren't around in a kind of short and mysterious manner."

"I've been out of town for a while. How did my team look?"

"Impressive. I watched a few innings. You've got some promising young players." He paused momentarily. "Go anywhere interesting?"

"Excuse me?"

"You said you were out of town. What took you away?"

"I was checking on some investment properties I own. Farm and ranch land out in the Midwest." He left it at that and was saved as the waitress reappeared.

"You gentlemen ready to order?"

"I'll have the wings medium with an order of fries and a refill on my drink."

"And how about you, darlin'?" she inquired of Dylan.

"I'll have the chicken sandwich, plain with just pickles. No side."

"What's the matter? You watching your waistline?" he asked with a smile after the waitress had departed.

He laughed. "Nothing like that. I'm having dinner with my family tonight and want to preserve my appetite."

"Hmm. I see. Well, while you were gone, the department made headway on one of your two cases."

"Which one?"

"The hit-and-run at Park and Central. Turns out you were not the target of an attack."

Dylan looked at him quizzically but said nothing, so he continued.

"We know for certain those two other vehicles were occupied by rival teenage gangbangers. Our GIU, Gang Intelligence Unit, got involved in the case after the pickup that rear-ended you was finally reported stolen. Turns out the owner was traveling abroad and reported it upon his return. From what we were able to determine, the two groups got into a feud on Treasure Island and chased each other, exchanging gunfire on a couple occasions before you were caught in one of the crossfires. I can say, unequivocally, this was not a targeted attack on you. You were simply in the wrong place at the wrong time."

Dylan processed the information in silence, and the chief waited patiently for his reply.

"What about the case on the trail?" he finally asked.

The chief exhaled and leaned forward, folding his hands on the table. "That one has gone cold. Because of your involvement, I assigned a couple of investigators to canvas the area. They spent several days at the site around the time of the attack, looking for the regulars, cyclists, walkers, et cetera. They came across one guy, a bicyclist, who witnessed the attack and said he spoke with you afterward. Said you were pretty beat up but didn't want to call us and left in a hurry. That true?"

He bowed his head slightly. "Yes, sir."

The chief nodded. "Anyway, the guy's a regular rider at that time of morning. Said he would recognize a good number of others he sees in that area and is very confident he's never seen those guys before. He gave us a description, which wasn't of much help, but he also said they appeared out of place. Said they didn't look like the typical people who use the trail and didn't fit the profile of the more nefarious characters that hang around the area."

"I see."

"Makes me believe that this wasn't some random road rage incident or a couple of druggies on bad trips. Feels more like a targeted attack. Any idea why someone would want to do you harm?"

He grimaced. "Nothing that comes to mind."

Their food was served. The chief dug in while Dylan picked at his sandwich. The chief had just cleaned the meat off a bone. "So. Who do you like?"

Dylan raised his brow.

"In the tournament, I mean," he said, nodding toward the television above him.

"UConn, of course."

The chief smiled sarcastically. "Ahh. A front runner. How long have you been a Husky fan?"

"Since I attended UConn as a student."

He smiled. "That's right. I knew you were originally a Yankee, but I didn't know you were the Connecticut version."

"Yes, sir. Born and raised in the Constitution State."

"I thought it was the Nutmeg State."

"The official nickname is the Constitution State, but either one works. How about you? Who are you rooting for?"

"I'm a Florida State grad, so, of course, I'm pulling for them."

"They have a nice team this year. They beat up on the Gators pretty badly a few weeks back."

The chief dipped his French fry in a sea of ketchup. "Indeed. But your Huskies are in a league of their own. They're favored to win it all again. What do you think of their coach?"

"I like him but, like most of Husky nation, probably because he's *our* guy. I suspect he doesn't have many fans from other teams."

"He does tend to get under people's skin."

The waitress appeared. "Can I get you anything else?"

"Not for me. Chief?"

"No. I'm all set."

"Just the bill, please," Dylan requested.

"No bill. It's on the house, per Ferg."

"Very well. Thank you," he replied, handing her a twenty-dollar bill.

"Thank *you*," she replied. "You gentlemen have a great afternoon."

Dylan and the chief walked out front in the direction of the police station. "Nice to see you, Chief. And thanks for the update on my cases."

He extended his hand, and Dylan shook it. "We're here to protect and serve," he said with a smile.

On the ride home, Dylan began to feel fatigued. He arrived at the house and initially fought the urge to nap, figuring he would catch up on some more work. He sat in his office going over some files on the computer for a few minutes before his eyelids became heavy. He finally relented, made his way upstairs, and collapsed on his bed.

Dylan woke up an hour later feeling refreshed. After he showered and dressed for dinner, he pulled the Escalade out of the garage and drove north on Gulf Boulevard, the road that ran along the Gulf of Mexico through the myriad barrier island beach towns from St. Pete Beach to Tarpon Springs. It was about a ten-mile drive up the coastline from his house to Indian Rocks Beach, where his grandparents lived, and Dylan enjoyed the relaxing vibe of the beach communities. He pulled into his grandparents' complex, an eighteen-unit building directly facing the gulf with breathtaking beachfront views.

The structure was only three levels above the covered garage, so Dylan ran up the staircase to the top floor, where his grandparents occupied a corner unit with northwest exposure. He knocked and was greeted at the door by his grandmother, who gave him a big hug and kissed him on the cheek. "My boy returns. I missed you so much," she said while still squeezing him tightly.

He looked up and saw his grandfather standing behind her.

"Long time no see there, grandson," his grandfather commented with a grimace. "Where've you been gallivanting off to all this time? Your grandmother misses you when you're gone so long."

"Nice to see you, Grandpa," he replied, shaking his hand firmly. "Why don't we wait for Mom and Rick, and I'll give you all the rundown together."

"They're already here. Left to go on a walk along the beach. They should be back anytime."

"Let's all sit out on the balcony. I'll serve drinks out there as soon as they get back," his grandmother added.

Dylan sat down in one of the cushioned chairs and was admiring the early stages of the sunset when his grandfather sat beside him. "So, how's that smoke-show girl pal of yours?"

He shot back an amused look. "I'll assume you're talking about Penelope. She's fine."

"Of course, I'm talking about Penelope. How many smoke-show girlfriends do you have?"

He smiled brightly, enjoying the exchange. "Only one at the moment."

The older man leaned in and lowered his voice. "She's a keeper. You ought to think about putting a ring on that finger."

Dylan laughed out loud. "Where do you come up with this stuff, Grandpa?"

"What nonsense is he spouting off now?" his grandmother interrupted as she made her way out to the balcony.

Dylan looked back and saw his mother and Rick standing behind her. He shot out of his chair and embraced her. "It's so good to see you, Mom. I've missed you."

"Not as much as I've missed you, son," she replied, planting a kiss on his cheek.

He stepped back and shook Rick's hand. "Nice to see you, Rick."

"Same here, Dylan."

They all took seats on the balcony in a semicircle around a large table facing the beach while his grandmother retreated to the kitchen. She returned shortly with a pitcher of mojitos.

"Thank you, dear," his grandfather replied, taking over and pouring everyone a drink. He remained standing and held out his own cocktail glass. "I propose a toast. The prodigal son returns. We'll spare the fatted calf and let Luigi handle dinner."

"Hear, hear," everyone said in unison amid the chuckling while they held up their glasses.

Dylan took a sip of his drink and exhaled, reflecting on how well it felt to be around his family again. "So, Dylan," his mother chimed in, "please tell us about your trip."

He had prepared a response to the inevitable question, careful to leave out any hint of the issues that caused him to leave town. "I had some business to attend to out west with some properties I own. I invited Penel along, and we decided to turn it into a working vacation. We started out in California before making our way to the properties and then just sort of freestyled from there."

"Where are these properties you own?" his grandfather inquired.

"In Nebraska and South Dakota."

"Christ sakes there, you're a regular land baron. How much property do you have?"

"Not sure exactly, but it's quite a bit."

"Quite a bit like a few hundred acres?" his grandmother asked.

He looked over at his mother and Rick, who were staring intently. "I would say quite a bit, like tens of thousands of acres."

His grandmother gasped, placing her hand over her mouth.

"You've got to be kidding me," his grandfather said. "Who mows all that property?"

"The cows handle the lawncare duties on the ranch. The rest of it is farmland. There's no grass, only crops."

"What do you grow?" Rick inquired.

"I don't grow anything. I lease the land out to farmers who mostly grow corn." He glanced over at his mother, who smiled proudly. He scanned his memory, trying to recall whether he'd ever told his mother about the investment properties, and came up empty. "Anyway, I checked on everything and met with the ranch manager."

"How did Penel enjoy the trip?" his mother asked.

"We had a great time. We both worked remotely in the morning and then went exploring in the afternoon." He continued with details for a while until all the questions were answered. After they headed across the street for dinner, he made it a point to steer the conversation toward other subjects.

# CHAPTER FORTY-NINE

DYLAN WAS IN HIS OFFICE early on Monday, and by midmorning, he had made his way through the balance of the work Shirley had left for him. He leaned back in his chair and reflected on how well she and Aengus had taken care of things in his absence. After a few moments, he wandered down to her office and delivered the balance of the paperwork.

"Here you go," he said, handing her the documents. "You're amazing."

"Tell me something I don't know," she replied with a confident smile.

"All right, I will. I really appreciate how you and Aengus handled things while I was away. When you prepare the payroll this week, include a ten thousand dollar bonus for each of you."

Her smirk temporarily morphed into a look of astonishment before returning to a somewhat warmer smile. "Thank you, Dylan. That's very generous of you."

"You're welcome. I sincerely appreciate the job you both did. Everything looks amazing around here, and I'm all caught up on my work. It's like I never left."

"Well, thank you again. I was about to come see you. Walt Jackman's office called to request a meeting. It's scheduled for ten o'clock tomorrow."

"Did they say what the meeting was about?"

"An update on the status of your audit."

He nodded but said nothing further before heading back to his own office. As soon as he sat down, Shirley buzzed his phone. "Esther for you on line one."

"Good morning, Esther."

"Good morning to you."

He brought her up to date on his decision to return home. "I was gone for a month, and I'm already caught up on my work," he concluded.

"You are blessed to have good people working with you. You can never underestimate the value of quality employees."

"I agree wholeheartedly."

"How is your family?"

"Everyone is well. I spent Saturday evening with them, and we had a good time catching up."

"Anything come up on the pesky matters you're dealing with?"

"I've managed to keep all that from them. I don't want my grandparents or my mom worrying about me."

"I understand. Any news on that front?"

"I met with the police chief on Saturday. Turns out the hit-and-run where I was shot at was some gang-related thing. Apparently, I was in the wrong place at the wrong time and got caught in the crossfire. The attack on the bike trail appears as if it will go unresolved, although the chief believes I was specifically targeted."

"I see," she replied, a trace of concern in her voice. "What about your IRS audit?"

"I have a meeting with my tax attorney tomorrow. Are you worried about me?"

"Is it that obvious?"

"Please don't worry. The chief was just expressing an opinion. There's a lot of unpredictable characters on that trail. It could have been just another case of wrong place-wrong time."

"Well, there's still the threat from the stranger in Tampa hanging out there."

He ignored the comment. "Your credit cards, phones, and computer are being FedEx'd back to you today," he continued. "You should receive them tomorrow. Please send me the credit card bill so I can pay you back."

"That's not going to happen," she answered.

He smiled. "Thank you for everything."

"You're very welcome. Just promise me you will be careful and watch your back."

"Of course. Take care of yourself, Esther."

"Please do the same."

Fanci was at her apartment on Monday morning when her cell phone rang. It was Kari. The pair had not spoken since Kari had dropped her off at home on Saturday. "Hello, sweetheart. Are you coming to work today?"

"I'm sorry, I just can't bring myself to come in. I'm exhausted. Every time I fall asleep, the nightmares wake me up."

"I understand. Listen, I didn't have a chance to tell you this, but I've received a job offer in Washington, DC, and I'll be leaving my position here soon. If you'd like, take the rest of the semester off. I'll give you full credit for your internship and a glowing final evaluation. And in a month or so, after graduation, you can come and work with me in DC."

The offer took Fanci off guard. She managed to lift herself off the couch and began pacing the small living space. "That's very generous of you. I think maybe I'll return home to Danbury and take some time for myself. Then I'll get back to you about coming to Washington."

"Very well. Don't worry about anything with your internship or your college. I'll take care of all that. There's just one other thing. You must promise me you won't say a word to anyone about what happened on Saturday night and trust me to deal with it."

"Okay, Kari, and thank you. You're so good to me."

"I told you from the beginning I value loyalty above all else, and you've proven to be a loyal and faithful assistant."

# CHAPTER FIFTY

DYLAN WAS JUST GETTING OUT of the shower after finishing a workout and light breakfast when his cell phone buzzed. It was Alex. "Hey, what's going on?" Alex asked.

"Where are you?"

"I'm in Tampa. Flew in yesterday. I'll be here all week. Where are you?"

"I got home Friday night. I'm actually getting ready to head over to Tampa for a meeting at eleven."

"Great. Let's grab lunch afterward and catch up. I'm looking forward to hearing all about your trip."

"Sure. Where do you want to meet?"

"How about the Boulon Brasserie at noon? Think your meeting will be over by then?"

"Should be. If not, I'll let you know."

"Text me when you're done, and I'll walk over and get us a table."

"Sounds like a plan. See you soon."

Two hours later, he was in his attorney's office in downtown Tampa, being escorted back to one of the smaller conference rooms with a view of the waterfront. Walt Jackman was seated behind his laptop computer, waiting for him. He stood and greeted Dylan. "Welcome back. How was your trip?"

"Very enjoyable, thanks, but it's good to be home."

"That's good to hear, and I have some news that may brighten your mood even more. I presented your offer to the IRS. They rejected it but did come back with a counterproposal. They've offered to close their file and pay you a settlement. Here's a copy of their written offer."

He slid a piece of paper across the table. Dylan read the letter, maintaining a stoic demeanor. He looked up at his lawyer. "Why the sudden change in their position?"

"I can give you my take on the situation." Dylan nodded, so he continued. "The service looks for wins, particularly low resistance ones. That's why they steer clear of billionaires. They avoid protracted battles with uncertain results. I suspect, at the outset, they had you categorized as non-combatant. When I rejected their previous offer and countered, I made it clear we felt everything was in order with your returns and that you were prepared to go the distance. I pointed out you've dug in your heels and have committed the necessary resources, and it's unclear to me how they could have misread the situation. I suspect they ran it up the chain of command and reevaluated their position when it became evident your case didn't fit the easy-win profile."

"I see. If I accept their offer, where am I at with what I've spent on fees?"

"I'd have to review our billing records, but offhand, I would say you would be slightly in the hole when everything is said and done."

He leaned back in his chair and looked away in thought, staring out the window at the view of the Hillsborough River before focusing back on his attorney. "Calculate your total bill on this and go back to them with that number as a best and final offer. Otherwise, we forge ahead."

Dylan observed as Walt looked down at his computer and began tapping some keys. "It's going to take me some time to update your bill, including costs, so I propose we accept their offer, and we'll write off any additional sums you owe."

Dylan had pulled out his phone to check the time before looking back up at Walt. "Done," he replied, standing and shaking his hand. "Thank you for all the work you put into this. If you'll excuse me, I have a lunch appointment."

"Sure thing. As always, we appreciate your business. You're a pleasure to work with."

He smiled and made his way out of the office. While he waited for the elevator, he texted Alex. "Leaving meeting now. On my way."

He immediately received a thumbs-up emoji in reply.

Dyland retrieved his car, drove across town, and found a parking spot in the garage next to Amalie Arena, home of the Tampa Bay Lightning hockey team. He walked across the street to the restaurant adjacent to the Edition and found Alex sitting at a table near the bar. He bypassed the line at the receptionist stand and made his way over. Alex jumped off his seat and consumed him with a bear hug. "Welcome back! I missed you so much," he exclaimed, loudly enough to garner a few stares.

"Okay. Easy there, big fella."

"I mean it. I really did miss you. And it didn't help that I had little female companionship to keep me occupied in your absence."

Dylan narrowed his eyes. "As I recall, you recently spent a weekend at my guest house with a friend."

"That was a few weeks ago. In fact, I called her several times over the weekend and again this morning. All the calls go directly to voicemail. Seems like she's blowing me off. First Ann and now Liz. Anyway, we're here to talk about your trip. Details," he said, holding out his hands and twitching his fingers toward his chest.

Dylan gave him a rundown, highlighting their adventures and the places they visited as they ate their lunch. Alex was uncharacteristically quiet and appeared rapt, hanging on every word. "Wow. Sounds like you had an awesome time. And I can't think of a better traveling partner than Penel. She's a keeper."

He smiled. "You sound like my grandfather. His exact words were 'You need to put a ring on her finger.'"

"Sage advice from a wise man. Now what about that other stuff? What's going on there?"

"It's pretty much resolved. My attorney negotiated a favorable settlement with the IRS, and the police told me, unequivocally, I was in the wrong place at the wrong time when I was caught in the crossfire after the car wreck. They seem equally confident the case on the bike trail will go unresolved but believe I was the target of the attack."

Alex seemed focused on his thoughts, his chin resting on his hand. "Hmm. So, I may have been right about that mysterious letter you received. Watch Ewe Ass."

"I hadn't thought about that, and I didn't mention it or the threat from the man in Tampa to Chief Thompson when he asked if I was aware of anyone who would want to do me harm. Anyway, what was the point? I honestly don't know of anyone."

"What about that climate change activist who paid you a visit?" he asked, suddenly diverting his eyes in the direction of the bar. "What was his name?"

Dylan winced. "Filmore, Barry Filmore."

"Look at the TV over the bar," he stated, astounded, a blank stare on his face.

"What is it?" Dylan asked as he turned slightly in his chair. He then turned all the way around to see a news headline with a photograph of a familiar face. The sound was muted, but the headline read 'Prominent Environmental Activist Found Dead.'

"Son of a bitch," Alex whispered as he glanced around at the nearby tables and leaned in. "If he was your guy, looks like you don't have anything to worry about now."

Dylan sat there in stunned silence. "Wow. Barry Filmore's dead." They were both quiet for a moment as they processed the news. "I'm not sure what the guy's deal was, but he obviously had a lot going on. Especially getting caught up in that counterfeit carbon credit scandal. It didn't seem like trying to extort money from me was worth his time."

"Who knows what makes a guy like that tick?" Alex commented. "Except money, of course. He was probably one of those guys who would chase down the last dollar to his own detriment."

"Think about it. A guy goes around shaking people down, and when someone rejects him, he exacts revenge. Seems like an inefficient way to do business."

"That's exactly how the mob does business. It's the deterrent effect. You make an example of one person, and everyone else falls in line."

Dylan frowned and shook his head. "That makes no sense. No one knows Filmore met with me, and I told him to get lost."

"Okay, so if it wasn't Filmore who ordered the hit on you, then who?"

"The hit? A little dramatic, don't you think?"

"You know what I mean. So what now?"

"I go about my life, but with a heightened sense of situational awareness."

Alex took a thoughtful sip of his iced tea. "What the heck does that mean?"

"Just like it sounds. I pay more attention to what's going on around me. In the car, I check the rearview mirror to see if someone's following me. When I'm out and about, I scan my surroundings. I make eye contact with anyone who approaches me and assess the situation."

"Okay. Sounds a little paranoid, but probably appropriate under the circumstances."

After lunch, Dylan drove home and found himself thinking about Barry Filmore. He'd found him to be a despicable character, but at the same time, he was curious about the circumstances surrounding his death and whether he, in fact, was responsible for Dylan's recent problems. As soon as he crossed over the bridge into St. Petersburg, his phone rang. The screen on his console indicated it was Esther. "Hello, Esther."

"Hello, Dylan. Where are you?"

"Driving back from Tampa."

"I read online the climate activist you were dealing with was found dead."

"I just finished lunch with Alex and saw the headline on the TV in the restaurant. What happened?"

"According to the article, his body was found by a maid in a rundown hotel off Route 1 in Westchester County. He died of a self-inflicted gunshot wound, and the day before, he transferred large sums of money through a maze of offshore accounts. The police are still investigating."

"Unreal."

"With everything that's been going on, I thought you should know."

"Thanks."

"I have to run. I have a phone conference in five minutes. Take care of yourself."

The call disconnected, and Dylan rode home quietly, consumed in thought, only to be disturbed each time a vehicle passed or approached quickly from behind.

Fanci was at her apartment when she received a call from Kari. "How are you, dear?"

"About the same."

"Have you seen the news today?"

"No."

"It was just reported that Barry Filmore is dead."

Fanci placed her hand over her mouth and gasped. "Oh, my God! What happened?"

"His body was found in a hotel room. In the unlikely event you are questioned by police, you are to not mention anything about Friday night. Simply tell them you haven't seen Filmore lately and you don't know anything about what happened. Do you understand?"

"Yes, ma'am."

"Good. I'm leaving for Washington next week. Everything is taken care of with your internship. I've instructed Ms. Bishop you will be finishing the semester doing independent study, and she has my evaluation to submit to your school."

"Thank you, Kari."

"Take care, sweetie. We'll talk soon."

# CHAPTER FIFTY-ONE

A WEEK LATER, KARI BALDWIN WAS working out of a temporary office in the Department of Education building while her new corner suite overlooking the Capitol was being renovated. It was late afternoon on a crisp, clear spring day in the final week of March, and the cherry blossoms were in full bloom. She left her office and decided to walk back to the Hyatt Hotel at the National Mall, where she was staying temporarily while she looked for a house.

As she made her way along Fourth Street, she observed two homeless men ahead of her. They were arguing loudly, but she could not make out what they were saying. Both wore dirty overcoats and were unkempt, with long hair and beards. She gave them a wide berth as she approached, walking along the very edge of the sidewalk. The confrontation became physical, and the pair began to tussle as she tried to pass. They crashed into her, almost knocking her off her feet. As she began to lose her balance, she felt a simultaneous stinging sensation in both of her thighs.

"Ouch. What that hell did you do to me?" she screamed at the men.

They were blabbering incoherently and continued to push and slap at each other, pulling her into the fray. She pushed back against the one closest to her and began screaming, "Get away from me!"

The other people in the area ignored the commotion and went about their business as if the threesome were invisible. She managed to extricate herself and walked briskly toward her hotel. She began to feel lightheaded, barely making it to her room before she collapsed on the floor.

# CHAPTER FIFTY-TWO

Two days later, Fanci walked into a dive bar in Ybor City. She was greeted by Sue, the regular daytime bartender, "Hey, Beth. How goes it?"

"Fine, Sue. Can I get a gin and tonic and send a couple beers over to my friends," Fanci said, indicating to the two large, bearded men sitting alone together at a table in the far corner of the bar.

"Sure thing, darlin'."

Fanci made her way over and sat down. She removed her backpack and placed it on the empty extra chair. They exchanged pleasantries until Sue brought their drinks over and retreated behind the bar.

"How did things go in DC?" she asked in a hushed tone.

"No problems. We got back yesterday."

"I got word from my job that my old boss, Kari Baldwin, died of an insulin overdose."

"That's a shame," the other man replied. "Was she diabetic?"

"I believe so. I used to see her inject insulin sometimes."

"You gotta be careful with that stuff. I'm diabetic myself. Too much insulin can be lethal."

"Well, I believe that concludes our business. You'll find your payment in the backpack. I do have a question, though." She glanced around the near-empty bar and leaned in over the table, dropping her voice to barely above a whisper. "When you shoved that gun in my mouth that night, was it loaded?"

"Of course," the man said with a sinister smile. "The same round your boyfriend ate."

She leaned back and maintained her normal voice level. "He's not my boyfriend. You are two crazy bastards."

"Us? You should talk. You're one psychotic bitch."

She smiled. "I'm outta here. My cab's waiting for me outside. I'll see you guys around."

"Just one thing?" the man added. "Why didn't you want your cut from the first job?"

"Didn't need it. I got my share after you gave me the bank account information and passwords."

"How much did you get?"

"Enough to call it even."

"You're not holding out on us, are you?" the first guy interjected.

She stood and glared down at them. "You were paid what we agreed. Consider my share your bonus," she replied as she stood and left.

She hopped into the back of the taxi. "Tampa Airport, please."

"Yes, ma'am."

She sat quietly in the back seat and stared out the window as the cab headed south on Interstate 275 and passed by the downtown skyline and the Westshore district. After the driver pulled off the highway and onto the airport exit road, she spoke up. "Please pull into the post office and stop at the drive-through drop box. I have a letter to mail."

"Yes, ma'am."

# CHAPTER FIFTY-THREE

THREE DAYS LATER, DYLAN WAS in his office when Shirley walked in with the mail. She placed the stack on his desk and pulled a letter off the top.

"You should read this," she said as she turned and hastily departed. Dylan picked up the paper. It was typed and unsigned.

DEAR MR TOMASSI
YOU DON'T KNOW ME AND YOU NEVER WILL.
THIS IS THE SECOND AND FINAL TIME I WILL WRITE.
I OWE YOU AN APOLOGY. I RECEIVED BAD INFORMATION REGARDING YOUR CHARACTER AND ACTED OUT IN AN INAPPROPRIATE MANNER. I HOPE YOU WILL FORGIVE ME FOR THE HARDSHIP I PUT YOU THROUGH. PLEASE KNOW THAT I HAVE FOUND THE LEARNING EXPERIENCE TO BE OF GREAT BENEFIT GOING FORWARD.

He stood and walked down to Shirley's office. "Where's the envelope that letter came in?"

"Right here," she replied with a smile, holding it up. "No return address and a postmark from the Tampa Airport post office."

He nodded and returned to his own office. He sat down and rubbed his temples, trying to make sense of what he had just read. His office phone buzzed. "Esther is on the line for you."

"Hello," was all he could manage.

"Good morning, Dylan. Is everything okay?"

"Uh, yeah. Sorry. I was just in the middle of something when you called."

"I need you to come and see me."

He was startled by the tone of her voice. "Is everything all right?"

"Yes. However, I'm working on something that has become quite problematic and I need your help."

"Please tell me what this is about. I'm worried about you."

"Trust me when I tell you I'm fine. All will be explained when you get here."

"Okay. How soon do you need me?"

"Next week will be fine."

Very good. I'll see you then."

He hung up the phone and stood pacing the room when his cell phone buzzed. It was Penel. "How are you, Dylan?"

"I'm okay, I think. How are things with you?"

"They would be much better if you were here. I miss you."

"I think I can help with that."

# ABOUT THE AUTHOR

Dan Romanello is an attorney and former Florida prosecutor. He is the author of the Dylan Tomassi novels, including the first book in the series, *PAPERBOY*. He lives on Florida's Gulf Coast.

**Like and Follow this author at:**

https://www.facebook.com/thedanromanello

https://twitter.com/TheDanRomanello